THE AWAKENING OF LIZZIE DANTON

SAVAGE

L.A. FIORE

ISBN-13: 978-1977937759
ISBN-10: 1977937756

Cover Model: **Jacob Sones**
Cover photo by **Scott Hoover**
Cover design by Melissa Stevens, The Illustrated Author
File creation, mobi and epub, by Melissa Stevens, The Illustrated Author
Typeset graphics, title page art and paperback and eBook formatting by Melissa Stevens, The Illustrated Author
www.theillustratedauthor.net
Editing by Editor in Heels, Trish Bacher
www.editorinheels.com

If I Ever Leave This World Alive…**Flogging Molly**
Carry On Wayward Son…**Kansas**
MmmBop…**Hanson**
Let Her Go…**Passenger**
Just Give Me A Reason…**P!nk**
Chasing Cars…**Snow Patrol**
Blackbird…**Doves**
Maybe…**Ingrid Michaelson**
More Than Us…**Travis**
The Story…**Brandi Carlile**
Breakeven…**The Script**

PLAYLIST

Run...**Snow Patrol**
Jeremy...**Pearl Jam**
Second Chance...**38 Special**
Jar of Hearts...**Christina Perri**
My Heart Is Broken...**Evanescence**
Light Outside...**Wakey!Wakey!**
What About Us...**P!nk**
Black Hole Sun...**Nouela**
Short Change Hero...**The Heavy**
Uninvited...**Alanis Morissette**
After All...**Cher (with Peter Cetera)**

For Melissa Stevens,

who brings my stories to life
through her art,
you have your own magic.

AUTHOR'S NOTE

Brochan (Bro-gan)
Fenella (Fen-nella)
The John Walker: high end of the Johnnie Walker brand
Laird: a person who owns a large estate in Scotland.
Cranachan: a Scottish dessert
Mo Leannan: a Scottish endearment meaning 'my love'

As children we are taught good from bad, right from wrong, but sometimes it isn't so black and white. It is how one handles the ambiguous area in between that defines her...or him.

—Lizzie Danton

PROLOGUE

The full moon illuminated the navy sky as wisps of clouds moved over the pale sphere. The few times he cased the castle, the forest that wrapped around it had been a symphony of sounds—wolves, owls, crickets. Tonight it was as if the creatures that roamed the dark knew a more dangerous predator was on the hunt. He knew of a door that never was locked, he slipped inside. Without a sound, he walked up the stairs and down the hall. His palm was sweating from both nerves and excitement as he pushed open the door, raised the gun and squeezed the trigger, spraying the bed with bullets. Surprise furrowed his brow when he flicked the lights on to find the room empty but for a small piece of paper addressed to him on the night stand. The first trickle of fear slithered down his spine. With shaking hands he unfolded it. Penned in dark red ink was written only one word.

Run

Panic coated his throat and the finesse he had entered with only moments earlier had fled. Bone-deep terror replaced it. He did as instructed and ran. Reaching the staircase, he felt the hair at his nape stand on end. He wasn't alone. The darkness took shape, staring back at him with ice-cold eyes. The last sound he heard was his own frantic scream for help.

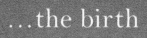

...the birth

of a monster...

CHAPTER ONE

THE HIGHLANDS OF SCOTLAND

1982

I don't like this. Abigail, I don't like it."

"It will be fine. You'll see."

"The doctors say it is a risk for you to carry a child. Why would you do this?"

"I want your child."

"But we discussed it. Your life is more important. We were considering adoption."

"It's not the same."

"So you tricked me. You got pregnant knowing the risks," he roared.

"I knew you wouldn't allow it, but I want this even with the risks. Please don't be upset. All will be well. You'll see."

"You deceived me."

"I'm sorry."

"I can't look at you right now." His anger was from fear. He couldn't lose her, but he *was* angry, so fucking angry. He shouldn't have left the house. He should have sought solace in a bottle of whisky. What he set in motion that night would destroy them all.

"Finlay." She reached for his hand.

He grasped it tightly. "I'm here."

"He's coming. Our son is coming." Nine months. She had made it, defied the odds. All *would* be well. He would make it so. If they could conquer this, they could overcome anything.

"One more good push, lass. I know you're tired, but one more push and you can rest," the doctor encouraged.

She was so tired, so very tired. She knew the doctors had been right and she felt fear for her son. Would her husband love him when she was gone? Or would he blame him? "Promise me, Finlay, that you will love our son. No matter what."

His face went pale. "We will both love him."

She wanted to believe that, wanted to believe she would be there for all of his birthdays, but she knew better. She was fading, but not before she saw her bairn. "Promise me!"

"Yes, I promise."

Satisfied her husband would keep his word she gathered up the last of her strength and pushed her son into the world. She knew it was a boy even before the doctor declared him as such. She touched his black hair and looked into his pale blue eyes. A lifetime of love she bestowed on him in that single glance.

"Doctor, her stats are dropping."

The doctor was already handing off the baby and trying to stop the bleeding. There was too much, too fast. "We need to stop this."

Finlay, seeing all the blood coming from his beloved, had forgotten all about their child. His only concern was for his wife. "What's happening?"

"Get him out of here," the doctor ordered.

"Save her. Save my wife."

The doctor worked quickly and efficiently, but his thirty years of experience told him there was too much damage to repair. When she went into asystole, he stopped working.

"What are you doing? Help her!" Finlay raged, seeing his wife lying so still.

"Get the paddles," the doctor ordered, but he knew it was just to appease the husband.

The nurse called, "Charging…clear."

No change.

"Again," he ordered.

"Charging…clear."

Another nurse touched her throat. "No pulse."

"Again."

"Charging…clear."

Finlay watched in horror as his beautiful wife slipped away.

"Time of death, twelve thirty-two am."

Finlay looked to the doctor and then to the babe crying air into his lungs before he settled on his beautiful wife and all the blood. His howls of anguish were heard on the other end of the hospital.

"Keep it away from me. I don't want to see it or hear it." If she hadn't deceived him, nothing that followed would have happened.

"It's just a bairn."

"I want nothing to do with it."

"You don't mean that. Think of Abigail."

"I didn't want it. She tricked me and it killed her!"

He had a pang of guilt, remembering the promise his wife had made him give, but then she had broken her promise to him and in doing so she died. Bled out on the table after pushing that thing out of her. It killed her. How the hell could he love something that killed what he loved most in the world? "Out of my sight, woman!"

"Will you at least name your son?"

"You want him to have a name, you name him." He walked away, needed to get drunk, anything to make him not feel the aching hole the loss of his wife created, or the hell he had brought onto himself.

Fenella and Finnegan had been with the McIntyre family from the beginning of Finlay and Abigail's courtship. The tragedy of their young mistress was heartbreaking, the cruelty of the father unthinkable.

"He will come around. He is in mourning, but he will come around."

Finnegan wasn't so sure Fenella was right. A man turning his back on his bairn, well, to his way of thinking wasn't much of a man.

"This babe needs a changing and some food. We're going to need formula," Fenella said as she cradled the wee babe in her arms.

Finnegan touched his dark hair, as soft as silk. "He's a sweet baby. I've never seen eyes that color blue before, pale like the moon."

"He is beautiful, but he'll be crying soon enough if we don't get him some food."

"All right lass, I hear ye. I'm going. What are we going to call him?"

Fenella didn't hesitate to answer; she knew what her young mistress wished to call the bairn. "Brochan."

Finnegan smiled his approval. "After the dear sweet lass' pa."

"Aye."

"And the laird?" Finnegan didn't hide his anger at the laird and his treatment of his son.

Fenella, always the more calm of the two assured him, "He'll come around."

The laird did not come around. He changed after he lost Abigail. He never left his study. Drank himself to sleep every night. Brochan was a sweet little boy. He didn't know the devastation his birth had caused. He didn't know that his ma had given her last breath to see him born. He didn't know that losing his wife, his father had lost himself. He didn't know that his father blamed him for her loss.

A few months after Brochan came home, Fenella went to check on him. He was already sleeping mostly through the night. She wasn't surprised because he was just that way, easy and sweet. She reached his room then stopped when she saw the laird standing over Brochan's crib. Her heart leapt thinking that Finlay was past his grief and ready to be a father. He would see Abigail in his son's features. She then noticed his hands curled into fists, so tightly the knuckles were turning white. She didn't know what he would have done had Brochan not stirred then fussed for his bottle. Fear for the child seeded that night, fear of harm coming to him at the hand of his own father.

BROCHAN
1987

"Ma, watch me."

"I'm not your ma, Brochan. Your mom was Abigail. We've talked about her."

"Ma is in heaven."

"Yes. You look like her. Her eyes were a darker blue, but she had the same black hair."

"Can I go to heaven?"

"One day you will."

"Will she know me?"

"Aye. A mother always knows her child."

"Will she love me?"

"Of course."

"Pa doesn't. Is it not the same for pa's?"

She got the look she did whenever I sneaked an extra biscuit, but it was scarier. "Your father is sad. He loved your ma very much."

"I look like her. Maybe he'll love me too then."

She looked sad now. "He does love you."

He didn't love me. I could see it when he looked at me. I didn't know what I had done. He never talked to me, but he hated me.

His car came up the lane and my stomach twisted in fear. He got mad at me even when I had done nothing wrong. I tried to please him, tried to make him proud, but he only ever looked at me with angry eyes. Finnegan had been teaching me to ride a bike. He said I was a quick study too, whatever that meant. I wanted to show my pa. Maybe if he saw I could ride a bike, he wouldn't be so mad. He would be proud.

The car stopped and Pa climbed out. He was a tall man. "Fenella, get the boy dressed for dinner. I have associates coming over. He needs to look presentable."

"Pa, look I can ride a bike! Finnegan taught me." His blue eyes looked over and I got so excited, my legs shook then the bike shook and then I fell right off. The stones of the drive cut into my knees. I tried not to cry, but did anyway when I saw the blood running down my legs.

"Shut him up or I will. And clean him up." Pa turned and walked inside without even asking if I was okay.

Fenella and Finnegan ran over. "You're okay, Brochan. We'll clean these cuts and maybe I'll give you a biscuit."

"Before dinner?"

"Aye."

I wanted a biscuit, so I tried hard to stop crying.

Finnegan's big hand came down on my shoulder and he squeezed in a way that made me feel loved, protected. "I bet that hurts, little man, but you'll be okay."

I wiped at my eyes and tried to keep the snot from running down my face. "Why does Pa hate me?"

"People grieve in different ways." Fenella's face went soft; it did when she was really sad. I didn't like seeing her sad, so I stood and bit my tongue so I didn't cry. My knees really hurt. "Maybe I could have two biscuits before dinner."

She smiled. "Maybe."

1989

"Ouch!" Pa pulled me from sleep when he yanked me out of bed by my hair. I smelled the whisky on his breath.

"You're evil. Before you even took your first breath you killed your mother. You're nothing but a monster."

He dragged me down the hall. "Please, Pa."

"Shut up."

"I'll be better."

"Your soul is dark. Nothing for you to do about it."

"I will be better. I will. I can be more quiet." I tried to walk and pull myself free, but his strides were long. I lost my footing on the stairs; my back and butt took the hit as he continued to pull me down them. He reached the front door. Fenella and Finnegan came running from the servant's hall, both dressed in their nightclothes.

"Laird, what are you doing?" Fenella demanded.

"You work for me. Remember that," he roared. "Anyone lets him in can pack and get the fuck out."

He opened the door; a blast of winter cold air hit me in the face. "You're nothing but an animal and animals live outside."

The heavy wooden door slammed closed in my face. I pounded on it, the bite of the cold going right through my pajamas. "Pa, please let me in. Please, Pa. It's cold. Please, please." My hands stung as I pounded on the heavy wood. I pounded for so long, my hands went numb and my shoulders ached. I curled up against the door and tried to convince myself I felt the warmth from inside coming through it. He would pass out and Fenella and Finnegan would let me back in.

I was frozen through when the door opened. My body so numb I didn't feel Finnegan's hands on me when he lifted me into his arms.

"He's like ice."

"He could have died," Fenella hissed.

"I think that was the plan." Finnegan was mad. I'd never heard him sound so frightening.

"When he learns you knocked him on the head," Fenella warned.

"He won't remember."

"We can't afford to get fired. Someone has to look out for Brochan."

"Aye. But if he ever does that to him again, I'll give him a taste of his own medicine."

"I'll hold your coat."

1990

Fenella wasn't feeling well. I sat with her and held her icy cold hand. She was sleeping now, but when she was awake she coughed so hard and so long it scared me. Finnegan was off getting her more medicine. I went to the kitchen to fill up her pitcher with water in case she woke and was thirsty. I didn't know my pa was home until I heard his heavy footsteps coming from down the hall. He stepped into the kitchen; his eyes were rimmed with red. He'd been drinking again. He studied the pitcher I held. I recognized the look. He moved fast, reached me in a few strides. Fisting my hair, he yanked me from the kitchen.

"You need to repent."

"For what?"

"Your sins."

"What sins?"

"You lived."

He dragged me to the small pond on the property, then into the pond until the water came up to his waist and my neck. Before I could gather breath, he held my head under. I flailed, trying to break free, even as my lungs burned for air. He didn't release me, he didn't let me up; he held me down so long the edges of my vision started going black. A sharp tug and sweet air filled my lungs; I inhaled greedily as I battled nausea. It didn't last long before I was thrust back into the murky darkness. He called it baptism. Over the next year, I would be baptized every week. He wasn't cleansing me of my sins. He was trying to kill me. Fenella wanted to report him to the authorities, had even risked telling her friend, Seamus, the local police, but he didn't believe her nor did the town; Finlay was such a good, kind man and not capable of the cruelties he was accused of. It was more believable that I was a troubled child. Fenella knew if Seamus came out to the estate to question Finlay, my father would fire her and Finnegan and I would be left alone in my nightmare. Every time I survived his abuse, stumbled to my room weak and exhausted, another little piece of my soul died.

1995

My father was away on business. How the man conducted business when he was insane, I didn't know. With him gone, it gave Fenella and Finnegan a chance to drive into Edinburgh to see a friend who wasn't well. I was in the kitchen working on homework when I heard the noise. It was faint, but it was coming from the lower level. On a few occasions, we had rodents getting into the stockroom. The last time I swear Fenella jumped twenty feet in the air. It was hilarious, but rodents could devour a pantry faster than Finnegan could kick back a pint. I grabbed a flashlight and headed down into the lower part of the castle. It was dark and cold and every time I got a chill, but not from the temperature. The dungeons were down here—small, stone cells with old iron gates and locks. People had actually been kept in those cells back in the time of my ancestors. Many left to die. I didn't know what was worse, starving to death or being feasted on by the rodents and insects.

I reached the stockroom, but I didn't see any rodents and nothing looked out of place. Pain exploded in my head. Disoriented and confused because no one was home, I didn't resist the pulling as someone manhandled me. It was only when I heard the distinct sound of a gate click close that my situation penetrated and with that came panic. I ran to the gates to see my father on the other side of them. He looked deranged. He had lied about his business trip. He'd planned this.

"Pa, let me out."

He laughed, a horribly twisted laugh.

"Don't do this." The baptisms were one thing, but this. He was completely mad.

"Let me out. Please, let me out!"

"Rot," he snarled then snatched up the flashlight I had dropped and walked away. The beam grew smaller and smaller until I was surrounded by nothing but darkness.

I pulled at the gates and clawed at the stone walls until my fingers bled. It was so cold, made even more so because of how damp it was. Then I heard the distinct sound of rodents, the scratching of their nails on the stone floors. At first I fought them off, but I was trapped in that cell for three days before a horrified Finnegan found me. I don't remember when it was I stopped feeling the rats on me, when I stopped feeling at all.

1998

"Brochan, stop! You're going to kill him."

My blood burned hot as it rushed through my veins. My hand cramped, my knuckles ached and still I didn't stop. There was a rhythm, a kind of beauty, as my fist made contact with flesh and bone.

Strong hands pulled me off Tomas. He would be eating out of a straw for a while. I grinned.

"Brochan!"

The teacher hurried over. She was new, not to the area, but she'd been away for a while studying and traveling. "You could have really hurt him."

"I *did* really hurt him."

"Why?"

"Why not?"

"I know you think that, really believe that you acted without cause, but something fueled that outburst. What?"

"He's a bawbag."

"Language. Why?"

"Look at him."

"Brochan. They're going to suspend you."

"I don't give a shit. I didn't ask to be here."

The big dude curled his fingers into my shoulder. "Don't talk to her like that. She's the only one who gives a shit about you."

"Fergus, language," Brianna chided then added, "Tell me, Brochan." It was her eyes. They were the windows to the soul; at least that's what that dick my pa always said. If that were true, my pa was fucked. The teacher's eyes were warm, kind…safe.

There had been a reason I pounded on the numpty; he had taken my St. Margaret medallion. The only thing I had of my ma's. Fenella gave it to me on my birthday. I uncurled my hand to show her.

She touched my hand and I wanted to recoil. Her hands were soft and warm as she curled her own under mine. Her eyes were bright, the green the same color of the hills that cradled our village. "I'm sorry he took that."

"Whatever."

A few days after I taught Tomas a lesson, I was in the kitchen with Fenella when we heard raised voices coming from the great hall. Finnegan appeared. "We have a problem."

We entered the living room to see my pretty, and seemingly sweet, teacher going toe to toe with Finlay McIntyre. "I've seen the bruises. It stops or I go to the authorities."

"Are you threatening me in my own home?"

"Yes. I've heard the rumors; the ones people insist aren't true, just the wild imagination of a troubled kid. They're true, every horrible detail. You will stop."

"Or what?"

"I'll make you. You don't scare me. You suffered a great loss, but what you're doing to your son is wrong. What would your wife say?"

His hand lifted. I ran into the room and stepped between them. For the first time his ire wasn't directed at me. "How dare you speak of my wife."

"You've done heinous things all in the name of your wife. She's rolling in her grave seeing how you're treating her child."

My father looked almost rabid, the spittle flying from his snarled lips. "You know nothing."

"I know she gave her life for her child and instead of holding onto that last piece of her, loving him like you did her, you've made his life hell. How you've gotten away with it for as long as you have I don't know, but I promise you it stops or I'll see your ass behind bars."

"He is a monster. He killed my wife," he roared.

"No. *You* are the monster."

Hearing someone say the words I felt distracted me so I didn't see Finlay curl his hand into a fist, wasn't fast enough when Finnegan shouted the warning. My father punched her in the face. Her head jerked back, her lip split before she crumpled to the floor. Every one had their limit; I had reached mine. I nailed him with a punch to the gut. But I didn't stop at one. I beat on him so hard and so long, he wasn't breathing when Finnegan finally pulled me off him.

That same night, the McIntyre ancestral home, my hell, burned to the ground.

...the

shadows...

CHAPTER TWO

LIZZIE
1992

My fingers touched the black wolf in the picture book I had brought home from school. He was supposed to be the bad one in the story. He was fierce and scary, but there was something pretty about him too. A banging on the door, followed by my father's angry voice, had me running to the corner. They would start fighting now. He wasn't here often, but when he was they screamed enough to keep most of the building awake.

"You got what you wanted, my fucking ring on your finger, but not anymore."

"You're going to divorce me? You never even lived here, never even gave us a chance."

"Why the fuck would I?"

"And your firm, those extremely conservative men. You think they'll be okay with you walking out on your wife and child?"

"They all have at least one mistress. A child out of wedlock, that would have turned their heads, leaving you won't even make them blink."

"You can't leave me."

"My lawyer is already drawing up the papers. You're one twisted bitch, bringing a child into this. You were a good fuck and even that got tired after a while. Getting pregnant, did you really think that would turn us into a loving family? The child carries my name so she will want for nothing, but you and me we're over. You can have this apartment and I'll keep you in the lifestyle you whored yourself to have, but know I already have another woman warming my bed."

"You son of a bitch." Something crashed against the wall.

"That's it, show your true colors, Norah. I *am* a son of a bitch. I never pretended to be something I wasn't. That's your thing."

"I'll ruin you."

"Don't threaten me. Remember Heather Craig? That's right, be afraid. I know where the fucking bodies are buried."

The door slammed, something crashed against it. I curled up as small as I could make myself in the corner of the room and cried. I was the child, that very unwanted child.

My mother appeared in my doorway. I started to shake. Kids feared the monsters under their beds or in their closets, but my monster was right out in the open. "You ruined my life. I wish you were never born."

She had said those words to me a lot and still they hurt, but this time I was scared too. When she walked away, I ran to the door and locked it. I grabbed the book, climbed under the covers and wished the big bad wolf were here to protect me…from her.

1997

"I should have insisted you wear the pink dress, the black just washes you out. Too late now, changing will ruin your hair. Do not slouch and do not pick on the food. You're a little wide in the stomach already."

Cold assessing eyes moved over me. Mother didn't like what she saw when her perfect lips turned down into a frown. "You are already slouching. Shoulders back, Elizabeth."

Her fingers bit into my shoulders as she forcibly pushed them back.

"Ouch."

"Stop being a child. You're ten today. I had planned to give you your present when your father was here, but if he keeps to his track record, he won't show for this birthday either."

It wasn't a package wrapped in pretty paper with a bow, or one of those fancy gift bags with all that lovely colored tissue paper. There were no balloons or streamers. No candles, just a gray envelope that had Stone Crest Academy written in the top left corner.

"What it is?"

"Boarding School in Vermont. You start in September."

"Boarding School?"

"Stone Crest Academy is very expensive. For the hundred thousand a year in tuition and boarding you might look a little enthusiastic."

Being abandoned was being abandoned; I didn't care how much it cost. "Yes, Mother."

It was my birthday and Mother was hosting a party. It wasn't a party for me; none of my friends had been invited, not that I had a lot of friends because Mother didn't approve of most and the few who actually got an invitation never came back a second time. She had a way of scaring people off. This was a party for her, another opportunity to show off to her friends.

"Do not embarrass me, Elizabeth." And on that note, Norah Danton turned and walked out.

Happy birthday to me.

I dragged my feet when I left my room and wondered how long I had to pretend. Mother usually drank heavily at these parties, so no longer than an hour. For that hour, I was the perfect little angel to all of her friends. I endured the cheek pinches, the assessing studies, and the comments under their breaths that they didn't think I heard because I was young, which to them was synonymous with stupid or deaf. When the mood of the party changed, I escaped to the urban garden on the roof of our building. The lights of the New York skyline twinkled in the distance as cars and people moved this way and that. Everyone was heading somewhere in a hurry. Maybe they were rushing to get to a party, or the birth of a child, or maybe it was just their family holding dinner so they could all eat together. Mother didn't eat, well unless it was in liquid form in a martini glass. My father never visited, but he did send me cards twice a year—one on my birthday and one for Christmas. Mother always opened them. She claimed she wanted to see the sentiment he wrote, not that he wrote any, but she was really taking the money he sent. I heard her on the phone with one of her friends saying she earned the money being stuck with the fat brat. I had been a means to an end, one that didn't end as she had hoped, so now she was sending me off to boarding school. I guess she didn't want the burden of a child anymore. I hated living here, but boarding school. My stomach ached thinking about it. I had only eight more years and I would be free. I didn't know where I would go or what I would do, but I would be free of her. I could endure eight more years, I hoped.

Stone Crest Academy looked just as you'd think; big, old, gloomy and cold. Mother drove down the long drive. "Behave with dignity, Elizabeth, you are a Danton."

When did I not behave with dignity? She held the reins so tightly I was barely able to think without her criticizing me.

"Will you visit at Christmas?"

"No," she exhaled on a huff. "I suppose there is no harm in telling you. I'm moving to California. My health isn't great."

Panic squeezed my chest hard. "But I'll be alone."

"Being alone isn't a bad thing. You'll have more time to focus on your studies. The curriculum here is very difficult and you, well, you will definitely be challenged."

In other words, I was stupid. "Why can't I go to boarding school in California?"

"Are you talking back to me?"

"It's a fair question."

"I'll make sure Stone Crest knows discipline is both welcomed and encouraged. After everything I have done for you, the sacrifices I have had to make, and this is how you speak to me?" Outside of finding my supposed flaws she did nothing for me. And I hadn't asked to be born and if I knew to whom I was being born, I would have definitely voted no. I was the consequence of *their* actions, but the threat of corporal punishment caused the boldness to flee.

She pulled up in front of the large black double doors, the crest of the Academy over them in stone. She turned to me. "Did you ever for a second think you are the problem? Both your father and I... what's the common denominator? You are, Elizabeth. Some people are impossible to love." After those brutal words, she climbed from the car. I couldn't get my hands to work, my stomach twisted and I felt sick. Was she right? Was I the problem? I managed to hide the pain, showing her would do nothing. She pulled my bags from the car, but she didn't walk me in to the registration office. We stood on the drive staring at each other with about as much warmth as two strangers would feel.

"Behave yourself," were her final words to me. Clutching my two bags tightly in my hands, I watched as my mother drove out of my life without a goodbye, without a kiss, without a hug. I wouldn't cry, crying didn't help, and still a single tear rolled down my cheek. I turned and looked up at the crest and felt a sickening sensation that as bad as my life had been, it was only going to get worse. I could do this, so I pushed my shoulders back and walked on shaking legs into the next chapter of my life.

Pain shot up my arm, but I bit my lip to keep from crying out. The ruler came down again on the same spot; the edges of my vision blackened. It was my third week here and I had dared to reach for a second slice of cake.

"Gluttony, Elizabeth, is a sin. Do you want to be a sinner?"

"No, Ms. Meriwether."

"Will you reach for seconds at dessert again?"

"No, Ms. Meriwether."

"That goes for all of you. Not knowing the rules isn't an excuse. We here at Stone Crest Academy are determined to turn out well-behaved and disciplined young ladies. Let this be a lesson for all of you. You're dismissed. Not you, Elizabeth. You can clean the dinner dishes as punishment."

Mindlessly, I started collecting dishes. This wasn't a boarding school; it was hell. Mother hadn't been kidding when she threatened to encourage discipline. Ms. Meriwether was the worst of the lot, an apparent convent drop out, she used her twisted version of religion as an excuse to hurt and punish. She was also the headmistress so her attitude trickled down to the rest of the staff. Her methods were wrong but they worked because I wouldn't be going for seconds again.

It took me two hours to clean up after dinner, which meant I would be up for most of the night doing homework, another punishable crime being up after curfew, but so was not turning in your homework. I was screwed either way. I dropped the dishrags in the basket and made sure all the lights were off before I headed to my room. Halfway there I realized I forgot my sweater. I turned back and noticed a light coming from the direction of the kitchen. My sixth sense was being honed here as well, so I didn't just march into the kitchen, I peered around the door. The sight that greeted me almost brought forth language that would have earned me soap in the mouth. Ms. Meriwether was sitting at the counter in the kitchen, but it was the two slices of cake in front of her that had me seeing red. If I were bigger and stronger, I'd be very tempted to walk right up to her and punch her in her hypocritical face. So much for practicing what she preached.

Every week mail was delivered and every two weeks we were allowed calls from home. Sitting in the dining hall, week after week, watching as the other kids received letters and packages from home was hard. On my birthday and Christmas my father continued with his tradition of sending me a card with money. I knew it was his assistant that arranged for the cards and still I kept them. The money I put in a sock under my mattress. I didn't have a roommate and no one came to my room, so it was safe.

My mother never called and she never wrote. She had quite literally washed her hands of me. Dumped me here and started over. I often wondered what she told my father because he was footing the bill for the place. Did she claim I was a problem child? That I was unruly and needed discipline? Most likely. Sometimes I thought to call him and set him straight, but he didn't care any more than she did. Sure he was paying for the school, but from what my mother told her friends he didn't feel the hit of my tuition and it was money that kept her and me out of his hair.

I often replayed my mother's parting words that the problem was me not them. I knew it wasn't true and still a part of me wondered. One day, maybe I'd find where I fit. I'd find a home. Maybe I'd even find someone who loved me. For now, I had to survive eight years of hell.

Strolling down the hall on the way to class, I wasn't paying attention and almost ran into someone.

"Sorry…" Nadine. She made the staff look nice.

"Watch where you're going, bitch."

"I'm sorry. I didn't see you."

"What are you, blind?"

"No."

"So you hit me on purpose."

Sweat dripped down my back. This was how it worked here. If it wasn't the staff, it was the older kids picking on the younger ones. Violence was fostered here, honed like a weapon. Her hand curled into a fist. I didn't run because that would only make it worse. I doubled over in pain when her fist connected with my stomach. My lunch rushed up my throat. She jumped back then started laughing, drawing the attention of others.

"Enough. Get to class. Elizabeth, clean this up." Ms. Beddle didn't reprimand Nadine, didn't ask what happened. That was how it worked here too. Don't ask; don't tell.

Nadine walked past me, shoving me with her shoulder. "See ya around."

For the next few years until Nadine graduated, she would go out of her way to bully me, but no one helped, no one ever stood up for me, no one cared.

2003

Drawing became my passion and coping mechanism. Any free time I had I used sketching. I learned that there was more to people than what you saw and I found translating that onto a canvas very therapeutic. Many of my images were of faces...dark, haunting images with empty eyes because there were a lot of those at Stone Crest. Sometimes when I looked in the mirror I even saw that emptiness staring back at me. The human spirit could take only so much before it broke and I could acknowledge my life to that point had broken a part of me.

I also learned I preferred being an observer to life rather than a participant. It was safer in the shadows, safer to document life but not actually live it. And with the life I had lived so far, I was ready for a little safe. My hope was one day to turn my observer ways into a career.

2007

I was going to throw up. My art professor entered one of my paintings in a contest and it won. It was a self-portrait. I called it 'Voices'. After I graduated from Stone Crest, I used the money my father had been sending me as the deposit on a studio in a building one step up from being condemned. I had to work double shifts at the diner to afford the place, but the lighting was perfect for painting. I worked and I painted until I had a portfolio to apply for art school. I wanted to get a formal education on technique. I had done it. Long hours, late nights and pinching pennies but I had gotten into night school. And now here I was, at an exclusive gallery where my painting was being shown. My professor was with me, but she was mingling. I was too nervous to mingle. I stood in a corner, watching as the who's who in the art world of Manhattan strolled around, many of whom stopped to study my work.

"Why did you call it 'Voices'?"

I almost jumped out of my skin before turning to the man who asked the question. He was older, probably in his fifties. Kind brown eyes looked back from a face that had lots of laugh lines.

"Your piece is exceptional, but I'm curious about the name."

"It's my interpretation of the inner struggle we all face at some point, the angel and devil on your shoulder trying to sway you to do right or wrong and how the line between the two gets blurred."

He touched his ear and I realized he was communicating with someone. Some collectors sent representatives to showings. His attention shifted back to me when he guessed, "Sounds personal."

"It is."

He was silent for a moment before he turned and extended his hand. "Alistair Duncan. My client wants the painting."

"It isn't for sale."

"He's willing to make you an offer."

I hadn't thought of selling my portrait. I loved it. It was my most favorite piece, but making a sale, my very first, it could be my foot in the door of a very difficult world to enter let alone be successful.

"He's prepared to pay $125,000."

My legs went weak and I almost sank to the floor. Alistair smiled. "I've shocked you."

"I've never sold my work before."

"His offer is more than fair."

"I know." I looked past him to my painting. As much as I wanted to keep it, I liked the idea of it going to someone who understood it and liked it enough to pay well over what it was worth.

"Thank you, Mr. Duncan. Please tell your client he has a deal."

"Excellent."

"May I ask who he is?"

"I'm sorry, my client likes his anonymity."

I understood, most collectors did. I learned that in art school, still it would be nice to know where my painting was going. "I hope he sees something new every time he looks at it."

"I've no doubt. Thank you, Miss Danton."

"Thank you."

As painful as it was to part with 'Voices' that purchase was the start of my career, the next chapter in my life.

2009

It was late; thank goodness the diner was still open. I had just finished a painting, an alley not far from my apartment in the garment district. It was like any other of the countless alleys in the city. There was something about the lighting from the streetlight when dusk fell, shining on the stones that made up the buildings along the alley, how the light reflected off the mica chips was beautiful.

The pancakes hit the spot. I hadn't eaten at all today. That happened when I was really moving on a painting. The coffee was hot and would probably keep me up, but then I'd be up anyway. A painting was never done after the last brushstroke for me. I stepped back, left it so I could return to study it with fresh eyes. I always found something I wanted to add.

Signaling the waitress for another coffee, a woman entered the diner. It was after eleven and she looked like she had just stepped off a fashion runway with her perfectly coiffed hair, her expertly applied makeup and her suit that was tailored just for her. She strolled through the diner on four-inch heels, an impressive sight. She scanned the diner until her eyes landed on me. It was tempting to glance behind me when she headed in my direction. Without a word, she slid into the booth across from me.

"Lizzie Danton?"

"Yes."

She extended her hand. "Cait Allen."

My painted covered hand curled around her French manicured one. "Hi."

"Your work is brilliant."

I had three showings since my first painting sold two years ago. They were small showings, but I couldn't describe how amazing it was when people not only showed up but also actually studied my work.

"Thank you."

"You're booking in small, off the beaten path galleries, where you're not the featured artist. I want to help you become the main attraction."

"How?"

"It's all about who you know."

Any artist worth her portfolio would jump at an opportunity like the one Cait Allen was offering, but in my experiences no one did anything for free. "What do you want?"

"I want to rise with a rising star."

At least she was honest. "Why me?"

"Because the first time I saw one of your paintings I cried. I don't cry, but there is something haunting about your work, something unique, and I know I can sell the hell out of that."

It sounded too good to be true. I told her as much.

"We can negotiate my fee. I just ask that you give me a chance."

The idea of my own showing, that was too tempting to turn down. "Okay."

Her face lit up. "Seriously?"

"Yes."

"You won't be sorry."

My feet ached, my face hurt from all the smiling, but I had just spent the night as the featured artist at the Coquette Gallery on

Fifth Avenue. Cait sat next to me on my sofa, our shoes kicked off, our feet up on my coffee table.

She dropped her head back on the sofa and stared up at the ceiling. "How fucking awesome was that?"

"I'm still riding the high."

Her blue eyes found mine. "You sold out, not just the show but all of your paintings."

"I'm still trying to get my head around that."

"It is just the beginning."

"I never would have been there tonight if not for you."

"You would have gotten there eventually. You're extremely talented; you just needed someone to market that talent, to push you into the spotlight."

"Thank you."

"My pleasure."

"Do you want to sleep here?" Cait had slept here often, working until the early morning developing marketing plans and scheduling, so she had clothes here and a toothbrush. In the year and a half we'd been together she wasn't just my agent. She had become my friend.

"Yep. Let's watch a movie. A scary one."

Thanks to Cait, I had started a new chapter in my life and so far I really liked this one.

CHAPTER THREE

BROCHAN
PRESENT DAY

Ashley curled into me. Her long arm wrapped possessively around my waist. Tall and rail thin, it wasn't a wonder she was a super model. I preferred a woman with a little meat on her bones. One who wouldn't break when I took her up against the wall, hard and fast. Ashley had been fun, but she was beginning to form an attachment. It was time to move on.

We moved through Edinburgh Castle, the charity event was being held in the opulent dining room. It seemed counterproductive to hold an event for charity by spending a small fortune to host it. Write a damn check. I wasn't here for the charity or for Ashley. I checked my watch; we were on schedule.

"I was surprised you said yes. You hate functions like this," Ashley purred as she ran her finger down my neck.

I did, but when an opportunity presented itself. "I'm a fan of the panda."

"I wouldn't have guessed that. Oh, champagne. I'm going to powder my nose. Grab me a glass."

She didn't wait, strolling off in her fuck me heels.

Ignoring the waiter and the champagne, I eyed the crowd until I found my mark—a heavyset man with an odd purplish complexion. Seemed to me his ex-wife should just wait for nature to take her course. The man looked like he was one foot in the grave already. Not my place to be the conscience or voice of reason. If you could pay my fee, there were no questions asked.

Harold Erskine, a solicitor, husband and father of three. He also had wandering eyes and hands. His flavor for the moment was a girl no older than eighteen, nearly the age of his eldest. His wife learned of his infidelity and filed for divorce. Harold didn't want to pay child support, so he was using his vast bank account and colleagues to find his wife unfit so his children could be sent to boarding school, cheaper than the monthly settlement he was paying currently.

I'd done my research. Harold was a randy cad, liked to fuck in public. A man his age messing up the sheets with a teenager would work in my favor. Normally, I liked a more hands on approach, but with a witness I had to sit this one out. Monkshood, a poison that was undetectable in an autopsy, added to the whisky he drank religiously before a fuck would bring about cardiac arrest. His wife wanted him humiliated. Croaking with his cock in a girl young enough to be his daughter during a charity event to save the pandas, yeah, that was fucking humiliating.

I checked my watch again. If he stuck to routine—the man was a stickler for routine, eating at the same bistro every morning for breakfast, parking in the same spot in front of his building, getting his clothes dry cleaned on the same fucking day every week—he'd be ordering that whisky any minute now. And like clockwork, he moved to the bar. I strolled through the crowd and came up beside him.

"Evening."

He looked over, a man impatient to get to the more sensual part of his night.

"Evening."

"Pandas," I said.

"What?"

"Saving the pandas." I looked around at the show of wealth, the flamboyance that had nothing at all to do with saving the pandas and all to do with status and showing off.

He understood when he laughed. "Just another excuse to dress up and be decadent."

The bartender placed his glass on the bar top. Harold slid the money across to him and grabbed his drink. "Enjoy your evening," he said kind of tongue in cheek and started away.

I moved with him and was careful to knock his arm only enough to get some of the whisky to spill over the rim. His focus shifted down to his pants and the small wet spot forming. I dropped the powder into his drink.

"Damn, sorry man."

Irritation rolled over his face. He didn't even acknowledge the apology. His honey was waiting. He kicked back the drink and placed the empty glass on the tray of a passing waiter. Grabbing her hand, he pulled her away. I didn't need to follow. When he croaked in the middle of a fuck, I was pretty sure her scream would alert everyone.

I went in search of Ashley. She was still in the ladies room. I joined her.

"What are you doing?" she asked then her eyes narrowed in understanding.

I flipped the lock and pushed her up against the door. Lifting her dress, I found her both wet and naked. Her smug smile turned into a moan as I fingered her clit.

"Condom is in my pocket."

She reached into my pocket, spent some time fondling me through the fabric of my pants, before she pulled my zipper down.

"Let me play."

"No."

"I want to taste you."

"Condom. Now."

Her pout was lost on me. As soon as I was covered, I lifted her leg, dug my fingers into her thigh and pulled her onto my cock. Her head fell back, her moan loud enough to be heard through the door. Her hands pulled through my hair, trying to drag my mouth down to hers. I didn't kiss. I fucked. She came, loud and long, before I emptied myself. The tingling at the base of my spine, the chills that moved down my legs, it was biology ... pure and simple.

"One of these days I'm going to get that magnificent cock in my mouth," Ashley threatened as she fixed her appearance in the mirror.

I wasn't going to be seeing her again. No point in telling her that. I reached for the door and held it for her. A few minutes after we rejoined the others, we heard the scream.

After dropping Ashley home, I called Gerard. He was my information man, the best in the business. He could find out anything on anyone.

"It's done," I said. "Has the money been transferred?"

"Aye."

"I'm taking some time."

"Why?"

"Personal reasons."

"You have a personal life?"

I disconnected the call.

On my way back from Edinburgh, I drove past my father's estate—the McIntyre ancestral home. The charred remains sat hauntingly on its hill. I owned it, the land, what was left of the building. I had enjoyed watching it burn. There had been just enough wood in the design to catch the fucker on fire. Developers wanted it, but I wasn't ready to part with it. I got an odd sense of satisfaction seeing what had been my nightmare nothing more than a pile of rocks.

My home sat on the other end of the small town. I hadn't had a stellar reputation, but after the fire I became a pariah. I didn't visit town often, but when I did people avoided me like the plague.

Fear fueled their behavior; I'd heard the whispers, the rumors. I did nothing to dispel their fears, partly because I didn't give a fuck, but partly because many of them knew what my father became and yet they did nothing…all but one. My former teacher.

There wasn't much in my blackened heart, but what little I had went to her, Fenella and Finnegan. Her cottage sat on rolling hills. She was forever outside working the gardens. I didn't get it. They died, you had to cut them back, replant. A lot of work for something that was so temporary. There was a heaviness that hung in the air as I approached the house. It had been growing stronger and stronger as her life slowly slipped away. When I knocked, it was a weary Fergus that greeted me. He didn't like me; he was right not to. We had something in common and as much as he disliked me, he loved her.

"How is she?"

Tears filled his eyes and rolled down his cheeks. I felt nothing, hadn't for a long time, but a phantom memory of pain burned in my gut.

"It won't be long now."

Such simple words, but when put together they were anything but.

A sickly sour scent filled her cottage. Even with the windows open, the smell of death saturated. Her room was at the end of a small hall. Her one time robust frame was frail. Her auburn hair had gone completely white and those green eyes that always sparkled with life were dull. Her head turned on the pillow and her lips curved up.

"Brochan."

I settled on the chair Fergus had vacated. I pressed a kiss on her forehead. She was cold and her skin was paper-thin. "She won't come."

Brianna was speaking of her niece, Norah Calhoun. The woman was a cunt. I didn't know her, but I heard the stories. The town still spoke of her. As loved as Brianna was, Norah was disliked just as strongly. She always wanted more than what she had. Lying and deceiving to get what she wanted. And she had hurt the one person who had given up everything to care for her because Norah left and never looked back.

"She has a daughter. I want to meet her."

"She's probably no better than her mother."

"She's my kin. The only kin I have left."

With kin like hers she was better off alone.

"My lawyer is looking for her, but there isn't much time."

That phantom pain was stronger and I was more harsh than I intended when I barked, "Don't say that."

"I've been dying for a while. I'm not going to thwart death again. I've made peace with it. If I don't live to meet her, be kind."

"I am many things, but kind is not one of them. Leave that to Fergus."

"You have kindness in you, goodness too, otherwise you wouldn't be sitting here with me now."

"I owe you a debt. I'm returning it."

"Bullshit. My dying wish is that you show my kin kindness."

"With Norah for a mother, you ask too much of me."

"Don't hold the sins of the parent against the child. You of all people should know that."

She always had a way of getting right to the point. "Fine. I'll attempt kindness until she proves she is no better than her mother."

"I have your word."

"My word doesn't count for much, but you've got it."

She took my hand into her small one. "It means everything to me."

I went home for a shower and a change of clothes before I returned to Brianna's. Fenella met me in the foyer.

"How is she?"

"Dying," I snapped then felt badly.

"I'm sorry, Brochan. I know how much she means to you."

That earned her a look. Despite what I had become, she too still insisted on seeing good in me.

"She has kin. Norah's daughter."

I knew the look well. Fenella showed it often, usually when she was watching those soaps she loved so much. Disgust.

"My feelings exactly. She wants to meet her before…" The thought of a world without Brianna in it had that phantom pain aching again. "I'm thinking she's better off letting sleeping dogs lie."

"'Tis normal to want to set things right." She twisted her fingers together. She had more on her mind. "I won't insult either of us and pretend I don't know where you go and what you do. 'Tis your life to live as you see fit and a part of me understands, but you are more than that. You don't see it, you haven't for a very long time, but you are more than that."

"I'm not."

"You are, Brochan. Finnegan and I will always be here, will always have your back, but one day I really hope you see that your father didn't break you, he only bent you."

It was a double-edged sword, their belief in me. It kept me grounded, kept me from spiraling too far out of control and that was the duality. It kept me from finally ridding myself completely of that fucking conscience they had both instilled in me, the one Brianna had taken up the torch on, feeding the fire of that dying ember.

"Speaking of which, Finnegan was looking for you."

My hands curled unconsciously, but I went to find him. I knew just where to look.

The room was dark, the smell of death clung to the air. Brianna's breathing was labored. Fergus sat at her side holding her hand.

"I'd like a moment with Brochan, love."

"Of course." He pressed a kiss on her forehead. He glanced at me giving a warning that I not upset her before he strolled out.

"Come. Sit."

I settled in the chair. She reached for my hand. "He doesn't understand why you do what you do."

I knew that. I didn't care.

"I understand it. I can't say I condone it, but I do understand it. There's a kind of justice in what you do."

"I'm not looking to right wrongs."

"I think you are. You just don't know it."

"Trying to make me good won't change a damn thing."

"See, that's your problem. You think you aren't good, but I know better."

I never understood her unwavering belief in me. I did nothing to encourage it. Did nothing to earn the respect of such a good woman. "I'm not good."

"You are, Brochan. A bad man would not be sitting here with a dying old lady. A bad man wouldn't be sad about it. I haven't been able to convince you, neither have Fenella and Finnegan, but my wish for you is that you meet that one person who will. I wish I could be there to see when someone breaks through that hard shell with nothing more than understanding. You'll fall, Brochan, and I hope you let yourself."

My eyes burned.

"I love you. I know you don't want to hear that, but I do. You are like a son to me. I wish I could have done more for you, stopped the harm before it happened."

"You did enough." I felt the tear roll down my cheek. I couldn't remember the last time I cried.

"Find happy, Brochan. Life is too short to live with hate."

I held her hand tightly as the years slipped away and I was that kid again, the one prepared to take on my monster to save my hero. My chest ached. "I love you."

Her eyes went bright before tears spilled out of them. "I know, but I do love hearing you say it."

Pain flashed over her face, her breath stilled. "Could you ask Fergus to come in?"

"Aye."

"We will meet again."

My own eyes filled, my reply no more than a broken whisper. "Promise."

"I promise."

I stood and pressed a kiss on her head, my lips lingered as I silently said my goodbye. Our eyes connected and she smiled. I walked outside as Fergus and Brianna said their goodbyes.

Two hours later, Brianna Calhoun, my savior, my conscience and my friend, died.

I was drunk. I didn't allow myself to drink to the point of intoxication thanks to my father, but the fucking pain I didn't want to feel damn near suffocated me. She was gone. It took almost a month, watching every day as her life drained away. Fergus, hard as nails, cried. Wept at her bedside when she took her last breath. After her funeral, I went straight from the cemetery to Edinburgh. I wasn't about to lose my shit in town. Edinburgh offered anonymity.

"Brochan."

I hissed out a breath when Ashley settled on the stool next to me, her hip practically on my leg. She hadn't noticed my condition. The woman was the poster child for self-centered.

"I haven't heard from you in a month. What's going on?"

I had no intention of telling her shit. "Busy."

Her head snapped to me. "Are you drunk?" Surprise shifted to interest as her lips curved up. "You're drunk. That might be fun." Her hand dropped to my lap, rubbing against my cock. I wasn't a eunuch; I grew hard.

"Maybe we should go somewhere and take care of that?" She leaned closer and whispered, "Let me suck you off. I'm told I am quite good."

I had no doubt. That was partly why I never let her suck me off, she got around, but also because there was an intimacy with blow jobs, a moment when you lost control, handed it over to the one on their knees. There was no way in hell I'd give that kind of control over to a vain bitch like Ashley. "I'll pass."

Fire flashed in her eyes. I fucking didn't care.

"Are you seeing someone else?" That pissed me off, the implication that we were together.

"I'm not even seeing you. We fuck."

Now she was pissed. "We fuck, that is all it is to you?"

"Yeah. And don't act all indignant. You aren't limiting yourself to fucking just me, so climb off the fucking horse."

"I would if you would let me in."

It always came back to this. She didn't want in anymore than I wanted her in. She wanted to lead me around by the cock, live under my roof and spend my money. I'd rather have stakes driven into my skull.

My focus wasn't great, but I tried to look her in the eyes when I said, "Not interested. Move on."

"Just like that?"

"Didn't put a ring on your finger, sweetheart."

"How dare you treat me like nothing more than a whore."

"You spread your legs for any man with money. That is the definition of a whore."

Even drunk, I stopped her hand from making contact with my cheek. "I'd be very careful," I warned.

"I can't believe I actually thought we might have a future."

"I can't believe you thought that either."

Her performance of outraged indignation was decent. Her parting words, "You'll be sorry." She stormed off and I called for another drink. At least the pain in my chest had eased.

Mac Donovan stood on his drive, his small estate rising up behind him and his pretty wife at his side. Two dogs playfully chased each other. Not a scene I thought I would ever see and certainly not from someone as ruthless as Mac Donovan. Pulling up behind his Range Rover, I climbed from the car and looked around. "You seem more the penthouse type, Mac."

He grinned as he approached. "We're all capable of change, Brochan." He didn't extend his hand, that wasn't Mac's way; he yanked me into a half hug. I tensed; it was instinctual. He knew why, but it didn't stop him. "It's good to see you."

"And you. Retirement agrees with you."

"That it does." He reached out for his wife. "This is Ava. Ava, Brochan McIntyre."

"'Tis nice to meet you. Mac speaks of you often."

"Nothing good I'm sure."

"Quite the contrary."

The dogs were rolling around, nipping at each other.

"Boomer and Champ, English Shepherds, six months old," Mac offered.

Ava wrapped her arm around Mac's waist, the gesture so easily offered and he moved into it, wrapping his around her. Content, peaceful, happy.

"We want children. Baby steps," Ava teased, but my attention jerked to Mac. The fiercest in the business and the man had stars in his eyes thinking about children.

Those eyes shifted to me. "What brings you out here?"

"I needed to decompress."

He knew what that meant, had been there a few times. Without missing a beat, he pressed a kiss on Ava's head. "We'll be in shortly."

"I'll start lunch." She surprised me when she took my hand. "It's really nice meeting you, Brochan."

She headed for the door, the dogs following her in.

"Best fucking thing to ever happen to me."

I believed him.

He turned and dropped his hand on my shoulder. "What's going on?"

"Brianna died."

Understanding moved over his face, his hand gave a light squeeze. "Oh, man. Brochan, I'm sorry."

I met Mac right after the fire at my father's estate. He broke apart a fight I was in. I was prepared to kill someone and all he had done was look at me funny. We talked that night, all night. He told me if I wanted to vent my anger in a more constructive way to call him. I had lived for so long with no power, at the mercy of someone who preyed on my weaknesses. He gave me a way to take that control back, to right the wrongs done to others. I wasn't virtuous, I'd sold my soul the first time I squeezed the trigger, but I had done it with my eyes wide open.

"Now that you're retired, settled with what looks like an idyllic life, do you have regrets?"

He gestured to the lane as we started down it. He pushed his hands into his pockets, looked ahead but his mind was in the past. "There will be those who see the world very black and white, but life is nothing but shades of gray. There can't be hard fast rules on what is right and wrong because nothing is that clear cut. A man kills someone for his wallet. That's wrong, but then you learn that he lost his job because his boss wanted him to cut corners and he wouldn't. His wife is sick and they need the insurance he had with his job. The man whose wallet he stole was the man who fired him. Does it make it right? Maybe not, but it makes his actions more understandable." His focus shifted to me. "You better than anyone know the ugliness that happens behind closed doors and so many times it's never brought to light. People know but turn blind eyes. Silence can be deadly. We smash open those fucking doors. No, I don't have any regrets at all. Life is what you make it. For some, the way I've spent my life is wrong, a sin, but my conscience is clear. And…" He gestured around him, "For those that believe in karma, I'm not the only one who feels that way."

He always had a way of looking at things that cut through all the bullshit. Still, ruthless Donovan a father…he'd make a good one. I wasn't above fucking with him though. "Children?"

"Yeah. Ava really wants them and she's still young enough to have them. Me, I'm getting old but I'm willing to try."

"You're what, forty-five? That's not that old."

"You're only a decade behind me." He patted my back. "Lunch will be ready."

"Thanks, Mac." It wasn't just for today, but for offering a hand when I really needed it. He knew. "It's what families do. Speaking of family, you're godfather to Boomer and Champ." He flashed me a smile. "Practice."

"Fucking hell."

LIZZIE

The gallery was packed; interested buyers strolled around the open space studying my paintings. I still hadn't gotten used to being a celebrity of sorts. I wasn't someone you'd recognize if I walked down the street, but in a setting like this it was both overwhelming and humbling when people stood in awe of my images. The dark edge to my work was sort of my signature. I sought what most thought of as ugly because even in the ugly there was beauty. An old gnarly tree, dead and rotting from insects and disease, but there was beauty in the way the branches had grown reaching for the sun and how the trunk, even crooked, held the weight of the one time majestic tree. The abandoned building, infested with rats and cockroaches, but the remnants of its former glory lingered in the hand carved fireplaces and crown moldings.

Cait approached. "You've got a buyer for 'Restless', but he'd like to talk with you first."

"Who am I talking to?"

"The tall hottie in the black suit." Cait leaned closer. "He's delicious, Lizzie."

Cait recently started cohabiting with her fiancé and she was on a mission to get me to find love and do the same. I dated, but I never found anyone I liked enough to date for more than a few months and certainly not move in with. She was in bliss and wanted me to be too. I loved that she cared, but that meant any man between the ages of twenty-eight and fifty were fair game for her meddling.

"I've no intention of licking him."

"Your loss." She touched my arm. "Have fun. I know you get nervous, but there is no reason to be. They are all here for you."

I knew that and still nerves had my stomach twisting. "I'll try."

She grabbed a glass of champagne from a passing waiter. "This will help."

I downed the whole thing then handed her the glass. "Here I go."

Cait studied me. She'd found the black sheath dress that hugged my figure. Had insisted her stylist pull my curly brown hair up into an elegant knot, and loaned me her Christian Louboutin black stilettos. "You look fantastic. Knock him dead."

I joined the man in front of 'Restless' a cemetery that was being relocated. It struck me as deeply disturbing to stir those from their final resting place just so a strip mall could go up. Still, there was beauty in the old caskets and in the knowledge that we were all part of the circle of life.

Dark eyes studied me, enough that I felt a little uncomfortable. "Ms. Danton?"

"Yes."

He held out a yellow envelope. "You've just been served."

I paced my lawyer's office; Harrison Billows was worth every cent I paid him. "My mother is suing me? On what grounds."

"She's contesting a will."

"What will?"

He scrolled a name on a piece of paper. "Joseph Masters. He's an attorney who represents the late Brianna Calhoun."

Hearing my mother's maiden name, my stomach squeezed tight. Was there another Calhoun like Norah out there? I hoped not. One was more than enough.

"Apparently this Brianna Calhoun is your mother's aunt. She left you her estate."

I didn't immediately hear everything he said because I was stuck on the fact that I had had a great aunt. The rest followed shortly after. "Her estate?"

"Yes, in Scotland. Brianna didn't know you existed. She only learned of you shortly before she died. Her lawyer is still getting her affairs in order."

"How does Norah know when I haven't even been notified yet?"

"Good question. I've called Joseph and he is very eager to meet you. You've an appointment today at three."

"If she lived in Scotland, why is her lawyer in New York?"

"He received his law degree in Scotland, but he also took the bar here. With you a US resident and Brianna being from Scotland, having a lawyer who practices in both countries simplifies things."

"Do I need to worry about this lawsuit?"

He actually snarled, "No, it's a nonsense suit. Joseph has assured me the will is ironclad, not to mention the bad blood between Norah and Brianna."

"Bad blood?"

"I'll let Joseph fill you in. Don't worry, Lizzie, we'll handle the lawsuit." He stood and walked me to the door. "I know you didn't know her, but I'm sorry for your loss, sorry you didn't get a chance to know her."

It hadn't fully sunk in, but I was sorry too. "Thank you."

The lawyer's office was understated, but elegant with antique furnishings and muted walls decorated with pretty landscapes done in watercolor. I didn't have to wait and was shown into an office where an elderly gentleman with a thick head of white hair sat behind a desk that looked a lot like the Resolute Desk. He stood as soon as I entered.

"Miss Danton, Joseph Masters. Thank you for coming. Please…" He gestured to the chair across from him.

"I'm sorry for the manner in which you learned of your aunt."

"Me too, but then nothing surprises me when it comes to Norah. I wasn't aware she had any living family."

"Your mother severed all ties with her family when she moved to the States."

Moved to the States? What was he talking about? "I'm sorry. My mother wasn't born here?"

"Your mother was born in Scotland. She moved to the States and never looked back. The only other family was her aunt, a Brianna Calhoun."

"And she died."

"Yes, quite recently. Her heart, she was only sixty-eight. She didn't know about you. It was very important to her that I stress that to you. She had no contact with Norah. To be quite frank, she scratched Norah from her life. The manner in which she left, her refusal to stay in touch, Brianna didn't want her toxic personality in her life anymore."

"I can sympathize."

"I'm sorry for that."

"My mother's loss. Aunt Brianna must have learned of me at some point."

"In her final months, she was getting her will together. She asked me to contact Norah. She hoped for a reconciliation before she died, her way of making peace. Your mother never returned a single one of my calls. But it was while I dug into your mother that I learned of you. When I told Brianna she had family it broke her heart because due to pride she never got to know you. It sickened her when she learned your parents had all but abandoned you. She couldn't make it right for you in life, but she wanted to do so in death, which is why you are here. All of her possessions, including her cottage in Scotland, she has left to you."

I opened my mouth but I had no reply. How did one reply to something like that? A woman I never knew left me everything. It felt wrong to even think about accepting.

"There is no one else?"

"Only your mother."

It felt wrong for me to accept, but it was really wrong for my mother to get her hands on it. Particularly now that she was trying to take it. "Don't get me wrong, I'm grateful, but..."

"It is a lot to take in."

"Yes, and not just the inheritance but learning I had family and missed out on meeting her."

"We don't have to do this today. If you would rather a few days to get your head around it."

"How did Norah learn I was being left Brianna's estate?"

He looked a little scary when he said, "I don't know, but I do intend to find out."

"Would Brianna have left the estate to Norah?"

"Had she not run away, yes. But not with how things were left. She sought reconciliation, but she wasn't a doormat. Her money was being left to the school where she taught and her cottage donated to the national historical register."

"But Norah learns it's being left to me and now she's crawling out of the woodwork to claim it."

"Yes, but she won't succeed."

I hoped he was right, but knowing Norah's track record it was possible she'd pull it off. I wanted to see it. In case Norah managed the impossible, I wanted to see the place where I actually had roots and a connection. "A cottage in Scotland."

"Yes, a lovely one in a small village called Tulloch Croft."

"I'd like to see where she lived, would like to know where I came from."

He pulled out a key ring and slid it across the desk. "Very well. I just have a few things for you to sign."

"I can't believe Norah. It's been twenty years that she's ignored you, but when there's something in it for her she reappears. What a bitch." Cait and I were having lunch; I called her as soon as I left the lawyer's office.

"Understatement."

"They won't let her win, right?"

"I hope not."

"A cottage in Scotland. It sounds magical. What do you think this Brianna was like?" Cait asked.

"She didn't get along with my mother and she left me everything, someone she never met. I think we would have had a lot in common.

My mother is cruel, but denying me the only other family I had was by far her cruelest act. How different my life could have been if instead of dropping me in Vermont, she sent me to Scotland... home to family."

"But you might not have found your art."

"True."

"You're going." She wasn't asking. She knew I was.

"Yes. I don't know what I'm going to do with the cottage. I'll most likely put it up for sale, but it's my heritage and considering the legacy of my parents, I want to see what else I'm made of."

"Makes sense. Plus Scotland, talk about inspiration. I'll take care of everything here. I'll get your utilities shut off while you're gone and stop your mail."

"I may not have scored big in the parent department, but I hit the jackpot with you. Thank you, Cait. I don't know what I'd do without you."

"You'll never be in that situation, so don't worry about it."

CHAPTER FOUR

LIZZIE

It wasn't possible to look everywhere at once, but I tried. I had never in my life seen such beauty as the landscape out the window of the cab. New York was metal, glass and concrete. Scotland wasn't overwhelmed with manmade, it was nature in its purest sense. Rolling hills of emerald green span for as far as the eye could see but the landscape changed nearly in a blink. The hills replaced with lochs edged by cliffs where the angry ocean slapped the jagged rocks. It wasn't a wonder this land was home to so many stories of myths and lore. It was stunning. My fingers itched to paint it.

Miles and miles stretched by with no sightings of other cars or people. The New Yorker in me grew nervous and then I saw the gates. I didn't know what it was about those gates that held my interest, but they stirred my imagination. Perhaps it was because there was nothing around them, just two large stone pillars and a set of black wrought iron gates. You couldn't see the house the gates were protecting, the woods that lined the lane were too dense, yet I found I wanted to walk down that lane and see it.

I'd asked the driver to show me the village before taking me to Aunt Brianna's. About a half an hour later, we drove through the center of her village, Tulloch Croft; built on the edge of a loch, charming stone buildings ran along one side of the two-lane road. Sailboats anchored just offshore. For a small village, it seemed to have everything—grocery, bakery, butcher, a pub, a post office, even a small train station. We backtracked a few miles to a long lane and at the end of it sat Aunt Brianna's whitewashed cottage. Gardens filled with color wrapped around the small structure. A stone barn sat perpendicular to it and a small stone wall ran along the lane. An older model Mercedes was parked in front of the barn. Behind the cottage was nothing but hills of green. I paid the cabbie, grabbed my bags and headed to the front door. The scent of heather carried on the light breeze. I didn't go inside immediately, too overwhelmed with a sensation I'd never before felt.

Home.

Inside was as charming as the outside with scarred wooden floors, antiques and an oversized sofa and chairs that begged for someone to curl up in. The kitchen was small, but the Agra stove was a thing a beauty. There was a fireplace in the kitchen, living room and bedroom. Photographs covered one wall leading to the bedroom. I could only assume the woman in most of them was Aunt Brianna. She had beautiful auburn hair that in her later life was chemically maintained. In many of her photographs there was a mischievous twinkle in her green eyes. More telling, she was smiling in every picture. Regret burned in my gut that I never got the chance to know her.

I was pulled from my study of the photographs when there was a knock at the door. Green eyes greeted me. The man was pushing seven feet tall. Wide in the shoulders and chest, even though he had to be in his seventies. My jaw dropped, the corners of his mouth tilted up. "You're the spitting image of Bri as a lass." He thrust his baseball mitt sized hand out to me. "Fergus Blake."

"Lizzie Danton."

Silence followed. He seemed friendly enough, but the New Yorker in me hesitated inviting in a stranger, particularly one as large as this one.

"You and Brianna were friends?"

"She was the love of my life."

It wasn't just his words, but the sadness that flashed in his eyes that had compassion overruling caution. "I'm sorry. Please come in."

The cottage felt much smaller with him in it. "Not as sorry as she was to learn of you so late. It broke her heart. Must have been a shock learning you had kin in Scotland. Brianna shared with me your story. Sorry, lass, you got dealt a bad hand."

"What doesn't kill us makes us stronger, right?"

"I suppose. How are you finding the cottage? I had a cleaning crew through it the other day when I heard you were coming. I had food dropped off too."

"It's beautiful. Thank you. Are you hungry? I could whip something up."

"No, lass. I just wanted to check in on you, make sure you arrived safely. I would have picked you up from the airport had I known your schedule." There was the slightest bit of censure in his words, but I didn't even know the man existed so I wasn't sure how I was supposed to have alerted him of my plans. He moved on. "Are you staying?" Direct. I liked that.

"For a little while. Brianna wanted me to experience my heritage, has given me an opportunity to do so, the least I can do is accept the gift offered."

"Smart lass."

I didn't want to put him on the spot, but he was here and he knew her, so I asked, "Would you like some tea? I'd really love to hear a bit about her."

His expression softened and my heart ached. He had loved her very much. To be loved like that, to love like that. He had lost her, but at least they had found that. He replied with a simple, "Aye."

He followed me into the kitchen. I started the tea. He leaned back against the counter and crossed his tree trunk sized arms.

"Brianna was always the life of the party. Never had a cruel word for anyone. Not even your mother, but that took effort."

"Did you know my mother?"

"Aye. Selfish from the day she was born. Her ma died in childbirth. Colleen, Bri's sister, she was a sweet girl, kind hearted like Bri. Your ma's dad was a sailor who didn't stick around when he learned of the baby. Bri tried, but Norah wanted more than this village, more than the Calhoun name, could offer. As soon as she could, she left. It broke Bri's heart, losing the last link she had to her sister, losing the last of her family. She kept tabs on Norah for a year or two, but Norah was just so...Brianna cut ties completely."

I brought the tea to the table and grabbed some cups. Fergus settled across from me. "My mother is still selfish and vain. Brianna was better off without her." I didn't want to tell him that Norah was after Brianna's estate, not unless it became an issue. No need for him to feel the thread of disgust that lingered in me at the knowledge.

"Yes, but in cutting those ties she didn't know of you."

"I found myself through my art. I don't know that I would have if I didn't live the life I did."

"I guess that makes sense."

"What did Aunt Brianna do, how did she spend her days?"

"She was a teacher. After she retired, she spent a lot of time gardening, hiking, she was trying her hand at jamming. She wanted to get livestock, sheep maybe some cows. She knew the work involved, but she didn't want to slow down just because she had retired. She was always the first at the hospital when a baby was born, the first to offer a hand when one was needed. She even took a local kid under her wing when he was having trouble fitting in, though the outcome of that wasn't one of her more successful interventions."

"She sounds amazing."

"She was. I miss her."

"I wish I had known her." I fiddled with my cup. "Can I ask why she didn't leave her estate to you?"

"She wanted a Calhoun to have this land, as is right."

"But am I taking your home?"

"No. We loved our cottages too much to part with them, so we used both." He took a sip of his tea. "You're here. That would mean so much to Bri to know her family had come home."

"I never felt home, not in any of the places I lived, but as soon as the cab dropped me off I felt it here."

"'Tis in your blood, lass."

"I believe that."

"We'll make a highlander out of you yet."

It wasn't until later that night that I found the letter resting up against the dresser in the bedroom, my name scrolled on it. Nerves caused butterflies in my stomach. My hand shook slightly when I reached for it.

> *Dearest Elizabeth,*
>
> *I wish this introduction happened in person. I blame myself in part for that. Pride and anger got the better of me for more years than I'd like to admit. Based on what I've learned of you, you understand better than anyone your mother's temperament. I did try to reconcile with her in my final months, but stubbornness runs in the family. I realize as I'm writing this, you will likely sell the cottage. I can't blame you; your life is in the States. I've seen your paintings. They are beautiful and yet sadness and loneliness weaves through them. It hurts to know you were out there alone, lonely. Had I known of you, I would have come for you. I hope you believe that.*
>
> *As an artist, I assume you can paint anywhere so maybe you will take a few months and paint here. Saying there is something special about the cottage and village will sound like the ravings of an old nostalgic woman, but there is*

something special about both. There's history and magic here, all one has to do is look.

Don't be surprised to see an old lady with ridiculous red hair in the moors. I do plan on visiting and often.

Your mother rejected her heritage, her past, her family, but Calhoun blood runs through your veins. This is your heritage, your past, your land, and your family. Even though we never met, I love you, Elizabeth. One day, a long time from now, we will meet. In the meantime, enjoy your journey of self-discovery.

Love, Brianna

Tears fell, but I let them. I ran my fingers over her handwriting, imagining the woman in the pictures writing it. She loved me. The words got stuck in my throat. I never had anyone say those words to me. Cait, sure, but for a woman I never knew to say it. What would life have been like if I had known her? If I had come when she was still the vivacious woman in those pictures? My mother denying Brianna and I a chance to know each other really was the cruelest of all her actions.

I unpacked and by the time I was storing my suitcases it was dark, but the cottage was so cozy. I had a fire burning; the lights were on low. Thanks to Fergus, the refrigerator was stocked, including a pint of soup from the local pub. While the soup heated, I gathered the photo albums from the living room. I poured over them; hours later I was curled up in front of the fire smiling at the life Brianna Calhoun had lived. My heart ached when I closed the last album, but after my chat with Fergus and these photographs I felt closer to her. I moved to the back door and glanced up at the moon. It was almost full in the dark sky. Resting my head on the doorjamb, I smiled even as tears brightened my eyes. "I would have liked to have known you. Thank you for giving me this, a piece of myself I didn't know existed."

A tingle teased the nape of my neck. I rubbed it away before turning from the window. I put everything back, cleaned up my dinner dishes and headed to bed. It was after three when I shut the lights off. My mind was racing, I didn't think sleep would come, but as soon as my head hit the pillow I was out.

The Highlands were magnificent. I spent the first few days just soaking it all in. There was something wild and untamed about its beauty. Mountains dotted the horizon, an almost rugged landscape where beauty survived despite the harsh environment. There was a house not far from Aunt Brianna's. It was tucked up against a stream, a small forest sat behind it, rocks covered in moss and little patches of wild flowers poked up here and there. Cottages speckled the landscape, but the focal point was nature whether that was the hills, the rocky terrain, the rivers that cut through the mountains or the wildlife that defied human settlements and still claimed the land as their own.

An elderly man with a walking stick and his dog moved slowly in my direction. I wished I had a paper and pencil to capture them.

He touched the rim on his hat as he passed me. "Evening, lass."

"Good evening." I was definitely not in New York anymore.

I had my phone to snap pictures; I wanted to capture the colors that seemed more vibrant than home. I had a little bag as well, to collect things like some twigs of heather, stones, maybe even some grass. I had ideas, paintings that would be different than my earlier work, that wouldn't have that dark edge because I didn't see darkness here, just bright, hopeful beauty.

I hadn't realized how far I had walked, but it wasn't the fact I was in town that had my feet stopping, it was the animal standing in the street. It looked like a cow, but it had long fur. It was blocking the road. Did cows attack humans? I was thinking no, but I did give him or her a wide berth. At least I tried, but two others appeared, much bigger than the first. The parents. The largest of the three mooed at me in what seemed like irritation. I didn't move and they continued to stare, like I was the one out of place. Maybe I was. Nervousness had me speaking my thoughts out loud. "I don't mean you any harm." The parents were flanking the calf, a clearly protective stance. "I'm not going to hurt you. I think we all know if anyone is getting hurt in this scenario it isn't you. I hope you're dairy cows because the idea of you being served up for dinner is enough to turn me into a vegetarian. Not really, I'm sorry to say I do love meat, but seeing you walking and talking…not really talking, well for you it is talking. Maybe I should stick to cheese while I'm here, just to be safe."

The hair at my nape stirred again. I rubbed it away even as I glanced behind me. A shiver moved down my spine when I saw the man leaning against a sexy black car watching me talk to cows. If I wasn't careful, people might start warning others to stay away from the crazy American. I was knocked off balance when the calf's head butted me in the stomach.

"Hey."

He mooed in my face and I swear it sounded like a laugh.

"Where do you belong because I am quite certain it isn't in the middle of town?" I asked that out loud to the cows. Yep, get the straitjacket.

"Hey, don't let them run off," a man called from down the street as he ran in our direction.

Don't let them run off? How was I supposed to keep them from running off?

One of the bigger cows started walking in the opposite direction of the man, the other two followed.

"No, wait. You're supposed to stay here." I actually jumped in front of them and put my hands up, like a cow was going to know that meant stop. They walked right around me. I dug into my purse for the granola bar I always carried because when I painted, I usually forgot to eat. I ripped off the wrapper. "Want some?"

All three heads turned to me. It was a good plan until they moved in.

"Oh crap." I broke off some and tossed it at the baby. Mommy and Daddy kept coming.

"Do cows like human?" I called to the man. He appeared, his laughing hazel eyes met mine over the cows' heads.

"No. They don't like human."

"I only had one granola bar."

"It was good thinking." He wrapped ropes around their necks.

"You're going to get them home by yourself?"

"Yeah. Thanks for the help. I'm Bruce."

"Lizzie Danton."

I didn't think I imagined his easy friendliness turning slightly cool. "Brianna's grand niece. I went to school with your mother."

"By the temperature drop, I'm guessing you had about as good a relationship with her as me."

I saw contrition before he said, "I'm sorry, lass. I fear you'll get that reception a lot around here. With Brianna's death, Norah is back in everyone's thoughts. She made it very difficult to like her."

"I understand that completely."

He studied me for a second. "Sadly, I can see you do." He offered his hand. "It is very nice to meet you, Lizzie."

"And you, Bruce."

"Welcome to Tulloch Croft. I better get these three home. My wife was just putting tea on the table."

"Are you sure you don't need help?"

"Aye, but thank you."

There was comfort knowing that Norah was a bitch to everyone. For a minute, I watched as Bruce walked three cows home, definitely not a sight I was used to seeing. Curious if I still had an audience, I glanced over to see the black car driving off. I continued on my walk. I reached the other end of town and intended to turn back, but my attention was drawn to the sight in the distance. The hills were lush and green and centered in the middle was a castle, or what remained. The roof was gone; the stone walls were jagged, like broken bones piercing through flesh. It was grim, bleak, sad and absolutely beautiful. I moved to get a closer look. Green grass grew up through the charred earth. The place had burned down some time ago and still it sat here abandoned but untouched. Why?

I walked through the rubble, reached what I imagined at one time was the front door. The sun tucked into the clouds when I stepped inside. The temperature dropped. It had been grand once upon a time. I could tell from the furniture, most of which was burnt beyond recognition, but there were a few pieces still recognizable that sat here and there. Paintings hung from the walls, carpets on the floor. Whoever owned this hadn't tried to save anything and stranger still, poachers hadn't tried to salvage it. Was it haunted? And if not, what was its story that it kept people at bay? I moved deeper into the castle, toward what had been the kitchen. It had been a grand kitchen. Had they large celebrations for the holidays? Had this space once teamed with staff, pulling the meats and breads from the ovens? Had a crew worked on nothing but sweets—fruited and spirit-laced cakes, fruit and meat pies? The sun moved from the clouds and how the rays shined down on the sad remains seemed almost ethereal. A glimmer caught my eye as the light reflected off something. As I grew closer, I saw it was a small medallion. It was only when I reached for it that I realized it was a necklace. It was charred so I couldn't see what it was of, but it felt warm against my palm. I didn't realize tears had gathered in my eyes until one rolled down my cheek. It was sad to see something so thoroughly neglected and to see the hints of life that had at one time existed here.

I was curious about the ruins, so I stopped at the small library in town on my way back to the cottage. Small was an understatement, with only a few racks of books, most of those being tourist books of the area and another of best sellers from the last few years. The librarian, Mrs. Wilson according to her tag, was an older woman with white hair pulled up into a bun. She glanced up when I approached her desk.

"Can I help you?"

"I was taking a walk and saw the castle just outside of town, the one in ruins. What happened there?"

I thought I saw fear flash in her eyes. She definitely crossed herself. "The McIntyre place. It burned down nearly twenty years now. The smoke from the fire was seen as far as Edinburgh, or so they say."

"Is there a reason it hasn't been taken down and the land cleared?"

She glanced around before leaning closer. "Only that the laird wishes it to stay as is. A memorial."

My heart twisted. "People were killed in the fire?"

"Aye, the old laird, the current laird's father. It was the McIntyre ancestral home since the eleventh century."

To lose his father and his home, that had to be hard.

It seemed the old woman didn't need me for this conversation as she continued. "The young laird is a cold sort. The truth is I don't believe he feels much of anything. Some even say he was born soulless. Our more superstitious townsfolk think he might even be…well not of this earth."

I didn't like gossip and I didn't like those who perpetuated it. I realized it was a small town and small towns fostered gossip, but I didn't have to listen. I was about to excuse myself until she said 'not of this earth'. What the hell did that mean? "Not of this earth?"

She leaned over her desk and whispered, "Supernatural." She then immediately crossed herself again.

Supernatural? Like what the Winchester boys battled every week? What nonsense and still I queried, "What, like a vampire?"

"No, a beastie for sure."

"A werewolf?"

"Aye." She crossed herself again. I entertained the possibility that she was pulling my leg for about ten seconds, but the look on her face. No, she was serious. Okay, so the librarian was crazy. I wondered if the laird knew about the rumors flying around about him and that the townsfolk spoke of him so candidly to strangers.

"Do you know this laird?"

"No, of course not. He stays to himself."

She didn't know him and yet she spoke with such authority, going so far as to call him a werewolf. I didn't blame the laird for staying to himself. If he made too many appearances in town they were likely to hunt him down with pitchforks and torches. "You don't know him and yet you say he's cold…a werewolf."

She crossed herself again. "Rumors. The town is small."

I wanted to educate her on the ugliness of rumors, but she was well into her seventies. She should know better.

"If he doesn't feel anything, why keep the castle standing?"

If she realized I was questioning her ridiculous comment, she didn't let on. "I don't know, lass. Maybe he gathers his powers from it."

"Powers?"

"Aye."

It was on my tongue to ask what powers did a werewolf possess, but it seemed unwise to challenge her delusion. Was she dangerous or a harmless crackpot? I wasn't really eager to spend any more time in her company to learn the answer to that. Thanking her was the polite thing to do despite the nonsense she'd shared. "Thank you for your time."

I reached the door and glanced back to find her watching me. Perhaps she'd start a rumor that I was a witch or a banshee. I supposed there were worse things to be. Curious I asked, "What is the young laird's name?"

"Brochan McIntyre."

CHAPTER FIVE

BROCHAN

"I t's done. Wire the remaining funds into the account."

"I told you not to call me on this line."

Fucking people. "I'll call you on whatever the fuck line I want. Wire the money. I'll wait."

"I want proof."

"I don't work that way and you know it. You have ten minutes to wire the funds before I pay you a visit."

Fucker was playing in a whole other league. I could hear the fear in his voice when he spoke his next words. "No need for that. One second."

The waitress set the highball of whisky on the table. I reached for it, savored the burn on my tongue.

"It's done."

I checked my offshore account to confirm the transfer was complete then disconnected the call. I leaned back in my chair and resisted the urge to pull a hand through my hair. It was time to retire. I was getting too old for this shit.

A woman entered the restaurant, led by the hostess. I checked my watch. Punctual. I knew she would be here; it was why I chose the place. Brianna Calhoun's kin. The town was abuzz about her. I wasn't sure if she was a skilled actress or really as innocent as she seemed. Knowing how much of a cunt her mother was I wanted to believe the former, but she hadn't known anyone was watching that day with the cows. She'd been talking to them and when she put herself in front of them and held up her hands, the first real laugh I'd had in years burned up my throat.

She glanced up at her server; her eyes were as blue as the sky. For someone so young, it was unusual to see the darkness that haunted them. Was it possible she wasn't like Norah at all and just another of her victims? I sipped my whisky as I watched her. She looked around, but not how most did. She wasn't checking out who was in the restaurant, she wasn't comparing herself to the other women in the place. She looked around like she'd just spotted a rainbow or a fairy ring with wonder and a little awe. I couldn't help throwing a glance around the place but there was nothing spectacular about it. What did *she* see?

She studied the menu, her brows furrowing. Her lips were moving; I watched the expressions rolling over her face. Her reactions went from the gamut of interest to gross, her lips even curling in disgust over a few things. I'd never seen anyone so animated over a menu. She settled on Scotch broth. After the waitress left, she reached into her bag and pulled out a pencil and scrap of paper. I couldn't see what she sketched, but the way her hand effortlessly moved across the paper she clearly had skill.

I tried to see Norah Calhoun in the woman but all I saw was Brianna, a younger, slightly broken version of her. Her meal arrived. She savored her soup in a way that suggested she had once known what it was like to have food withheld. I'd experienced that enough to recognize it easily in others.

Despite myself, Brianna's kin intrigued me. I had said I would show her kindness and the kindest thing I could do for the lass was to stay away from her. I didn't leave until after she had, and curious I walked passed her table to see what she had been sketching she had left. My hand actually shook when I reached for it because what she'd drawn were the gates to my home. Instinct had my focus jerking to the door. I didn't believe in coincidences. In my line of work, I couldn't afford to. She had drawn my home. Did she know who I was to Brianna? Was she intending to cash in on more than Brianna's inheritance? She was in for a rude awakening if she thought to come at me. Perhaps the apple didn't fall far from the tree after all. I headed to my car while I reached for my phone to call Gerard. It was time to learn more about Miss Danton.

"I need you to look into a Lizzie Danton."

"Client or mark?"

"Neither."

"So why the interest?"

"I don't pay you to ask questions."

"I know. You're getting it for free."

He was an ass, but he was the best in the fucking business. "Just the highlights."

"Give me fifteen minutes. I'll email it."

Hanging up, I dropped the phone on the passenger seat. I was curious about Miss Danton because there was a look in her eyes that lingered like a shadow or a ghost despite the awe and wonder; a look that once upon a time stared back at me from the mirror. Lost.

Gerard was fast; the notification of incoming mail came as I parked in the garage. I went right to my study, flicked on the lights and settled at my desk. Pulling up his email, I started to read.

Rodney Danton made his money in investments, running one of the most lucrative firms in Manhattan. He was a self-proclaimed womanizer, changing up his arm candy like one would shoes. Norah Calhoun. He hadn't appreciated her cunningness until it was too late.

I stood and walked to the bar for a shot of whisky. The man had some morals, agreeing to marry the mother of his child, a child brought into the world through deception. Miss Danton. What was life like for her, being the reason a man was shackled? I had been on the other end of it, responsible for the death of someone's love. She had been the tether tying her father to her mother in a match he didn't want. And her own mother had done that to her, used her as no more than a pawn. That was cold, even for me.

I downed the whisky, savoring the burn, and returned to my desk. Rodney dropped a bunch of money on the problem and walked away. Norah kept up pretense for ten years before she gave up and dumped her kid at boarding school. There was very little about Miss Danton during those early years, likely foisted off and neglected. After boarding school, she returned to New York and was accepted into art school. She had a healthy savings and yet she put more into it than she took out. She lived very frugally. There were no friends of note, except her manager who it seemed was her only and closest friend. No boyfriends, no children anywhere. For all intents and purposes, Lizzie Danton wasn't so much living as she was going through the motions.

Leaning back in my chair, the anger surprised me. Norah knew Brianna was here, knew she could have foisted her child on a woman who would have loved her, cared for her and given her a life. She had deliberately kept the two apart. And in doing so, she had hurt one of the three people in this world I actually cared about. She'd answer for that.

I understood now the haunted look in Lizzie Danton's eyes. What it didn't explain was why of all the things in the area to sketch—Tulloch Croft had countless sights more interesting—she chose my unassuming gates. It was careless to leave questions unanswered. I wasn't careless.

LIZZIE

Brianna's grave was in a small cemetery in town. Heather grew wild around the stones. Hers was a simple one with bright green young grass sprouting up through the dirt. A large bouquet of flowers rested across her grave. My guess, Fergus had been by.

I knelt in front of it. I wasn't even sure what to say to her and yet she had been family, blood, and I had found her too late. Emotions,

I hadn't realized were so close to the surface, had tears filling my eyes.

"Hi, Aunt Brianna. It's Lizzie. I don't really know what to say, but I do hope you can hear me. Thank you for bringing me here and giving me a chance to see where I come from, to learn more about my family. I'm an artist, oils and watercolors mostly. I'm not married and I don't have children. I'd like to one day, but I've never met anyone I wanted to step into all of that with. I've spent much of my life alone. I guess you grow used to your own company when it's all you have. Your home is beautiful. I've gotten so much inspiration being here. I can't wait to set up an easel. I met your Fergus. He misses you; he helped get me settled. I do intend to stay for a while and I hope I do see you on the moors. I love you, Aunt Brianna. I know we never met, but I feel it. I don't know how that's possible but it is. I guess I should mention that Norah is contesting the will. I'm conflicted with your generosity aimed at me, but I absolutely will not allow her to get her hands on your legacy. Our lawyers are confident the suit will be squashed. You didn't miss out on anything, Aunt Brianna. Believe me, your life was much better off without her in it."

A twig cracked, my head snapping in the direction to see a man standing not far from me.

"Sorry to intrude."

So why was he?

"You're Brianna's kin from the States, aren't you?"

He was being rude interrupting me, but I didn't need to be. "Yes. Lizzie Danton."

Extending his hand, he stepped closer. "Tomas O'Connell. You're from New York City. This must be a change for you."

"Yes, but a good one."

"What are you going to do with it?"

"Excuse me?"

"She left you everything. What are you going to do with it?"

I realized it was a very small town and everyone knew everything, but even for a small town he was out of line. Not even Fergus had asked me that and he was Brianna's other half.

I had no intention of answering him, so I stood. "I didn't realize it was so late. I'm expecting a call at the house. It was nice to meet you."

His eyes narrowed. I hadn't fooled him, but I didn't care. It was more than a little creepy that he approached me in a cemetery and peppered me with questions he had no business asking. I didn't wait for him to reply and hurried from the cemetery. As I was leaving, Fergus arrived.

"Hey, lass. I was going to check in on you after I visited Bri."

I didn't realize how hard my heart was pounding. Seeing Fergus, it started to slow. "I was going to grab a bite at the pub. If you want, I'll wait for you there."

"I'd like that."

I expected the scrutiny of those in the pub when I entered. It was a small town; I was sure everyone knew everyone's business. Not to mention Bruce had warned that Norah had not been liked and I was her daughter. They didn't start throwing things at me. *That* was a surprise.

"Sit anywhere," the bartender called from behind the counter, an older gentleman with a shock of red hair and a generous belly. A waitress, no older than eighteen, strolled immediately over but more out of curiosity than efficient service.

"Can I help ye?"

"Please. Do you have coffee?"

"Aye."

"A cup of that please."

"And to eat?"

There was a board behind the bar that listed the dishes offered. I hadn't a clue what any of them were. "I'm not familiar with the menu."

She flashed me a smile, the meaning was clear, 'no shit'. "We can do a Scottish breakfast of eggs, sausage, black pudding, beans. Or Cullen skink, a soup of haddock, onions, potatoes."

"I'll have that."

"You got it. You're Brianna's grand niece."

"I am. Did you know her?"

"Everyone knew her." There was a bit of censure in her words.

I didn't need to explain, but I did anyway. "I didn't know I had a great aunt."

Her brows furrowed. "Your ma didn't tell you?"

"No."

She leaned closer. "Seems to fit with what people say about her. She is not at all popular around here."

She was definitely outspoken. It was refreshing. "I'm definitely getting that vibe."

"Stop badgering the customers, Bridget."

"Just being friendly." She winked as she strolled back to the bar.

The door opened and Fergus entered. "Pull me a pint, Blair, and a plate of haggis."

Haggis? Yuck.

He pulled the chair out opposite me and sat down. "Seeing the sights?"

"I am. I would like to take a trip to Edinburgh and farther north to Culloden Moor."

He did the sign of the cross. "Terrible history, beautiful place."

Thinking about my odd conversation with Tomas I said to Fergus, "I met Tomas O'Connell at the cemetery."

"You did? Odd place for him."

"I had the sense he followed me in."

Fergus flashed me a grin. "He just might have. He likes the ladies, the prettier the better."

"He asked me what I intended to do with Aunt Brianna's inheritance."

Fergus' brows furrowed. "Not his business."

"No."

"He is blunt as stone."

I thought it was more than that, but Bridget returned with our food so I let it go. Fergus drank his pint in one swallow and called for another before he started digging into his haggis. I knew what haggis was, but I had to admit it smelled delicious. My soup certainly was.

The door opened again, this time a hush fell over the place. Fergus wiped his expression and yet his focus was glued to the newcomer. Curious as to who would cause such a reaction from the dynamic man across from me, I twisted my head to the door. It was the man that watched me with the cows that day. He was dressed entirely in black, the fabric stretched tight across the muscles of his shoulders and biceps. He wasn't a beautiful man, his features were too severe or perhaps it was his expression that looked to be carved from stone. Not even his pale blue eyes softened his appearance because they were cold, like chips of ice. He strolled to the bar in an easy, yet deceiving stride because I was sure he was very aware of everyone in the pub. His focus never shifted to me and yet a shiver went down my spine in awareness, like prey when sensing a predator. A bag was waiting for him. Not even the friendly Bridget met his gaze, focusing too hard on filling the sugar containers. He dropped a few bills on the bar top, grabbed the bag and as silently as he entered, he left. It took a minute before the noise level in the pub resumed.

The words were out before I even considered them. "Who was that?"

"Brochan McIntyre."

My eyes flew to the door. *That* was Brochan McIntyre, the man who was or was not a werewolf? I could admit he had a presence, one worthy of the rumors circulating around about him. Still, he was only human...I was pretty sure.

"You would do well to stay clear of him, lass. He's a kind of trouble you don't want knocking on your door. I'm not kidding, Lizzie, steer clear of him. Some people don't want fixing."

"What does that mean?"

"Just that help doesn't work when the one you're trying to help doesn't want it."

Brochan intrigued me, even more so now. Besides, I liked forming my own opinions so I told a little white lie, "I'll steer clear."

"Good. Now finish your soup and we'll split a cranachan."

"I don't know what that is."

"Trust me, it's delicious."

I needed groceries. I had gone through what Fergus had brought. I wasn't sure what to expect of the markets, particularly the food, but I was looking forward to the experience.

The parking lot was a challenge; it sat on a kind of rise and all the cars were tilted at slight angles. The land surrounding the parking lot was muddy from the constant run off. Any car that rolled into that mess would take quite an effort to dig out again.

The market wasn't much different from the markets in the city, but then I was used to smaller markets. Wooden shelves lined much of the store and there was a small section for fruits and vegetables. One difference, there was no meat department or bakery because both the butcher and bakery were right down the street. Another difference, the packaging was brighter than at home with lots of loud colors. It was pretty and definitely eye catching.

I recognized some labels: *PG Tips, Cadbury* and *Walkers, Robertson's* and *Crosse & Blackwell,* but I had fun strolling the aisles because there was a lot not found at home. Like canned haggis. Perhaps haggis was like scrapple, a Philadelphia favorite but how it was made was not something you needed to know.

I reached for a can and read the ingredients. It didn't sound too terrible. Could I really be in Scotland and not try their national dish?

"It tastes better than it sounds," a deep voice said to my right. I started to reply as I turned to him but the words got stuck in my throat when I saw Brochan McIntyre. My head tilted back to see his eyes, a blue so light they almost looked white. There was no smile on his face and no warmth in his gaze.

He gestured to my hand. "By your death grip, I'm guessing you are on the fence as to whether to buy it."

Why are you talking to me almost rolled off my tongue. Based on all the accounts I had heard of him, he was a loner and a scary one at that, and yet he was encouraging me to buy canned haggis.

"What does it taste like?"

"A hearty stew, kind of like shepherd's pie."

"But it's made from a sheep's heart, liver and lungs."

"Traditionally. Nowadays, it's usually beef or lamb...sometimes liver is added. When in Rome, right?"

He strolled toward the register before I could reply. I still held a death grip on that can of haggis but for an entirely different reason. The town's werewolf just encouraged me to purchase it. I dropped it in my basket. My focus was no longer on the market or the loud and brightly colored stock. I had expected Brochan McIntyre to have fangs or claws or be antisocial. I hadn't expected small talk in the grocery store.

I paid for my things and headed to my car. Distracted, I didn't notice the small crowd until my name was called. The crowd parted to show Tomas O'Connell leaning against the back of his beat-up truck. An unpleasant feeling moved through me, the scene causing a wicked case of déjà vu.

"Evening, Lizzie."

The town was ready to crucify Brochan, but it was Tomas I found grating. He acted far too familiar for someone who didn't know me at all.

"Tomas."

"We were heading over to the pub for a few pints. Want to join us?"

"No, thanks. I'm working this evening."

He pushed from his truck and approached. I continued to my car. "Yeah? Doing what?"

My business wasn't any of his business, so I answered being as vague as possible. "I'm painting."

"What are you painting? Already making the place your own."

Moron.

That sexy black car pulled up across the street. Brochan. Tomas' head whipped around but not before I saw the look that crossed over his face. Hatred. He turned back to me and moved in a little closer.

"You'll want to stay away from him," he said as he gestured to the car. "Dude is bad news. He thinks he's tougher than he is, but he's still trouble." Tomas leaned even closer and touched his temple. "I don't think Brochan is right in the head."

His posse started to laugh, egging him on. That was why it seemed so familiar. It was Nadine all over again. I didn't know Brochan, but of the two it wasn't Brochan's character I found lacking.

I closed the trunk. "Didn't you ever hear the expression, if you don't have anything nice to say..."

He didn't like that, his lips curled into a snarl, but my focus had shifted behind him. At first I thought I imagined it, but no, his truck started rolling. Never had I seen karma swing back so quickly. I could have told him, alerted him that his truck was about to roll into the muddy swampland. I didn't. I even went so far as to linger a few seconds to make sure the truck gained some momentum to do the most damage before I offered a farewell and climbed into my car. I waved then drove off. I had just reached the road marker indicating I needed to stop when I heard him cursing. The sexy black car was still there; I drove right by it and my heart slammed into my ribs when he pulled in behind me. Despite what I had told Tomas, there were enough warnings shared about Brochan McIntyre that I'd be stupid not to heed them; so having him behind me was a little scary. It crossed my mind he was only making sure I got home safely, since I had deliberately allowed Tomas' truck to go down that ditch. But he was rumored to be cold and unfeeling so why would he care? I felt my pulse all over my body; it was throbbing so hard and fast. I turned off at the lane to the cottage and held my breath. The sexy black car drove past. My hands were shaking as I continued down the lane. When I reached the cottage, I locked myself in then double-checked the locks. I kept all the lights on that night.

Aunt Brianna's white Mercedes was old. I didn't know much about cars, but I was guessing it was circa nineteen sixties or maybe seventies. The interior was in surprisingly good shape. She started when I took her out the other day, not at first, but after coughing out some black smoke she roared to life. There was the slightest floral scent in the car, her perfume. The realization brought a smile even as my heart twisted a bit. Unfortunately, my good luck with the car didn't last. I made it just outside of town when she died. I stood on the side of the road, staring under the hood without a clue as to what I was looking at. Cait had put an app on my phone before I left, she knew me so well, so I was able to find the closest garage. It was going to take at least an hour for the truck to get here. I'd sightsee, but I was in the middle of nowhere. It was the main road into town and still there was nothing on either side of it but fields for as far as the eye could see. I didn't have games on my phone. Cait had offered to add some, but I had been adamant that I'd never have time to play them. She did load up a bunch of songs. I scrolled through the list and at one title I actually laughed out loud. Hanson. Cait apparently had been obsessed with them as a kid. I'd seen her rocking out to them a few times. In honor of her, I selected 'MmmBop'. To my shock, my feet started tapping to the beat. I had teased her enough over the years, but the joke was on me. It was a very catchy tune, enough that by the end I was dancing to it. I didn't know how many times I replayed the song, shaking my booty on the side of the road. I didn't hear the car until it pulled up alongside me, that black sexy car. The passenger window rolled down. My face was on fire because I had been really getting into it, a song my friend loved when she was ten.

Mortifying.

I peered into the car.

"Car trouble?"

I answered in my head because there was a disconnect from my brain to my mouth. For a loner, Brochan was pretty social.

"Is a tow truck coming?"

Even if one weren't coming, I'd have lied. Self-preservation. "Yes, any minute now."

"That's Brianna Calhoun's car."

"I didn't steal it." *I didn't steal it?* What the hell was wrong with me?

He had the blankest expression, like the muscles in his face didn't work, so his deadpanned reply surprised me. "Good to know."

He didn't drive off, didn't say anything, just stared. I wasn't sure if he was waiting for me to do something, maybe dance again because I definitely had a groove going on when he pulled up. The silence dragged out so long it got awkward. I almost asked if he wanted fries with that just to break it.

"Did you try the haggis?"

"Not yet."

"You're Brianna's kin."

"Yes."

"What's your name?" Did he want to know because I was Brianna's kin or to report me as the crazy lady dancing on the side of the road to Hanson? I wondered from what direction the paddy wagon would come.

"Lizzie Danton."

He offered no reply. Not his name, not welcome to town, not a critique on my dancing. Nothing.

"And you are?" I knew who he was, but he should have offered.

A beat or two of silence followed my question before he answered, "Brochan McIntyre."

"Thanks for checking on me." Though I didn't really have the sense he cared one way or the other, so it was odd that he stopped at all. I thought of his home, charred and ruined and almost opened my mouth to ask why he allowed it to remain that way, but the intrusive conversation with Tomas popped into my head. It wasn't my business.

More silence followed before he shut off his engine, climbed from his car and strolled to Aunt Brianna's car. He leaned over to inspect under the hood, my eyes following the motion. Shamelessly, I studied his shoulders and back and the defined muscles the shirt didn't hide, then to my horror my gaze moved lower to his faded jeans covered ass. What the hell was I doing?

"Why didn't you ever visit her?" My attention jerked to his face to find him studying me out of the corner of his eye.

"I only learned of her when her lawyer called. She sounded like an amazing woman. I didn't know you could miss someone you never knew." Her photos, how much I would have loved to know why she chose to hang the ones she did. To watch her interact with the butcher, a stodgy man who actually smiled when sharing stories about her. She had a life here, but more, she was loved and she was missed. I didn't know her, my only family and I learned of her too late.

I didn't realize Brochan had turned and was now studying me, a lot like the other day when I was chatting with the cows. Remembering that, I felt my cheeks burn. I shook it off and gestured to the car. "Any luck?"

Before he could reply, not that I was holding my breath for one, the tow truck arrived. A kid climbed down, but his focus was on Brochan's car. "Nice wheels." His attention shifted to Brochan and I swear he looked even more interested in the car's driver.

"Thanks again for stopping," I called to his retreating form. Not surprising, he didn't reply.

"Do you know him?" the kid asked.

"No."

"But he stopped for you."

"He recognized the car."

"Brianna, she was a cool lady. Hey, wait. You're her kin from the States."

"Yes."

"Cool." Then he sobered. "Sorry, I mean…sorry. Sweet lady. Funny too. Do you want a ride back to the cottage?"

"If you wouldn't mind."

"Not at all."

"They're still adorable. And I told you it was a very danceable song. I still rock out to it too."

"Not to an audience like this man."

Cait chuckled, "You should have taken his picture."

"Yes, because that would have been the icing on my crazy cupcake. Let's get a selfie, scary, sexy man."

"Sexy? You didn't mention sexy."

"He was sexy, but he was more scary."

"I don't understand you. A handsome stranger stops to help you and you think he's going to kill you."

"I can't explain it. It was just a vibe. I'm not into crystals and all that, but this dude definitely had a dark energy."

"I think you're letting your surroundings influence you."

"Maybe. I'm thinking about staying here, Cait."

Silence.

"I never felt like I belonged in New York, but I feel something here. And to be living on the same land my ancestors lived on. I have a family I never knew of. Sure, they're gone, but they're still here in a way. I can't wait to set up an easel."

"I thought that might happen. I know you never really felt like you fit here. I'm happy for you, Lizzie, and I can't wait to see how you translate this new chapter in your life into your art. I am sad though, because I don't want to lose you."

"You won't lose me, it will just take a little longer to see each other."

CHAPTER SIX

LIZZIE

The area between my shoulder blades tingled again. I'd been feeling that same sensation for the last week. I had the distinct impression someone was watching me, but whoever it was might as well be a ghost because I never saw them. Maybe it was a ghost; maybe it was Brianna. She had said she'd be stopping by often for a visit. The thought made me smile.

I studied my painting. I was behind the cottage and though there were endless images I could have captured—her gardens, the hills, the cottage itself—I found it was the woodpile that stirred my creative juices. The wood was weathered, several seasons from the look of it. Long, green grass grew around it. I guess weed whacking wasn't big here. And mushrooms, those beige and brown mushrooms that popped up when it was particularly wet, grew on many of the logs. It struck me as whimsical and had I been home I likely wouldn't have looked twice at the pile, let alone paint it, but in this setting I could imagine the sprites that called the woodpile home. And as I painted, I painted those sprites. Delicate, iridescent wings, long, willowy bodies and bright eyes in colors like purple, pink and green. My work was usually dark, a vein of sadness weaved through the images that though beautiful were also tragic. But this, it was light, almost hopeful. And I realized as I studied the happy image I was bringing to life that the weight of sadness I'd carried since I was a child wasn't so heavy here.

Birds took flight from within a patch of trees, as if they'd been scared off. Likely an animal, but I was feeling fanciful so I called out. "Aunt Brianna?" It was shockingly easy to hold a one-way conversation with a ghost. "I painted sprites. I don't paint sprites. My work has always run toward the dark, but not here." I touched a leaf on one of the trees, emerald green with veins forming a pretty pattern. I'd have to bring my sketchbook out later to capture a few of them. My thoughts turned a bit melancholy. "She was wrong to turn her back on you. She was wrong to ignore your wish to reconcile, but thank you. I've never felt home, not anywhere, but I do here. Clearly, since I'm painting sprites. I wish you were really here. That we could actually have this conversation, that I could hear your laugh and see your smile. I missed that, we missed it, but your photos paint your picture so beautifully." I hadn't expected the tears. I wiped them away; today was a happy day. "I should probably get back to painting before someone happens along and sees me talking to myself. I'll hang this painting in the living room, over the fireplace. It belongs here."

"Miss Danton."

I jumped ten feet in the air then spun around while cursing, "What the hell."

The curse ended abruptly when I saw who the intruder was. Brochan McIntyre. What was he doing here? If he was contrite for scaring ten years off my life, I couldn't tell. He strolled toward me then around me to study my painting. He glanced from the canvas to the woodpile before those pale eyes landed on me.

"Brianna would have liked that."

I joined him in front of the canvas, studying my work with a critical eye but there was nothing I would change about it. It was different from my usual work, it was enchanting.

My focus shifted to him. "Why are you here?"

His answer intrigued me. "I don't know."

"Do you want something to drink? Tea?"

"I never much cared for the stuff."

"Whisky?"

"That I'll take."

We moved inside. He stood by the fireplace in the living room while I got our drinks. After handing him his, I settled on the sofa. "You knew her."

"Aye."

"Did you know my mother?"

"No, but I've heard stories."

"You're wondering which one I'm like."

He turned to me then. There was absolutely no inflection in his tone. "Her dying wish was that I show you kindness."

"Why?"

"You were her kin and she was forever seeing more to me than there is."

Somehow I doubted that. From all that I'd heard Brianna called it like she saw it.

"Knowing my mother, you have to be wondering if I'm here to take advantage. In your shoes, I would be wondering the same."

"Are you?"

"No. I'm here because I spent my life being alone, so to learn I actually had family who wanted to get to know me. How could I not come?"

"And the inheritance?"

I'd be angry at what he implied, but he was looking out for Aunt Brianna, showing the side of himself that he insisted didn't exist. "I make a good living. I don't need her inheritance. I'd have come if she lived in a box by the river."

He drank the whisky in one long swallow then placed the glass on the table. "I've kept you long enough." He started for the door but stopped when he reached it. I thought he intended to say something else, but he didn't. I sat on the sofa as the door closed quietly behind him wondering what the hell that had been about.

***

Danny from the auto shop gave me a loaner car. It had been two weeks since I arrived in Scotland. I spent part of the day working, the light had been perfect, but I couldn't get those gates out of my head. There was something about them, mysterious for sure, but also forlorn. Were they once the grand entrance to a castle that now lay in ruins while Mother Nature reclaimed her land? I hoped the gates were open so I could find out. Halfway to my destination, the loaner car started spilling out black smoke, the engine started knocking then it just died. My cell had died; I had forgotten to get the adapter. I sat in the car and watched as gray clouds came rolling in. There was nothing to do but walk. I hoped the weather held out until I reached my destination. The words were barely out of my mouth when lightning flashed then thunder rumbled seconds before the rain. I was soaked to the skin almost immediately, but I was drenched when I reached the black iron gates. They were open. Dense woods lined the long drive, with some trees so tall they would have blocked out the sun had it been visible. The canopy provided a relief from the rain. The lane widened and my feet just stopped. It was dark, the rain was coming down in sheets, and still I had never seen a more beautiful sight. Tucked within the pine trees that surrounded it was a castle, one that was definitely not in ruins. It felt as if I'd stepped into the pages of a fairy tale, as if the castle had sprouted up right along with the trees. I had never seen anything more beautiful. The stone was red, like the color of faded terracotta. Hundreds of glazed windows, chimneys and turret towers came together in stunning harmony. My feet propelled me forward, but it wasn't shelter and a phone that motivated me, it was awe. There was a cobblestone path that wrapped around the castle, right on the edge of the forest. The back was whimsical with the castle and its surroundings blending harmoniously together, the front was landscaped and meticulous, the wild vegetation tamed back. Emerald green lawns stretched out in the distance and a circular drive, with a stunning marble fountain, greeted visitors. A turret that was only missing Rapunzel rose up to the clouds. Two urns, larger than me, spilling over with flowers, flanked an exquisite mahogany door. It was the most welcoming entrance I'd ever seen. What looked like newer construction sat on the far side of the courtyard, a twelve-car garage that I had no doubt was filled because why else build it. The design kept to the original style of the castle and blended in beautifully. I fell in love. I knocked, I needed to call for a tow, but I wanted to see the inside. Would it be as magnificent as the outside?

An older man pulled the door open. Dressed formally in a black suit, I had the distinct impression he was the butler. He glanced at me, then behind me at the rain before he stepped back. "Come in."

As soon as I stepped inside, my breath caught in my lungs; it was even more beautiful on the inside. A small staircase brought you down into what I could only assume was the great room. The intricately detailed plastered ceiling was three stories up, the walls were a muted gold on top and a patina cherry wood on the bottom. The floors were the same cherry, more brown than red and old. Chunky furniture was arranged around the enormous space creating little clusters. The floors were partially covered by old rugs in bold colors. Massive crystal chandeliers ran down the length of the room. A grand staircase rested against the right wall.

I realized the butler stood stoically as I gawked. I pulled myself together. "My car broke down and I don't have a cell. Could I use your phone?"

A woman wearing gray trousers and a pale pink sweater set appeared from one of the halls. "You are soaked to the bone, you poor dear. You need a shower and some hot tea or soup."

What? No. "Thank you, but that's not necessary. Could I just use your phone?

The butler hadn't moved. The woman pushed past him. "Finnegan, make yourself useful and put on the kettle."

On second thought, tea sounded nice. Something warm; I was quite cold.

"The laird."

The woman turned to the butler and put her hands on her hips. "Do you think he would rather she die from a cold on his front steps." She didn't wait for a reply, escorting me toward the grand staircase. I wanted to see more of the castle, but I was a stranger. They were strangers.

"I'm sorry for intruding. It wasn't my intention. I drove by the gates when I first arrived in town and I was very curious what lay behind them."

She continued up the stairs. "The white room is the closest. You can shower there."

A shower? Getting naked in a stranger's home? She didn't know me, why would she offer that?

"I'm a stranger off the street. I could be a serial killer."

She stopped midway up the stairs and turned to me. "Are you?"

"No...are you?" It was reasonable to ask because she was being awfully nice about it, almost luring me in with kindness. Was there an elaborate torture chamber in the basement, complete with a creepy man in black leather and a mask? I almost turned and ran down the stairs.

"Not the last time I checked."

"Is it like a national custom to invite rain-soaked strangers into your home for a hot shower and tea?"

"If it isn't, it should be. You'll catch a cold if you don't warm up."

She had a point. "You're very kind. Thank you."

Pleased that I acquiesced, she continued up the stairs.

"How many rooms are in the castle?"

"One hundred and forty-five."

A hundred and forty-five rooms, imagine the heating bill. "Are they all named?"

"No, but the name is fitting for this one. "

She pushed open a pair of hand carved wooden doors. She was right; it was fitting. The white room was stone, a pale stone made up the walls, the vaulted ceiling and the floor. In the middle of the room was the largest bed I'd ever seen. The bedding was white, the window treatments were white. The bedside tables were white. The only color came from the paintings on the walls, bold and stormy paintings.

"I feel like I've just stepped into a fairy ring, it's too beautiful to be real."

"It's real all right. Takes forty of us to keep this place going."

"Are you sure about me taking a shower? I don't want to get you in trouble with your boss. I can call for a tow and wait with the car."

"He's not home and even if he were, he wouldn't turn you away on a night like this. You just worry about getting dry and warm. I'll worry about the laird."

"Thank you. I'm Lizzie."

"Fenella, 'tis nice to meet you, Lizzie. There's a robe in the closet. When you're done, leave your clothes in the bath, one of the parlor maids will retrieve them. The kitchen is at the other end of the great hall."

The door closed behind her and for a few seconds I didn't move. I was standing in a Scottish castle, in a room fit for a princess. I wished I had my phone. Cait was never going to believe it. I moved to the window, the rain pelting against them, and caught a glimpse of the almost full moon in the early evening sky. I thought of Brochan. If he were a werewolf, his night was coming. I smiled at my silliness then felt the chill so hurried to the bathroom. Stone sinks, pewter faucets, a huge glass shower and even a crystal chandelier, elegant yet modern. I peeled my clothes off and climbed under the hot spray. It felt so good. I hadn't realized how cold I was until the soothing heat touched my skin. I could have spent an hour in the shower, but I kept it to a few minutes. After I dried off and donned the robe, I made my way to the kitchen. The scent of something delicious wafted down the hall. Fenella looked up when I entered, but she frowned instead of smiled.

"Your face is flush."

"It's colder than I'm used to."

"Let's get some warm soup into you."

"It smells delicious."

"Potato, leek, mushroom soup. I also have tea."

"You're very kind."

"Highland hospitality," she said with a smile. "Where is your car? I'll call a tow truck."

"About two miles toward town, a green car. I don't know what kind."

"I'll be right back. You finish your soup."

She returned shortly after. "Your clothes will be dry soon enough. Would you like to see the library? It is one of my favorite rooms."

"Can I help with cleaning up?" She looked horrified, like my offer was a scandal. "Absolutely not. While your clothes dry, you can curl up in front of the fire and read."

That idea sounded lovely. "Thank you."

I could live in the library, two stories of books wall to wall on three of the four walls. A spiral ladder to get to the second level, library ladders to reach the higher shelves. The windows went from floor to ceiling; a huge stone fireplace that was large enough for me to stand in took up the fourth wall.

"I would never leave this room."

"Aye, it's beautiful. Keeping the books dust free is a never-ending job. We've one parlor maid whose only job is this library."

I supposed that made sense because once she finished the room, the books she started with would be dusty again.

"Enjoy," Fenella said before she disappeared.

Discomfort faded as I walked the perimeter on both levels; it was an eclectic library of rare books, classics, textbooks, how-to books and best sellers. I selected a current New York Times best seller I'd been wanting to read and curled up on the sofa. I lost track of time. A sound from the hall startled me. Glancing up, I was surprised to see it was dark outside. My clothes still weren't done. It wasn't just the heavy footsteps approaching, but the warning that moved down my spine and froze me in place. A large shadow appeared in the doorway and I gulped down a cry of panic. It moved farther into the room and I realized it was a man, a very large man. With how the room was laid out I didn't have a great view of him, but I could see he was dressed in a tuxedo. He headed for a small bar set up at the far end of the library as he pulled his tie off and flicked open the top few buttons of his stark white shirt. Pouring two fingers of something, he studied the liquid in his glass, and then he emptied it in one swallow. He placed the glass on the table and started walking out. Recognition hit even before those pale eyes turned to me. Of all the castles in the entire world, I found myself in *his* library. What were the odds? I didn't gamble, not ever, but maybe I should.

"Lizzie Danton. May I ask why you are in my library?"

I stood, clutching the book like a lifeline. "I passed your gates when I first arrived and I had to see what was beyond them."

"Why?"

It was a simple enough question but outside of curiosity, I didn't know why his gates in particular held my interest. "I honestly don't know."

Those pale eyes moved down my body taking in the fact that I wore only a robe. "Where are your clothes?"

"Drying. The loaner car from the garage died halfway here. Then it rained."

"The rental car died too?"

"Yes, I'm a car killer." He had a reaction to that, but what he was thinking I couldn't say. Again he didn't move and yet something in his expression seemed to soften. I put the book on the table and hurried to the door. "I'll get out of here."

"Fenella will have already prepared a room for you. The lane will be impassable with this rain." Said with the same amount of enthusiasm one would have when going in for a colonoscopy. He didn't want me here. I couldn't really blame him. I was the crazy lady who danced on the side of the road and spoke to cows—the woman related to Norah—so seeing me curled up in his library was surely not a sight he liked.

I thought he was leaving but instead he turned and pushed his hands into his pockets. "Why are you here?"

"In this library or Tulloch Croft?"

"Both. Did someone send you?"

"No, well Mr. Masters told me of Aunt Brianna, encouraged me to visit."

Temper flashed in his eyes. "Doesn't explain why you're in my library."

"I explained that."

He pulled something from his pocket and slammed it down on the table. "Explain that."

Fear trickled down my spine. Had Tomas been right about Brochan not being right in the head? The man was acting crazy. I looked down at what he demanded I explain. Fear gave way to curiosity. I drew that, the gates to his home. My eyes jerked to his face. "How do you have that?"

"I watched you draw it. Why the fuck are you drawing the gates to my home? Who the fuck sent you?"

He might be crazy, but he was pissed too. Did he think I was here to steal from him? Or lure him in with my charms so I could get my hands on his home? That was insulting, but I was here uninvited and he knew enough about my mother to wonder if I was like her. "I didn't know you lived here. Like I said, I saw them when I first arrived and they caught my attention. I'm an artist. I paint. Those I want to paint." More curious than was wise I added, "Why do you have that?"

He didn't answer and instead asked, "You mentioned you didn't know you had an aunt. How is that possible?"

"My mother is a vindictive bitch."

"She's a cunt."

"You do know her. I didn't know I had an aunt because my mother dumped me at boarding school when I was ten so she could move across the country and start over. She only had me to get to my father, when that failed she cut her losses. I'm sure it never occurred to her to ask Aunt Brianna if she wanted me. Or maybe it did and she is just such a bitch she wanted us both to be alone. I really don't pretend to understand Norah."

His lips formed a frown. "And your father?"

"She trapped the man into marriage by getting pregnant. What kind of relationship do you think we had with me being the child that bound him to her?"

"Why did you let Tomas' car slide down that slope?"

The swift subject change was dizzying and for a second I was confused until I remembered he had been there. He would have seen me staying silent as Tomas' car rolled into a situation that took several hours to remedy, or so I heard. Not my finest moment and yet I had no guilt about it. I wasn't sure I liked what that said about me. To him I replied, "I've had a lot of experience with bullies. He was being one."

"Bullying you?" His voice was clipped, as if he was angry.

"No. You. The town talks about you. I'm sure you know that, most just curious and a little afraid. They have the oddest notions, so ridiculous they're comical, but Tomas was being cruel. He called you touched. I absolutely cannot abide bullies. He deserved to have his truck caught in that mud."

"What else did he say?"

It was how he asked that, like a snake toying with his prey before he went in for the kill. Fear bloomed again. "That I should stay away from you."

"You *should* stay away from me," he warned before he walked out of the room.

He was probably right and yet I found myself intrigued. From all accounts, Brochan McIntyre was a loner and yet I was standing in his castle, invited, however reluctantly, by the werewolf himself. Yes, I was definitely intrigued.

I returned to the white room to find a nightgown resting on the bed along with a new toothbrush. I changed, brushed my teeth, then pulled back the heavy comforter and climbed in. The bed was comfortable and warm. I fell asleep instantly.

I didn't know what woke me, but the navy sky was turning purple and red as the sun started to rise. I dressed and went in search of Fenella. She was in the kitchen, the heavenly scent of something wafting toward me.

"Morning, lass." She turned then frowned. "Are you feeling okay?"

I wasn't. My throat hurt and I felt a little lightheaded. I was coming down with something. "I'm okay. Thank you so much for letting me spend the night. I'm going to head back."

"I'll let the laird know. He can give you a ride."

Despite my feelings from last night, reality returned with the sun. I was a stranger in the man's home, one that was fed and given a room. I still couldn't believe how kind they had been about it. I didn't think the same hospitality would be extended in the States, but maybe I was wrong. Either way, I was a little embarrassed to be here and I definitely wanted to be gone before the laird stirred. Not to mention, I had the sense he thought I was my mother's daughter and that pissed me off.

"No, that's okay."

"It's a long walk."

"I like walking." And I did. It helped me think and it brought inspiration.

"Will you have some breakfast first?"

"Thank you, but I'm not hungry." I glanced around the modern kitchen of a medieval castle and couldn't help the smile. "It really is a wonderful place."

"Maybe you'll come back."

"I'd like that."

She wiped her hands on her apron. "I'm sorry for your loss, lass."

"You knew Brianna?"

"Aye, she was a good woman."

"Brianna knew Brochan, didn't she?"

"Aye, one of a very few that did."

There was a part of me charmed that the stoic Brochan hadn't been able to resist Aunt Brianna's charismatic personality, but there was another part of me irritated because he knew Aunt Brianna, so why did he assume I was like my mother and not her? Whatever. Curious though I asked, "Did you know my mother?"

"Aye."

It was how she said it, yep she definitely knew Norah. "The expression the apple didn't fall far from the tree, that doesn't apply to Brianna and Norah."

"Nor you and your ma from what I can tell."

The smile lit up my face. "That is the nicest thing anyone has ever said to me."

She laughed; she thought I was joking. I wasn't.

"I'll show you out." She gestured to the door. "There is more to him than meets the eye."

I suspected that was a huge understatement. "I have no doubt."

We reached the door and she held it open for me. "Enjoy your walk."

"Thank you." I crossed the threshold but glanced back at her. "I'd love to paint this castle. Maybe your laird would consider it. I'd gift the painting to him. I have a website, some of my portfolio is on there. He can also Google me."

"Why would you do that?"

I glanced out at the woods that hugged the property and the juxtaposition of the tamed and tended gardens that butted up against that wild beauty. "Because when I walked down that lane yesterday it quite literally took my breath away."

"I will pass on the offer."

"Bye, Fenella."

"See you soon, Lizzie."

CHAPTER SEVEN

BROCHAN

My hands fisted in the pockets of my trousers as I watched Lizzie Danton walking down the drive. Fuck. Damn that fucking conscience. I didn't need it, didn't fucking want it. I wanted to turn my back, but I could hear Brianna and Fenella, even Finnegan, in my head. "Fucking hell."

Fenella was just entering the library as I was leaving it. She was giving me her stink eye, that frosty look that condemned without her needing to speak a word. What the hell did she want? I let the woman sleep here, fed her, and clothed her. It was the clothes, or lack of them, that stirred something left well enough alone. "Our guest is walking home."

"I saw."

"I think she's coming down with a cold."

"Fucking walking in the rain will do that."

"Not her fault the car broke down." She narrowed her eyes at me before she added, "And it's not her fault she's kin to Norah Calhoun. Remember, she's kin to Brianna too."

I didn't pay my staff to lecture me. They weren't staff; they were family, but I ignored that. I was halfway down the hall when Fenella called after me, "She wants to paint your home."

That stopped me, my head swiveling to her. "She said that?"

"Yes. Said you could Google her to see her portfolio and that she would gift you the painting."

I didn't need to Google her. I was familiar with her work. But after my interrogation last night, why the hell would she offer that? "Why?"

"Because the sight of the castle from the lane took her breath away, her words."

It was the view from the lane that sold me on this place; more specifically the feeling of peace it evoked, a foreign, but not unpleasant feeling. Fucking hell.

There were a few broken branches blocking the drive. By the time I got the Range Rover out of the garage, it had been about an hour since Miss Danton left. Halfway back to the village, I saw the body on the boulder. My chest grew tight thinking harm had come to her; the unwanted sensation annoyed the hell out of me. Pulling over, I climbed out to hear Lizzie Danton talking to herself. She had a bizarre habit of talking to things, like those cows and Brianna's ghost. Her words that day had lingered because despite the shit she'd seen, she still had it in her to paint fucking sprites...to try for happy. I couldn't decide if she was the most well adjusted person of my acquaintance or the craziest. I wondered if she'd spent any time in a mental facility.

I couldn't make out what she was saying, didn't really care. My goal was to get her ass back to the cottage. That would ease the nagging from my fucking conscience. I stepped closer, to peer down at her, her eyes went wide then she screamed. She jumped off the boulder like it was on fire.

"What the hell! Didn't you ever learn not to sneak up on someone resting on a rock?"

I ignored that ridiculous question. She was pale and there were dark circles under her eyes. "You don't look so good."

"Nice. Scare the shit out of me and then insult me. Seriously, charm school was completely lost on you."

She had the oddest way of communicating. More surprising was the urge to grin at her nonsense. "I'll give you a ride to the cottage."

"No, thank you. I wouldn't want you thinking I was after your car, or your house and heaven forbid, you. I'll walk." She started walking away but stopped and turned back. "And why assume I was like my mother? You knew Aunt Brianna, but you interrogated me like I was after something. Never mind. I don't care what you think."

She did care. I saw how deeply it cut her to be compared to her mother. Another unfamiliar sensation curled in my gut. Guilt. I shook it off. "You can barely stand."

Temper burned behind her eyes, but she acquiesced. "Fine."

She didn't wait for me and walked to the car in much the way a child in temper might do. She yanked open the door and dropped into the seat. I climbed in, felt her eyes on me, but when I looked over her focus was out the window.

"How many cars do you have?"

"Eight."

"Why?"

"Why not?"

She muttered something then asked, "Why are the villagers freaked out by you?" She turned in her seat to face me. "They think you're a werewolf."

I'd heard that rumor. Was actually rather fond of that one. "Maybe I am."

I glanced over at her and she was contemplating the real possibility that I was a werewolf. Damn, if I didn't want to grin.

"I don't think so, but I'll be sure to stay inside on the full moon. Can I ask you something else?"

"You can ask." The implication that I probably wouldn't answer was clear.

"Why don't you tear down the castle on the other end of town?"

The only sign I showed that I'd heard her was the slight tightening of my hands on the steering wheel. "How do you know it's mine to tear down?"

"The town librarian. She's very free with information on you, even when she's making it up. She was the one to inform me of your werewolf tendencies."

"It's a memorial." That was the reason the town came up with. I let them believe it because the truth was harder to hear and would only confirm I was the monster they already believed me to be. I liked seeing my father's legacy burned to the ground. I liked knowing there was nothing left of him or his ancestors. I was responsible for the extinction of a clan…my clan.

"I'm sorry." It wasn't the apology for my loss that stirred something in me; it was how she offered it, like a person who had known true loss. The only one in her life worthy of that kind of emotion was Brianna. A woman she never knew and yet she felt her loss as poignantly as I did. If I had a heart, it would break at the evidence of just how lonely Miss Danton was. Rejected, abused, abandoned for the curse of being born. I knew how that felt all too well.

I pulled up in front of the cottage. The car hadn't even come to a complete stop and she was out of it. She was halfway to the door when she called from over her shoulder, "Thanks for the ride."

She had just unlocked the door when I called back. "You can paint my house."

Her head twisted and I didn't miss the joy in her expression before she wiped it. "Thank you. I won't get in your way. I'll work on the lane. If the lighting is good, I'll start tomorrow." Then she disappeared into her cottage.

The knife didn't hit dead center. I blamed the lack of aim on Miss Danton. Reaching for another blade, I emptied my head of everything but the target and the cold steel between my fingers. The second when the blade took flight, the soft hiss as the knife displaced the air and the decided sound of it hitting its mark was a kind of music. Dead center. I reached for my Auto Mag and spent the next hour hitting the same hole on the cardboard cutout, but I was distracted. It had been three days and Miss Danton had not returned. I cleaned my gun and stored it away then went in search of Fenella. She was in the kitchen making lunch.

"Have you heard from Miss Danton?"

"No. I was going to ask Finnegan to check on her. She was coming down with something. The idea that she is alone in that cottage fighting a cold breaks my heart. The poor dear."

"I'll go." Her smile had my hands curling. "Don't get any ideas."

"I didn't say a thing."

"You're thinking it loudly enough." I grabbed my keys. Fucking women.

The cottage was quiet when I arrived. I parked and climbed from the car, taking a moment to look around. Memories tried to surface, I pushed them down. I knocked. No answer.

I knocked harder. Nothing.

Something was wrong. I picked the lock. It was subtle, but I recognized the scent of sickness. The cottage had stunk of it at the end with Brianna.

"Miss Danton," I called as I moved through the living room to the bedroom, where the smell was the strongest. For a second, it wasn't Miss Danton but Brianna that last day. I shook it off. She was breathing, I could hear her from the door, but it was labored. Closing the distance, she was pale, yet her cheeks were flushed with fever. I brushed my fingers over her forehead; she was burning up.

"Miss Danton." She stirred, her eyes opened.

"Why are you here?" A little fire, a good sign.

"I'm taking you back to the castle."

She brushed my hand away. "I'm fine. I just need sleep."

"I'm not asking."

"You don't want me there anymore than I want to be there."

"You're sick. Fenella is an experienced healer." I didn't wait for a reply as I lifted her from the bed and carried her to the car.

LIZZIE

I woke in the middle of the night shivering. My throat was on fire and I ached everywhere. I didn't even have the strength to climb from bed. I curled deeper in the warmth and hoped in the morning I felt better.

I woke when voices entered my room. Why were there people in my room? My eyes were open and yet I had trouble focusing. I was so cold I couldn't stop shaking. I tried to talk, but no words would come out.

"Hush now, dear. She's burning up with fever." That sounded like Fenella. Why was she at the cottage?

A deep voice said, "Get the doctor." Finnegan? He was here too? A warm hand touched my cheek. It felt so good, I moved into it and fell back to sleep.

The weight of my suitcases caused my arms to ache. I didn't even like her and yet my heart was breaking. She was leaving me; I was unlovable. No one would ever love me. Please don't leave me. I don't want to be alone. I can try to be lovable.

"Lizzie, sleep." I felt heat on my cheek; a soothing stroke that lured me back to sleep.

I woke again. That same deep voice said, "You need to drink water." A strong hand wrapped around my chin. "Take a little."

It was cold and felt so good sliding down my throat. "Not too much."

"I'm thirsty."

"Sleep."

It was dark outside when I woke again. I was disoriented and so weak. I tried to climb from bed. "You aren't ready for that."

My head jerked, which brought on a wave of dizziness. Brochan sat in a chair across the room. I wasn't at the cottage. I pinched myself hard. He was still there.

"How am I here?"

"You never showed to paint. I went to the cottage to find you burning up with fever."

"You went to the cottage. Why?" He didn't answer. "You were quite determined to see the last of me. Did you heal me so I was of sound mind and body for when you toss me from the window?"

"I've spent the last three days keeping you alive, so tossing you out the window is counterproductive."

The deep voice, that soothing voice was Brochan? What the hell had I said to him in my delirium? "Wait, three days?"

"We didn't want to give you antibiotics because we weren't sure if you were allergic, so you had to fight it off."

I didn't understand why he was the one caring for me, but he was. "Thank you."

He studied me for a few seconds before he added, "You remind me of Brianna."

Was he making amends? Putting us back on even ground? That didn't seem to fit with the man everyone believed him to be.

"Are you hungry?" he asked.

"A little." He stood and stretched. "I'll have some soup brought up."

"Why are you helping me?"

"Because Brianna would want me to."

"Who was she to you?"

"My conscience." He walked out before I could ask him to clarify that odd comment.

Fenella brought me the soup. I didn't eat much before I fell back to sleep. When I woke in the morning, I was still weak but I felt much better. She settled next to me on the bed and handed me a cup of tea. "You look better."

"I feel better."

"I Googled you. Your work is beautiful, but haunting."

"A little piece of me is in my work."

"I think I'm sorry to hear that."

I sipped on the tea. "Brochan cared for me."

"Yes."

"Why?"

"I think you remind him of Brianna."

He had said that. Then it dawned. "Brianna died in the cottage, didn't she?"

"Aye. Brochan was there."

"He loved her."

"He did, but he would never admit it. He believes emotions are a weakness. He doesn't like having weaknesses."

"Where is he?"

"He postponed a job to care for you. He left a little bit ago. I don't expect him back for a few days."

"What does he do?"

She grew oddly quiet. "I don't rightly know."

She knew, or suspected, but she wouldn't share. That was interesting. It definitely wasn't a nine to five job. I was curious.

"He said I could paint."

"Yes. He had your supplies brought over. They're in the garage, in a cart attached to a tractor to make it easy to get to and from."

That was unexpectedly thoughtful.

"He offered you this room while you're working."

"I'm going to take him up on that. The mood strikes at odd times, it will be nice to be here to work when it does."

She took the cup from me. "You look like you could use more sleep."

"I've been sleeping for days, but I am tired."

"The flu can do that. Rest, lass."

I settled back under the covers as my eyes grew heavy. "Thank you."

"Sweet dreams."

My bare feet made no sound on the stone floors as I ran, my heart pounding behind my ribs. I glanced back feeling him growing closer even as I pushed

myself to move faster. Fear trapped the scream in my throat. I ran, but I went nowhere. There was no escape. I was going to die. He made no sound, but the hair at my nape stirred. He had found me. I turned to face him, to force him to look me in the eyes. He was clenching a knife so tightly in his hand the knuckles were white. Blood was smeared across his cheek, soaked into his sweater. He moved with slow but determined strides as he closed the distance between us. Those pale eyes were lifeless when he lifted the knife.

I jerked awake, the scream dying on my tongue. It had only been a dream, but what a dream. My hands were shaking when I reached for the glass of water on the nightstand. Glancing at the clock, the sun would be rising soon. Throwing my legs over the side of the bed, I was concerned at how weak I still felt. In my current environment, I couldn't help but think of those from back in the day without the benefits of modern medicine. A common cold could be deadly.

I showered and changed, then stripped the sheets from the bed and brought them down to the laundry room I had spied the other day. I was up before Fenella. There was peanut butter in the pantry and bread on the counter. The protein would help with the weakness. The mournful cry stopped me mid-smear. At first I thought I had imagined it, but then I heard it again. The nightmare flashed through my head and even knowing I was being ridiculous, I felt a chill as the hair on my nape stirred. I waited, even contemplated following the sound to the source, but silence followed. Feeling a little shaky, and not just from low blood sugar, I stepped outside using the kitchen door and headed to the garage for my art supplies. The key was in the tractor. I had never driven one, but it was very similar to a car. When I reached the lane, I forgot all about the haunting cry because the timing was perfect. The sky was washed with purple and red as the sun broke over the horizon. I brought my phone; I had finally purchased the adapter and good thing I did because I wanted to take a few shots of the sky to capture the colors. Blending took time and I wanted the colors to be exact.

Painting was my release. Stroking the brush across the canvas was the only time when I felt completely at peace. Though seeing this place for the first time had stirred the same sense of calm. Not the inside, that was much like its master…beautiful but cold.

Outside, nature took care of the warmth the inside lacked. The trees, the grass, the sky and clouds provided the backdrop that turned what could have been a monstrosity into a whimsical and magical setting. It really was exceptional.

My cell pulled me from my thoughts. Glancing at the phone, it was Aunt Brianna's lawyer.

"Hello, Mr. Masters."

"Lizzie. How are you?"

"I'm painting, so I'm very good."

"How do you decide what to paint in a place like Scotland?"

"It's not easy, so I'll be painting a lot."

The cheeriness left his tone. "The reason for my call. We now know why Norah is contesting the will. As it turns out the land the cottage is on is not zoned at all, so one could push and get granted the rights to build multi-family residents or even commercial."

Fury twisted my stomach into a knot. "She doesn't want it at all, she wants to sell the land to a developer."

"Yes. The will is ironclad, but she apparently has the money to waste all of our time." Silence followed.

"There's something else."

His exhale was audible. "She is arguing that you staying in the cottage while the will is be contested puts you at unfair advantage. She's demanding you move out until the decision by the judge is made."

I was so pissed I almost knocked the easel over in my rage. And despite wanting to scream, my voice was barely over a whisper. "That woman abandoned me at ten and now she crawls out of her hole to try to steal my heritage, a heritage she turned her back on?"

"I'm afraid so."

"She isn't going to win."

"No."

Brochan had offered me a room while I worked, that was something. "She can't take Aunt Brianna's cottage, Mr. Masters."

"I won't let that happen."

"I'm temporarily staying at a client's residence while I paint his home. I'll have my stuff out of the cottage by tomorrow."

"I'll let them know. This is good, Lizzie, you are showing you are cooperating. It will go a long way with the judge."

"Just win this."

"You have my word."

I almost tossed my cell; what a fucking bitch. Karma better come back around for that cow. It hadn't yet, not if she was rich enough to toss money around on a lawsuit she likely wasn't going to win. If I ever saw her again, I was punching her in the fucking face. The mood was ruined, so I loaded my stuff back into the cart. Maybe Fenella had alcohol somewhere.

Fenella hooked me up with a very tasty glass of wine and while she cooked dinner, I kept her company. "Can I help?"

"How are you with peeling potatoes?"

"There is no one better." She laughed then put the bowl of potatoes in front of me. She didn't use a peeler; she used a paring knife. A challenge, but I was up to the task.

"How did the painting go?"

"I was set up just as the sun started to rise. The colors were incredible. I took a picture." I reached for my phone as she walked behind me. "Look at those colors. That's how I want to capture Brochan's home. In the shadows coming into the light, the luminous sky, the wash of colors. Makes it seem otherworldly, doesn't it?"

"Aye."

"I had to cut the painting short, unfortunately."

"Why?"

"Actually maybe you could help me. My estranged mother has crawled out of the woodwork and would like to contest Aunt Brianna's will." The pan Fenella had been holding crashed to the floor. I jumped up; she turned and I froze. She was livid. "She's what?"

"Contesting the will. It gets worse. She wants to sell the land to a developer."

"You're not kidding."

"I wish I were. I also have to move out because she made the argument it is unfair for me to be staying in the place, gives me an unfair advantage."

"'Tis yours to stay in."

"I know, but I'm going to pack up my stuff tomorrow. I don't have much, but that leaves me with the dilemma of needing a place to stay once I finish the painting."

"You'll stay here."

"That's sweet, but I don't think Brochan would like that."

"He'll insist on it."

"Doubtful. Is there an Inn nearby?"

"In the town, but you'll stay here."

I wanted to stay here. There was still so much I hadn't seen, but it was extremely unlikely that Brochan would extend the invitation.

"Perhaps tomorrow I could get a ride to the cottage and then into town to look into a room."

"If you wish, but you'll have to cancel the reservation."

"He's a rather reluctant host, so I'm curious why you think he'll agree to this."

"You're getting kicked out of your aunt's cottage, a cottage she wanted you to have. Not to mention that hag is trying to tear down the heritage she walked away from. Brochan will definitely insist you stay here. He'll want that lawyer's name too."

The more difficult this was for Norah, the better as far as I was concerned. In fact, it might even be worth a trip home to see my father. I had a feeling she took him to the cleaners before he was free of her. He might be looking for payback.

The following day, Finnegan dropped me off in town on his way to run errands. I wanted to inquire about a room at the Inn despite Fenella's insistence I stay at the castle. I also hoped to find art supplies. On my way to the Inn, I almost changed directions when I saw Tomas leaning up against the wall of the pub. My heart hammered because I had intentionally let his truck roll into that mud and though he wasn't an intellectual giant, he'd know I had. Bright side, we were in the middle of town with lots of people.

He called when I was half a block away. "It took four hours to get my truck out of that mud." He fell into step next to me. "You let it happen."

I didn't confirm or deny it. I hoped he would walk away, I knew better. He was just like Nadine, a bully.

"I heard you were up at Brochan's place. What was that like?"

The man had an unnatural interest in Brochan; there was a story there.

He only lowered his head and yet it felt like he was invading my personal space. "Are you spreading them for him?"

What? Of all the...I stopped walking. "What is your problem?

"What's it like with a killer?"

Where the hell did that come from? First it was the librarian and now Tomas, spewing nonsense about a man who, from what I'd seen, kept to himself. What was with this town? Engaging a crazy person was not wise. I continued on.

"Do killers fuck like the rest of us or are they rougher...dirtier?"

This dude was nuts. The town had all kinds of theories on Brochan and yet they had a lunatic walking amongst them and no one seemed to care.

"Holy shit. You don't know." At my completely blank stare he added, "You're messing up the sheets with a hitman."

Why the fixation that I was sleeping with Brochan, I didn't know, but seriously this dude was whacked. "Have you ever sought help for your condition?"

He was the one with the blank stare now. "What condition?"

"Insanity."

And it was insanity. Fixated on Brochan and, like the librarian, not shy about dishing out shit on him. It really wasn't a wonder Brochan avoided town.

He ignored that. A smug smile curved his lips. "You feeling like you need a shower now?"

I didn't know much about Brochan. He was cool, aloof and standoffish, but he had also extended a room to me during that storm and had nursed me back to health when I was sick. Not one characteristic defined him. The same couldn't be said of Tomas. He was ugly...right down to the bone.

He wasn't expecting the smile; it grew even wider at his look of confusion.

"I understand why you're so jealous of him; sexy as hell, smart, rich. And look at you? Your biggest accomplishment was getting your secondhand truck out of the mud."

"You fucking cunt." His hand raised, I leaned in tempting him to do it.

"Go ahead. Hit me. By your own account, I'm fucking a killer."

Fear joined hatred in his expression. His hand lowered. "Watch your back, bitch. He's not always around."

He stormed off and my knees went weak. I shouldn't have provoked him. He was nasty and crazy. I pulled a shaky hand through my hair and continued to the Inn. I didn't know which was more unbelievable, Brochan being called a hitman or a werewolf.

By the time I reached the quaint Inn, I had stopped shaking. Pulling the door open, the scent of heather hit me. A roaring fire burned in the fireplace. The reception desk was just to the right of it. A woman, who looked oddly familiar, greeted me.

"Hello. May I help you?"

"I wanted to inquire about a room."

She looked harder, like she was trying to figure something out. "You're Brianna Calhoun's kin."

"Yes."

Her voice cooled. "Her cottage is not up to your standards?"

Wow, Norah really had made it difficult.

"Quite the contrary, but Norah has decided to resurface and contest the will. I've been asked to vacate until the judge makes his decision."

Contrition showed now. "I'm sorry, lass."

"You are not the first person in town to assume I'm like my mother."

"'Tisn't right all the same."

"Knowing my mother, I understand."

"I do have several rooms available."

"I'm working on a commission so I have a place to stay at the moment, but I'll be in touch if I need that room."

"A commission?"

"I'm a painter, oils mostly."

"Oh, how lovely. There is certainly a lot to choose from in this town."

"It's magical."

"Aye, it is."

I offered my hand. "Lizzie Danton."

"Molly Addison. If you've eaten at the pub, you've met my daughter Bridget."

"I thought you looked familiar. It's nice to meet you, Molly."

"Enjoy your stay in Tulloch Croft."

"Thank you."

I headed for the door and she called after me. "Welcome, Lizzie."

CHAPTER EIGHT

BROCHAN

Pulling around the drive, the shit from the last three days crumbled away. It was why I bought the place, the calm in the middle of the fucking storm. I drove around back. Finnegan was waiting.

"Is the room ready?"

"Aye." I popped the trunk, the man twisted and strained against his restraints.

"You'll die for this motherfucker," he snarled.

"No, you will." A punch to the face silenced him. Throwing him over my shoulder, I carried him to the refitted dungeon. I tossed him into the cell, and then kicked him for good measure. "No food or water until I say."

"Aye."

I drove the car around the front, parked then grabbed my bags and headed inside. Laughter greeted me. Miss Danton.

I forgot I had offered her a room while she painted. I only had because she hit a nerve, picked at a scab left well enough alone. That wasn't entirely true. I wanted her to paint my house. If anyone could capture the mystery of this pile of rocks, it was her. Her work was both haunting and inspired. Darkness existed in her, the colors, the harsh brush strokes, and the images. I suspected her darkness came from abandonment and abuse, but her renderings tainted by that darkness were magnificent.

Reaching my room, I dropped my bags and headed to the shower, stripping on the way. My side ached. Washing the dried blood from my body, I replayed the events leading up to me taking a bullet to the side. It only grazed me, but it still hurt like a bitch. It had all gone exactly as I planned, right up until the end. I had been distracted and that almost cost me. Drying off, I pulled on a tee and some sweats then rubbed my hands over my face. In a few days, I'd visit my guest. Torturing someone was exhausting.

Fenella was preparing breakfast when I entered the kitchen, but it was the coffee I was after. I never took to tea; I preferred strong coffee.

"Morning, Brochan."

"Fenella."

"Is everything okay?"

She hated what I did, I knew she hated what I did, but that was just her way. She cared. I wouldn't go into detail because I didn't want to upset her.

Instead I asked, "Where's our guest?"

"Painting."

My focus instinctually moved to the windows. I'd like to see her work, watch as she conjured the images that, unlike most things in my life, actually stirred something in me. My attention shifted to Fenella because she was fidgety. That meant she had something on her mind.

"What's wrong?"

Her head snapped up like she was shocked I could read her so well. I'd known her my whole life, why the hell wouldn't I know her moods.

"Lizzie won't mention it, I'm sure, but I feel you need to know."

This is why I didn't socialize. I couldn't fucking be bothered with other people's problems. I really just didn't give a shit. Fenella on the other hand, like Brianna, made it her mission to help everyone. Bloody annoying.

"You've a mind to say it and I'm standing here so spit it out."

"Norah Calhoun is contesting the will."

My coffee mug stopped halfway to my mouth. "Come again?"

"Lizzie heard from Mr. Masters. Her mother is contesting the will and more, they made her move out of the cottage until a verdict is reached."

I went cold as ice, my fingers curling into the mug. "Why?"

"I don't know all the details, but needless to say Lizzie is really pissed."

I slammed the mug down on the counter and went in search of Miss Danton. By the time I reached the lane, I was seething. Then I saw her. Mist curled at her feet, like a fairy popping up from the world beneath ours. I shook my head; where the hell had that come from? Maybe it was blood poisoning from the gunshot, but dressed in sweats, a tee and riding boots she looked ridiculous and oddly sexy. My cock stirred at the sight of her. Clearly it had been too long since my last fuck. My gaze moved to the canvas and that sense of peace I felt whenever I came home, hit like a punch to the gut. It was my home and yet it felt alive. The stones pulsed with life and evocative as if the Highlanders would at any minute appear over the rise, returning from raiding and warring. It was dark, romantic and poignant.

She didn't hear me approach and jumped a bit when I said, "Miss Danton." She had paint on her cheek, but it was the dreamy look in her eyes that caused my blood to heat. She was painting what she saw in her head, the images evoked by my home. It would be fascinating to spend some time in her mind, to see the world as she did. She wasn't a dreamer, ugly had touched her too, and still she could create heartbreakingly beautiful images like the one on that canvas.

"Welcome home."

I tipped my head to the canvas. "Magnificent."

Her lips curved up even as her cheeks turned pink. "It's a work in progress..." Her focus moved back to the canvas. "But it is my best work without a doubt."

Remembering what brought me out here, my tone went hard when I said, "I heard Norah is contesting the will."

Her fingers tightened on the brush. "She's a bitch."

"What do you know?"

She put the brush and palette down and walked from the painting. My guess, she didn't want the emotions fueled by thoughts of her mother to compromise it. "She wants the land. It is not zoned so she's hoping to sell it to a developer."

"Motherfu—"

"Mr. Masters assures me the will is ironclad, but it is infuriating that when there is something in it for her, she resurfaces. The ironic part, Aunt Brianna would have left it to her had she shown any interest in her family."

"Aye, but had she shown interest she wouldn't be inclined to tear it all down."

"True. I'm contemplating a trip to New York. My father never cared for her, hated her actually. I'm guessing she did a number on him before she moved on. He's a very powerful man in his own right. He might be interested in helping to squash this. He's certainly vindictive enough."

How had this woman come from such parents? "You'll stay here until this is resolved."

She twisted her head. Temper burned behind those eyes now. She didn't like being told what to do. I almost smiled. "Thank you, but I was looking into staying at the Inn."

"You're here already. There's plenty of room and you want to be here. That..." I gestured to her painting. "Is proof."

I'd hit it on the head. We both knew it. She got points for not arguing, for not letting pride overrule common sense. "Thank you."

I turned to leave and winced. My fucking side was on fire.

"Are you okay?"

"Aye."

She didn't believe me, but she didn't push. She got points for that too.

LIZZIE

"I can't believe she's doing this. Unbelievable, but tell me what you need."

Cait wasn't just my agent; she was my go to for everything. She had contacts everywhere. It would be easy for her to get the info on my father. He wasn't someone found in the yellow pages. Numbers to his company sure, a direct line to him was harder.

"I want to cover all bases, so I would like to talk with my father."

"You want his help."

"Yes."

"What makes you think he'll help you?"

"I don't, but I do know there is no love lost between him and my mother."

"Fair. Okay, I'll get you his info."

Curious as to what was causing the noise in the courtyard, I looked outside. "Holy shit."

"What?"

The sight that greeted me was completely unexpected as was my body's response to it. Several places stirred to life, damn near throbbed. Brochan was chopping firewood, but it was the sight of him in his faded jeans and white tank, more specifically the muscles of his shoulders, chest and arms accentuated from his efforts. And I had said the man wasn't beautiful. He glanced up; I jumped out of sight.

"What is it, Lizzie?"

My heart was pounding and not for having gotten caught staring. It was impossible not to be intrigued by the man. He was so reserved and mysterious and undeniably dangerous. Even knowing better, warning myself to stay away, I was on the slippery slope of attraction. A sure dead end when the recipient was the poster child for unavailable.

"Lizzie?"

"I may have failed to mention I was painting scary, sexy man's house."

"No way."

"Yeah, it's a magnificent castle, Cait, and the image coming to life on the canvas is my best work yet."

"I can't wait to see it, but what does that have to do with your holy shit."

"I'm staying at his place while I'm working. Convenient, plus now that I've been kicked from the cottage, a lifesaver."

"Unusual for you, but makes sense. Still not seeing the connection."

"He's currently in the courtyard, chopping firewood."

"Ah…that nice?"

"Yeah."

"Get his picture."

"We're not teenagers, Cait, I'm not taking the man's picture unbeknownst to him."

"Fine," she huffed, just like a put out teen. "I'll get the info on your father."

"How's Ethan?"

Her voice went soft. "He's wonderful. He's taking me away for the weekend."

"Oh, well don't worry about getting my father's info now then, it can wait."

"Are you sure?"

"Absolutely."

"As soon as I get back."

"Where are you going?"

"He's surprising me."

"Sweet. I want to hear all about it when you get back."

"Deal. Talk soon."

"Have a great weekend."

I dropped my phone on the table. I tried to resist the urge to look out the window, but I did. Brochan wasn't alone. A woman stood with him. His household staff was over forty people, though I never saw any of them except Fenella and Finnegan. It was like they moved through the walls or something. The woman was likely one of them, but it was the familiarity between them that suggested there was something more to their relationship. It wasn't my business, so I tried to put the sight of them out of my head as well as the pinpoint of jealousy it stirred.

The castle was so big a person could seriously get lost in it. I think I was lost. I was exploring because how often does one have access to a medieval castle? I was curious about what Brochan did for a living to afford such a place, hitman and werewolf aside. No one talked about it, like at all; the one time I brought it up, the normally chatty Fenella acted like she'd had her tongue surgically removed. His business trip after I was sick only lasted three days and when he returned he was even more withdrawn than usual. Not that I knew the man very well, but I was an observer and he was a subject I found I couldn't help but observe.

I found a back staircase, narrow stone steps that spiraled deeper into the castle. I ran my hand along the cold, stone walls to keep my balance. My heart raced because I was envisioning a torture chamber somewhere in the bowels of the castle. Or a dungeon.

The lower I went, the darker it grew. I should have brought a flashlight. I hadn't thought about electricity but it was unlikely the place was wired down here or if so, very little because who would actually come down to this part voluntarily? I doubted even Fenella's staff cleaned here.

I had just reached the bottom when the hair at my nape stirred. I wasn't just cold, I felt anguish, as if the cruelties inflicted here lingered, saturating the stone…becoming part of the structure and the legacy. Who had lived here and what unspeakable acts had they performed that it still resonated so strongly all these centuries later?

Then I heard the mournful cry, like an echo from the past. I ran all the way back upstairs.

BROCHAN

I didn't usually bring work home, but the fucker shot me. I had a gun to his head at the time, but I missed his gun. That pissed me off, more so because I was distracted thinking about a certain houseguest. My next punch broke his nose.

"Dylan Daniels sends his regards."

The man's face paled. It should. Dylan's sister was on life support after this jackass hit her, driving after having consumed his body weight in alcohol. He walked away from the crash without a scratch. Walked out of the trial with a mere hand slap because his father had connections.

I grabbed his hand and broke his finger. "I can't abide fucking drunk drivers."

He didn't look pretty when I was done with him. I reached for the gun from the waistband of my jeans. Leveled it at his forehead. His eyes went wide in fear. I squeezed the trigger.

Pulling out my phone, I called the cleaners. I glanced down at my hands, the bloody and busted knuckles. It wouldn't do for my guest to see me like this.

Finnegan knocked about twenty minutes later, escorting the cleaners. He gave me not even a glance before he offered, "We'll handle this. Perhaps you should clean up."

"Where is our guest?"

"Last time I saw her, she was heading to her room."

The loch wasn't too far and the moon was still rather full. "Thank you, Finnegan."

He nodded then got to work. I never understood why he was so accepting of what I did. Maybe I should ask him. I strolled upstairs and out the door off the kitchen. I moved through the woods, knew the way easily in the dark. I took it often enough. Light from the moon danced off the calm surface. My gut twisted, slight but undeniable...the remnants of abuse lingered decades later. Finlay and his baptisms, it took me years and relentless discipline to overcome my knee-jerk fear of water. He laughed, the asshole laughed as I coughed up the water to open my lungs, but it was the look in his eyes that had been terrifying. He hadn't wanted me to cough up that water.

I kicked off my shoes and reached for the back of my shirt. A tickle between my shoulder blades told me I wasn't alone. My pulse pounded and my cock grew hard. Miss Danton. Something about those innocent, wounded eyes and the images she created. She stirred me in a way I never felt before and I was feeling reckless enough to ignore the trouble fucking her would bring. I stripped then turned. I'd been hunting long enough to easily track a prey. My gaze shifted in her direction and for a second I stared into the darkness knowing she was out there watching me. Part of me wondered if she would admit to watching if I called her on it. In my experiences, lying came too easily to people. Honesty was rare and that truth calmed the restless beast that wanted her. And I did want her. I'd be a fool to not admit it. I'd be an even bigger fool acting on it. I dove into the cold water. It felt like thousands of needles pricking me at once. I liked the cold. It reminded me I was alive. I felt when she left. I ignored the persistent whisper in my head that she made me feel alive too.

Returning home, I showered then headed to the library for a nightcap. I expected to see Miss Danton, since she seemed to like the room as much as I did. The library was empty. A fire was roaring. I had Finnegan to thank for that. Moving to the small bar in the back, I poured two fingers of whisky and downed it. I was just pouring another when Fenella entered.

"Would you like something to eat? You missed dinner."

"No, thank you."

"Lizzie missed dinner too."

"Perhaps she'll want something in her room."

"I'll ask her when she gets back."

I stopped pouring and looked at Fenella from over my shoulder. "Gets back?"

"I was just in her room to turn down her bed and she isn't there. I thought she might be in here."

It was cold out and growing colder. I left the glass and headed out of the library. "Get some blankets and hot tea ready. I think Miss Danton is out in the woods."

"At this hour. What on earth for?"

"She followed me to the loch."

"In the dark." She hurried from the library. "I'll get right on it."

LIZZIE

I was still shaking when I reached my room. I was being fanciful, but that mournful cry in the dungeon really sounded like a banshee or some other mythical creature. A werewolf? No, that was ridiculous and yet I wasn't as successful dismissing the thought as nonsense. It was an old castle; who knew what horrors happened in the dungeon back in the day.

I walked to the window and pushed it open. The cold air felt really good on my flushed face. The moon was still almost full, the ethereal light it cast made the forest around the castle seem almost magical. I saw the shadows move; Brochan was heading into the woods. I glanced at the clock. What was he doing in the woods at this hour? More curious than was healthy, I hurried out of my room and down the stairs. Once outside I had to look up at the tower to get my bearings before I followed in the direction he had been going.

It was cold. I should have grabbed a jacket. It took a few minutes for my eyes to adjust and still I wasn't sure how I managed to walk through the forest and not trip over something. I wasn't walking long when the trees thinned to reveal a lake. My feet just stopped. There was magic in these woods. It was beautiful; definitely something I needed to see during the day. The moon was bright, reflecting off the surface of the lake, which made it very easy to see Brochan on the other side of it. He kicked off his shoes, reached for the back of his shirt and pulled it forward over his head. I should walk away and give the man privacy, but he dropped his pants and I couldn't get my feet to move. He was all muscle, like he was carved from marble. It took effort to get a body like that, to keep a body like that. My focus had been on his ass so when he abruptly turned, I got an eyeful as my body warmed and a throbbing started between my legs. He was hard. I thought it shrunk in the cold. I pulled my gaze from his cock to his face to find he was looking right at me. A chill moved through me. He couldn't see me, so how did he know I was here? For a beat or two we stared across the distance at each other and then he dove into the water. That snapped me out of it and I turned and hurried away. He knew I was watching him. I tried to reason to myself there was no way he knew I was there, but somehow I knew he did. How embarrassing. So distracted getting caught being a peeping Tom, I got turned around. It was cold, I was lost and it was too dark to see anything. Unlike at the lake, the trees blocked out the light of the moon. I couldn't even see the turrets to the castle because the trees were so tall. I walked around for what felt like an hour but the view didn't change. Dense woods. Fear stirred because what lived in these woods? My pace picked up as my imagination ran away with all manner of threats, including werewolves. I almost cried in joy when the trees thinned out ahead. Hopefully Brochan was still swimming. I didn't even care my showing up would confirm I'd been watching him. He knew the way home, but more importantly he was scarier than anything we might meet in these woods. It wasn't the lake though. I stepped into a circle; the trees had long ago been cut down. What remained were eight stumps about ten feet tall. I approached the closest and saw the carvings. I couldn't make them out, but someone had done carvings into the tree trucks. It looked to be some kind of ceremonial circle. I wondered if Brochan knew of this place and what it was? Interest shifted to worry because it was really cold; I couldn't stop my body from shaking. Was it possible I could die out here? Would they even find me before the animals started feasting? Continuing on seemed stupid, so I sat down and rested up against one of the carved trees.

I entertained the idea of calling for help, but the thought of large predators roaming the forest kept me silent. My teeth started to chatter and the shakes now were uncontrollable. I pulled my legs up to my chest. I had read once when freezing it was important to keep your torso warm, to keep the blood flowing. It hadn't felt this cold earlier. Just how much did the temperatures drop at night?

The sounds of the forest kept me company and I wondered what type of animals or insects made the various noises. There was music in their sounds, a harmonious song that soothed some of the fear away. Until I started thinking about those same insects crawling up my legs, down my back or in my hair. I was too cold to move, but now that I put that unpleasant thought in my head I was certain I felt little legs crawling over my skin. I could be sleeping in that lovely bed right now or in the library curled up by the fire. Suddenly the sounds of the woods silenced as if someone hit the off switch. A predator was out there, and knowing my luck, I was what it hunted. What would it be, a bear or a wolf? What Scottish man-eater was going to feast on me this evening? I should have stayed in my room and even thinking that, a part of me wouldn't have missed seeing Brochan stripping by the lake. It was a nice way to leave the world, with that image burned into my brain.

Brochan stepped into the circle and I nearly wept in relief. Watching him move, yeah, he was definitely a predator. At that moment, I could even believe he *was* a hitman. He moved with grace, that long, strong body eating the distance between us. I was happy to see him, but that quickly turned to wary because he looked pissed.

"What the fuck are you doing out here this late?"

Self-preservation screamed that I confess the truth. "I followed you."

He yanked me from the ground and roughly pulled the jacket on me that he carried, but it was warm so I didn't protest.

"I saw you from my bedroom window. I was curious."

He had the most intense glare. It was like kryptonite, I was powerless against it. The truth kept tumbling out. "Before I could make myself known, you started to strip."

His brow rose.

"I should have left then, but…"

"But what?" Was he enjoying my discomfort? I swear it looked like his mouth tilted up slightly.

Don't say it. Don't say it. "I've only painted a few nudes, but your body is definitely one I'd love to paint. You're exquisite." My shoulders slumped. I said it. I blamed the cold.

He didn't reply, but he did lift me into his arms effortlessly. He was strong, but he was also warm. I curled into him.

"You just got over the flu. Are you trying for pneumonia?"

"I got turned around."

"Easy enough to do."

"What is this place?"

He didn't even glance around as he headed out of the circle and back into the woods. He also didn't answer me.

"Do you often skinny dip at night?" *And if so when and what time?* I wanted to add that to my calendar.

"Yes."

"It's kind of cold to go swimming."

"It's a form of discipline."

"Is that important to you, discipline?"

"Yes."

"The woods stopped talking."

He glanced down at me like I'd lost my mind.

"Before you showed up, there were sounds from animals and insects but they stopped when they sensed you. I'm not convinced you're a werewolf, but you are definitely the scariest predator in these woods."

Why the hell did I say that?

His reply was so low I almost didn't hear it. "You would do well to remember that."

"I'm not afraid of you."

Those pale eyes landed on me, but what brew behind them I couldn't say.

"You're scary, intimidating too, but I know a kindred spirit when I see one. Life hasn't been very kind to either of us."

I was feeling tired, so I rested my head on his shoulder. Maybe I was imagining it, but he seemed to hold me closer. The rest of the walk back was in silence.

Fenella was waiting for us in the library. Brochan set me down on the sofa and taking the blanket from Fenella, he roughly wrapped it around my shoulders. I smiled at the gesture. He glared then walked to the bar in the corner.

"Oh dear. You're an ice cube."

"I got lost in the woods."

"Why were you in the woods?"

"I followed Brochan. I was curious what he was up to so late at night."

A ghost of a smile touched her lips. "Did ye think he was going to shift into something?"

"I wasn't sure. That or maybe he was offering a sacrifice."

She chuckled, "The town is filled with superstitious nitwits."

Brochan returned and pushed a glass filled with an amber liquid in my hand. "Drink."

I blamed the cold, it froze the section of my brain that handled impulse control because I took the glass from him and said, "You aren't going to get me drunk, big boy. I can hold my liquor."

Twenty minutes later I was seeing double. Fenella brought in a tray of hot soup and tea. Brochan sat in the chair across from us, staring into the fire. He was sexy and that feeling I was trying to run from grew stronger.

Fenella handed me a cup of soup. I asked, "There's a circle in the woods. Do you know what it is?"

"A circle? Oh with the trees. No, I don't."

"There are all kinds of mystical things here, aren't there?"

"Many, though some are imagined," Fenella replied.

"Like werewolves?" My eyes darted to Brochan, who was now looking at the whisky in his glass.

"Yes, like werewolves."

Thanks to the alcohol, I had a loose tongue and I almost mentioned the conversation with Tomas, but talking about it gave it more meaning.

"Well, I'm off to bed." Fenella practically jumped from the sofa. I wasn't the only one to find her departure sudden because Brochan looked up at her too. "Enjoy the rest of your evening." She all but ran from the room.

"That was weird." I glanced at Brochan who was watching me, but I didn't know what he was thinking. Maybe it was the alcohol, maybe it was the setting, most likely it was the man, but I was feeling a little reckless. *Don't go there.* I stood. "I think I'd like a book."

I strolled around the library, chancing glances at him. He had reached for his own book, one that was on the table by the fire. Looks were deceiving because he appeared both calm and at ease, but I'd bet money he was like an engine revving, just waiting to take off from the starting line. He wore power and danger like a second skin.

I found a book, flipped to the end but didn't like it, so put it back and reached for another. I read the endings to four books before I found one I liked.

"What are you doing?" Brochan was no longer reading. The book rested in his lap and his focus was on me.

"Reading the ending."

"Before you read the book?"

"Yes."

"Why?"

"If I don't like how it ends, why would I waste my time reading the whole book?"

"If you know the ending, why bother to read the story?"

"Because a book is a journey. The ending is only part of that journey."

His brow rose.

"What? It's like life. Where you end up isn't as important as how you got there."

"I have never before heard that logic used for books."

"But it makes sense. Doesn't it? You're thinking about reading the ending to that book…" I gestured to the one on his lap. "Aren't you?"

"I already know the ending."

"Ha! See."

He lowered his head but not before I saw the grin. My heart stopped, what a sight. We spent the next few hours reading... together, sort of. It was nice.

CHAPTER NINE

LIZZIE

I was working on the painting, had moved into the solarium which had lots of great natural light and good ventilation.

"Miss Danton."

The brush wasn't near the canvas or there would have been a streak of purple across the image. "How does a man your size move so quietly?"

He approached, but his focus was on the painting. "You've captured more than the image. It pulses, like it's a living breathing thing."

"The castle kind of is. It's stone, but all the stories it could tell. All the lives it touched. I believe some of that lingers, becomes part of it. Haunted houses, I think they're haunted because there's more darkness than light in their history."

His eyes seemed to have gone flat, but then his focus shifted to me and I wondered if I had imagined those lifeless eyes. "Yesterday, the circle you asked about. It's a healing circle. I thought you might like to see it in the daylight."

So he did know what the circle was. Why share with me now, and not last night? Curious, but I didn't ask. Instead, I teased him, "Inviting me to see the circle. Are you feeling okay? Maybe you shouldn't take late night swims when it's so cold."

It was just a grin, a barely there one at that, and yet, like last night, the transformation in him almost had my jaw dropping.

"Shall we?"

"Yes." I quickly rinsed off my brush and placed it on the palette. "A healing circle, do you know anything else about it?"

We headed out of the solarium as he explained, "The carvings on the pillars were for the Celtic goddesses, the hag in particular as she was a healer. It was believed if you were ill, spending the night in the circle would heal you."

"Do you have any idea how long it's been there?"

"The carvings are very worn. It's possible the circle dates back to when the Ferguson clan owned the land back in the thirteenth century."

"It's one of the things I really love about Scotland, Europe in general...the history and continuity."

"Not all history is good, some is better forgotten."

I hadn't imagined the harshness of his words. We stepped into the woods—the place was very different in the daylight—wildflowers, little streams ran here and there, the variety of trees, the shapes of their leaves and colors.

"It's magical."

"The woods?"

"At night it was a little scary, but seeing it during the day. It's beautiful. I love that you didn't tame the back of the castle. The contrast of the tended gardens and lawn against the wild woods...I kind of feel like Little Red Riding Hood." I glanced over at him. "Fitting since I'm keeping company with the big bad wolf."

He snarled, much like a wolf. "Fenella was right. There are a lot of superstitious nitwits in town."

"Still makes you wonder how the rumor got started about you being a werewolf."

It wasn't anger, but more like weariness when he replied, "People fear what they don't understand. A werewolf is a killer."

His choice of words, did he know the other rumor about him? Was it possible there was some truth to it? I should be alarmed, even scared, but I wasn't. In fact, I even felt the need to defend him.

"A werewolf is a man who shifts during the full moon. The instinct of the wolf is to kill, but there's more to him than those basic instincts. One only needs to look to see."

I'd have made a pact with the devil to know what he was thinking. We reached the circle and my feet just stopped. Chills danced down my arms. "It's magnificent."

Brochan stood near one of the pillars. I joined him, but my focus was on the carvings. He was right; it was hard to make out the images. I had to touch it. Something done centuries ago and it was still here, a link from the past to the present. Standing in that circle, I was overcome with emotion. I hadn't realized tears were in my eyes until I heard Brochan ask, "Miss Danton?"

"All the people who came here, the ill and the family of the ill, looking for a miracle ... clinging to hope. It's heartbreaking because you know most probably didn't make it."

He studied me. I wiped at my eyes. "Sorry. I'm not usually a crier."

"How do you do it?"

I met his gaze. "Do what?"

"Feel so much. Isn't it exhausting?"

"Yes, but I'll take that over not feeling at all."

In the morning, I woke to the sound of bagpipes. I thought perhaps the pipes were like that haunted wail I'd heard the other day, just another ghost from the past, but the longer I lay there the more I realized there were indeed bagpipes outside. I jumped from bed and ran to the window. The lawn was filled with activity. There were obvious tourists walking around—cameras hanging from their necks, fanny packs around their waists and canteens in their hands. Stands had been set up, like at a fair, to sell food and souvenirs. A man dressed in a kilt stood off from the others, a lonely looking figure, shrouded in mist, or maybe the painter in me added the mist. His hauntingly beautiful song carried on the wind. How the hell had they set up so fast and why hadn't anyone mentioned it to me? In studying the scene I realized there were quite a few men wearing kilts, women too. Glancing at the clock, it was only eight in the morning. What was going on? I quickly dressed and hurried downstairs. In the kitchen, Fenella and several others were whipping up biscuits, as cookies were called here, and cakes. Her smile greeted me, and she answered my question before I asked it. "Highland games."

"What's that?"

"A lot of fun. Go see."

"Can I help in here?"

She waved me out of her kitchen. "Go on now."

The day was bright and cool, the perfect day for outdoor festivities. Farther down the lawn, the games were being played. Men and women dressed in their family's tartans were competing in wrestling, shot put, hammer tossing, relay races and more. It was the event at the far end that held my attention. Men were tossing logs, cabers, which looked to be over twenty feet long. They were tossing them. Holy shit.

"Are you thinking of trying that?"

I jumped at his voice, but surprise turned to pleasure that Brochan was teasing me. I didn't hide the smile. "No, but it's amazing. Have you ever done that?"

"When I was a lad."

"How long is that caber?"

"Nineteen feet and six inches and weighs about a hundred and seventy-five pounds."

"Damn."

There was another game involving a pitchfork, a burlap bag filled with something that was being tossed with an overhead throw to fly over a horizontal bar. "What's that?"

"Sheaf tossing."

"I think I need to try my hand at something."

He turned to me and though his expression gave nothing away, he was teasing me again. "The caber toss?"

"No, obviously, but there has to be something I can try."

"There is," he said cryptically. "Come with me."

I felt giddy that he was offering to join me for at least part of the day. I didn't understand the rumors about Brochan because I really enjoyed his company…probably more than I should.

I did the sheaf toss and shot put, I even tossed a caber. Sure, I was competing with kids and they kicked my ass, but it was so much fun. Caleb, a little boy of seven, had just whipped my ass at the caber toss. I walked over and shook his hand.

"Nice toss."

He smiled. Too shy to answer but I just knew he'd be bragging to all his friends about his victory.

"Are you hungry?" Brochan asked when I joined him after my very sad performance on the caber field.

"Yes, getting my ass handed to me makes me hungry."

We stopped at one of the stands. Brochan ordered a Cornish pasty and a bridie. As the woman fetched our food, I asked, "What's a Cornish pasty and bridie?"

"They're similar, both are seasoned beef wrapped in pastry. The Cornish pasty also has carrots and potatoes, the bridie is just beef and onions."

"Sounds good."

He ordered us each a pint of ale.

"Which do you want?" he asked.

"You decide."

He handed me the Cornish pasty and after the first bite my eyes rolled into the back of my head. "This is amazing."

"Try this." He handed me the bridie.

"Do you want to try this?" I asked as I held out the pasty. I wanted him to say yes, the idea of eating from something his mouth was on. Please say yes.

He didn't say yes, he just took the pasty, his eyes on me as he took a bite. Was he thinking the same thing? I couldn't tear my gaze from his mouth then realized what I was doing and took a long drink of ale to cool down.

We strolled through the activity and I was feeling a little off because the punch of lust and attraction came out of nowhere. Maybe not out of nowhere, more likely creeping up on me slowly but surely.

"Are you going to try any of the events?" I asked.

"I hadn't planned on it."

"Why?"

"Part of the rules is wearing your tartan. I won't wear my colors."

Bitterness laced through his words. He lost his father, but it didn't sound as if they had a good relationship. My heart went out to him because I understood. Looking at the people around us though, his tartan wasn't just his father's. There was a long line of McIntyres that had worn it before him.

"I get it. I think you know that, being familiar with Norah. I wouldn't share a fucking tissue with that woman. But seeing all these people, the generations—babies to white-haired men and women—those plaids are bigger than any one person. Their tartan links all of them, every generation. I wouldn't turn my back on that. I wouldn't give anyone that kind of power over me."

He was watching me when I glanced up at him. His silence was meaningful. We had reached the castle.

"Excuse me," he said before disappearing inside.

I was disappointed he left because I had been enjoying his company, but I had been too familiar with my comments. I didn't know the details of his relationship with his dad and I wouldn't be thrilled with comments from the peanut gallery on my relationship with my mother.

Fenella stepped outside not long after Brochan left. "There you are, lass. I was just going to look for you. Are you having fun?"

"Yes, it's wonderful. Brochan just left. He was showing me around."

Her face lit up. "He was?"

"Yes. Does he host this every year?"

"Aye, for many years now. Finnegan and I took him to the games in Edinburgh when he was a wee lad. He loved it."

They didn't talk about his father and from the way she spoke I had the sense his father hadn't been in the picture much. At least he had Fenella and Finnegan, and Brianna. There was no question they loved him; he'd had family and that made me smile.

Fenella's gasp turned my head in the direction she was staring. Mine wasn't a gasp, but a punch of lust that almost knocked me off my feet. Brochan stepped from his castle dressed like his ancestors. His stern face and cool blue eyes did nothing to deter people from staring. His kilt hung from his narrow hips. The white shirt and tailored jacket hugged the muscles of his chest and arms. His muscled legs ended in hose and those black shoes everyone was wearing. It was the single sexiest sight I'd ever seen. He moved in that controlled way he had, the practiced moves of a predator. His destination was me. Another emotion, stronger than lust, moved through me seeing him wearing his kilt. He had found something in my words to change his mind. I had a feeling he didn't change his mind often.

He said nothing, just offered his arm. I fell a little bit in love with him in that moment.

"I like your ensemble," I said shyly.

He didn't acknowledge me, his focus was straight ahead, but I saw his lips twitch. How could people be so wrong about him?

We reached the caber field. He took off his jacket and handed it to me.

"What's that called?" I asked of the pocket thing sitting over his kilt.

"The sporran." He looked up and grinned. "Kilts don't have pockets."

My heart fluttered, but damn this man was dangerous.

For the next hour, I watched as he tossed a caber. Halfway through he took off his shirt. Watching as that powerful body moved, the muscles straining under his golden skin with his efforts. I wanted a canvas and paint. Holy hell I needed to paint him. I wanted him life size, just like that, on my wall. I wanted him, period. It was stupid to deny it.

He joined me, dripping with sweat despite the cool temperature. My mouth watered thinking about licking him dry, every inch.

"I need a shower."

I almost offered to wash his back. I bit my tongue.

He took his shirt and jacket from me as we walked back to the castle. My tongue was tied. I couldn't form a thought because I was battling the strongest case of attraction I'd ever felt. He headed for the door, but stopped. He said it so softly and that made the impact even stronger. "Thank you."

He disappeared inside before I could say anything. I stood there, unable to move.

Fenella appeared. "You got him to wear his tartan. I can't tell you how many times Finnegan and I have tried and failed. What did you say to him?"

"Only that his tartan is more than just his father and that I wouldn't let anyone keep me from my family history."

"He listened to you." She turned to me. "I think because he knows you're kindred spirits."

An ache started in my chest. "He didn't have a relationship with his dad, did he?"

"Ah, lass. It was more complicated than that."

She touched the thin white scar under my eye. "How did you get that?"

"Nadine, my tormentor at boarding school. She was mean. Picked on kids younger than her. Always looking for a fight, but she never fought fair. The staff let her get away with it too. I never understood that. I got whacked with a ruler my first weeks there because I had reached for a second dessert, but she victimized kids and they turned a blind eye. She always had a posse with her, those who were spared her torment. Instead of steering clear or standing up, they egged her on. Even knowing it could have been them she beat on, they encouraged her and laughed while doing so. I got more than a few black eyes courtesy of Nadine."

"I'm sorry to hear you had a difficult childhood too."

"It's why I started painting. I had to believe there was something beautiful in the world. I hadn't seen it personally, but people wrote songs about it, books, and poems. Life for me had been one never-ending nightmare. Painting saved me."

"That explains the darkness of your work."

"I don't see it so much as dark. I see it as finding beauty even in the ugly. It was what I did."

"Let's walk," she suggested, but was already heading down the lawn. She had a faraway look, as if she had slipped back in time. "Brochan's dear sweet mother died in childbirth. Finlay loved Abigail. She was his whole world. When she died, he was lost. I won't make excuses for what he did. There aren't any. He took that loss, that pain and put it on Brochan."

Horror twisted in my gut. I had expected bad, but I hadn't expected evil. "He put her loss on his son?"

"Aye. He was such a sweet boy; from the day he was born, sweet and innocent. It seems like only yesterday he was chasing butterflies on his little two-year-old legs. There is so much of his mother in him, even now, her kindness and calm deposition. Finlay didn't see any of that. The older Brochan grew, the more twisted Finlay became. I won't go into detail, that's for Brochan to share, but I will say he was not safe around his father. He endured a lot and it didn't break him. But everyone has their limit. I can't tell you how hard it was for Finnegan and I to see the change in him from that sweet and trusting little boy, to the hard and closed off man he is now."

His thank you earlier touched me in an entirely different way, learning what demons he battled and how somehow I had gotten through.

"Why are you telling me this?"

"Because I want you to understand."

"Understand what?"

"Why he is the way he is." She glanced up at the house. "I'm needed in the kitchen." She said nothing more, just took my hand and squeezed before she left me with my thoughts.

BROCHAN

My kilt hung from my closet door. Fenella had had it cleaned. I couldn't believe I'd worn it. I had almost burned it in the fire, but I felt that connection Miss Danton mentioned, that link to the past. It was why it had been spared; even wishing to bring about the extinction of the McIntyre clan, I hadn't destroyed it. Apparently, I lacked conviction.

I'd acted like an adolescent, foolishly trying to please my girl. My girl? She wasn't mine. She was a houseguest, Brianna's kin, and also the woman who, despite my best efforts, kept drifting into my thoughts more often than she should. The look on her face though, she felt it too. Whatever the hell was brewing between us, it was mutual.

Curious what she was up to, I went in search of her. Right outside the great hall, I found her. Resting my shoulder against the wall, I crossed my arms over my chest and fought a grin. Miss Danton was trying to look under the paintings in the great hall... every single one. The paintings were bolted to the wall due to their size and weight. After a few, she was beginning to see the pattern. She stepped back, dropped her hands on her hips and blew her hair out of her face. She looked annoyed, slightly frustrated, and fucking adorable. She glanced my way then did a double take. I enjoyed watching her cheeks turn pink from her embarrassment.

"Hey," she called.

"What are you doing?"

Her eyes narrowed. She looked annoyed again. "What did you think I was doing?"

"I haven't a clue, which is why I asked."

"I was trying to find the television."

"Under the paintings?"

"Rich people hide safes behind paintings. Why not televisions."

"You want to watch television?"

"I just finished painting for the day and I was hoping to unwind, but I'm too tired to focus on a book."

"Even one where you skip to the end."

I had the sense if I was anyone else, she would have stuck her tongue out at me. She had that look, one of a petulant child, but on her it was oddly cute.

"There's a television in the library."

"I looked there first. I didn't see it."

I gestured for her to precede me. "I'll show you."

Something was on her mind; she seemed fidgety. She didn't make me wait long before she said, "You wore your kilt."

Instinct for me was to evade, but I found that wasn't instinct around her. "You had a persuasive argument."

She twisted her fingers together before she added, "It's a really good look on you."

Those shyly spoken words went right to my balls. Yeah, whatever was happening, she felt it too.

We reached the library and I led her to the back where a smaller sitting area was set up. The look on her face was priceless. She thought I'd lost my mind.

"There's no television back here."

I slid the panel that looked to be part of the bookcase to reveal the television. Her eyes widened, but instantly turned to slits. "How is that any different than behind a painting?"

It wasn't, but it was fun getting a rise out of her. "What did you want to watch?"

"A movie would be nice. Do you have pay per view?"

"Yes."

"Maybe a superhero flick, *Superman*, *Avengers*, *Thor*, *Wonder Woman*, *Batman*, but only the ones with Christian Bale. Who is your favorite superhero?"

My blank look wasn't lost on her. I rarely watched television.

"Have you ever seen the movies I mentioned?"

"No."

She had a thought on that but kept it to herself. "I think *Avengers.* You'll watch it with me, right?"

I'd stay for only a few minutes. "For a bit."

"We need popcorn. Tell me you have popcorn?"

"I have no idea if we have popcorn."

"I'll go. You cue up the movie." She ran from the room then peeked her head back in. "Maybe when it gets dark we can watch a scary movie. I both love and hate scary movies."

I couldn't believe I was actually looking forward to watching a ridiculous movie with superheroes of all things. I was a thirty-five year old man who killed people for a living and yet here I was preparing to watch a movie with a woman I couldn't get out of my head. I was fucking losing my mind.

She returned; cheering as she held a bag of what I assumed was popcorn over her head. "I got us soda too."

I was on the sofa, left her the chair. She had other plans; sitting so close she was practically on top of me. She crossed her legs and put the bag of popcorn between them. I wasn't sure if she was teasing me because I had teased her, but the idea of putting my hand between her legs to get the popcorn, coupled with her ass resting on part of my thigh, yeah I was hard and growing harder. Where the fuck was my discipline?

"Hit play. You're going to love it."

I wasn't even going to watch it.

She knocked my arm with her elbow and handed me the soda, but her eyes were glued to the set.

"Have you seen this before?" I thought she had, but with how excited she was maybe I misunderstood her.

"Yeah, a dozen times at least. It's awesome. There's a second one, we can watch that after this."

The opening credits rolled. I placed the soda on the table and prepared my excuse as soon as the movie started, not that I thought she'd care. She was already in the zone and it was just names flashing on the screen.

Two hours later, I understood her enthusiasm.

"You liked it," she said knowingly.

"I did."

"The second one is awesome too, unless you have something else to do."

I had plenty to do, but at the moment there was nothing else I wanted to do but sit in my library with Miss Danton, who made my body ache in all the right ways, and watch as the *Avengers* kicked ass.

I reached for the remote then glanced at her from the corner of my eye. "We need more popcorn."

LIZZIE

My pillow was very hard. Was my head resting on a rock? I slowly woke and felt a little disoriented until I saw the television. I glanced down and noticed it wasn't a pillow, but Brochan's thigh. A thigh that had a bit of drool on it. I wiped at my mouth and sat up. The television was off; Brochan's head was resting on the sofa back. He was sleeping. I didn't want to wake him, but I did want to see the awesome man that was Brochan McIntyre sleeping. He didn't look peaceful, even in sleep his expression was stern. There was a line between his brows. I wanted to rub that line away. I wondered what he was dreaming about. Did he dream?

His head turned and his eyes opened, those pale blue eyes that I had thought looked icy, but there was nothing cold about them now. "We missed the ending," he said.

"We can watch it again."

"It's cold. I'll start a fire."

He stood, stretched that tall body and walked to the fireplace. He'd watched television with me; he'd let me drool on him. How was it the townsfolk had such crazy notions about him? I joined him, resting against the wall as he worked.

"Why do the townsfolk think you're a werewolf? The rumor had to come from somewhere."

I noticed the muscles in his back and shoulders tensed. I wouldn't push, but I did think he should know Fenella had shared a bit about him.

"Fenella told me part of your story."

His head jerked up.

"Not details, just that you didn't have any better a childhood than I did."

He finished with the fire then moved to the bar. "Do you want a drink?"

A little whisky would be nice. "Please, what you're having."

He splashed a few fingers in two highballs and handed me one. I sat on the sofa closest to the fire.

"What was Brianna like?"

He took the seat across from me. The easiness from early was missing, but I understood how the past could haunt. "She was fierce and loyal. Pigheaded and convinced she knew best." His gaze flickered to me. "You remind me of her."

He was teasing, but it warmed me to know I was like her. "It's fascinating that Aunt Brianna raised my mother and yet she is nothing like her. How someone can be so different from the person who helped form them into the person they became."

"Your mother is an anomaly, it skipped a generation."

I liked he thought so.

It was a risk mentioning Tomas, but I was curious how he'd react. I took a sip of the whisky and enjoyed the warmth that followed. Carefully, I said, "I ran into Tomas in town the other day." If looks could kill. "I see the animosity is mutual."

"He's a dick."

"I agree." I debated if I should continue. Curiosity won out. "He had some very interesting things to say about you." Our eyes met. "He said you were a hitman."

It was his lack of reaction that twisted my stomach into a knot. "It's true?"

He said nothing, but it was an affirmation. I was mildly alarmed at the revelation. My only reference for hitmen was from movies and television. Regardless, I never thought I'd be sitting across from one. Knowing that when he left on business after I was sick he was off killing someone was definitely unnerving. Even being unnerved, I didn't feel fear because this was Brochan. The same man who had nursed me back to health, had let me use his lap as a pillow, had put on his kilt and tossed a caber in some sense for me. In the time we'd spent together, I was learning there were many layers to him. A hitman was only one.

He didn't take his eyes off me, challenging me or waiting for me to run away.

"How did you become a hitman?"

Surprise flashed in those pools of blue. "That's it?"

"Were you expecting me to run screaming from the room?"

"At least cross yourself. The folks in town all do when I'm near."

"Is it jarring to hear you're a hired killer? Yes. Am I in shock? Probably. But killing is what you do, not who you are."

"Did you just say that?"

"It's true. You spent the afternoon watching the *Avengers* with me. You took me to the healing circle and showed me around the Highland games. Are you ruthless, cold even? I imagine you need to be, but there's more to you than that. Besides, I've thought about killing people and not just in passing like when someone cuts you off in traffic and then honks at you. No, I've thought hard about killing a few people. If I had a little more guts, I might have followed through."

His expression was priceless. He thought I was nuts.

"Would you prefer that I run screaming from the room?"

"It would be more understandable than your easy acceptance."

"I've seen ugly too. Maybe because I have I understand better than most what we do to cope with that ugly."

He finished his whisky then stood. "I'm not sure if you're a curse or a gift." He placed his glass on the table and walked out of the room.

"Funny, I was wondering the same about you," I said into the empty room.

I was heading into town to have lunch with Fergus. My thoughts drifted to Brochan often since last night. I had thought I'd be more freaked out this morning, having the night to process that the man I had been keeping company with was a killer. I wasn't freaked. In fact, I found him even more fascinating. I understood now why the townsfolk thought he was a werewolf; he was beautiful and deadly. Tomas' behavior, knowing that he was right about Brochan, didn't make sense. Why taunt a man who made a living hurting people? Did the dude have a death wish?

I arrived before Fergus. Bridget seated me. "Coffee?" she asked.

"Please."

The door opened and Fergus strolled in and called to Blair, "A plate of haggis." He really liked his haggis. I had yet to try the can I bought, the can Brochan had encouraged I try.

"I see that look, lass, but it is delicious. You should try it."

"I'm talking myself into it."

His laugh sounded like a gun blast. He folded himself in the chair across from me. "I haven't seen you around."

"I'm working on a painting."

"How's it going?"

"Really well. That's understating it. I've never been this excited about a piece before."

"I'm not surprised. 'Tis Scotland." He definitely had country pride.

I rested my arms on the table. I had to tell him about Norah. I didn't want to because I didn't want to set the mood for lunch, but he needed to know. "I do have some news that isn't great."

His large brows furrowed. "I'm listening."

I explained the situation with Norah. His expressions were both scary and not surprising. Bridget returned with our food.

"I don't understand how that woman is kin to Brianna and you."

I wondered that myself but had no answer except for Brochan's. It skipped a generation.

"Thank you for telling me. Joseph is good, really good. If he says he has this, he does."

I was relieved to hear that, still the journey to the verdict was going to be trying.

Fergus started digging into his haggis. "What are you painting?"

I hesitated sharing because I knew he'd have an opinion on my choice of subjects. "Brochan McIntyre's home."

His fork came down with force, his eyes snapping to me. "Lass, Brochan is bad news."

"I'm just painting his castle." I didn't mention the attraction, or that I was growing to like him or the fact that I knew he was figuratively a big bad wolf and it didn't make a lick of difference regarding the aforementioned attraction.

He wasn't appeased. Did he know about Brochan's profession? "Why is he bad news?"

"Haven't you noticed that his eyes are empty?"

I didn't see empty. In the beginning I saw hard and closed off. Now I saw interest. And even if they were empty, my own had been empty once too.

"I watched him nearly beat a kid to death. He was sixteen, old enough to know better. Tomas' jaw was wired shut for eight weeks."

Tomas? Now that was interesting. I wanted to break his jaw and I hardly knew the man.

"Why did he beat him up?"

"Is there any reason to justify beating someone nearly to death?"

The correct answer was no, however nothing was that black and white. And Tomas, the man grated and I hardly knew him. I think if I had to spend any amount of time with him I'd probably cause him physical harm too. "No, but there can be factors that make people do the unthinkable."

"He's been doing the unthinkable his whole life. He has no remorse, no empathy. I'm telling ye, lass. Stay away from him."

Interesting that Fergus didn't see what I did, but Aunt Brianna had. "I appreciate the warning, but I've learned from personal experience that things are not always what they seem. You might be right about Brochan, but I prefer forming my own opinion."

The smile came out of nowhere. "You sound just like Brianna. Fine, form your own opinion, but I am not above saying I told you so."

"So noted."

On the way back to Brochan's, I detoured to his family's ancestral home. This place hadn't been a home for him and I suspected it wasn't a memorial so much as a reminder. Still, there was history here. He had family that had lived on these lands for centuries. It seemed to me it might be cathartic for him to learn about the others who came before him. Possibly now after the Highland games, he might be receptive to looking into them.

I fiddled with the medallion I had found. I carried it with me. I'm not sure why. I should return it to Brochan, but I found comfort in it. Maybe because it had survived what had to have been an inferno and still it had endured. I felt a little bit like that. I had endured the inferno. I was singed a bit, but I was still in one piece.

I hadn't realized I wasn't alone until that deep voice startled me. "What are you doing here?"

I expected to see anger when I turned to him. Instead, I saw nothing. He wasn't even looking at me, his focus on the ruins around us. What happened here? Fenella and Finnegan adored him; Aunt Brianna had loved him. That wasn't usually the case when someone was so hardened and removed from others. According to Fenella, he had been a sweet and loving child, so what had his father done to him to turn him into the man he was now?

I didn't think he was waiting for an answer to his question, but I gave him one anyway. "It's peaceful."

I didn't imagine the harsh exhale. "It is now."

I wanted to ask what I didn't know; I wanted to know what his father did to him. Instead, I bit my lip.

"There used to be a pond over there."

I glanced where he gestured, but all I saw was green grass.

"It's gone now. I had it drained then filled in. Under our feet, there used to be an intricate maze of halls lined with cells. The dungeon. I had it filled in with cement."

"It's not a memorial, is it?"

For the first time since he arrived, those pales eyes sought mine. "No."

"I don't know what happened to you, but I understand better than most the damage that can be done by those meant to love and protect us. And based on what remains, whatever happened was unimaginable. I think it makes you human to erase the memory of the one who did harm to you."

He didn't reply but his focus never wavered.

"Fergus told me you once broke Tomas' jaw."

There was a flicker of what looked like satisfaction that sparkled in those eyes. "Aye."

"I bet he had it coming."

"That he did."

"I'm not sorry I let his truck slide down that embankment."

Another flicker, but this time it was understanding or maybe comradery. "I can see you aren't."

"He's a dick."

"You are one of a few who see that."

"People see what they want. An easy smile and the good ole boy act and people are blind to what's under that, but someone who doesn't hide behind an easy smile, who doesn't always have a quick reply, and they see trouble. I've seen the masks people wear. I think only people who have truly seen what lurks beneath are skeptical of those who are too agreeable too often."

"It was Brianna who stepped in that day. She tried so hard to fix me."

My heart stilled then nearly swelled right out of my chest at his confession. He was lifting his mask, even if just a little, to let me see a bit of the man underneath.

"I don't think she was trying to fix you, Brochan, because you're not broken; you're just bent."

His eyes went dark but what fueled that reaction I didn't know. He practically snarled at me. "Are you for real?"

So taken back by the venom in his words, I answered absently. "I don't know what you mean."

He turned away, his long strides putting distance between us. "Please don't..." I didn't finish because I didn't know what I was willing to beg him to do. I just knew that there was a man under the mask that I wanted desperately to know.

BROCHAN

"Damn you." I stood over Brianna's grave as a war raged in me. "Did you know? Did you know the one you sought was the one you cursed on me with your dying breath? She learned what I am, what I do, and didn't even bat a lash."

I didn't understand half of what I felt...anger was there, but it was the other unknown feelings that baffled and enraged me.

"I don't want it. I don't want her." And yet even saying it I knew I was lying. Being around her, it was the same peace I found at my home, but stronger. Just her being brought a calm in me I never felt before. Calm and oddly alive...almost drunk on the knowledge that someone understood the darkness because she too lived there. And damn Brianna because she knew. It wasn't Miss Danton's pretty face that broke through; it was her pain, her own demons that made her understand. And even understanding me, it wouldn't end well. Just by the nature of who I was, her knowing me was only going to bring her more pain.

"I'll hurt her, but that won't stop me from claiming her. How is that being a good man, the one you were so convinced existed? Heaven help her with what you've set in motion."

CHAPTER TEN

LIZZIE

I drove to Edinburgh. I wanted to see the castle, I needed art supplies, but I'd save that for another trip. My destination for this trip was New Register House, the lovely Italianate building located in New Town Edinburgh. I planned to research my own ancestors, but that wasn't what brought me here now. I didn't know the full story of Brochan, but I had deduced the reminder he sought in leaving his home in ruins was of the horror inflicted on him. I couldn't imagine what kind of horror by his father would elicit so decisive and definitive a retaliation, but there was more to the McIntyres than just his father. I had been of a similar mindset when learning of Brianna. I had been prepared to dislike her because of her connection to Norah. I would have been wrong to do that. So my goal was to research the McIntyres, to give Brochan his family back. At least that was the hope. If it turned out they were all like his father, no one was the wiser.

I was given a desk and a computer terminal with instructions on how to look up the McIntyres by way of registries—births, deaths, marriages and parish. Perhaps there were other living McIntyres and not all of the clan's history burned with the castle. The first name that popped up was Finlay McIntyre and his marriage to Abigail Stewart, followed by the birth of their son and her death. My father wouldn't have given a shit if Norah croaked on the table when she delivered me. But someone who loved his wife, a love that was real and strong and pure, if you lost a love like that was it possible it could twist you? Would it turn your love to hate? Would you focus that hate on the one you believed to be responsible, an innocent babe? Fenella had said as much, his father blamed him for his mother's death. I ached for Brochan, an innocent babe guilty of nothing more than being born. That was me too, abused solely because I existed, but his father had been a monster if he had blamed Brochan for his wife's death. No pain or loss justified that. She died to give him a son and he turned on that son. Poor Abigail, poor Brochan. I changed my search. It wasn't his father's family Brochan needed; it was his mother's.

Stewart was a very popular name, so for the next few hours I went through lists and lists of marriages, deaths and births. It took time following the trail back from Abigail, but knowing how much my life improved learning of Brianna, knowing there was more to me than my parents, I wanted Brochan to experience that. Why? That wasn't a question I was ready to answer. I knew very little about him. I understood him, I was attracted to him, but I only knew the tip of the iceberg when it came to him. Going down the path I felt myself being pulled toward was one I unequivocally knew there would be no coming back from. However it played out, Lizzie Danton would never again be the same. I was just beginning to find myself. I wasn't sure I was ready to lose myself so soon.

I spent the entire afternoon jotting down names and creating a rough draft family tree. Marking marriages, children and deaths. Next step would be the internet. Googling the names still living. I wondered why Fenella and Finnegan never thought to do it, to find her family. I'd ask Fenella when I returned to Tulloch Croft.

On the steps outside the Register house, I referenced my tourist books for the shopping district. I was going to dinner tonight at a French restaurant, one of a few places I hoped to try. The reviews were wonderful and I liked that it used seasonal Scottish produce in their offerings. I needed a dress. Well, I didn't need one I had one, but I wanted to shop. I rarely shopped. Most of my clothes I bought online or Cait bought them. Cait. It had been too long since I talked to her. I reached for my phone. As efficient as ever, she answered on the first ring.

"Cait Allen."

She hadn't checked her phone before she answered. That was her formal, business voice. I mimicked her, "Lizzie Danton."

"Lizzie! Oh my God. It is so good to hear your voice. How are you? Where are you? Are you having fun?"

Chuckling, I attempted to answer all of her questions. "I'm good. Currently, I'm in Edinburgh in search of a dress for dinner. And yes, I am having fun. I love it here."

"I can tell. Are you still thinking about staying?"

"I am, but that is kind of dependent on what happens with the cottage."

"Speaking of which, I have the information on your father. I'll email you. He still has an office in New York and one in Boston. I have direct numbers for both."

There was a knot in the pit of my stomach thinking about speaking to my father, but I would. Norah wasn't going to win, no way.

"I did a little research on him too. He never remarried after your mom and he doesn't have any other children."

"I should hope not. He couldn't handle the one he had."

"I'm sorry, Lizzie."

"It's fine. It's all water under the bridge, but thanks for getting the info. How was your surprise weekend?"

"He took me to Vegas. I thought I would hate Vegas. I loved it. We're going back."

"I've never been."

"It was crazy and loud and wild and just electric."

"I'll have to check it out. I need your fashion sense. I'm going to dinner tonight at a restaurant that is business attire."

"You need a cocktail dress and get black, very versatile and it is a great color on you."

Not according to my mother it wasn't. All these years later and I still remembered that. The damage our parents were capable of doing to us.

"There are a couple great little boutiques. I'll text you their addresses. Don't forget shoes."

"You love this."

"I do and I think you will too. Any update on your scary, sexy Scotsman?"

"That is a whole other conversation."

"So there is more."

"He fascinates me, Cait, and partly because he and I share a similar background."

"I'm sorry to hear that."

"It connects us though. I can't even really explain it, but he gets it because he's been there. It's not just empathy, he really understands."

"I like that you have that. Sorry that either of you need it, but I like that you have it."

I did too. "I have a dress to buy."

"Send pictures."

"I will. I miss you, Cait."

"I miss you too."

BROCHAN

"It's not empathy. She's been there; she gets it. And there's just something about her." I glanced down at my companion as I flexed my fist. I had really been getting into it; my breathing was labored. "I don't know why I'm telling you this. Maybe because I know it won't leave this room."

Wide fearful eyes stared up at me. Blood dripped down his cheek from the cut over his eye. He only replied in grunts, but the gag inhibited his talking. I cracked my knuckles then slammed them into his face again. His front tooth popped out.

"She knows what I do. Understands it."

He moaned when my fist connected to his temple. He may have even blacked out. I grabbed the pliers and started on his fingernails. "She talks to herself. A lot." He howled when I yanked his thumbnail from his finger. I held it out to him. "She has a devious streak too, intentionally letting that douche's car roll into the mud." I yanked out another nail. "Just the fact that I'm talking about her." The man was whimpering. He was almost at his breaking point.

"Only one way to stop people like you. You can't use it if you don't have it." I grabbed the knife. He screamed around the gag, his eyes completely dilated from fear. My cell rang.

I glanced at the ID before I answered. "Fenella."

"Brochan, how are you?"

I glanced down at my mark struggling to break free. I pointed the knife at him and he nearly expired on the spot. I grinned. "I'm good."

"Are you working?"

"Even now, yes."

"Oh. Well…you answered the phone. This is kind of awkward, never mind. I don't want to keep you from…but I wanted to let you know that Lizzie is in Edinburgh."

I was losing it because I felt my mouth turning up in a smile. "She is?"

"Yes. I thought maybe you could meet up with her."

"Edinburgh is a large city." That didn't matter I'd find her. It was what I did.

"Like that matters."

Again my lips twitched. It was a slippery slope, this feeling thing.

"I'll let you get back to ah…work. Show Lizzie the sights."

I dropped the phone on the table. An evening with Miss Danton, my day was looking up. My focus shifted back to my mark as the grin morphed into a sneer. "I'd say this won't hurt, but that would be a lie."

LIZZIE

I checked myself in the mirror of the hotel, turning this way and that. I wasn't sure about the one shoulder design on the rack, but I loved it. The chiffon beaded dress fell to mid-thigh, one shoulder was completely bare, the other ended in a long, flowing sleeve. The color was not black, but a charcoal gray. My wild, brown curls were pulled up into a knot and I'd added a little mascara and lip gloss. The Sophia Webster crystal beaded silver sandals were an extravagance, but they were so damn pretty. I even bought a little silver clutch. I didn't recognize the smiling woman looking back at me in the mirror. Checking the time, I grabbed the room key and clutch and hurried down to the waiting cab.

From the outside, the restaurant didn't look like much, but inside was simple and elegant. The color palette very neutral with splashes of color coming from the orchids at the table, but more importantly the dishes. The entire restaurant was designed to be the canvas for the cuisine. It was very clever and very effective. The hostess saw me to my table, one that was set for two. A restaurant of this caliber shouldn't have two place settings for a lone diner. I assumed the server would remove the second setting when he saw I was dining solo.

The menu was a little overwhelming and partly because I didn't know what half of it said. I'm not sure what had me glancing up when I did, but if I hadn't I would have missed the sight of Brochan McIntyre entering. At first, I thought I was hallucinating. I had been thinking about him a lot throughout the day, but watching the hostess stand a bit taller, seeing the slight flush coloring her cheeks—he wasn't a hallucination. I forgot all about the menu and just stared. In the back of my mind I wondered what he was doing here, more specifically how he knew I was here, but at the moment I was enjoying the sight of that tall, hard body dressed in an elegant black suit. The man was handsome and striking and he was also heading to my table. I glanced down at the second table setting.

"Miss Danton." His pale eyes looked darker, heated as he moved them down my body.

My greeting could have been better. "How did you know I was here?"

He flashed me a grin. Yes, he grinned. "May I?" He gestured to the empty seat.

"Please."

He folded his tall frame in the chair and glanced at the hostess. "A bottle of Chateau Lafite 2012." Those eyes were on me immediately after. "Are you enjoying our fine city?"

"How did you know I was here?"

"In this restaurant or Edinburgh?"

I had said similarly to him once. He was teasing me. The smile couldn't be helped. "Both."

He didn't reply immediately, his focus was on my mouth and I felt the heat of that stare from my head right down to my toes. I reached for my water in the hopes it would soothe the burn.

"Work brought me to Edinburgh. Fenella called, told me you were in town."

"That doesn't explain how you are here now?"

"I tracked you down."

I had said he was a predator. He was an even better one than I thought to be able to hunt me down in a city this size.

His face closed off; it was only then that I appreciated how animated he'd been. I didn't like how he could turn it off so quickly. "Would you prefer to dine alone?"

"No!" I said that loud enough to attract the attention of several tables around us.

He grinned. I really liked that grin.

"I would enjoy your company."

"Have you decided on what you want?" he asked.

Him. I wanted him. I had from the moment he encouraged me to buy a can of haggis. He was waiting, watching. I dropped my eyes to the menu. "I don't know what half of it means."

"Would you allow me to order for you?"

"Please."

The server returned with our wine and went through the production of uncorking, pouring a splash. Once Brochan approved it, the waiter served me then Brochan before leaving the bottle and disappearing as quietly as he appeared.

"It's a Bordeaux. Quite good too."

It was better than good. The flavors exploded on my tongue, some lingered longer than others. "It's delicious."

Brochan ordered for us both before he reached for his wine. "So what brought you to Edinburgh?"

"Research."

His brow rose at my vague answer. "On?"

"I'd rather not say just yet."

"Very well."

"You said work brought you here, that went well I hope." Even as I spoke the words, I realized what I was saying. That I hoped his killing of someone had been successful. Silence followed before we both laughed out loud. My own cut short to hear that melodious sound from Brochan.

"Aye, it went well."

"Can I ask you something?"

I regretted asking when the brightness in his eyes dimmed. "Yes."

"Never mind."

"What do you want to know, if I have a code or do you just need to be able to afford my fee?"

"I know you have a code."

"How do you know that?"

"Because I'm looking, Brochan. I see you."

His hand flexed and a dark but wildly sexy look entered his expression. "What did you want to know?"

"Does it help? Righting the wrongs, does it help push back the darkness?"

"Yes." There was so much behind that simple word. "Are there sights you hope to see while here?"

Normalcy. We both deserved that. "I'd like to see the castle."

"You have an unusual interest in castles, Miss Danton."

"We don't have castles in the States. I doubt Edinburgh Castle will come close to your home, but I still want to see it."

Silence followed for a few seconds. His voice seemed softer when he said, "Edinburgh Castle is pretty spectacular."

"Your home is spectacular. That view from the lane is unparalleled. How the castle rises up with the trees. I've never seen anything to compare to the beauty of that."

His reply was so softly spoken I almost missed it. "I have."

Our eyes connected and I would have given up years of my life to know what he was thinking.

The moment was over when he said, "Where are you staying?"

"A hotel on Hill Street. What about you?"

"High Street...old world charm and exceptional service. I've taken the liberty of reserving a room for you there. When we're finished dinner we can go back to your hotel and..." He paused long enough for me to know I wasn't the only one filling in the blanks with something that had nothing to do with collecting my things.

Sexy thoughts aside, I was surprised by his offer. I wasn't eloquent when I asked, "Why?"

"You've a mind to sightsee, I know the area. Being in the same hotel simplifies things."

"Why take me sightseeing?"

He took a sip of his wine. "Why not?"

"You don't strike me as the tour guide type."

"I'm happy to hear that."

"So why join me?"

"Maybe it is for solely selfish reasons."

Where my head went with that and the delicious chill that moved right down my body felt really nice. "What reasons?"

"Witnessing you discovering that my home is in fact nicer than Edinburgh Castle."

He grinned again and holy shit I needed to paint that. Heaven forbid he actually smiled; I'd probably die from the beauty of it. As excited as I was at the prospect of spending time with Brochan, his radical attitude shift toward me was confusing.

"What changed? Our last meeting you demanded to know if I was real before walking away."

He was spared in answering when our first course arrived, scallops in a citrus glaze with dandelion greens. It was exceptional. It wasn't until our main dishes were delivered—Gigot d'Agneau Pleureur, lamb that was grilled over the potatoes served with it so those starchy lovelies absorbed the juices—that he answered me.

"I'm not a good man, Miss Danton, despite what you might think. I need you to understand that. I'm not about to turn a new leaf and become a pillar of the community. I'm not looking for absolution and I'm not looking for a happily ever after. I just like hearing another voice in the dark."

He was even more damaged than me and it broke my heart knowing he wasn't just saying the words. He truly meant them, but I could be that voice in the dark for him.

"So we'll see Edinburgh Castle tomorrow."

His eyes met mine; he knew what I was offering too when he said, "First thing."

CHAPTER ELEVEN

LIZZIE

"Holy shit." My eyes bugged out of my head. Edinburgh Castle was amazing. With it sitting at a higher elevation than the city that surrounded it, it looked like a beacon…a sentry. Brochan and I were in his Aston Martin. Yes, the man had an Aston Martin DB11 in charcoal gray.

"Can you imagine what it was like back in the day, before the city rose up around the castle?"

"Magnificent."

"Fair warning. I'm going to want to see all the rooms and I will linger. Paint colors, fabrics…all day, Brochan."

"So noted."

"How many rooms does the castle have?"

"Sixteen hundred."

I jerked my head from the tour book making myself a little dizzy. "Sixteen hundred. This might take longer than a day."

He chuckled. It was a nice sound. "Only a few are open to the public."

"Can you imagine your staff tending to sixteen hundred rooms? You'd need a huge staff, hundreds. The mind boggles."

"How many rooms are in your place?"

Pleased that he asked I answered, "Four. I have a one-bedroom apartment. Bedroom, kitchen, living room and bathroom...simple and cozy."

"And small."

"Yes, very."

We parked. There was a line to get in, but we didn't have to wait. We were whisked passed it and shown to a private entrance. "What just happened?"

"I'm a benefactor. I don't have to wait in line."

We were led into the great hall. It was massive. There were swords along the walls, hundreds of them. And the beautiful paneled wood walls carried to the arc ceiling with its buttresses. A huge stone fireplace took up part of one wall and would have been perpetually burning back in the day. This room would have been where the clan spent most of its time according to our tour guide, a pretty woman with auburn hair and green eyes. Eyes that were undressing Brochan even while she delivered her spiel flawlessly. If he noticed, I couldn't tell. Women and their bad boys, like death and taxes, one of life's constants.

We walked around for hours. Right before one o'clock, we were escorted upstairs to see the cannon shot off the turret. History oozed from the place and how much I wished I could go back in time and see the castle in its heyday. So many people, if given the choice, would travel to the future to see what became of the world. Not me. There were so many moments in the past I wanted to see—dinosaurs, Ancient Greece, the discovery of electricity, the Wright brothers' maiden voyage and the Highlands when it was ruled by clans. A violent and savage time and still I wished I could see it.

"What are you thinking?" Brochan asked.

"Just wishing I could go back in time."

He had a thought on that, but instead asked, "Since you have a fondness for old buildings, how about we hit Inchcolm Abbey?"

"Lead the way."

"Maybe we could stop and get something to drink." It was exhausting touring through ruins.

The words had just left my mouth and we were turning a corner to find a sidewalk festival, one that featured beer.

"Scotch ale, you need to try it."

"I'm not really a beer drinker."

"This isn't beer."

Clearly Brochan took his ale seriously. It was a sampling, but with as many stands set up along the street someone could get good and drunk on the samples.

"Most towns have their own preferred ale. Microbreweries are popping up all the time."

It wasn't what we were discussing but the fact that we were discussing it. Brochan was usually so taciturn, so despite the fact that the conversation circled around ale, I was happy to be having one with him.

He handed me a paper cup. "Try this."

My first thoughts were it was bitter and heavy. I could see the Highlanders back in the day drinking it though. It was thick enough to be a meal.

"By your expression, I'm guessing you don't like it."

"It's bitter."

"We'll try another."

We tried eight and with each sample, the taste improved but that might just be because I was now mildly drunk. He handed me sample nine and I grinned the grin of a slightly inebriated person. "You're trying to get me drunk."

"Then I've succeeded."

I pointed at him in surprise that he was teasing me and the ale sloshed over the rim of the paper cup. "That was funny."

"You need food."

"I couldn't eat food. My stomach is filled with ale."

He reached for my hand and I froze. It felt nice, really nice, but it was the fact he had done it. He glanced back at me when I didn't follow him.

"You're holding my hand."

"Is that a problem?"

"No."

"Food?"

"Okay."

Maybe it was because I was drunk but the cheese and crusty bread was the best I'd ever tasted. There were stands of jams, just jams. I tasted a few of those too. They were even selling seafood, like US festivals sold hot dogs and chicken fingers.

"Brochan, why do they call them chicken fingers?"

We were walking down the street, feasting on cheese. What kind of cheese I didn't know, but I'd ask him later when I'd actually remember. He turned his head and regarded me before he said, "I don't know."

"Chickens don't have fingers."

"Good to know."

"That makes me happy."

"That chickens don't have fingers?"

"You teasing me."

He said nothing, but there was the slightest softening around his eyes.

We walked for a little while in comfortable silence before he asked, "How do you do it?"

"Hold my liquor? It's a gift."

He chuckled, the sound so sweet because it was so rare. I almost asked him to do it again.

"Find the happy."

"Because otherwise she wins."

He reached for my hand again. "We've more old buildings to see."

I held his hand tighter. "And a restroom."

We ended the day in a pub. I was pretty sure we'd walked the length of Edinburgh and I saw many of the restrooms in the city thanks to my binge on ale.

Once we were settled at our table, Brochan spoke, "I think we've seen enough old buildings to satisfy even you."

"That was a lot of fun, thank you."

"What were you planning for tomorrow?"

"I was hoping to see Culloden Moor."

"It's a few hours away. It might be best to check out and stay somewhere closer."

"You want to join me?"

He didn't answer right away and when he did my tummy quivered because there was so much behind his simple answer. "Aye." He added, "I'll make arrangements to have your car sent back to Tulloch Croft. We can take my car."

"Drive to Culloden in your Aston Martin? Yeah, twist my arm."

He grinned. "There's one last thing you need to do today."

Kiss you. I really wanted to kiss him. Badly. A mistake, no doubt, but I didn't care. Instead, I asked, "What?"

"You need to try haggis."

"No." My stomach was already feeling a little queasy, that would surely send me over the edge.

"It's not as bad you're thinking."

"So you say."

"You can not travel to Scotland, to Edinburgh, and not try haggis."

"Is that documented somewhere?"

He only arched his brow in reply before he added, "One bite."

"I'm not getting out of this, am I?"

"No."

"Fine. One bite."

He ordered the haggis, I ordered the fish and chips and water and wine. I intended to wash the taste out of my mouth with everything and anything. I will say, it did smell good when it was placed in front of him. The bite was a huge mouthful and he knew what he was doing because the bastard had the nerve to grin as he handed his fork over.

"That is not a bite."

"It's a highland bite."

"You made that up."

"Eat."

I studied it, sniffed it, and then I closed my eyes and got it over with. The joke was on me because it was good. "Is that mashed parsnips?"

"Yes. Not as bad as you thought, is it?"

"It's good." I forked up some fish. "This is better."

It was thinking about our day that had me asking, "What do you know about your home?"

He leaned back in his chair and reached for his ale. "It was built by the Ferguson clan back in the twelve hundreds. In the seventeen hundreds a wealthy English lord bought it to appease his young wife's wish to live in the wilds of Scotland. They didn't live there long. As beautiful as the highlands are, back then it was a harsh environment to live in. A young, English rose wouldn't stand up to the climate. Over the years it had a few owners, the last of which were Americans hoping to open a hotel. Good idea, bad location. They need to be closer to tourist areas for that to succeed. I bought it about ten years ago and dropped a small fortune into restoring it."

"Well, it's amazing."

We were interrupted when a shadow fell over us. Looking up, unease moved through me to see Tomas. What the hell was he doing here? He wasn't alone; a woman was with him. She was beautiful; tall, thin with long delicate limbs. Her eyes flickered to me and a chill moved down my spine before they settled on Brochan. "Hello, lover."

It took effort to not react to her words, her intention I was sure. Brochan was much better at it than me. His expression was cold and blank.

"Have you met my girlfriend?" Tomas was being smug, his arm going around the woman.

Her eyes were only on Brochan. "Who's this?" she asked as she slid her gaze to me. She wasn't impressed with what she saw.

I was saccharine sweet when I held out my hand. "Lizzie."

She looked at my hand like it was a sewer rat nipping at her designer shoes. Her red lips curled up into a snarl. "How do you know Brochan?"

How was that any of her business? Brochan agreed. "Not your concern." Ice should have formed from Brochan's cold shoulder.

I held her cool glare. "I don't know him. I'm just using him for sex."

She didn't like that. Brochan on the other hand...his eyes warmed.

"How do you know Tomas?" I intentionally used her words back at her, but it had the added effect of talking about Tomas like he wasn't there. He wasn't so stupid that he didn't pick up on the slight. If looks could kill...

She moved her hand down Tomas' chest. "I don't. I'm only using him for sex."

I wanted to stick my tongue out at her. She was touching Tomas, but she was thinking about Brochan. It was clear there had been something between this chick and Brochan and he had been the one to end it because she wanted him back.

"He has some very interesting things to say about you, Brochan."

It was the first time Brochan looked at her. If I had been on the receiving end of that glare, I would have peed myself. She wasn't immune. I was tired of the conversation. They each had their own reasons for standing there, but I didn't care. They weren't ruining our evening with their bullshit.

I dropped my arms on the table and huffed out a breath in boredom. "Honey, I've got plans for this man. If you're done with whatever this is, could you hurry it along?" I thought she might take a swing at me. I enjoyed twisting the knife. "Please go be outraged elsewhere because no one at this table gives a shit."

"Nicely said, mo leannan." Brochan's fingers touched mine.

I didn't know what that meant, but I liked how he said it. Sure, it was for the chick's benefit and still my body warmed. His eyes shifted to our unwanted visitors. It was fascinating to watch the transformation, heat to ice in a blink. "You're still here?"

She hissed, Tomas cursed. I swear it looked like one or both of them were going to hit him, both thought better of it. She stormed out, Tomas following in her wake.

"That wasn't a coincidence," I said.

"No."

"She's clearly scorned, but what was Tomas' motivation?"

Brochan said nothing, but he was thinking plenty. He changed the subject. "What's happening with Brianna's estate?"

"You're changing the subject, that's fine, but he has it out for you. I don't have to tell you to watch your back, but I will anyway. Regarding Brianna's estate, no news is good news, I think. I've been assured the suit is frivolous, but I do want to see my father. I don't want her to just not win." I glanced down and played with my food. It was spiteful, cruel and still it was how I felt.

"You want her to suffer."

"I do. We're taught right from wrong. We're taught to talk through our problems, to find a solution without violence. But it's all bullshit." I leaned closer and dropped my voice. "It's why I understand what you do. Sometimes it really should be an eye for an eye. I admire that you have the conviction to be that balance." Words failed me at the sight of Brochan. He looked dangerous and sexy as hell. He stood, dropped money on the table and grabbed my hand.

"What's wrong?"

He said nothing as he dragged me from the pub. We reached his car. He unlocked the door and held it open. He sounded odd, distressed maybe, when he said, "Get in." Something was brewing, but the trouble was I couldn't tell if the storm was one I wanted to get caught in.

We spoke not a word during the ride back to the hotel. We reached my room. He followed me in but didn't move any farther than the door. I waited, afraid he wouldn't share what was going on in his head and even more afraid that he would.

He started to pace and even pulled a hand through his hair. Seeing a man usually so cool and reserved coming undone was fascinating to watch. He stopped and leveled those pale eyes on me.

"People can empathize; Fenella and Finnegan, even Brianna, have tried, but unless you've experienced the truly ugly in the world even compassion can fall on deaf ears to someone touched by it."

He moved closer and my lungs constricted because in that moment, as he bared a part of himself to me, I knew whatever happened from this point on I would never be the same.

"That day standing in the rubble of my nightmare, it wasn't empathy you shared. You understood because that has touched you too."

He moved so close and yet he didn't touch me. Not physically, and still I felt him as if he were. We were bound by something stronger than lust and desire, even heartache and pain. We had both survived.

"I'm not looking to be saved, Miss Danton, but I've never wanted a woman as badly as I want you." He brushed his thumb over my lower lip in an achingly sweet gesture. "But you need to know that road is a dead end."

Dead end or not I'd been heading down it from almost the minute we met. "I don't care."

Those pales eyes warmed; they damn near burned as he moved them over my body. His hands followed, leaving a trail of heat that seared my skin like a thousand little fires were being ignited by his touch. He took his time, tracing the curve of my shoulder, the line of my collarbone, one finger running down my throat. My hands itched to touch him and yet I couldn't get them to move. I was transfixed and hypnotized by the delicate, sensual onslaught his light touch stirred. His head lowered, my lips parted. A hiss of air escaped when he pressed a kiss to my neck, right in the spot that caused those lovely chills. Cool air hit my stomach as he lifted my shirt over my head. Slowly, he ran his hands down my body; his palms on my bare skin broke something loose inside me. I felt alive, truly alive for the first time in my life. He worked the zipper on my jeans then dropped to his knees to pull the denim from my legs. His fingers curled around the silk of my panties and he pressed his nose between my thighs.

He inhaled.

"So fucking sweet."

Yanking the silk off, he buried his face there as lips, teeth and tongue feasted. The orgasm didn't so much build as it exploded. I had never felt anything like it. Overwhelming, all consuming and slightly terrifying that he could bring that out in me.

He stood and I reached for the snap on his jeans, hoping to give back the beauty of what he just gave me. He stepped out of my reach and kicked off his shoes. He had boundaries and was making those very clear. And control, he had to maintain it even during sex. His focus never left me as he slowly undressed. I squeezed my legs together when he dropped his jeans and briefs. He fisted his cock and pulled. My mouth watered. He was beautiful. I was under his spell, totally and completely, captivated as I watched him pleasure himself. He knew what he was doing, stirring me, teasing me, readying me for him.

It was then I noticed the condom.

"Let me."

He ignored that and rolled it on. My stomach flipped, my heart skipped a beat and my clit spasmed when he moved me back against the wall. His fingers dug into my thighs as he lifted me and wrapped my legs around his waist. I tried to kiss him; he turned his head and buried his face in my neck.

It was deliberate, the way he claimed me. He was barely holding it together, easily seen from how ragged his breathing turned, and yet he entered me like he was making a statement. He wouldn't kiss me, he wouldn't let me kiss him, but he took his time joining us. That was very telling; the smile wasn't one he would see. I didn't rush him because I was enjoying the torture, every magnificent second of it. He filled me so completely it hurt a little before he stopped moving. The first quiver of the next orgasm started those delicious chills. He touched my chin, lifted my gaze to his and when he had my complete attention he started to move his hips. Slowly at first, the moan dragged from my throat because it was torture, the sweetest torture. Then it turned rough and wild as his control slipped. A scream tore from my throat as my body found its release, my nails dug into his shoulders as I jerked my hips into his rhythm to prolong it. A growl rumbled up his throat, right before his body stilled, his cock pulsing and twitching inside me. I tightened my legs around him and held him there. It was several minutes before he carried me to the bed for round two.

CHAPTER TWELVE

LIZZIE

It was late, almost three in the morning. Brochan hadn't stayed. After exhausting both of us, he went back to his room. The man didn't want me touching him, so actually sleeping with him wasn't going to happen. My body ached. It was a good ache after the hours we spent fucking. I didn't usually like that word when describing sex, but that was what it had been. There had been very little emotion; it was biology, pure and simple. Contradictory and curious because the man I had been spending time with felt things, deeply. He didn't show it, had a nearly bionic control on his emotions, but he wasn't the cold, unfeeling man people believed him to be, who I believed him to be once upon a time. For whatever reason, he held back earlier. What would it be like if he let it out? My body gave a pleasant shudder thinking about it. Perhaps it was wiser to keep that reined in. I might not live through it.

Brochan said he wasn't looking to be saved. I wasn't looking to save him. I understood some wounds cut too deep and his seemed to cut right to the bone. My mother was cold and manipulative, but I believed his father had been evil. The fact that Brochan could care about anyone—and he cared about Brianna, Fenella and Finnegan—showed the resiliency of the human spirit. His father hadn't broken him, dented up and damaged, but that sweet boy Fenella remembered was still in there. He was just hiding. I wasn't about to bring him back into the light. I lived in that darkness too. Sometimes people didn't want out. Like he said, sometimes we just wanted to know we weren't alone in it. But what would his life have been like had his mother lived? Who would he be had she lived? I didn't know, but I did know I liked the man he was.

Perhaps his father's grief broke him, but one had to wonder if he didn't have that ugliness in him all along. People lost people every day, every second. Most didn't turn into what Finlay McIntyre had. I think it could even be argued that what he felt for Abigail hadn't been love at all. It was obsession. Love stemmed from something good and healthy. Obsession stemmed from something ugly. Brochan didn't want love. He made that very clear during our hours of sex. He refused the intimacy of a kiss; and though he touched and tasted every inch of me, he wouldn't allow the same to be returned. What was sad, he had love from Fenella and Finnegan, from Brianna. Maybe one day he'd realize that.

In the morning, I finished packing when there was a knock at the door. My hands shook and my stomach flip-flopped. "Stop being silly. It was just sex."

Reaching the door, I pulled it open on Brochan. My heart hammered in my chest. Would he be different after last night? He didn't enter; just stood in the hall and asked, "Are you ready?"

Not really the greeting I was hoping for. "Yes, I was just finishing packing. Do you want to come in?"

"No."

I tried to hide my reaction to his decisive no and turned to close up my bag. "I'll meet you outside in a few."

"Lizzie."

It was the first time he called me Lizzie. I looked back at him.

"If I come in, we won't be leaving today or tomorrow...for the whole fucking week. If you're okay with that..." He stepped into the room.

The wave of lust started with a tingling of my scalp and moved right down my body, but a week with him and I would fall too fast and too deep. If I had any chance of surviving him, I had to be smart.

"I really do want to see Culloden."

He reached for my bag that sat at the door. "I'll meet you at the car."

"Brochan?"

He glanced back.

"I wouldn't survive a week."

His expression softened, but he said nothing and walked away.

It was awkward. Sitting in his car, so close to him I could touch him. I wanted to touch him. I had to link my fingers to keep myself from giving in to the urge. He hadn't wanted my touch last night; I felt fairly certain he didn't want it now.

A half an hour of complete silence and I was going mad. We had two and a half hours left. I wanted to ask him what he was thinking, but that was a classic mistake. Asking a man about his feelings. He'd probably toss me from the car. I didn't want to think about mine because I wasn't sure I knew any better than him how I felt. We had to talk about something though. The silence was maddening.

"Do you think the Loch Ness monster is real?"

He turned his head to me. My eyes moved to those lips, remembering how they felt on my skin, wishing I had felt them against my own.

"What if it really is some prehistoric creature? So many people have claimed to see it. And if he is real then are the creatures of myth and lore real?" I turned toward him because this was something I had pondered and often. All those stories written and passed down, they had to stem from something. I wasn't convinced humans had good enough imaginations to make it up.

His focus was out the window when he asked, "Like werewolves?"

"I have it on good authority that werewolves do exist. Mrs. Wilson was quite adamant."

"We've had a full moon. I didn't change."

"Yes, but I didn't see you on the full moon. Next full moon."

He glanced over and dropped his voice to a seductive whisper. "Are you thinking of keeping me preoccupied during the next full moon?"

It was how he said it that caused the ache between my legs. "It's a plan."

"A good plan," he deadpanned.

I laughed out loud.

BROCHAN

Lizzie was getting her sketchpad. We didn't find an inn before we stopped at Culloden. I leaned against the car and waited for her to collect her things. Last night had been a mistake and one I wanted to repeat. She didn't need the kind of trouble I would bring into her life. I didn't need the kind of trouble she would bring into mine. Acknowledging that didn't do shit because it wasn't just lust I felt for her. I wasn't a werewolf, but I was a monster. For the first time in my life, it didn't claw to get out and that was because of her.

She walked passed me, her focus on the field and the monument. Small stone grave markers dotted the open field, the markers of the fallen clans.

Bright eyes turned to me. "Can you feel it?" A noticeable shiver went through her. "It was brutal. You can still feel it." Her hand shook as she flipped open her sketchbook. "The cruelty man does upon themselves. It was the end of a way of life, wasn't it?"

How she could feel such passion for something that happened so long ago, I didn't know but I admired it. "Aye."

"Warriors, proud of their heritage and they were forced to conform, to become something they weren't." Her eyes turned to me. "Why try to tame something into being what it isn't? I don't understand that."

It was then, hearing those words from her, that I stopped trying to fight it. She'd found a way in. Rocked by the significance of the moment, my voice was rough when I answered her. "It all comes down to power and control."

Silence followed as I watched her work and how easily she brought the pain and the beauty to life. It was another aspect of her that could grow addictive…she didn't give up. She took the hits and yet she got back up, brushed herself off and kept going, kept finding the good in the bad and the beauty in the ugly.

Hours later we were in the car on the way to the inn. Her focus was somewhere else and I didn't try to engage her. I brought her bags up to her room after we checked in. I had intended to give her time, despite the gnawing need to touch her; she had other plans. The door had barely closed at my back and she was pulling off my shirt. Hot eyes looked into mine, a challenge as her hands found my abs. I shouldn't allow it, especially not with her when her touch actually had power over me, but I wasn't in control. She had it, maybe she always did. Her eyes stayed on mine as she lowered her head and pressed soft kisses down my body. I was so fucking hard. She worked the snap on my jeans, yanking them down so my cock sprung free. Her small hand closed around me and I bit my lip and curled my hands into fists as I struggled to stay sane.

She dropped to her knees and I almost fucking wept. Stroking me softly, she touched her tongue to the tip. My legs went weak. I'd never been more turned on.

Her lips closed around my cock as she pulled me deep. Squeezing the base, she sucked then ran her tongue along the underside, swirling it around the tip. Her heel pressed against my balls as she squeezed. She kept up the onslaught until I couldn't hold it back.

"I'm going to come."

She replied by sucking harder. My fingers curled into her hair as my hips twitched and I blew…the best fucking orgasm of my life. She swallowed hungrily, like she was savoring my taste. I yanked her to her feet, thrust my hands into her hair and for a second I acknowledged I was stepping right off the edge before I slammed my mouth down on hers. She tensed in surprise before she grew as hungry as me. Her tongue warring with my own as I thrust it into her mouth, tasting her and me. I worked off her shirt, flipped open her bra and palmed her breasts. They fit my hands perfectly. Her nipples were hard as I twisted them and tugged. She straddled my thigh to ease the ache. I carried her to the bed. Her back hit the mattress as I yanked off her jeans and panties then thrust two fingers into her. Her back arched, her tits rising up to meet my mouth. I tongued her nipples, thumbed her clit and curled the fingers in her pussy, hitting the spot that made her moan.

"I want you inside me when I come," she pleaded.

Grabbing the condom from my jeans, I rolled it on. Lifting her hips, I settled myself between her thighs. Her eyes opened, desire stared back. I thrust forward, my own eyes closing as she closed around me like a velvet fist. She linked her feet behind me and moved with my thrusts. Our gazes locked, her hand moved down her body where she played with her clit. She was close when she bit her lower lip. She came on a cry. I came seconds later.

LIZZIE

"Haggis. You need to keep your energy up," Brochan teased as we checked out the room service menu.

"Fish and chips."

"Haggis has more protein."

"Then you should get it. I wouldn't want you getting tired."

The glance he threw me was wicked.

My body warmed even as my heart sighed. Earlier hadn't been a fuck and it hadn't been impersonal. He had let me touch him; he'd kissed me. Whatever had held him back our first night together, he'd willingly crossed that line. I didn't know what that meant, if anything, but I knew I was in serious danger of falling for him.

While he placed our order, I climbed from the bed to get a robe. I felt his eyes on me, glanced over my shoulder to find his eyes were on me. I walked back, pulled the sheet down, climbed onto the bed and straddled him. He continued placing our order, his voice deceivingly neutral considering I was rubbing myself against his hardening cock.

I moved slowly at first, pressing down to feel him pushing against me before tilting my hips to rub my clit against him. He dropped the phone in its cradle, but he didn't reach for me. He just watched as I pleasured us both. Dropping my hands on his shoulders, I brought my breast to his mouth; his tongue touched the tip and still he didn't touch me, only his tongue. He teased the one breast before I guided the other to his mouth. He grew harder, my hips moved faster until I felt the first tingles of my orgasm.

"I'm clean," he growled. "I want inside you. Are you on the pill?"

"Yes."

He reached for me then, almost brutally his fingers sank into my hips as he lifted me up and brought me down at the same time his hips jerked upward. It felt like he was tearing me in two.

Glorious.

He flipped us, pulled my hips higher and really started moving, driving into me in hard, deliberate thrusts.

"Reach for it," he demanded. I felt his body tensing with his own orgasm, but I was already there. He buried his face in my neck as we rode out the pleasure. The knock at the door came sooner than either of us expected.

His head lifted and he gifted me with a smile. My heart hiccupped at the sight. "We need clothes."

I couldn't answer since I was stunned speechless seeing him smile.

He bit my lip before he climbed from the bed and tugged on his jeans. I watched as he moved to the door. I wasn't falling. I had already fallen.

We sat on the bed eating. It felt so natural. I was feeling a little off because I had never thought I'd find myself here, happy, but I was. Brochan gave me that.

"What did you think of Culloden?"

"Poignant and terribly sad. I read a little about it, knew how brutal it had been. I didn't think I'd feel anything, but I did. It lingers, all that death haunts it."

He was thoughtful before he asked, "What's next on your list?"

"I don't know. Do you have any suggestions?"

"There are a few scenic spots on the way home that you'll want to see."

The change in him was almost as profound as the change in me. Funny that two damaged people could find what they lacked in each other. "Okay." I hadn't realized I intended to say what I did next. "You kissed me."

"I did a hell of a lot more than kiss you."

Despite his words, his expression wasn't quip.

"Why?"

He looked me right in the eyes and answered simply, "You make me feel."

As if to prove his point, he pushed our empty plates to the floor, grabbed and rolled me under him. We spent the rest of the night doing nothing but feeling.

We stood on a cliff of green, the transition from land to water was blunt—a nearly vertical cut through the rock down to the beach. Water stretched out for as far as the eye could see. The colors, the grass wasn't emerald or pine, it was a blending of them, a blanket that was vibrant and lush. The water was sea foam green close to the shore before turning sky blue at the horizon. As a painter, the palette took my breath away.

"It's like someone just cut this part off." I glanced over at Brochan whose focus was on me. "I've seen pictures, but seeing it in person…I don't have words. If someone told me as a kid I'd be standing here looking at this, I'd have thought they were insane."

"I felt that way the first time I stood here." His focus shifted to the horizon. "Beauty to rival the ugly I grew up with."

My heart broke because if this beauty rivaled the ugly, his childhood had been really, really ugly.

I didn't want to push him to talk about it and I had the sense he wasn't ready to talk about the ugly, so I asked instead, "You never did say how you became a hitman. Is there like a school or online training?"

His focus shifted to me, humor in his eyes. I liked seeing that, liked knowing he was willing to show me that.

"I met Mac. I was a young kid with a lot of anger. He helped me channel it."

"Mac?"

"My mentor."

"You had a hitman mentor?"

He turned to me and actually smiled. Like last night, the sight of his smile distracted me, but it also inspired me. "Don't move," I almost shouted. I reached into my bag and pulled out a small pad of paper and a pencil.

He had moved, the smile was gone and he was looking at me like I was crazy.

"I wanted to sketch your smile. It's so rare, I needed to document it for proof."

He moved in and my body went weak.

"Maybe we shouldn't stand so close to the edge. You make me feel off balance," I whispered.

That smile returned. I would sell my soul to see that smile replace the blank look he'd mastered. He dragged me farther away from the cliff then he dragged me to ground.

"People might see." There was no one around and we hadn't passed a car in forever, still we were right out in the open.

His hand moved under my shirt, up to my breast. He tugged on my nipple. "Do you really care?"

His mouth replaced his hand. Nope, I really didn't care.

I can take that off my bucket list." We made love outside. If there were any satellites directed in our area, whoever was watching would be getting an eyeful. Instead of embarrassment, I wanted a repeat.

We reached another scenic sight, Brochan parked and climbed out. "That was on your bucket list?"

"No, but it should have been."

He laughed; the sweetest sound.

"You need to do that more often too," I said.

He ignored me. "What else is on your bucket list?"

"Seeing the pyramids. Bungee jumping and skydiving, though I don't know I have the guts to do either. Getting shot."

He stopped walking and his head jerked to me. "Getting shot?"

"Yeah, to see what it feels like."

"Why the fuck would you want to know what that feels like?"

"It's a bucket list." I suppose he had a different perspective since he likely was shot at often.

"And punching my mother. Knocking that critical and dismissive look right off her face."

He grinned. "That one I get."

I looked around as we walked along a winding path through a forest of old trees, the branches twisted, gnarly and covered in moss. Wildflowers grew in the grass. The way the sun diffused through the foliage looked like mist. In the distance was a stone cottage. Smoke from the chimney curled up into the evening air. I expected to see sprites and fairies darting out from the cover offered by the trees. "It's like we stepped into a fairy tale."

"Maybe a Grimm brothers one. I'm a werewolf, remember."

In this setting, I could believe he really was.

"How did you find this?"

Some of the easiness faded. "Years ago, I wanted to see more of Scotland than my part of it." His expression grew serious. He touched my hair, rubbing a few strands between his fingers. "I told you I wasn't a good man. I'm not, Lizzie."

"And I told you doing bad things and being a bad person are not the same. I've spent time with you. You're not a bad person."

He looked almost boyish and my chest ached seeing again the glimpse of who he could have been. He conceded, "Okay, then I do bad things. Very bad things."

"Like I said before, I've thought about doing those bad things too. My mother and Nadine, I've spent countless hours thinking of the most gruesome way to kill them. But it isn't just them. Tomas, Ms. Meriwether, Ms. Beddle."

He looked up at the sky. "You're a witch, woman."

Out of character for him and utterly charming, I teased, "I thought only I talked to myself."

"She was a witch."

"Who?"

"Brianna."

"Why do you say that?"

"Because she gave me you and damn her, she knew I would want to keep you."

No words would come. He had rendered me speechless. He knew it too. "I've left you speechless."

He had. Completely.

So we didn't talk, he kissed me instead.

I hadn't been able to think of anything but Brochan's confession. He wanted to keep me. He was in luck because I wanted to keep him too. Even riding the high of his confession, I noticed the closer we got to his home the quieter he became. Had he ever talked about it? I found talking about it made it less than it was, smaller, easier to let it go. Maybe if I shared, he would too.

"My mother used to think I was fat." Even looking out the window, I saw his attention shift to me. "I wasn't. I'm not rail thin like her, but I wasn't fat. She would have our cook prepare meals that were mouthwatering; mashed potatoes with a pool of butter in the center, juicy cheeseburgers and grilled cheese that just oozed with cheese. She'd have the table set with the fancy dishes and linens. The first time she did it I thought things were going to be different, better. My younger self believed I had finally gotten a mother. She came to dinner in one of her designer gowns, and asked me to dress up too." Remembering even her small acts of cruelty had a humorless laugh moving up my throat. "She always bought me dresses one size too small. It was her way of convincing me I was fat. Her dinner was a martini, a bottomless martini. And me, I sat at that table laden with food but I wasn't allowed to eat it. Our conversation consisted of her saying 'you're fat...you can feel how fat you are because that dress barely fits you'. For an hour I was forced to watch her get drunk while all that delicious food went cold. The cook tossed it. Such a waste when there were people right down the street starving, but my mother insisted it all be tossed out."

I felt his attention, but I didn't look over. "One time there was a man, the first one she brought home. I was maybe seven. He made me uncomfortable because even though he was there to see my mother, he spent an awful lot of time with me. On one of his visits, my mother said she had to run out to the store. My mother didn't shop unless it was for clothes and shoes and most of that she had a personal shopper for. At the time I was too young to truly appreciate what was happening and still I was smart enough to know I didn't feel safe around the man. I was on the sofa, trying to make myself as small as I could be. He joined me and sat so close his leg was touching mine." I wiped the tear away, my stomach even now revolting at what my mother had tried to set in motion.

"He brushed my hair from my shoulder, told me how pretty I was."

"He didn't..." Brochan's voice turned my attention to him. He was looking straight ahead but his hands were fisting the steering wheel so hard he could have left finger marks.

"No. I threw up all over his designer clothes. My mother came home, grabbed me by the hair and hauled me to my room. She locked me in there for two days. Screaming that I ruined her one chance at happiness. He was a very rich man, he would have continued to keep her in the lifestyle she had grown accustomed and all it would've cost her was her child's innocence."

It was a risk, but it was a risk worth taking. "Have you ever talked about your childhood?"

Silence.

"I'm a great listener if you ever find you want to."

The rest of the trip was made in silence. We pulled around the drive; Finnegan appeared to help unload the car. Brochan threw the car in park then looked over at me. There was something on his mind, but he said nothing, just touched my cheek, the touch was achingly tender. "I have work. I'll be back in a few days." His phone had buzzed a few times on the way back, a sound I hadn't heard during our time together. He'd silenced it or even turned it off. I smiled inwardly.

He brushed his thumb along my lower lip before pressing slightly and running it along the inside of my lip. His eyes met mine when he brought that thumb to his mouth. He climbed from the car and disappeared inside; I wasn't able to move until Finnegan appeared, pulling the door open.

"Good afternoon, lass."

Lust made my reply sound like a frog gave it. "Hello, Finnegan."

"I trust you enjoyed Edinburgh."

"Yes, it was beautiful."

"Perhaps you'd like a cup of tea?"

I linked my arm through his. "I'd like that. Give me a few minutes and I'll join you in the kitchen."

Reaching my room, I pulled out my cell to call Cait. I moved to the window, my favorite place in the room. "Hey, Cait."

"Lizzie. How are you?"

"I'm good." Resting my head on the wall, I couldn't help the smile. Good was an understatement.

"What's wrong? You sound funny."

"I'm happy."

She didn't tease because she knew those words rarely came from me. "The place or the man?"

"Both."

"Hold on. I have someone on the other line. Let me get rid of them." I turned to Brochan's painting. It was done and it was absolutely my best work.

"I'm back. Details, leave nothing out."

"We spent the past few days together. He showed up at the restaurant—"

"When you were dressed to the nines, that night?"

"Yes."

"Sweet."

"He took me sightseeing. I wish I could explain that to you, the significance. He's seen even more ugly than me, Cait, and yet he played tour guide. He even took me to Culloden Moor."

"There's more, what are you leaving out?"

"We made love."

I would have heard her scream even without the phone. "Hot damn. And?"

"I'm in love with him."

She sobered. "Is that a bad thing?"

"No, but I don't know when it happened or even how, but I feel things I've never felt, Cait."

"Like colors are brighter and a lightness in your chest that makes you feel like you might float away."

"Yes. Is that how it is for you and Ethan?"

"I thought it would fade, well not fade but maybe I'd grow used to it. It's been four years and it's still the same."

"You both need to visit. I don't know how this suit will go, and I'm planning a trip home to see my father, but whatever happens you both need to visit. If you don't believe in a higher power, this place is powerfully persuasive."

"And the painting?" Ever practical and the reason I couldn't do what I did without her. She never lost focus.

"I have a few works in progress, two of them are staying here, but I have enough ideas. I can't wait to get started."

"Do you need me to make arrangements for anything?"

"I don't want to leave, but I need to follow up with the lawyers, see my father, so yeah. Could you get me a flight back at the end of the week?"

"I understand why you're dragging your feet with your father; that's going to be awkward."

"The enemy of my enemy, right?"

"I'll send you the itinerary."

"Thanks, Cait. I can't wait to see you."

"Me too. We'll go out and celebrate."

I disconnected and absently tossed the phone on the bed. I was in love with Brochan. I did feel like I could float, but more, I felt alive. I had been going through the motions since I was a kid, sleeping through life. He woke me up. I hoped I could do the same for him.

I entered the kitchen to the smell of something buttery. "What is that?"

"Shortbread. I thought we'd have some with our tea," Fenella suggested.

"I love shortbread. Can I help with the tea?"

Her eyes narrowed. "No, lass. You seem different."

"I feel different." I realized I said that out loud by their matching goofy grins.

I tried to play stupid. "What?"

"Take a seat and tell us all about this trip."

"I don't kiss and tell," I teased.

Fenella jumped on that. "But there was kissing?"

Finnegan's head snapped to her. "Leave the lass alone."

We settled around the table and while she poured the tea Fenella asked, "Why did you go to Edinburgh?"

I had almost forgotten what had sent me there. "I wanted to do some reach on Brochan's family."

"Why?" Finnegan asked.

"I had hoped to give him his father's family, to show him his father was just one of many and a bad egg to boot, but I realized it's his mother's family he needs." I reached for my tea. "Is there a reason they're not in his life?"

Fenella placed her cup in its saucer. "Finlay forbade us from contacting them. After the fire, I always had the sense that Brochan believed his past burned in the fire."

I understood why he'd feel that way, but he hadn't buried his past. He carried it around with him like a shield. "He didn't."

"I know." Fenella glanced over at Finnegan. He nodded and I wondered why. "I've been working on something. Come, I'll show you," she admitted.

She took me to a part of the castle I had not yet seen. The servant quarters but her room was no servant's quarter. It had been redesigned, several rooms turned into one. "This is beautiful."

"Aye. Brochan had it done for us."

They were together. I had wondered. "You're married."

"Forty years."

She walked to her bed and pulled out a trunk from under it, opening it to reveal a large leather book. "This was Abigail."

She flipped the cover and staring back was a beautiful woman, the same black hair her son had inherited. The eyes were the same shape but hers were a deeper blue. "She's beautiful."

"She was, inside and out." Fenella flipped through the book of mementos and photographs of Abigail and Finlay.

"They look happy."

She smiled as she brushed her fingers over a picture of a very pregnant Abigail. "They were."

"He loved her."

"Deeply," Fenella confirmed.

"That makes his behavior toward his son harder to understand. I'm guessing Brochan hasn't seen this?"

"No."

"I started a family tree of the Stewarts. Names and addresses for those still living. Maybe you could put that with this and at some point give it to him."

"To what end, lass?" Finnegan asked.

"I didn't want to come here. I thought Brianna would be like my mother and I didn't need another Norah in my life. But I've changed. Learning of Brianna, seeing her life, knowing I'm connected to that. I'm not the same person I was when I arrived. Knowing Brianna has made me part of more than I was. I think Brochan needs that. I caught a glimpse of the boy you knew, he was different in Edinburgh, but as soon as we started back for this place he retreated behind his mask."

"At least you saw under it. Not many have."

I wasn't sure they would answer, but I needed to ask. "What happened to the McIntyre estate?"

She didn't even hesitate to answer. "Brochan's version of a cleansing."

I think deep down I knew Brochan had set the fire, but just how horrendous had his father been to cause him to do that?

"What happened to his father?"

Finnegan ended the conversation. "That's enough. It should be Brochan that tells the rest."

Fenella added, "He's our son in every way that counts. You're the first woman to break through. Don't give up on him, please."

"I have no intention of giving up on him."

A shudder of relief moved through her and it broke my heart. They were so worried about Brochan, but he wasn't the only one suffering. The healing needed to happen for them too. It wasn't much, but it was a start when I offered, "His painting is done and he loves the library..."

"Over the fireplace would be nice," Finnegan added with a smile.

"Would you help me hang it?"

They answered in unison, "Absolutely."

CHAPTER THIRTEEN

BROCHAN

Leaving Lizzie in the car, I was determined to finish up quickly whatever the hell it was Gerard had been ringing me about nonstop for the last hour. I thought Mac had been insane settling down, but he had it right. He gave up the ugly for beauty. Maybe it was time for me to do the same. Strolling to my office, I pulled out my phone and called Gerard.

"Fucking hell, Brochan, keep your fucking phone on."

"What's so damn pressing?"

His hesitation had the hair on my nape stirring. I stopped moving. Whatever it was, it wasn't good. "Gerard?"

"Fuck man, I hate to have to tell you this but…"

My blood iced.

"It's Mac. Shit…he and Ava, they're dead."

It felt like a gunshot to the heart, the pain that exploded in my chest. I stumbled, hitting the wall as I nearly lost my balance. "Say again?"

"I'm sorry, man."

That lightness was swallowed by the shadows. Mac was dead. Ava. He was out, he was happy; he had made it to the other side. "When?"

"Two hours ago. A hit. One shot each."

My hand curled around my phone so tightly it should have crushed in my palm.

"Who?"

"I'm still working on it."

"Why the fuck would someone come at him now?"

"Grudges man, in your line of work there's always someone gunning for you. Retired or not, doesn't matter."

I thought of his pretty wife, teasing him, wanting his children. Her only crime was falling in love with a monster. That pain grew stronger. Lizzie.

"I'm heading to his place now."

"I'm sorry, Brochan."

I disconnected but I didn't move. He had thought his karma was good, that he could mark his soul and end with the fairy tale. But karma had just taken a little longer to come back around. That was the fate for monsters. Believing otherwise was fucking foolish. The last few days, I had been foolish, really fucking foolish. Her taste was still on my tongue and for the first time I regretted the path I had taken.

The police had already been through. I ducked under the crime scene tape and down the hall I had walked only months earlier with Mac. His face changing, shifting to what I understood now was love when he saw Ava. Someone took that from them. I moved into the living room, my legs going a little weak seeing the bloodstains, two, right next to each other. Did he make him watch as he killed her? Was the last thing he saw his wife, his love, staring back at him with dead eyes? At least they died together and if there really was a better place after this one, maybe they'd get a second chance.

Outside I stood in his drive staring at what should have been his happily ever after. Rage and sorrow burned through me as I dropped to my knees and roared to the heavens. I would make it right; I would avenge Mac and Ava. My head hung as the tears welled. We'd come to the end of the road; it was time for me to let Lizzie go.

In less than twenty-four hours after their deaths, Gerard had found both the assassin and the one who hired him. I took out the hitman first, one shot to the head, but I took my time with the one who hired him. The brother of one of Mac's marks, a man who had beaten and killed his girlfriend for the crime of not having his dinner on the table. Her father hadn't gotten justice in the courts; he had found it with Mac. I enjoyed the pain I inflicted on him, enjoyed watching him break until he was nothing but a whimpering, broken man. I shot him in the forehead, on his knees like Mac and Ava. No one would claim him; no one would find him. The cleaners took care of that. Boomer and Champ were being held at a shelter. I collected them, both looking for Mac and Ava, their tails wagging in anticipation, jumping around me and each other, thinking I was bringing them home. My chest grew tight as I kneeled down next to them. They licked my face, unconditional love, even for a stranger.

"They're gone. You're stuck with me now."

I had let it in, those fucking feelings, but it was a double-edged sword. You couldn't feel joy without misery. It was better to not feel at all.

LIZZIE

I was trying to recapture that cottage Brochan had showed me. I wasn't getting the colors right. I was close but I was missing a dimension. As I blended paint, I heard the heavy footfalls. I didn't hide my joy when I saw Brochan strolling into the solarium. Joy turned to lust at the look on his face. I'd called him a predator and that's what he was, and I was his prey.

He didn't say hello, just grabbed my hand and pulled me from the room, out of the castle and down the path leading into the woods. I didn't speak either; I was too busy thinking about all the things we were only moments away from doing. I thought maybe we were heading to the lake, but he pulled me deeper into the woods until we reached a little cabin. It was charming from what I saw. The door closed and my shirt was off, my bra followed. I liked his form of hello when his mouth closed over my breast, hot and hungry. He worked the snap of my jeans, his hand slipped inside my panties, two fingers slipped inside me. My eyes closed on a moan and my head fell back against the door. His free hand cupped my breast, rolling the nipple as he tugged on the other with his teeth. He dropped to his knees and yanked my jeans and panties off. His mouth replaced his hands. Digging his fingers into my thighs, he lifted me, pressing me back against the wall, holding me in place with his mouth. Curling my fingers into his hair, I ground my hips into his face. Another growl rumbled in his throat when I came. He didn't stop eating. Somehow he carried me to the bed. My back hit the mattress and he was pulling his shirt off. His jeans followed. He moved like a big, sexy cat when he climbed onto the bed. My focus moved from his cock up his body to his eyes. They were distant. Something was wrong, but then he lifted my hips and buried himself deep.

We both moaned. His focus was on where we were joined. Mine was on him as he moved harder and faster. It scared me, when I reached the edge, the intensity of the orgasm. He pulled out, flipped me onto my stomach, lifted my hips and slammed into me again going so deep. He didn't stop as he moved so fiercely I felt my body climbing again. I didn't think it was possible, but I crested and rode another wave of pleasure. His arm wrapped around my waist as he drew me even closer, his cock sinking right to the heart of me. Then he froze. The sound he made when he finally came was the sexiest sound I'd ever heard. He pulled out, his cock sliding between my ass cheeks. He was still hard. I couldn't believe I felt my clit quiver.

He flipped me over and thrust a hand in my hair; he wasn't distant now. He looked vulnerable as if he was letting the mask slip when the only sound in the cabin was our labored breathing. Love swelled in me. I grabbed his head and pulled his mouth down to mine; filled the kiss with all I was feeling but didn't think he was ready to hear. I tasted myself on him and went slightly wild. Sliding my hands down his back to his ass, I squeezed while rubbing myself against him. He assaulted my mouth, like a hungry man. Lips, teeth and tongues warred, our bodies moving together, finding that perfect harmony. I needed more. I dragged my mouth from his and shimmied down the mattress as I kissed my way to his cock. He stood; I sank to my knees and swallowed him down my throat. He'd have bruises on his ass, but I couldn't get him deep enough, couldn't suck hard enough. His body tensed. Working the sac between his legs, his control slipped. He cradled my head, pressing his fingers into my scalp, as he fucked my mouth. My clit ached to the point of pain; I touched myself to ease it. When we came it was together.

Several orgasms later, I was on my stomach and Brochan was lying on top of me. We were too tired to move.

"That was a fantastic way to say hello," I mumbled into the mattress.

He said nothing as he climbed from the bed; I turned to watch him. The man wasn't shy about being naked, moving to the fireplace to start a fire without a stitch of clothing. And as lovely as the sight was, the distant look in his eyes was back. Something was wrong.

"Are you okay?"

"Yes." But he wasn't.

"Did something happen while you were away?"

"Nothing you need to worry about."

As intense as he'd been during our lovemaking, he was retreating back into himself just as thoroughly.

"Brochan, talk to me."

He glanced at me from over his shoulder. "When are you going home?"

In the fireplace an orange flame sparked to life but as the cabin warmed, I grew cold. "The cottage or New York?"

"New York."

"I need to visit, but I was thinking about staying in Tulloch Croft."

"Why?"

The word hit like a slap across the face. Sitting up, I covered myself with the sheet. I felt exposed and not just because I was naked. "Why?"

He glanced back at me. His eyes were empty. "Yes, why?"

"I thought that was obvious."

His sardonic laugh sliced through me. "I knew you were innocent, but not that innocent." Who knew words could eviscerate. "It's lust, sweetheart, hot sex, not the fairy tale you're looking for."

"Why are you doing this?"

He wouldn't look at me. I yanked the sheet from the bed and got toe to toe with him. "What just happened wasn't lust, it was so much more and you damn well know it. Why are you doing this?"

Looking into his eyes, Brochan wasn't there. The man who sat with me when I was sick, the one who encouraged me to eat haggis, the man I had fallen in love with. He was gone.

"What happened when you were away?"

"Nothing. I told you going in, this was a dead end. You walked into it with your eyes wide open."

The first true pang of fear hit then because he really was ending us.

"Please think about what you're doing. Another voice in the dark, remember? I don't want you to go back to the silence. I don't want to go back to the silence either."

I understood Fergus' comment about empty eyes, because there was nothing looking back at me.

"Why are you shutting me out?"

His reply was no louder than a whisper and cut as efficiently as a well-honed blade. "Miss Danton, you were never in."

I closed my eyes as his callous words pierced my heart, not a fatal blow, but a slow agonizing bleed. I'd lost him and I had no idea why. I walked to my clothes. I didn't speak because I couldn't. The only sound in the cabin was the crackling fire. I dressed. At the door, the tears started but he wouldn't see them. "I didn't imagine it. Despite your callous words, you felt it too. I would have been that voice in the dark for you. I would have fought for you, Brochan, because I do see you, but there's no point when it's you I'm fighting." The click of the door closing behind me was so final, the end of something that could have been the best thing to ever happen to either of us.

"I'm sorry to hear you're leaving. Will ye be coming back?" Fergus and I were at the pub having lunch. I was going back to New York, but I couldn't leave without saying goodbye. I hadn't touched my soup. I hadn't eaten in two days. It was a different kind of hurt I felt, far more devastating.

"Yes. Once the lawsuit is decided."

"What will you do with the cottage?"

I didn't know. I had thought to sell it but I couldn't. A part of me still wanted to live there, but I wasn't so sure how that would work with Brochan being so close. Despite knowing there was no future for us, that wouldn't stop me from wishing for it.

I didn't want to get into that with Fergus so I was vague. "I'm not selling it. My hope is to live there."

"I'm happy to hear that."

"How are you?" He looked tired.

"Every day it's the same, waking up, remembering she's gone, and learning to find the happy even when I feel like shit. She'd want me to, would be quite angry if I was lamenting on her loss."

I couldn't help think of Finlay McIntyre and how he hadn't just lamented on his wife's loss, he'd taken that loss out on his son.

"I'm thinking I might do a little travel. Brianna and I wanted to see Hawaii. We never made it, maybe I'll see it for both of us."

"Hawaii, that sounds like fun."

"I've never left Scotland. She and I traveled throughout Scotland when we were younger, but I think I'd like to see a bit of the world." His eyes lowered to the table as he picked at a knot in the wood. "I wish she could see it with me."

I reached for his hand. "She is with you."

"Aye, lass. She is."

"Oh, Lizzie, I wish you wouldn't go. You were reaching him." Fenella hadn't stop crying since I told her I was leaving. I hated causing her more pain, but staying wasn't an option. "You said you wouldn't give up on him."

I had called a cab. My bags were already loaded and my paintings had been shipped home. I hugged her, her body shaking as she cried. "I didn't give up on him. He gave up on us."

"You'll come back?"

I wiped the tears from her cheeks. "Yes."

Finnegan wrapped an arm around me and pressed a kiss on my head. "You're a good lass."

"Something happened when he was gone. He was different that day, looking for an excuse to end it. I can't stay, but I would hate to think he was drawing even more into himself."

"I'll look into it." Finnegan promised.

"Please visit us again," Fenella pleaded.

"I will. Oh wait." I hated seeing the hope in her eyes thinking I was changing my mind. I reached into my purse and pulled out the medallion. "I found this in the rubble."

Her hand curled around it. "St. Margaret. This had been Abigail's. I gave it to Brochan."

I felt guilty for holding onto it for so long. "I'm sorry. I should have returned it sooner. I found it oddly comforting."

"I'll make sure he gets it." She touched my cheek. "Have a safe trip home."

"Thank you." I looked behind them at the castle. I didn't see whimsy when I looked at it now. Dark, isolated and lonely, but it was still beautiful. Just like the beautifully damaged man who owned it.

CHAPTER FOURTEEN

LIZZIE

I stared out the window of my studio, the same space I had started my career. The hustle and bustle of New York happening all around me, people heading to work, children hurrying off to school, happy couples getting married and making love. Life went on. I followed the rain as it rolled down the window. Never in my life had I felt the devastating emptiness that threatened to consume me. You couldn't miss what you didn't know; those words were accurately and painfully true. What hurt more, he had felt it too. I hadn't wanted to leave, I hadn't wanted to give up, but fighting him was pointless.

I had hoped he would realize that the darkness wasn't so dark when we were together. I had hoped he'd call, damn near willing my phone to ring, but it had been five weeks. I accepted the truth. What had only just started between us was over.

I turned back to the canvas and picked up my brush. A slash of color here and there as the image came to life. I spent every waking moment in my studio. I had to get what was inside me on the canvas. I wanted the pain and the anger, needed to translate that into my art. It was my way of processing and dealing, my therapy. Stormy and angry, but the image before me was also magnificent.

I heard Cait's heels on the floor and nearly sighed. I didn't like being alone too long with my thoughts.

She stopped next to me, cocked her hip. "It's dark and haunting yet hopeful. How the hell do you conjure that with just paint?"

"You should have seen it in person, Cait. I think maybe that little parcel is what heaven looks like."

"You're different," she said as she touched my hair. "In a good way."

I was different. More dents, more pain, but I was stronger too. "I learned something about myself. I can be happy. For those few weeks, Cait, I was so happy."

"Asshole."

"He's not. He's just damaged, more than is reparable I think. I realized something else while I was away. No one has ever stuck around. People move in and out of my life, but not you. Not Ethan. I don't say it enough, but I love you, Cait."

"You're going to make me cry and this isn't waterproof mascara." She cried anyway then pulled me close for a hug. "I love you too." She stepped back and wiped at her eyes. "How bad?"

"Not very if you're a raccoon."

"Funny." She disappeared into the bathroom but called out, "I have news."

"Good news, I hope."

"I think I found my dress."

That was news. She and I had been looking forever for a dress and though we had come close a few times nothing was exactly right.

"Where?"

"That little boutique off Fifth Avenue." She peeked her head from the bathroom. "She's holding it for me. I couldn't buy it until you saw it."

I felt those damn tears again. I was bent but not broken, lonely but not alone because I had Cait. "When are we going?"

"Whenever you're free."

"Now works."

Cait stood on the platform in front of four mirrors that reflected back her smiling face. She was right; the sleeveless dress was perfect with its plunging necklace, a keyhole back, ivory lace bodice, A-line blush-colored tulle skirt and court train. What really sold the dress was how comfortable and happy she was wearing it.

"It's perfect. Cait, you have to buy this dress."

"Right? I think my hair up."

"Yes. Flowers tucked in, no veil."

Her eyes sought mine in the mirror. "That's what I was thinking too."

"Four months to go," I said.

"So much still to do."

"But you've got your dress."

"Yes, I do."

I stood on the sidewalk and stared up at my father's building. I had spoken to his assistant to schedule the meeting. I had been prepared for him to turn down the invitation. I wondered if he thought it was a shake down. Did he think I was like my mother?

I dressed how I would for a show, needed the confidence my work clothes brought me. A simple black dress, high heels, my hair pulled up in a knot. I wasn't as nervous as I thought I'd be. He was technically my father, but this meeting was about two people who had something in common, Norah.

At the front desk I was given a badge and sent to the twenty-eighth floor. A woman in her forties greeted me when the elevator doors slid open. "Miss Danton?"

"Yes."

"Maria Carson. Mr. Danton's assistant. Please follow me."

She led me down a long hall to a set of black double doors. Nerves hit when she pushed one door open and gestured me through it. Rodney Danton stood behind a massive black desk. His back was to me, but he turned as soon as I entered. He was tall, wide in the shoulders. His hair was mostly gray, but it made him look distinguished. I had his eyes.

"Elizabeth."

"Lizzie, please."

"Thank you, Maria."

The door closed quietly behind her.

"Have a seat."

My legs were shaking as I walked to the chair, so I was happy to get off them when I sank down on the soft leather.

"This is a little awkward," he announced.

"A little."

"You're an artist."

"Yes. Oils mostly."

"I've seen some of your work. The images are flawlessly executed, but it's the feeling in the pieces that jumps off the canvas that makes your work really stand out."

That was how I felt about it. Hearing he got it was an affirmation I didn't know I needed. "Thank you."

"I'm sorry I wasn't a father to you."

"Please, let's not go there."

"Children weren't in the plan. I'm too self-absorbed to be a parent. I knew that. Norah didn't care."

"I'm not here to give you absolution. Father material or not, my life was hell and my only crime was being born. I'm sorry you have guilt, but nothing you say or do will change that. I'm here because that bitch is trying to do what she always does. I found family. Too late, because she died, but for the first time in my life I felt connected to something…someone. It was bad enough Norah kept us apart while Aunt Brianna was alive, but now she wants Aunt Brianna's legacy just so she can tear it down. I won't let her do that."

He transformed before my eyes. The man across from me now was a little scary. "What's being done?"

"Aunt Brianna's lawyer and mine assure me the suit is frivolous but she's seeing green. I don't think she'll give up so easily."

"She is a piece of work that woman. She'll back off. I'll make sure of it."

He was so confident, almost arrogant. "You have something on her."

"When dealing with a woman like her, it's smart to do your homework."

I wanted to know what he had on her, almost opened my mouth to ask, but I didn't. I was getting rid of the ugly in my life. Norah was nothing but ugly. I didn't need it.

I stood; he walked me to the door. "Thank you."

"It's the least I can do."

RODNEY

I stared at the door. My daughter had grown into quite a beauty, nothing like her cunt of a mother. I hadn't wanted children, had wanted the child even less when I'd been tricked into fatherhood. I wasn't so much of a monster that I'd take my fury out on an innocent. Instead, I dropped money on the problem and went on with my life.

From time to time I checked in on her. Was pleased the child that beared my name had turned into someone with integrity and grace. I may have even offered a hand a time or two. She was my child after all.

Norah Calhoun had surfaced; the bitch was like a bad fucking penny. The fact that I put my cock into her countless times sickened me. I knew some of the most cutthroat men in the business and she put them all to shame. Norah wasn't a young woman anymore and there were too many younger, prettier trophy wives. She needed a new way to keep herself in the lifestyle to which she had become accustomed. A big fat development deal would set her up for life.

I settled back at my desk and reached for my phone. This call I would enjoy making. Being the one to foil her plan for the cash infusion she so desperately wanted, knowing how she had done absolutely everything to crawl out of poverty, was a kind of poetic justice.

The call connected and was answered on the first ring. "Mr. Danton calling for Ms. Calhoun."

A few seconds later she greeted me, "What the hell do you want?"

"As pleasant as always." I knew the smile would have pissed her off. I leaned back in my chair. "I just had a visit from our daughter."

Silence followed before she asked, "What the hell did she want?"

"My help in getting you to back off. Poking your greedy little nose where it doesn't belong."

"I don't belong? I fucking lived there. That woman raised me. My mother was her sister. That cottage, that land is mine."

"Still a cunt."

"Fuck you."

"No thanks. It was only average when you were young and tight."

"Son of… did you call just to insult me?"

"Definitely a call worth making, but no. I realize now that you're older and not able to secure a rich husband, you are looking for a new revenue stream, but you'll leave Lizzie alone."

"The hell I will."

"I've gotten where I have in this business because I make it my business to learn everything there is to know about my associates. The same can be said of wives. I've learned some very interesting things about your friend Heather. Do you remember her?"

"That was ages ago." There was fear in her voice.

"You weren't as clever then as you are now. There are some questions as to the timing of your departure and your poor friend. The authorities have been looking for you, but you fled so quickly then changed your name, your look. The case is still open. Did you know there is no statue of limitations in Scotland?"

"You bastard."

Anger turned my voice hard. "It is amazing to me that you do nothing but cause destruction and yet you can actually sound indignant, as if you're the victim. Let me make this very clear. Leave Lizzie alone or I'll see your ass hauled back to Scotland."

She uttered the words so softly I almost didn't hear them. "I should have smothered her."

Alarm rose up to meet fury. "You touch a hair on her head and I will fucking hunt you down. There will be nowhere you can hide. And hear this, I won't be looking to lock your ass up." I hung up before I hunted her down now. I'd have to warn Lizzie. It wasn't likely Norah would strike out at her, but when an animal was backed into a corner who knew what it would do.

CHAPTER FIFTEEN

BROCHAN

That fucking painting. It was like she had crawled into my soul, to the small part that still felt, and pulled out what lived there and splashed it all over that canvas. I stood with my hands in my pockets, needed them there so I didn't reach for the whisky as I could still see her and our last night together. She didn't understand it had been done for her, but telling her would have made her dig her heels in, would have had her fighting harder. She'd seen enough ugly in her life, she didn't need more of it because of me.

Her face that last night, not just wounded but devastated. I saw it every time I closed my eyes. That was my penance for tossing away the one person who completely understood every dark part of my soul.

Fenella entered the room carrying a book. Boomer and Champ lifted their heads from their naps by the fire. She'd been giving me the cold shoulder since Lizzie left. Finnegan followed her in. He wasn't any happier with me. She tossed the book on the table, fire in her eyes when they landed on me.

"We have stood behind you every day since your first. Through it all, even when you decided to become a killer for hire, we never faltered because that is what family does, but damn it I can't stand behind this. You had happiness right in your hands and you tossed it away. Your father let his pain destroy him. He couldn't find his way out and you...you're acting just like him but it's self-hatred that will be your end." She started for the door. "Lizzie went to Edinburgh to research your family. She thought to show you that the McIntyres were more than Finlay, but instead she gave you your mother's family. Names, addresses of all those still living."

She reached the door and looked back. "Knowing Brianna linked her to something, changed her, gave her a foundation in which to build on. She wanted you to have that too. Her hope was for you to build on it together, but like your father you turned your back on the best thing that ever happened to you." She walked out and tossed over her shoulder, "You can make your own fucking dinner. Boomer and Champ, come."

They hurried out. She'd feed them.

Finnegan's silence cut just effectively as Fenella's words. I didn't share about Mac, what the hell was the point. What they wanted for me was a fairy tale, but fucking fairy tales weren't real. Mac and Ava were proof of that. That foundation could crumble; it could be leveled with nothing more than one perfectly aimed shot. I glanced down at the book. Alone but for the ghosts that haunted me, I settled on the sofa and picked it up.

LIZZIE

Sitting in Joseph Masters' office I was reluctantly impressed with how quickly my father handled my mother.

"She dropped the suit. Her lawyer faxed all the appropriate papers to me just this morning." Joseph looked up from the fax. "I'd like to know what your father used as persuasion."

Despite what I had said earlier, I was curious too for her to change her tune so quickly. His threat carried more weight than her greed, so it had to be something significant.

"What happens now?"

"It's yours. I'm having the title for the cottage transferred to your name. The funds are ready to be deposited into your account."

I was grateful, wanted that link to Brianna, but going back to Tulloch Croft wasn't happening anytime soon. "Thank you, Mr. Masters."

"I'm very happy it all worked out." He removed his glasses and rubbed his eyes. "But I want to warn you. From what I know of Norah Calhoun, I urge you to be cautious."

"Do you think she might try something?" I wasn't sure she had the balls to confront me. I wasn't a helpless child anymore.

"I think you know her better than I, but I've been doing this job for a long time. Some people when pushed push back. Your mother seems the type to push back."

"To what end? She lost."

"The win or lose mentality is assuming the person in question is acting logically."

If he was looking to scare me, he succeeded.

"I'm sorry. I've upset you. I just want you to be careful, at least until things settle down."

"I'll be careful, but my mother is a bully. She attacks those she deems weaker than her. I haven't been that person in a long time."

"All right." He stood and offered his hand. "Congratulations."

"Thank you for everything."

I had just reached the door when he asked, "Will you be returning to Scotland?"

When it no longer hurt thinking about it. "Some day."

"Water damage, Lizzie. That stupid toilet flooded into the living room. The landlord is dealing with it, but I can't have Ethan and my anniversary dinner there. Nothing like chateaubriand and eau de toilet water."

That was a visual. "Have it here."

She looked up from buttering her bagel. "I don't want to kick you from your place."

"Nonsense. I'll be in the studio anyway. When is it?"

"In four days. Are you sure?"

"Yes. Do you need help bringing anything over?" Dinner wasn't just dinner, she liked to stage her apartment to fit with both the event and the food.

"Would you mind?"

"No, especially if you save me some of whatever deliciousness you create," I offered with a hopeful grin.

"Deal." She took a bite of her bagel. "I have some shopping still to do. Do you want to come with me?"

"Yeah, let me get my coat." It wasn't my coat I was retrieving. Cait had been eyeing a *Moncler* coat for years. It was an extravagance, one she was on the fence about indulging in. I bought it for her. Silver lining to the heartache of Brochan, the reminder to show the ones you love that you love them. I pulled the black, quilted puffer coat from the closet. She didn't see it right away because she was checking her phone.

"Are you ready?" she asked and glanced up. She did a double take before her jaw dropped. "Holy shit."

I held it out to her.

"For me?"

"It's just a small token."

"Small? Three grand is small? It's even prettier in person."

"Try it on."

She moved from around the counter and then stopped. "I have greasy fingers." She hurried to the sink and washed her hands before she joined me, but she didn't take the coat. Instead, she hugged me around the coat. "Thank you."

We shared a moment before she declared gleefully, "Okay, let's get this baby on."

She moved like a runway model, reminding me of the day we met, the turning point for me, from living in hell to finding the path that would lead to happy. "It suits you."

"It's so warm, and soft." She grabbed my hand. "Let's go show this off."

Seeing how happy it made her, I made a note to do little things like it often. Showing people you loved that you loved them was a good thing.

BROCHAN

I stared into the flames lost in thought. My mother's family, the names and addresses Lizzie had compiled, there were more than I realized and many of them lived within driving distance. From time to time, I'd get invitations for events that I blew off. I hadn't given them a second thought, hadn't realized that their desire to reach out to me wasn't just about me. It took Lizzie to get me to see that. She had been the link to Brianna's sister and it was because of that link that Brianna's dying wish was to meet her, to see in Lizzie her beloved sister one last time. Lizzie giving me my mother's family, she understood I was their link to my mother and that it hadn't just been my father who lost her. I'd never considered that before, too wrapped up in my own hell to think about anyone else.

"This just came for you by way of special courier." I turned to see Finnegan carrying a white envelope. He handed it to me and was halfway to the door when he said, "Fenella asked me to tell you that dinner is at seven."

I guess I wasn't in the doghouse anymore. He reached the door when I called to him. "Finnegan?"

He turned. "Aye."

"Why the easy acceptance for what I do?"

A shadow moved across his face. "My best mate went out to get milk. His wife was home with their young babe. He just went down the street. Walked in on a hold up. The animal didn't even hesitate; shot him in the face. He held on for a few days before he died. They never caught him. His wife lost her husband; his son lost his father and all because he went out to get milk. What you do is brutal, but the world is brutal and at least you are on the right side of it."

I was beginning to understand just how much of a dick I'd been. I had never even considered their lives outside of mine. Why they stuck with me, I didn't know. "I'm sorry for your mate."

He nodded. "Don't be late for dinner." He winked then disappeared.

I turned over the thick card stock before ripping it open.

> *Dear Brochan,*
>
> *By now you have met Elizabeth Danton and if you are reading this letter, you have turned her away. How I know this, let's just say it's women's intuition.*
>
> *I understand why you've chosen to live a life on the outside. I think I might have done the same had I lived through what you did, but my dear boy you aren't living. What your father did to you, it can't be undone, but by separating yourself from others you're allowing him to keep doing it.*
>
> *I didn't get to meet Miss Danton. Perhaps she is like her mother and if so, well done for tossing her out. But perhaps she is just another victim. Another lost, lonely soul looking for a place to belong.*
>
> *You knew her, you would know best the kind of person she is, but I will say this. If she eases the pain, if she makes the world just a little bit brighter then you are a fool to walk away from that. You've been in the shadows long enough, dear boy. Allow yourself to step back into the light.*
>
> *Love,*
> *The nag who loves you, Brianna*

She was still maneuvering me from beyond the grave. That meddling...I almost fisted the letter and tossed it in the fire. I didn't. I read it again and then again. I missed her. I still didn't understand why the woman wanted so badly to believe there was good in me, that I cared? My eyes drifted to the painting hanging over the fireplace...it hit like a punch to the gut. It did every time I looked at it. Fucking stupid to lie to myself. About Lizzie, I cared a whole fucking hell of a lot. "Shit."

I was a grown man, but I stood there lost as to what to do. I wanted her, I feared for her, but I fucking wanted her. I found myself in a position where I needed some advice and there was someone who had been offering that my whole life. It was time I listened.

Leaning against the doorjamb, I watched Fenella moving around the kitchen. I had long ago told both her and Finnegan they weren't required to work. That had been the extent of my kindness, offering them a life of leisure. They could have left. They owed my family nothing and yet they stayed. They taught me how to fly a kite and how to roller skate; they had kissed my wounds when I hurt and they tucked me in at night. They didn't owe my family, they were my family and I never acknowledged it. I got so wrapped up in my own shit that I took for granted the two people who had never left my side. Who have had my back since the day I was born. Lizzie gave me that too. She opened my eyes to what was staring me right in the face.

"Fenella."

"Dinner's not ready yet," she said as she continued to whip whatever was in the pot.

"I'm sorry."

The whipping stopped and she turned.

"I never thanked you for sticking around, for not just caring for me, but for..." I glanced down, my fucking eyes burning, but she deserved the apology and the tears. She was crying too. "For stepping in and being my family...my mom."

She knocked me off balance with her hug. My arms came around her, a hug that was long overdue. She pressed a kiss to my cheek then stepped back. "There's nothing to say thank you for, it's what families do."

"I fucked up with Lizzie."

"Yes, you did."

"There's a reason."

"This sounds like a conversation that requires tea with a kick." She busied herself with putting on the kettle, getting the cups and saucers. I moved to the cabinet for the whisky. She plated up biscuits and I smiled remembering as a child she always had biscuits.

We settled at the table. "You might want a few sips of that before I get started."

Worry clouded her pretty eyes, but she took a few sips and then I told her about Mac and Ava. Watching the emotions move over her face was hard, had my own feelings rising to the surface despite my best attempt to lock them up.

"Oh, Brochan." She reached for my hand. "No wonder you sent her away."

"You think I was right to?"

"Of course not. It was bloody stupid, but I get it."

The chuckle felt natural, so did sitting here talking with her. I had denied us this. I *was* fucking stupid.

"You need to go to her." Fenella's eyes widened and I could see very clearly what she was seeing…the fairy tale ending, the look across the crowded room, the fucking blue birds singing. She loved romance; she loved happily ever afters. I pulled the letter from my pocket and handed it to her.

"What's this?" She was already reading it. Her smile was bittersweet. "If I didn't know any better I would think she was the supernatural one."

"She's a witch."

"Aye. I think you might be right. She's right too. It's time to step into the light, Brochan, and there's a really bright one whose heart you broke. She's right over the pond."

"How do I handle that? Just show up with flowers. Hey, sorry I was a fucking bawbag. We good?"

She glared. "No. You need to make a grand gesture."

Ah shit. I was afraid to ask. "Like what?"

"I don't know. You'll know when the time comes."

"Wouldn't my flying across the pond to see her be the grand gesture?"

"You broke her heart and basically kicked her out of your house."

She had a point.

"So until this grand gesture magically appears, what am I supposed to do with myself?"

"You have the unique opportunity to see Lizzie in Lizzie's world. Maybe you'll understand better what that grand gesture should be after watching a day in her life."

"So stalk her."

"It's not stalking, it's observing."

"You want me to fly across the pond and stalk a woman until I come up with some grand gesture. Am I getting this right?" Maybe she wasn't the right person to talk to about this.

"Do you have a better idea?"

No. "No."

"The important thing, Brochan, don't let her slip through your fingers."

CHAPTER SIXTEEN

LIZZIE

I walked from my room, slipping in my earrings. "You have everything?" I asked Cait. The chateaubriand smelled amazing.

"Yes." She looked up from slicing the tomatoes for the salad and whistled. "You look beautiful. I love that dress. That's the one you bought in Scotland."

"Yes."

"It's fantastic."

I had intended to work in my studio, but I decided to treat myself with an evening at the Met and dinner.

"Wear my coat," Cait said.

"No."

Her hand went to her waist. "I'm not using it and you have nothing in your closet to complement that dress. Wear my coat."

"But you just got it."

"And I wore it for the last four days, even when I was in my apartment. Wear it. It wants to be worn, not stuck in a closet."

"Okay. I'll wear it."

Her expression softened. "Your eyes aren't so sad."

"I don't feel so sad."

"I'm happy to hear that."

I looked around my kitchen. It had never seen so much activity. "Maybe I should get a hotel room. I think someone is getting lucky tonight."

"There's nothing wrong with our bedroom," Cait said as she smiled.

"If you change your mind, call me." I went to my room, grabbed my clutch and tossed my phone into it. Sliding on her coat, I fell a little in love.

"This is amazing."

"I know, right?" She wiped her hands and walked around to join me. "Have fun."

"You too. Tell Ethan I said hi."

"Will do."

We hugged then she walked me to the door. "Now off. I have to finish dinner before I get all dolled up myself. My man is coming over."

"Love you, Cait."

"Love you back."

I adored the Met. I visited it several times a month. In the beginning, it had been inspiring and now it was like a home away from home. Regardless of what was going on in the world, inside these walls art transcended all the obstacles humans erected for themselves. It was our link to the past, to the future, a constantly changing documentary on humans and their impact on the world.

There was a new exhibit featuring artwork on loan from some of the biggest collectors in the city. It was a chance to see pieces one wouldn't have access to—Van Gogh, Warhol and Picasso. I took my time studying the pieces—brushstrokes, color saturation, negative space. Halfway through the exhibit I nearly forgot how to breathe when I saw 'Voices' hanging in the same room with arguably the greatest artists ever. 'Voices' was my very first painting, the self-portrait that had been acquired for way over what it was worth, the painting that started my career. I never knew who purchased it. I scanned the caption next to the painting. My knees went weak when a name popped out at me, the benefactor who had loaned the painting to the museum. Rodney Danton. My father. My father was the anonymous collector whose generosity had started my career.

I was a little unsteady as I walked to one of the benches and sat down.

My father had been my benefactor. It didn't change anything, well, maybe it changed a little. I wanted to call Cait, but she was busy celebrating her anniversary.

A tingling started at my nape. I hadn't felt that sensation since Scotland. My eyes stung. Instead of dinner, I wanted noise, people, and alcohol.

Sex on the beach, the cocktail, was delicious. Sex on the cliffs, the act, was delicious too. I chuckled to myself. They should make a cocktail for that. I signaled to the bartender that I wanted another then looked around at the club. It was one of the happening places in the city. People crushed on the dance floor, bodies lining the walls. I didn't really get the scene. I preferred a quieter setting, like a library in a castle with a sexy and dangerous Scotsman. It was a good thing I didn't have his number because I felt a drunk dial coming on.

The stool on my left opened up, but not for long. A man settled there, not that I looked but the size of his shoulders gave it away. "Evening."

I glanced over. "Hi."

"Can I buy you a drink?"

I almost opened my mouth to shoot him down like a duck. Was it ducks hunters shot? And why? Did they eat them? They should. Killing and not eating your kill was wrong. Well, not with humans. The idea of Brochan eating his kill was gross, but he was allegedly a werewolf. Did werewolves eat their prey? I needed to brush up on my supernatural facts. I glanced over to find the man was staring at me. I hadn't answered him; too busy talking to myself. I was about to answer when the bartender appeared and set my drink down. "I just bought a drink." My eyes met his; they were blue, not pale like the moonlight, but still pretty. I threw caution to the wind. "How about my next one?"

"You're on."

I thanked the bartender and got a chin lift in reply. I might start doing that; efficient and it looked cool. The man ordered a drink then turned to me.

"What's your name?"

"Lizzie."

He held out his hand. "Clark." It was a nice hand, but when it wrapped around mine it didn't make my heart skip. But then, *his* was the first and likely the last to stir that feeling.

"What do you think of this place?"

I replied by lifting my hand and tilted it from side to side as I sipped on my drink. I really liked sex on the beach, partially because it numbed me. The persistent pain I'd felt since I left Scotland was just a dull ache. The uncertainty I felt about learning the role my father had played in my career, no longer right on the surface. I wasn't advocating drinking as a coping mechanism, but right now it felt good. "It's very loud and crowded."

He grinned. "It's a club." He took a sip of his beer. "What do you do?"

"I'm an artist. There is actually one of my works hanging in the Met at the moment."

"Fancy."

It was fancy and amazing and a little bittersweet that my father had been in my life even then but never made himself known.

"What about you?" I asked.

"Banker."

There were a lot of bankers in Manhattan. A woman pushed between us to get to the bar. She waved her painted nails toward the bartender. "I need water or I'm literally going to die."

I looked around her to Clark and said loud enough for her to hear. "Why do people insist on misusing the word literally? This chick is going to die if she doesn't get water, so we should either break her fall or step back."

The chick glared at me from over her shoulder. I smiled. Clark laughed.

A song started pumping through the speakers. My feet itched to dance. I jumped from my stool. "Let's dance."

I didn't wait for him, pushing my way through the bodies until I reached the floor where others were moving to the beat. It felt good to just let go, to think of nothing but my body moving to the rhythm. Clark reached for me and I almost pulled away, but I didn't. The one I wanted holding me wasn't here. He'd let me go; maybe it was time I did the same, even if it was just for one song.

BROCHAN

My hands curled into fists when he touched her. He pulled her close and my fists squeezed tight as I envisioned doing the same to his skull. Did she not have any sense of self-preservation? She had three drinks and was now dancing with a stranger, close dancing with the fuck. If his hands moved to her ass, I was fucking breaking them off.

Watch a day in her life, she said, look for the grand gesture. Yeah, that gesture would be to not kill her and him…fucking hell.

"Hey, baby. Want a dance." A blonde pressed into me, her hand moving south.

I caught it. I didn't even look at her. "Fuck off."

Lizzie lifted her hands into her hair, closed her eyes and swayed her hips to the beat. My cock went hard. She was flirting with disaster but the shadows behind her eyes were gone. Drunk, but at least for the moment happy. Two days I'd been 'observing' her. She never left her studio except with her friend Cait. She was thinner than she'd been in Scotland. That light behind her eyes was gone. She was still hurting.

I'd seen her reaction at the museum, walked past the painting before I followed her out. I almost lost her because I'd been unable to pull my eyes from the painting. It was Lizzie, but a darker, sadder version of her, the Lizzie who existed before Scotland. The one who was reemerging after Scotland. I read the caption and understood her reaction. Her father owned her painting. I wondered how that came about? I'd be paying him a visit.

Lizzie stopped dancing then rubbed the back of her neck. In the next breath, her head turned and she looked right at me. Fuck. I saw her eyes widen and that light was back. I slipped into the shadows, her eyes searched then that light extinguished. She didn't stay after that. Saying her goodbyes to the fuckhead, grabbing her bag from the bar and heading out for a cab. I made sure she got in one then I followed her home.

LIZZIE

"This is delicious," I said as I stuffed a mouthful of beef in my face. I had missed dinner. This hit the spot. Cait and Ethan were both leaning over the kitchen counter watching me. They looked to be holding back laughter.

"What's so funny?"

"You're drunk," Ethan said.

"Tipsy," I clarified.

"Drunk," Cait corrected.

"Fine. Drunk."

"You're lucky you got home okay." Cait wasn't wrong.

"There was a guy."

"What guy?"

"Clark. He offered to buy me a drink. We danced. He was nice."

"Did you give Clark your number?"

"No," I said then added, "You're probably right about being drunk because I swear I saw Brochan at the club."

Cait straightened, interest on her face now. "Seriously?"

"I blinked and he was gone. I'm sure I just imagined him. He looked good. Bastard."

"You're reaching the anger phase."

"No. I don't think I'll reach the anger phase. As much as I want to be angry with him, I get why he did what he did. I don't know what triggered it, but I understand it."

"So what about this dude, Clark?" Ethan asked.

"He's nice and cute, but..." I found I preferred dark and dangerous.

"But he's not Brochan," Ethan finished.

I touched my nose.

Cait poured me a glass of water. "You need sleep."

She was right. I glanced around my clean kitchen. "I would have cleaned up."

"Why? We made the mess." Ethan walked around the counter and pressed a kiss on my head. "Thanks for giving us your place for the night."

I gave him a chin lift, like I'd seen the bartender do. I wasn't cool enough to pull it off apparently when he asked, "What's wrong with your neck?"

"Nothing. You're welcome."

Cait kissed me then they both demanded I lock up, waited in the hall until they heard me turn the locks. I took my plate to the dishwasher, grabbed my glass of water and turned off the lights. I got ready for bed and climbed in. I thought of Brochan. He hadn't really been there, but for just a second I thought he'd come for me. I closed eyes and slipped my hand into my panties. I touched myself as I remembered and when I came I turned my head into my pillow and cried.

I was in the market, memories of my first meeting with Brochan teasing me. Would I ever be free of him? I had brought the can of haggis back with me. I wasn't going to eat it; the can sat on the counter because despite how it ended, that had been a good memory.

Speaking of memories, a voice from another aisle had the hair on my arms standing on end. It couldn't be. I turned down the aisle. It was.

Nadine.

The years had not been good to her. She was only a few years older than me, but her hair was almost completely gray. Lines marred her face but not laugh lines. At some point she had given up on herself because she was overweight and dressed like a homeless person. I wondered if she was homeless? What hadn't changed, she was still a bully. The woman on the receiving end of her cruelty looked terrified. As I grew closer, I realized the scene was over a parking spot. Nadine accused the woman of stealing her parking spot. Seriously? People stood and stared, some even had their phones out to record and post on social media, but no one stepped in and offered aid. People sucked. We needed more Brochans to thin out the fucking herd.

"Nadine. Just as vile as ever."

Her head snapped in my direction and the full force of her ugliness slammed into me like a freight train. It was a jolt, but I held my ground.

"Lizzie Danton?" she sneered then raked her gaze down my body and up again.

"In the flesh."

The woman was forgotten as Nadine moved closer. I glanced down at her fisted hand. It was a much bigger hand than in our youth. It would cause significantly more damage, but I met her glare with one of my own.

"Just as scrawny as you were in school," she chuckled and even looked around as if the crowd would egg her on. Had she not grown at all? She was exactly the same, but age and life experiences had me seeing her more clearly. Her best years were over—sad enough considering what those years had been like—but she was desperately clinging to them. It was kind of sad. Under the bully she was pathetic.

"You haven't changed at all."

She thought I was being cruel, referring to her physical appearance. Her hands lifted. "Say it again, bitch."

"You're going to hit me with all these people watching?"

Glancing around, taking in the phones aimed at her, she lowered her hands. "Not worth it. You're nothing. You always were. Your own parents didn't want you, but did that stop you...always doing the right thing, always looking forward, always hopeful."

Part of me softened toward her because underneath all that ugly was a jealous little girl who was dealing with the pain of her own abandonment. All the anger I'd carried around for her dissolved; she no longer held any power over me. It was freeing to rid myself of that weight. It felt so good I smiled, one that took up my whole face. Nadine thought I was nuts when she took a step back.

"Goodbye, Nadine." And it was a goodbye. I was leaving her and all her ugly behind. I headed back to my cart. She didn't even miss a beat when she turned back on the woman and started in on her. I was free of the ugly, I was free of her, but the bitch needed to be taught a lesson.

I turned around, walked right up to her, pulled my hand back and broke her fucking nose.

"Damn," I hissed and shook my hand. That hurt, but seeing all the blood as it poured from her nose made me smile. I turned to the subhumans that were capturing the moment on their phones instead of helping Nadine. "Make sure you get all of that, fucking Spielberg wannabes." I walked right out of the grocery store. My hand ached like a bitch, but I felt really fucking good.

***

"She's going to sue you," my lawyer, Harrison, said as he paced behind his desk. I left the market and went right to him. After some of the adrenaline faded I realized there would be repercussions.

"I know. There were several people who captured the moment. Why do people do that? Need to capture every incident of humans at their worst?"

"Confirmation that as much as our lives suck, it could always be worse," he said then asked, "What were you thinking?"

I shrugged my shoulders as I held the ice he'd gotten for me to my knuckles. "It was a cleansing."

"Next time, max out your credit card like other women."

"Are you being a misogynist, Harrison?" He was far from it. He had a wife and four girls that he doted over. I just liked fucking with him.

He gave me the eye, the one he gave often to lawyers on the other side of the table.

"If she makes noise, I'll handle it. Which reminds me. I've been meaning to sit you down to discuss your will. I know you're young, but given your circumstances, if something should happen to you as your next of kin your mother would inherit unless you specify otherwise."

"I hadn't even thought of that. This is why you get the big bucks."

He shook his head in good humor before he stressed, "We need a sit down and soon."

"Okay. Thank you, Harrison, and sorry for adding to your work with Nadine."

"As your lawyer, I'm appalled. As your friend, I say right on."

BROCHAN

Pulling on my gloves, I yanked down the fire escape and headed to the top floor. Seeing Lizzie in that market. Fuck, she'd been magnificent. She'd faced down one of her ghosts and walked away with a fucking smile on her face. Staying in the shadows had been hard, but her light was coming back. She was doing what she did, getting back on her feet.

The window to the apartment was open; I slipped inside. Checking my watch, it wouldn't be long now. Minutes later, the door opened. She was talking to herself, mumbling as she flicked the lights on. I knew the moment she knew I was there.

Jerking around, she snarled, "Who the fuck are you?"

I stepped from the shadows. "You don't know me, but I know you, Nadine." Fenella had shared what she'd learned about Lizzie's childhood during our chat. This wasn't the grand gesture, but it was going to feel fucking good.

Fear flashed across her face and she turned for the door. I was faster. Fisting her hair, I dragged her to a chair and pushed her into it. Terror widened her eyes. She stuttered when she asked, "What do you want?"

I pulled out my tool set and unrolled it. She gasped then sobbed. I reached for one of my knives, touching the razor sharp tip to my finger. It happened so fast she didn't have time to react; the blade was so sharp she didn't feel the cut until it started to bleed down her cheek in the same place she'd scarred Lizzie. Shaking fingers lifted to the wound. She pissed herself.

"I'll make this really simple. Forget you ever knew Lizzie Danton." Understanding shined in those eyes. "You go after her for what happened earlier…" I pinched her broken nose and twisted it. She screamed. I shoved a gag in her mouth. Her eyes bugged out as panic had her body convulsing. I leaned into her and she went stone still. "They'll never find your body."

Satisfied I'd made my point, I collected my tools and slipped out the same way I slipped in.

"I'm sorry, sir, I tried to stop him."

"I'm going to have to call you back." Rodney Danton ended his call then looked past me to his bewildered receptionist. "It's fine, Elsie."

"Yes, sir."

Lizzie had his eyes. He stood and walked around his desk. He was older than I was expecting, but he wore power like he wore that expensive Italian suit. I had to give Norah a bit more credit because playing this man…that had taken some impressive skill. I wanted to gauge Norah's response to her dreams going up in smoke. It was smart to keep your friends close and your enemies closer.

"I don't believe I've had the pleasure."

"Brochan McIntyre."

"May I ask why you're barging into my office?"

"Norah Calhoun."

I recognized the look since it was the same one I had when thinking of the bitch.

"How do you know Norah?"

"I know Lizzie."

He wasn't able to hide his reaction when his eyes widened. "You know Lizzie?"

"You squashed the suit."

Surprise this time but he answered, "I did."

"How did she take it?"

His brow rose. "What makes you think I know?"

"Let's not fuck around. A man like you gets an opportunity to stick it to a woman like her, you're going to take it. How did she react?"

"She wasn't happy."

"Do you think she's capable of coming after Lizzie?"

"Norah is a more behind the scenes type, though..." He grew thoughtful for a minute. "She made a comment before she hung up that I didn't like, not just the words but the venom behind them."

"What did she say?"

"That she should have smothered Elizabeth."

Red-hot rage flooded me. That fucking... "Coming from a woman like Norah, I think that's a reason to be alarmed."

"What do you need from me?"

He may not have been a father to Lizzie when she was younger, but at least he was willing to take on some responsibility now. "It might be smart to get eyes on Norah."

"Done."

"You bought Lizzie's painting."

"Who are you to her?"

"Long story for another time."

He didn't like being the one questioned. Tough shit. "Yes, I bought her painting."

"She's your daughter, maybe it's time you got off your ass and started acting like a father." I was done here. I headed for the door.

He called after me, "How do you know she'll want anything to do with me?"

"I don't, but you owe it to her to make the effort."

CHAPTER SEVENTEEN

LIZZIE

I wish you had been there. I'll probably get sued, lose all of my worldly possessions, but I don't care. It felt so good." Cait and I were having lunch following my meeting with Harrison.

"People were filming it?" she asked before she lowered her fork and picked up her phone. It was her super power, navigating her phone. Not a minute later, she turned her phone to me and there I was, live and in color, punching Nadine in the face.

"Play it again."

"Man, you really socked it to her. I bet that did feel good, but unless she's a complete twit you are definitely getting sued. She has proof."

"Whatever. Harrison set up my work as a LLC. She can sue but only my personal assets; all of my money is tied up in my paintings. She won't get much."

"Smart."

"That was all Harrison."

"We're going out tonight."

"We are?"

"Yes. I want to get dressed up and go somewhere with alcohol and dancing."

"Why?"

"Because Ethan is out of town and I want to party."

"Sounds like a plan."

She then reached for her bag and pulled out a folder. "You haven't had a showing in a while, so here are your options."

I smiled at Cait being Cait and then we spent the rest of lunch deciding which gallery would feature my next show.

Cait arrived as I was finishing getting dressed. "There's wine on the counter if you want a glass," I called.

"Do you want one?"

"Yeah. I'll be right out."

I finished with my hair, spread some gloss on my lips and grabbed my clutch. Cait held out a glass to me. She looked sexy in her fire engine red dress.

I whistled. "Where did you get that?"

"Ethan. It's my way of including him tonight." She took a sip of wine. "I needed this. I've been crampy all day...totally premenstrual."

My glass stopped halfway to my mouth. I hadn't had my period in a while. I was usually very regular.

"What's wrong with you?" she asked.

"What's the date?"

"October ninth, why?"

It had been well over a month since I left Scotland. I lowered my glass as my hand unconsciously moved to my belly as the most profound feeling filled me. "I'm late."

Cait looked from my face to my stomach. "How late?"

"Enough."

Her glass came down on the counter with a bang. "Before we get crazy, let's make sure. I'll run down the street for a kit."

Before I could answer, she was gone, the door slamming closed behind her.

Cait and I stood in my bathroom staring down at the three pink positive signs. She bought three different brands, just to be sure. Seeing the confirmation that I was pregnant, that I was carrying Brochan's child, I ran to the toilet and hurled.

"Oh Lizzie." Cait was there, holding my hair back. "This is a good thing, right?"

"Yes. Definitely yes." I sat back and wiped at my mouth.

She touched my belly, her eyes filled with wonder. "There's a baby in here, but I thought you were on the pill?"

"I was, but I forgot to take it once or twice while in Scotland."

"That'll do it."

I was pregnant. I dropped on the stool. The revelation was both thrilling and terrifying. I had to tell Brochan, but dropping a child on him knowing how his own childhood had been, I'd be tethering him to me just like my mother had done to my father. I hadn't intentionally done it, but I was still binding a man to me who didn't want to be there. Unlike my mother, this baby would never know a day that he wasn't loved, deeply and completely. I touched my stomach again. I was going to be a mommy.

Her voice grew soft. "Do you still want to go out?"

"Yes."

We decided on a little jazz bar. It wasn't packed body to body and the music was soothing. Cait ordered us both club sodas with lime.

My thoughts were wrapped around the knowledge that I was pregnant. Cait's question interrupted them, "When are you going to tell Brochan about the baby?"

"Not telling him isn't an option, but I don't know when or how. A letter. Hey. How are you? You're going to be a father. Or better yet a phone call, especially since the man doesn't usually talk. Sharing he'll be a father to dead air, that sounds like fun."

"Maybe he'll surprise you."

"He didn't want me in his life, Cait. For whatever reason, he didn't want me there and now I'm binding him to me. I feel kind of like my mother—"

Cait leaned forward so fast I almost spilled my drink. "Don't you dare compare yourself to your mother."

"I'm not. Believe me, but I'm still forcing his hand."

"Last I checked it takes two to make a baby."

"You're right. We're both equally responsible, but the difference is I want to be with him."

"Well if he's foolish enough not to want you and his child in his life, you have Ethan and me."

Despite being worried, that made me smile. We weren't your typical family, but we were one all the same. "Auntie Cait and Uncle Ethan. That has a nice ring to it."

She laughed, "Yes, it does." She reached across the table. "You won't be alone, Lizzie. You're never going to be alone again."

My eyes stung and I needed to use the bathroom. "I have to pee."

Cait chuckled, "And so it begins."

I tossed my cocktail napkin at her. "Clown."

"I'll come with you." She linked her arm with mine. "We need to get those books."

"What books?"

"You know, the what to expect books?"

I looked over at her. "How do you know about those books?"

"What? I'm getting married. We have thought about children."

"Auntie Lizzie."

"Let's get you through your..." She waved her hand at my stomach "First."

We reached the hall to the bathrooms. "No lines. Unbelievable," Cait said. "Upside of coming to a smaller club."

Someone came up behind us. I was reaching for the door when a hand closed over my mouth and I was jerked back against a hard body. I felt the knife at my throat.

Cait turned but before she could call for help the man snarled, "Scream and she dies."

"What do you want?"

"Your money. Just the money." He nodded to Cait. "Collect it."

I held my purse out. Her hands were trembling as she pulled our money from our wallets. She held it out to our assailant when her eyes moved behind us. I could feel the dude looking around, edgy but more than from fear, like he was on drugs. The tip of the knife pressed into my neck and for a second I thought he was really going to kill me. Then I was free and I didn't waste time trying to figure out how, I just hurried to Cait; she grabbed me and pulled me close as I looked back at our attacker. I almost rubbed my eyes because I couldn't be seeing what I was seeing. Brochan had my attacker by the throat, holding him three inches off the floor. What the hell was he doing in New York? And how the hell was he here now?

"Brochan?"

Cait's head snapped to me. "That's Brochan?"

We both looked back when we heard the crack as he slammed our attacker's head into the wall. The man went limp.

"He's definitely scary. I'm not sure about the sexy yet," Cait whispered.

It was a jolt when those pale blue eyes landed on me, but I was moving past scared and right into angry. "What the hell are you doing here?"

"Making a grand gesture."

I was sure I hadn't heard him correctly, but no Cait had the same baffled expression I felt on my face.

"A grand gesture?"

Our attacker stirred, Brochan kicked him in the gut. It was then I noticed the red blooming on his t-shirt. "You're bleeding."

"It's a scratch."

"I've never had a scratch bleed that much." Brochan glared at Cait. "What? I'm just saying."

Worry for him trumped confusion. "We need to tend that."

I got a look. Sure, he was a killer and probably got cut all the time, but he was also my baby's father and damn it he wasn't going to stand there bleeding. "You have a car?"

"Aye."

"My place. Now."

The ride back was silent. Brochan was silent because that was who he was, me I was biting my tongue and Cait was waiting in anticipation for the fireworks to start. Once in my apartment, I headed to the bathroom to get the first aid kit. The door closed behind me. Brochan stood in front of it.

"What the hell are you doing here?"

"In your apartment or the States?"

My heart squeezed, both at the memory and that he remembered it too. I shut that shit down. "Both."

A strange look entered his expression before he offered, "I received a letter from Brianna."

Even angry, my heart softened remembering the letter she'd left for me.

"She knew I would turn you away."

"She said that in a letter?"

"Aye."

"One you received after she died?"

"She's a witch, remember?"

I did, but the memory only brought an ache. He seemed to realize that when he added, "I had a talk with Fenella, she told me I needed to make a grand gesture."

I almost laughed not just at the fact that Fenella had offered that advice, but that Brochan actually followed it."

"So you flew to New York to make a grand gesture?"

"Aye."

"How long have you been waiting to make this grand gesture?"

"Long enough to know you have absolutely no sense of self preservation."

"First, ouch, second, did it ever occur to you that just coming to see me was a grand gesture?"

He rolled his eyes heavenward and hissed, "I told her that. She said it had to be grander."

This momentarily charmed me, the unsure, completely out of his comfort zone, Brochan. It didn't last though as the memory of our last time together reared its ugly head.

"Why the grand gesture? It was just lust, sweetheart, hot sex."

He leaned in and dropped his voice. "Now isn't the time for that conversation."

There were too many feelings stirred by those words, but he was right. Now wasn't the time. And grand gesture aside, he'd hurt me. I wasn't above giving a little of that back. "There isn't a conversation. That ship sailed."

It was probably not wise to taunt a killer so I moved past him. "I'll tend your wound in the kitchen." I hurried away.

Cait sat at the counter. She was polishing off the bottle of wine we had opened earlier. "That's a pretty big scratch," she said, gesturing with her glass at the cut along Brochan's side.

It wasn't a scratch. It was deep enough to need stitches. Stubborn bastard wouldn't go the emergency room. At least he'd let me clean it. I couldn't even appreciate seeing his beautiful body again because of the blood staining his skin. He didn't move. The entire time I was disinfecting and washing the blood from his body he stood completely still.

"Are you okay, Lizzie?" Cait asked and then added, "I've lived in Manhattan my whole life. That was my first mugging."

The shock of seeing Brochan had the mugging kind of slipping my mind, which was bizarre because I had been held at knifepoint. "Strangely, I'm fine."

"Well, you've other things on your mind than a pesky two-bit criminal." She took a sip of her wine. "I missed part of the show when you two were in the bathroom. So what the hell is this about a grand gesture?"

Brochan growled, "That's the last time I go to Fenella for advice."

I couldn't help the grin, mostly for Fenella that he'd come to her. She must have been over the moon.

I glanced up at Brochan. His pale eyes were on me. There was a lot going on behind them.

"I think Brochan and I need to talk."

"My cue to leave."

"No. Ethan isn't home and you're already here. Sleep here tonight. We'll get a hotel room."

"Are you sure?"

"Yes."

"I'm not going to argue." Cait put her glass in the sink. I got her some water and walked her to bed. She took my hand before I left. "He's here, Lizzie and from the sparks flying around, I think he wants to be with you too."

I kissed her on the head. "Sleep. I'll see you in the morning."

BROCHAN

Lizzie had been quiet since we left Cait. She kept looking down at her hands. They were clean and yet I knew she was seeing my blood because she'd been rubbing them on her lap as if to wipe it away. "I need a shower. Shit, I don't have a change of clothes."

"I'll buy you some."

Irritation moved into her expression, annoyed I was taking over after how we left things. Her focus shifted to the floor.

"Lizzie." I touched her chin and lifted those wounded blue eyes to me. "You've had a difficult night. Let me take care of you."

Her expression softened before she whispered, "Thank you."

I didn't like the lost look in her eyes, so I tried to lighten the mood when I asked, "Where does a Scotsman stay when in this big, bad city?" I'd checked out of the last hotel this morning. Nature of my job, I didn't stay too long in the same place.

Her lips curved into a slight grin. "The Plaza."

Lizzie was showering when I returned. I knocked. "I have your clothes."

"You can bring them in."

The stall was frosted, but her silhouette against the glass had my cock going hard. I wanted to join her. Wanted to wash her back, then her front, then fuck her boneless. Later.

I put the bag on the counter and walked out. She called, "Thank you."

Detouring to the mini bar, I poured three mini bottles of whisky in a glass then walked to the balcony. Fucker had a knife to her throat. I went cold thinking about what could have happened if I hadn't been there. Fate teased my neck; I was beginning to wonder if fate went by another name like say, Brianna. And despite how we reconnected—Fenella and her damn grand gestures—Lizzie was here with me. Only a fool would blow the opportunity to atone. I took a sip of the whisky. New York, I liked the crowds, the noise, and the lights. The city that didn't sleep.

Lizzie stepped out onto the balcony. The cashmere sweater and yoga pants were too big. Even the socks were big, but she looked comfortable, warm and fucking adorable. My heart twisted. My hands itched to touch her. Instead, I took a sip of whisky and focused on the burn down my throat. "Are you hungry?"

Her focus was on the view. "Beautiful, isn't it?"

"Yes."

"I could eat."

"The room service is quite good here."

She leaned her hip against the railing and tilted her head. A ghost of a smile touched her lips. "Not your first visit."

"No."

Her smiled faded. "Why are you really here, Brochan?"

I looked down at my drink. "Thank you for the painting."

Her expression softened.

"I've lost hours looking at it."

"I love that you love the painting. I even love that you're here, but you were cruel the last time I saw you. I know you well enough to know something happened, but you didn't share it with me. You cut me from your life. You gave me a glimpse of something I've always wanted, and then you yanked it back. I can't do this with you. I can't turn it off, I can just move on. I'm trying to move on, but you're not making that easy."

She waited for me to say something and when I didn't she walked back into the room. Maybe I *was* a fucking fool. I had caught a glimpse of it too, but then I saw the two bloodstains and how brutally it could be taken away. I finished my drink and walked inside. Lizzie was calling for a cab. For the first time in my adult life I felt panic and fear that she would walk out that door and I'd never see her again.

"Don't go." She looked over with tears in her eyes.

"I'm sorry. I'll call you back." She wouldn't look at me as she hung up the phone.

"What do you need from me?" A risk, but to keep her I would give her anything.

Sad eyes lifted to mine. "Tell me what happened that last night?"

LIZZIE

A shadow drifted across his face. He was so still.

"My father was a broken man after my mother died. I became the focus of his pain and despair. After Brianna confronted him, after his estate burned down, that was when I roamed. No place in mind, just away. I had so much anger, didn't know what to do with it. I knew I was heading down a path that would have led to my death or jail. Mac Donovan, he came into my life when I really needed him. He was the one to show me there was another way to handle the anger, an outlet. My mentor, my friend…the father figure I never had."

I remembered him mentioning Mac. I wanted to flee the room because I so didn't want to hear what came next.

"He retired, got married. Ava, his wife, she wanted kids. He had found it, that elusive happiness. That day we returned from Edinburgh..." He lowered his head and I felt his inhale from across the room. Pain laced through his next words. "They were murdered, both of them, execution style." Only his head turned, his pale eyes bright. "Her only crime was loving him."

We didn't meet; we crashed into each other. Mouths fused and bodies entwined. His fingers dug into my thighs, lifting me. My legs wrapped around his waist like a vice. He fisted my hair, tilting my head to kiss me deeper. I yanked on his tee. He jerked back only long enough for me to get it over his head before his mouth was back, tasting, exploring, invading. His hand found the bare skin of my stomach, his touch setting me on fire. He moved it up slowly, his fingers dancing along the underside of my breast. Hot eyes met mine when he pulled my sweater up, his mouth replacing his hand, closing over my breast, sucking it deep. I held his head, moved into his touch, wanted him to take me deeper. I hit the mattress, my sweater hit the floor. My pants and panties followed. He stripped, but instead of him taking me hard and fast, he pulled me up so I was kneeling in front of him, our naked bodies touching from chest to thigh. He cradled my face, his thumb lightly stroking my cheek. A tear slipped down his face. I kissed it away.

"His killer made him watch. The few seconds where he lived in a world without her, knowing the only reason she was gone was because of him." His voice broke, "That could have been you."

I choked down a sob; he closed the distance and kissed me, raw, real and fueled by love. He lowered me back on the bed, his body moving into the cradle of mine. When he joined us, like his kiss, it wasn't hard or fast. It was slow, deliberate and so achingly sweet. My hands moved over him, his mouth never left mine as our bodies moved together. His hands curled around my thighs and he pulled me closer. When we peaked it was together. Neither of us moved, savoring the love, the shared pain, the moment that changed us both. His head lifted stealing my breath because there was no mask. I saw him, all of him, every inch of his tragically beautiful soul. Quietly, purposefully and a little shyly he brushed my hair from my face and spoke the words that burned on my heart, seared my soul and sealed my fate, tying me to this beautiful and complicated man. "I love you."

I touched his lips; wishing to hold those words, to physically feel them as all the emptiness inside me was filled with love for him. "I love you."

He pressed into me, as he grew hard, "Say it again."

"I love you."

His hips moved.

"Again."

"I love you."

His mouth slammed down on mine, stealing the words before I could say them. He wasn't gentle as he moved almost violently, claiming me with each thrust of his hips. My arms wrapped around his neck; I pulled him closer, kissed him deeper and let myself fall because we were falling together.

I woke, stirred from sleep. Brochan was sleeping. Turning to him, I thought of Mac and Ava. Their story had hit me really hard and not just because Mac had clearly been a father to Brochan and he lost him so brutally, but because it could have so easily been Brochan and me. It didn't change anything. I'd rather a day with him than a lifetime without him, but it drove home how dangerous the world was he lived in. It was also a reminder of how short life was and how it could change in a blink. Mac and Ava had wanted children some day, but some day would never come for them.

Rubbing the line between his brows, I whispered, "Brochan."

"I wondered how long you were going to stare."

He was awake. I should have known. The man probably didn't sleep. His eyes opened and love looked back.

"I have to tell you something."

He glanced at the clock. "At three in the morning."

Now that I was actually doing it, those damn nerves came back in force. I climbed from bed, putting distance between us in case this didn't go the way I was hoping it would. He was out of bed and walking around it toward me. I put my hand up to stop him. "Stay there."

"What's going on?" His expression was slightly terrifying. "Lizzie, just say it."

So I did, dropped the bomb without any pomp and circumstance. "I'm pregnant."

You could have heard a pin drop. He looked like a statue; he didn't even blink. He just stared at me with an expression I could not for the life of me discern. The longer the silence dragged on, the more worried I grew.

"Say something."

Nothing.

Was he mad? Did he think I deceived him? "I was on the pill, but I forgot to take it a few times. I was so caught up in the, well everything. We weren't...I didn't..." I hung my head because he didn't want this, but I did. With quiet conviction I whispered, "I'm keeping him."

It felt like I hit a wall even though I hadn't moved. His arm went around my waist and he pulled me close as he gently fisted my hair, pulling my head back for his kiss. I didn't react, too overwhelmed, then I tasted his tears. My hitman was crying. I curled my arms around him, pulled him closer and kissed him back.

BROCHAN

Lizzie was still sleeping. I hadn't slept at all. I watched her. She was pregnant; she was carrying my child. I hadn't thought I wanted kids, but kids with her; it was crazy to want something so badly. My cell rang. I almost ignored it, but then I saw Rodney Danton's name.

His greeting, "Norah is in town. It's likely nothing, but I thought you should know."

"Any idea why she's in town?"

"No. Knowing her she's just looking to spend money. I'll keep eyes on her. Have you spoken to Lizzie?"

I'd done a hell of a lot more than speak to her. "Yes."

"How is she?"

"Why don't you find out for yourself?"

"She isn't going to want to see me."

"You're her father. You were the one to turn your back, not the other way around."

"There's a lot of water under the bridge."

"Then buy a fucking boat."

He chuckled, "I like you." He sobered quickly and asked, "Dinner tonight?"

"When and where."

Fucking hell, I was getting as bad as Brianna with the meddling, but Lizzie had given me my family. I could help with maybe giving her back hers.

Cait was green. I had never seen that, but she was so hung over she was actually green. She did drink the whole bottle of wine.

"I feel like shit. How bad do I look?"

I'd seen corpses with better coloring.

"You look beautiful."

I jerked my eyes to Lizzie at such a blatant lie, so she wasn't above lying to her friends to spare their feelings. I'd have to remember that. Her gaze met mine. There wasn't contrition; there was a warning for me not to contradict her.

"Do you want me to whip you up something greasy. It does help."

"No. I want to die. Just let me die."

"You're not going to die."

"I'm glad Ethan is not here. I'd be getting the lecture on over doing it." She grabbed Lizzie's hand. "There was a reason for overdoing it. Between that stupid ass mugger and then the preg—" Her mouth slammed shut as her eyes darted from Lizzie to me.

"He knows."

Her eyes went wide. "He does?"

"Yes."

"Thank goodness. I thought I let the cat out of the bag." She had a funny look on her face when she said to Lizzie, "You know what? I think I will take something greasy."

"Okay. I'll make you an egg sandwich."

"That sounds delicious."

I stood, she pointed. "You stay. We can chat."

It was how she said it. I was a man who had seen and done pretty much everything. I earned my living from breaking the human spirit and yet the prospect of a chat with Cait made me want to hurry to the door.

She waited until she heard Lizzie in the kitchen. "What are your intentions toward my friend?"

It wasn't any of her damn business and had it been anyone else I'd have walked out, but this was Lizzie's family and so I sat back in my chair and crossed my legs. "To marry her."

Her expression almost drew a smile. She looked like a guppy. "Seriously."

"I love her and she's carrying my child."

I didn't realize using the L-word would start the waterworks, but Cait, as if on cue, started to cry. Big, fat tears were rolling down her cheeks. I had skinned men alive, removed their fingers. Once I even cut a man's heart from his chest, but seeing Cait cry I got a little queasy. What the hell did I do with that? I looked around for tissues; she improvised and used the sheet. I threw a glance at the door. What was taking Lizzie so long?

"You love her?"

"Yes."

She sat up in bed, fisting the now snot covered sheet. "How will you support her?"

I had a feeling telling Cait what I did for a living might send her screaming from the room or she might reach for her stiletto heel and bury it in my chest. I was getting out of the business though, so I told her a half-truth.

"I have family money."

She didn't like that. Her eyes narrowed. "A man of leisure. They tend to have wandering eyes and hands."

The only wandering my eyes and hands would be doing was on Lizzie's body. Speaking of which, maybe I should go do a little of that now. My dick twitched at the idea.

"Well?" She looked indignant. "Are you a wanderer?"

"No."

Her expression changed to one of genuine concern. "She's been through a lot. Please don't be one more thing she has to survive."

It was because of her concern and love for Lizzie that I leaned forward and looked her directly in the eyes. "She owns me heart and soul."

The tears started again. "Good answer."

I think she was about to use the sheet to blow her nose, but Lizzie entered and glanced at both of us then handed her a napkin. I stood. "We're doing dinner with your father tonight at seven."

She looked adorably confused. "Wait, What?"

"I'll pick you up at six." I pressed a kiss on her head and walked out. I'd had enough emotions for one day. I needed to go hurt something.

It didn't take much to find the asshole from last night. Prick held two women at knifepoint but the fucker goes to the emergency room because he got a knock on the head. And people called me a monster. The nurse had been helpful when I inquired about my dear grandmother; odds an old woman had been brought into the ER were damn good. Her interest wasn't my grandmother, it was my cock, but her distraction got me a glance at the admissions sheet from last night. Only one treated for a concussion.

He lived in a shit apartment that probably should have been condemned. Seeing the knife at Lizzie's neck, the fucker tried to cut corners to improve his lifestyle by daring to touch what was mine. He'd paid for that.

I slipped on my gloves and moved silently down the alley and up the fire escape. He was on his bed sleeping or maybe the concussion took care of him for me. He stirred then jerked up. Or not. Recognition came swiftly. He tried to move; a punch to the jaw knocked him back on the bed. I straddled him, then shoved his own sock in his mouth. His eyes went wide with fear. I pulled out my knife and he whimpered. "This is for touching what's mine." I sank the blade into his gut, right to the hilt. He screamed around the gag. I pushed deeper then I twisted it.

CHAPTER EIGHTEEN

LIZZIE

There was an awful lot happening all at once. Learning I was pregnant, Brochan stepping back into my life, telling me he loved me and now dinner with my father. I felt like I was on an amusement park ride and there was a part of me that wanted to get off. Not really, but I wouldn't mind if the ride slowed down.

Brochan held my hand and I was grateful because despite having seen my father already, knowing now the role he played in my life—being the catalyst for my dreams coming true—I was nervous.

"How did this dinner come about?"

"I stopped in to see him when I first arrived."

"Why?"

"He didn't do right by you. Someone had to hold his feet to the fire."

I smiled to myself and moved closer. "You do realize that's another grand gesture, right?"

He actually huffed. "I fucking do now."

I wanted to laugh but he was irritated, so I held it in. "And dinner?"

"He called, told me your mother was in town then asked after you."

"Wait? Norah is in town?"

"Yes."

"Why?"

"I don't know. He's got eyes on her." He looked down at me. "He cares."

I never knew a person could experience conflicting emotions and in such intensity. Like right now. I was happy my father cared and really pissed that he waited so long to show it.

"It would have been nice if he cared when I was a kid."

"No question."

"When I was just starting out, an anonymous benefactor purchased a painting, my first. That sale was what kick started my career." My eyes found Brochan's. "It was my father."

"I know."

Of course he knew. We arrived at the restaurant. He held the door for me. I reached for his hand. He squeezed, silently telling me I wasn't alone. My father was already at the table. He stood when we approached.

"Thank you for coming," he said in way of greeting. Brochan held out my chair before he folded himself in the chair to my left.

"Would you like a drink?" my father asked.

"Water, please."

The smallest of grins curved Brochan's lips before he turned to my father. "Glenfiddich, neat."

Once our orders were placed I gathered up my nerve. If we were going to try for some kind of relationship, he had to own up. I was rather direct when I asked, "Why did you stay away?"

He'd been expecting the question and still he didn't jump to answer it. He didn't have a pre-rehearsed one. He got points for that.

"I never wanted children…" He raised his hand when I tried to object. "I know it doesn't make it right. Having one with the woman I did, it made it easier to pretend I didn't have a child."

"How?"

He leveled with me. He got points for that too. "Because in my mind you were your mother's daughter."

"I'm not my mother."

"I know. I spent so long hating her. It's an unproductive emotion, hate, and look what I missed out on…a chance to know my daughter."

Was it too early to get emotional from the pregnancy hormones? Because damn if I didn't feel tears. I changed the subject. "How did you get Norah to back off on the suit?"

"She dropped the suit when I mentioned Heather Craig."

Brochan's blank expression was proof he didn't know who that was either. "Who's Heather Craig?" I asked.

"She was your mother's friend in Scotland. She died. Your mother fled Scotland not long after."

"Are you saying she had something to do with her death?" I should be horrified by the possibility, but I wasn't.

"One night after too much wine and sex she was rambling on about it. She never said she did it, but she was unnerved, as unnerved as I've ever seen her. She said the case was still open, that they were looking for her. I looked into it; the case is closed. It was a suspicious death, but without sufficient evidence it was ruled accidental and closed a few years back."

"Why does she think the case is still open?" I asked.

"She's probably too afraid to query it, afraid they're still looking for her and that by doing so she might give up her location, but she'll eventually figure out that my threat is empty."

"You need to keep eyes on her." Brochan sounded a little scary.

"I will."

I changed the subject because talking about Norah was giving me a stomachache. "You bought 'Voices'". My comment caught him off guard because he hit his glass on his dinner plate. He looked back at me almost shyly. "Yes."

"Why?"

"Because it quite literally took my breath away."

My body shook hearing him say words I too had once uttered when looking at Brochan's home, but my father was saying it about my painting. Brochan started stroking my hand with his thumb.

My father added, "The beauty on that canvas came from within you and that was when I realized you were my child and not hers."

It didn't make everything okay, but it helped.

"I wasn't there for you when you were a child, but I want to be now. If you ever need anything I hope you know you can come to me. I know this is late but..."

"Better late than never."

We'd just entered the hotel. Cait was crashing again at my apartment. I moved into the room and kicked off my shoes. My father consumed my thoughts on the ride back, but now I was watching Brochan as he removed his jacket. He'd packed a jacket when he came here to make his grand gesture. The stark white cotton of his shirt was snug across the muscles of his back and shoulders. He was elegant and yet I knew he was lethal; it was a seriously sexy combination. I loved him, he loved me, we were having a baby and yet I didn't know what came next for us.

"What happens now?"

He turned, those pale eyes moving down my body starting those tingles. I grinned. "Not this very moment, I mean what happens next?"

He turned and pushed his hands into the pockets of his trousers. "I'd like to go home to Scotland and I'm hoping you want to come with me."

Relief nearly had my knees going weak. It was what I wanted. He looked nervous; like I was going to say no. "I never wanted to leave Scotland."

He had no outwardly physical reaction to that, but I knew how much my words meant to him.

"Listening to my father tonight, all the hate and all the ugly, it's like a cycle. I don't want to hold onto my anger for my mother, to find myself thirty years from now still holding onto it." I touched my stomach. "We didn't have any control over how our lives started, the abuse and the pain, but we have the control now. We're going to be parents. It's time to let it go. We can teach by example. Our baby will know what we never did…safety, love, and happiness, and in doing that we stop the cycle."

I hesitated to finish because I was crossing a line, but for our child's sake, for his, I did.

"I know what you do, knew it before anything started between us. I understand it, understand why you went down that path, but what you do is another cycle."

His expression went tight and I felt the wall going up. It hurt, but I kept going. "You're still reacting, Brochan. And what will you tell your child when they're old enough to know what you do for a living. I once told you that I admired you for having the courage to be that balance, but maybe it's time to find balance in a different way."

"I love you and we'll make it work if you can't give it up because I don't want to lose you. You said once you weren't looking for the happily ever after, but it's right there. All you have to do is reach for it."

Silence followed and for so long I felt cold to the bone. I left him and headed to the bath, I needed a hot shower. Stripping on my way, I climbed under the spray. Maybe I was wrong to say that to him. Asking him to change, that hadn't been my intention. I just knew there was so much more to him and maybe he too was caught in a cycle.

I heard him enter the bathroom. He stepped into the shower. The water sprayed over him. I stared at the knife wound, one he had gotten protecting me, paralyzed by what came next.

He wiped the water from his face then touched my lips, the lightest brush of his thumb. "You're right."

I nearly wept.

"I thought it was control, but I'm still reacting just in a different way." He touched his lips to mine, nipped my lower one. "I was already retiring."

I leaned back. "You were?"

"I was growing tired of it all, but now there's you and the bairn." His expression grew mischievous when he turned and pressed me against the shower wall. "I've been thinking about another line of work. Was told recently that I have a beautiful body." His hand moved down my back to my ass then over to my thigh. His fingers dug in and tilted my ass up. His legs moved between mine. "A famous artist mentioned how much she'd like to paint it."

The moan couldn't be helped because of both the idea of painting a naked Brochan and because his cock was sliding down the crack in my ass heading to where I really wanted him.

His hand moved around my front, over my belly before moving lower. He touched my clit at the same time he pushed into me. My ass lifted more as I bent lower to give him better access. He moved so slowly, taking his time drawing out the orgasm. Right before I came he whispered in my ear.

"I'm ready to cut out the ugly too because I'm surrounded with beauty."

BROCHAN

"We have somewhere to be this morning and after I have the rest of the day planned." I wanted to stay in bed, though watching Lizzie move around wearing nothing but my tee was giving me some ideas too, like getting her back in this bed so I could lift up that cotton and eat.

Distracted, I didn't realize she had stopped getting dressed and was staring at me. "I have an OB appointment."

Lust took a backseat as my eyes moved to her stomach.

"I kind of hoped you would come with me."

"Absolutely."

I'd never grow tired of seeing her smile. I climbed from bed. Her smile turned into something a bit more wicked and hungry. She kept talking but her focus wasn't on my face.

"After, I thought I'd show you around my old stomping grounds." She was looking at my cock. I fisted it; her eyes flew to my face.

"First one to the shower…" She ran past me. I called after her, "Eats last."

The shower turned on. "Then hurry up, I'm hungry."

Hearing the heartbeat of our baby was surreal. Lizzie had a death grip on my hand, I was happy for it because I felt a little unsteady.

The elderly doctor had a soothing bedside manner, though he'd probably delivered countless kids so this wasn't earth shaking for him as it was for us.

"You're about eight weeks. The baby has a nice strong heartbeat. You need to start prenatal vitamins. You'll also want to start coming in for routine exams, just so we can monitor your baby's development."

"We'll be heading home, back to Scotland." I loved that she thought of my home as hers.

"That's okay, just make sure you find a doctor at home. I can send the records from today."

"We have a family physician. I'll give you his information before we leave."

"I'll write the prescription for prenatal vitamins. Make sure you're drinking lots of water. Despite what you've heard, you don't really need to eat more because you're carrying. In fact, maintaining a healthy weight during pregnancy will help reduce complications like gestational diabetes. You, however, are a little too thin so try to make sure you're eating enough during the day. Your baby's due date is mid May."

She was too thin because of me. Guilt twisted in my gut but seeing the wonder on Lizzie's face, I let it go. We were moving on, finding our own version of happy.

We stood outside the doctor's office. Lizzie reached for my hand. "Wait until we tell Fenella and Finnegan they're going to be grandparents."

I could already see her expression and it brought a smile.

"You need to do that more often, smile."

With her, that was very likely to happen. "Where to now?" I asked.

"We'll start at the beginning."

We were on the Upper East Side, standing in front of a high-rise. It was cold, sterile and not at all Lizzie. "I lived here until I was ten."

"It doesn't suit you."

"No, but there's an urban garden on the roof that was lovely. I never knew who kept the garden, but I escaped to it often. Looking out on the city, all the people going about their lives, it made my world seem not so small."

Her parents were assholes. At least her father was trying now.

"For the next eight years I was at Stone Crest. That's not a trip for today. So, I'll show you where I went to art school then we can get something to eat."

Her world had been very small. I bet intentionally done by her mother. Holding her close, separating her for the purpose of abusing her. I recognized the pattern since my own father had done the same, or had tried, but I had Fenella and Finnegan. Lizzie had had no one. There was a part of me that wanted to hunt down Norah Calhoun; if anyone deserved to be on the receiving end of my particular skill set, it was definitely Norah. But Lizzie wanted to leave all that behind. That was lucky for Norah because I would have really enjoyed torturing her.

Lunch was at the diner where Lizzie had worked double shifts to afford her apartment that was now her studio. She was taking me to see that next.

"This is where I met Cait. She strolled through that door looking for me. My work made her cry."

"How long ago was that?"

She thought about it for a second. "Wow, eight years. Funny how time flies."

I'd hate to not go back to Scotland, but if she wanted to stay. "Are you sure you want to leave this?"

"It was never home. None of the places I lived felt like home. I've only ever felt that in Scotland."

Brianna strikes again.

"Doing this today, there's something else I want to do. Are you still looking to make a grand gesture?"

"I'm fucking never living that down."

"Not likely," she teased.

"Yeah, I think I still have more atoning to do."

"We're going to need my father too."

LIZZIE

"This is where she sent you?" We'd taken my father's private plane to Vermont to visit Stone Crest Academy. At the moment, we were standing in the exact place I had stood all those years ago watching as my mother drove out of my life.

There was anger in his eyes and guilt. "I didn't know, Lizzie, but I should have made it my business to know. I'm sorry."

"I survived it, but I hate thinking of others having to survive it."

"And you think getting rid of this Ms. Meriwether is the answer."

"She is still the headmistress and she's the worst of the lot. Her behavior trickles down."

"Cut the head off the snake." Brochan had it exactly right.

"The threat of an investigation might be enough to get her to retire. She's nearly at retirement age already," I reasoned.

"If not, I'm prepared to go through with an investigation and a lawsuit," my father confirmed.

"More importantly, it is crucial that whoever replaces her wants to be there, wants to be the driving force of good for these girls. They need someone to hold their hands not smack them."

My father had been horrified and furious to hear I'd been a victim of corporal punishment, particularly since it was illegal in Vermont.

My father held open the door. "Let's make the woman an offer she can't refuse."

I had knots in my stomach walking down the hall, memories slamming into me, none of them good. The girls we passed I saw in colors, but they weren't bright and vibrant. They were dull, as if the color had been washed out. I remembered feeling that way. My hope was to bring some light back to this place.

Ms. Meriwether sat behind the same desk. She was older now, her brown hair mostly gray, the lines on her face cut deep around her mouth and eyes, but she still had that arrogant, dictator-like attitude. As a kid I had feared her, as an adult I realized she was just another bully.

"Lizzie Danton. When my secretary told me of this meeting I must confess I was surprised. We can count a rising artist among our alumni. Are you here to give back to the place that helped you to achieve your success?"

Was she for real? "I am here to give back, just not in that way."

She linked her fingers. "What can I do for you?"

"You can retire."

Her cool façade cracked slightly. "Excuse me?"

My father stepped in. "I have a team of investigators on standby."

"Investigators? Whatever for?"

"Corporal punishment is illegal. I'm sure you know that."

Her face paled slightly but she rallied. "We do no such thing here, despite what your…daughter might have said."

"And I'm not about to take your word for that. I've already been in touch with the Board of Directors. They were concerned by the reports, more about the potential law suits that will arise when it is learned how you discipline the children here."

"You can't threaten me. I have held this post for thirty years."

Furious, I slammed my hands down on her desk. "And for thirty years you've fostered fear. These girls come to you scared and lonely and feeling abandoned and you play on those ugly emotions, perpetuate them so even when they graduate they stay silent about what goes on here. I did. I survived it and I tried to put it in the past, but I'm not covering my eyes anymore. You need to be held accountable, and these girls that are dumped here by parents that can't be bothered, they need to know they have a family here."

"How dare you speak to me like that!"

I curled my fists. "You're lucky I'm only speaking to you, you bitch."

"Lizzie." Brochan's calm voice cooled some of the rage. I stepped back and tried to get a handle on the rest of it.

"You're missing the point. You are already as good as out. We're offering you a way to retire with dignity and not be fired with disgrace. A courtesy you don't deserve, but we are trying to rise above the sewer you're swimming in." My father's voice was ice.

She stood, her chair slamming back against the wall. "I will not be pushed out. I'll fight this."

She walked to the door; her hand had just curled around the knob when a knife came flying through the air to land mere centimeters from her head. She jumped back. For the first time since this meeting started, there was fear in her eyes.

Softly spoken and ice cold Brochan said, "We tried it the nice way. Now we're going to do it my way."

"Where the hell did the knife come from? You actually carry a knife on you?"

Brochan didn't answer me, just sipped his whisky.

My father was on his third. "It might have been nice if you mentioned your boyfriend is a...what exactly are you?"

"It's not important. He's out of the business," I said quickly.

He gulped the last of his whisky and poured another. "I will say, for an old woman she ran pretty damn fast."

I chuckled because he was right, she had run pretty damn fast, after she drafted her resignation letter and signed it.

My father looked over at Brochan. "You wouldn't have actually done the things you said you would do."

Brochan replied with a blank stare.

"Holy shit. You would have." He took another drink. "I'm glad you're on our side."

"She's out, but you really need to make sure whoever replaces her isn't just like her."

"The Board doesn't want the backlash and I've been given assurances that I can have someone monitoring the situation to make sure her replacement is working."

"How did you manage that?" I asked.

"I did what Brochan did, but instead of a knife I used a pen."

"Stone Crest should help form those girls but through good means not fear. I hope that happens. It wouldn't have had a chance if not for both of you. Thank you. Oh and I guess now is as good a time as any to tell you you're going to be a grandfather."

My father froze, his gaze moving from me to Brochan then he poured himself another drink.

We made plans to meet my father for lunch before we left for Scotland. After the shock of learning he was going to be a granddad, he'd seemed pretty animated. Maybe he'd be for my child what he hadn't been for me. Time would tell. I had him in my life because of Brochan. He was rocking at the grand gestures.

We reached my apartment. As soon as he closed the door, I pulled off my jacket and yanked off my tee. He dropped the car keys on the table and pushed his hands into his pockets, his focus on my hands that were moving to my jeans.

"Do you know what I realized today?" I asked as I slipped my jeans off.

"What?"

I reached for my bra, my eyes on him. "We're the lucky ones." I was over his shoulder and halfway down the hall to my bedroom before my bra hit the floor.

"We're heading back to Scotland." We were at Cait and Ethan's having dinner. I was ready to go home. I wanted to see Fenella and

Finnegan, I wanted to see the lane; I wanted to get settled, nesting the book called it.

Cait's fork stopped midway to her mouth. "When?"

"As soon as we can make the arrangements."

"I've never been to Scotland. Have you Ethan?"

He chuckled, "Can't say that I have."

"I bet it's beautiful."

"Are you looking for an invitation?" I wanted her to come; I wanted to show her the beauty of Brochan's home.

"Me? What? No...yes."

I looked over at Brochan. His expression gave nothing away but he said, "Whatever you want."

"Can you get off work, Ethan?"

"I've over a month of vacation days accumulated. I should use some."

"So we're doing it. You don't mind, do you Brochan?" Cait used her puppy dog eyes.

"No."

"Hot damn. Scotland. I can't wait. Oh wait, I need new clothes, plaids and wools and boots. I need new boots."

Ethan lifted his glass of wine. "Here we go."

CHAPTER NINETEEN

LIZZIE

"Holy shit. You live here?" Cait's face was pressed up against the window as Brochan drove the car around the circular drive. It had been ten weeks since I left.

Finnegan and Fenella were waiting out front, as were two large beautiful dogs. There was affection in his voice when Brochan said, "The pups got big."

As soon as I climbed from the car, Fenella had me in a bone-crushing hug. "You're back." She pushed me away while still holding my upper arms then pulled me back for another hug. She was crying.

"It's so good to see you too."

She held me away again. "I didn't think you were coming back and it broke my heart because you and he..." She glanced over at Brochan who was introducing Cait and Ethan to Finnegan. "You are perfect for each other."

"I knew that, he does now too."

"I know. I see it in the way he looks at you."

"How have you been?" I asked as I wrapped an arm around her waist as we joined the others.

"Mad, annoyed, but I knew he'd be successful. I've been cooking in preparation for your return home."

Home. I looked behind us to the magnificent castle made so because of the man who owned it. She was right. This was home. I smiled at her. "He came to you."

"Aye."

"That had to have felt good."

Tears welled. "There are no words."

I squeezed her then called, "Cait, Ethan, this is Fenella."

As they said their hellos I joined Brochan who had two beautiful dogs jumping up on him but when he ordered them to sit, they did. "These are Boomer and Champ." He looked back at the dogs. "And this is the lady of house. You are to protect her when I'm not home."

Both dogs turned to me as if they understood exactly what Brochan had said. Like those cows, maybe they really did.

"Lady of the house?" I teased him even loving that he called me that.

"You're my woman and you're carrying my bairn; you're the lady of the house."

"We need to share the news with Fenella and Finnegan."

"When we drop the bags in our room."

"Our room?"

He yanked me close and whispered in my ear, "I'm not sneaking around my own house to fuck my woman. You're in my bed."

I wasn't going to argue. "Maybe we could give Cait and Ethan the white room."

"Done. Let's share the news and eat because I have plans for you," he said. My entire body throbbed. He added, "No clothes required."

Finnegan pushed the doors open to Brochan's room and I had to catch my breath. It was sparse, elegant and so totally Brochan. The panel walls and ceiling were black, thick crown moldings that were detailed in the corners were also black. The floors were a dark wood with no area rugs to adorn them. The windows went from floor to ceiling and were draped in black chenille. A twelve-armed crystal chandelier hung in the center of the room. The bed was huge and looked like a sea of black and the headboard was gray and not much taller than a sofa table. There were books piled on one side, but it was the small silver frame on the other side that had my heart squeezing in my chest. I walked over and picked up the picture, the one I had sketched of Brochan's gates. He'd not only kept it, he'd had it framed. Our eyes met from across the room.

"Why did you want us to join you?" Finnegan asked.

Brochan crossed the room to me and wrapped his arm around my waist, pulling me tight to his side. He looked down at me, giving me the honor of telling them.

With teary eyes and a full heart I said, "We're pregnant."

Finnegan processed the news first when he smiled, something I hadn't seen him do. Fenella took a minute but when it sank in, she broke down into tears. I broke down into tears when Brochan hugged her and whispered, "You're going to be a grandmother."

She recovered quickly and reached for my hand. "You boys go down and entertain our guests. Lizzie and I will join you shortly."

Finnegan dropped his hand on Brochan's shoulder. "I think we need to crack open the John Walker you bought me for Christmas last year."

"Come with me," Fenella said after the men had left. In her suite of rooms, she led me to the walk-in closet that was a room in and of itself. She pulled open a drawer; the smell of cedar filled the space. She lifted a small garment. Tears hit my eyes.

"This was Brochan's," she whispered. "I kept some of his things hoping one day he'd have children of his own."

My hand shook as I took it from her, seeing a little Brochan with those pale eyes small enough to wear it.

"You'll need a nursery. I have his old crib, but I think it might be better to buy something new. Safety reasons.

"I agree. I'd like the baby in our room."

She approved by the smile that touched her face.

"You need blankets, clothes, nappies, mobiles...you'll want to paint the room. I have numbers for contractors."

"I think we should paint the room, you, Finnegan, Brochan and me."

She started to cry again.

"And we'll definitely need a trip to Edinburgh to shop. We can bring the men; they can carry our bags."

She was feeling too emotional to speak so she wiped at her eyes and simply said, "Aye."

Brochan and I were in the cabin, his plans for me that required no clothes. I was a little hesitant since I didn't have fond memories of the place. Brochan was determined to correct that and lying naked on top of him on the floor in front of the fire, sated and happy, he was doing a fine job of changing my opinion.

"I can't believe Cait tried haggis with no arm twisting."

"She didn't just try it. She liked it."

She did. She had two servings. Dinner had been a bit of everything. Fenella really had been cooking in preparation. After dinner, a weary Ethan and Cait called it a night. They had no sooner left the library, and Brochan was dragging me to the cabin.

"What is this place?"

"A hunting lodge, likely built around the same time of the house. I used it when they were renovating the castle. It's been used from time to time."

"By who?"

"Wanderers."

"How do you know?"

"There had been evidence when I temporarily moved in that someone had been living here in this century."

"You don't lock it?"

"It's technically mine, but no. I don't see the harm. Someone gets turned around, like you have a habit of doing, and they have somewhere to catch their breath."

I leaned up on my elbow. "That's very kind of you."

He pulled me back down. "It's not kind, it's practical. They use this instead of banging on my door and bothering me with their bullshit."

That sounded more like Brochan.

"Speaking of getting turned around. There are several places in the woods that the land just drops, a far enough drop you could hurt yourself. And with the dogs, they wander. You need to be careful when you're out there."

"Okay."

Silence fell and I had the sense there was something else on his mind, something more than lodges and drop offs. Before I could ask what was troubling him he said, "We're cutting the ugly from our lives." He wrapped me in his arms before he stood and dropped me to my feet. "Get dressed. I have to show you something."

It was late as we walked through the woods. The moon was barely a sliver in the night sky, but Brochan didn't need its light. He knew the way. He hadn't said anything since he told me to get dressed. We reached the castle but instead of the front door or the one off the kitchen, he took me to another door that led lower into the castle.

At the bottom of the stairs was a hook holding a flashlight. The beam of light reflected off the dirty stone floor and the grates. The dungeon. A chill moved through me.

"Brochan, why are we down here?"

He didn't answer, just led the way deeper into the dungeon. There was a door at the end of the hall. Several padlocks kept whatever was behind that door from getting out.

Brochan stopped and I caught a glimpse of his face. Tormented. I wanted to hold him, wanted to take it all away, instead I did what he needed most. I listened. "My father didn't die in the fire."

I hadn't realized I was crying until my vision blurred. "You locked him up down here?"

He gestured to the window that sat high up on the door. My feet wouldn't move, too afraid of what I would find behind that door, more afraid that I wouldn't be able to understand why Brochan had become a monster to deal with one.

Brochan knew it too when he whispered, "His accommodations are nicer than he'd find in a mental hospital, which is where he really should be."

Peeking into the room, it was larger than I expected, and furnished like the house above with old rugs on the stone floors, sofas and chairs, a little eating area. Paintings hung on the walls, a large bed sat in one corner. He'd even run cable for the television with DVR that was tucked in the corner.

"A nurse comes three times a day. Feeds him, cleans him. Talks with him not that he understands. His mind left him a long time ago."

That woman I'd seen with Brochan. She was his father's nurse.

"But why keep him here at all?"

He didn't answer but he didn't have to. Hatred, vengeance was what kept the broken man buried in the darkest part of the castle, Brochan's hatred.

"That kind of hatred is really dark stuff."

"He used to leave me outside in the cold in the middle of winter. He'd drag me from bed by my hair in the middle of the night. Called me an animal and animals slept outside."

I went numb.

"He used to hold my head under at the pond, cleansing me of my sins he claimed. When I'd gasp for air, he'd laugh even while wishing I wouldn't cough air back into my lungs. On the only occasion that Fenella and Finnegan left me alone because they believed my father was away on business, he locked me in the dungeon. He'd tricked us, dragged me down there and left me…no food, no water and no light. Rats and spiders nipped at me but by the time a furious and horrified Finnegan found me three days later, I'd stopped fighting the rodents. It was the same time I stopped feeling."

His beautiful eyes, lifeless now, looked down at me. "My only crime was being born."

All that I lived through, my mother's cruelty, my father's indifference, Nadine's abuse, the loneliness, none of that broke me, but listening to Brochan dispassionately retell nightmares from his childhood that would make even Satan shudder, that broke me. I lowered my head because it wasn't just tears but rage, a burning rage powerful enough to have a grown man locking away his tormentor in his gilded hell. He touched my chin.

I spoke from the heart when I said, "I would have let him burn."

He pulled me into his arms.

"He can't hurt you anymore."

He cradled my face, love looked back. "No, he can't. Tomorrow, I'll make arrangements to have him moved." He wiped the tears from my cheeks and smiled. "No more ugly."

BROCHAN

Cait and Ethan climbed into the Range Rover. Lizzie was taking them into town. She had intended to drive Brianna's car, but since it was hit or miss that the thing would work I wasn't risking them getting stranded. It had been two days since I shared with her my darkest secret. Finlay was being moved to a private hospital; the staff was arriving shortly to collect him.

She dropped her purse in the car, ducked her head to say something to Cait then strolled over to me. Her softly whispered words that night, how she would have let my father burn, I hadn't been able to get them out of my head. I had worried showing her my father's prison would be the thing that turned me into a monster in her eyes. We were cutting out the ugly, but I didn't have remorse for locking him up. I could go to my grave with a clear conscience. To hear that she thought so too was all I needed to knock that weight from my shoulders. As she had done with Nadine, I was free of him.

"I'm going to show them town and then get a bite at the pub."

"You don't have to leave."

"I would like to be here for you, but I think this is something you, Fenella and Finnegan need to do. It's kind of a cleansing for all of you."

I cursed Brianna for sending me Lizzie, but I was going to erect a monument to the woman. Even in death, she was looking out for me.

Lizzie got up on her tiptoes to kiss me, but she still wasn't tall enough. I lifted her up and pressed her close. Her arms went around my neck, but she didn't kiss me; she looked me in the eyes saying without words how she felt. Then she pressed a kiss on my mouth. "See you later, handsome."

I squeezed her once and dropped her to her feet. She was halfway to the car when I called to her, "Enjoy the haggis."

Her laugh carried back to me before she climbed in the car and drove off.

I walked inside to where Finnegan, Fenella and Anastasia were waiting. Anastasia had been my father's nurse for the last year. We had a steady stream of them since none stayed longer than two years. "Are you ready for this?" Fenella asked.

"What's he like today?"

"The same as usual, nasty. Now that he's moving, this is a good time to give you my notice."

There was a moment of silence, before she and Fenella broke out into laughter. I didn't blame her; it was why I hired people because I didn't want to be anywhere near him either. He was an infection, a plight on society. He deserved to be locked up and the key tossed.

We reached his room. Outside of when I came with Lizzie, I hadn't visited him since his incarceration. As soon as she unlocked the door, I heard him. He didn't need anyone in the room. It was the same rhetoric, his poor beautiful Abigail, me...the devil. I didn't listen. The only reason I was here was to help pack up his shit. I was figuratively free of him and soon I would be literally free of him.

He stopped talking when we entered. He looked over at us, hope in his eyes that it was his beautiful Abigail. All these years later and he was still hung up on her; of course he was trapped in his mind, trapped in that time when his life ended with her death. He didn't recognize us, not even me. He spared us a second or two then got back to his delusional nonsense.

"She lied. She lied…shouldn't have lied, shouldn't have…no baby, no baby, NO BABY."

Finnegan shot me a look. I knew the story that Abigail had been told having a child could kill her. She wanted a baby so badly that she deceived my father and got pregnant. And all these years later, the ravings of a madman who was still tormented by how that deception cost them everything.

"Just once, only once. If she didn't lie…should have stayed home. Only once, shouldn't be baby, just once. Didn't want my baby. Don't want hers."

"Are you hearing him?" Fenella asked "What baby?" She turned to Anastasia. "How long has he been going on about this?"

"A couple months."

I looked over at Finnegan. "Do you know what he's talking about?"

"No, but I do remember days after he learned Abigail was pregnant, after their huge argument, he locked himself in his study for a few days."

"I remember that. Abigail was so worried when she couldn't get through to him, but he was a changed man when he reemerged. He was still worried, but he got on board, for her," Fenella added then she went as white as a ghost.

Finnegan reached for her. "What's wrong?"

The first night I found Finlay standing over Brochan's crib, he had received a phone call earlier in the day. Do you remember? We could hear him tossing stuff in his office."

"What are you saying? That he was pissed at my mother for getting pregnant so he went off and fucked another woman?"

"That day, he must have found out there was a baby."

Finnegan looked over at me. "Only once."

"Why the fuck would he care? She was gone. Just the spawn that killed her was left." I was furious. For all of his devotion, he was nothing more than a fucking cheat. He was old, he was completely broken, and still I moved right into him, grabbed him by the shirt collar and slammed him up against the wall. Fear shined through the crazy.

"You fucking made my life miserable, tried to break me, kill me, because you lost your precious Abigail, but you cheated on her. You put your cock in another woman when the love of your life was carrying your child. You're a fucking fraud."

I released him; he slid to the ground crying. "I'm done with this. Pack his shit or don't, but I want him the fuck out of my house."

LIZZIE

I found Brochan at the loch. Dusk was falling, but I managed to find my way. Cait and Ethan had called an early night, still adjusting to the time difference. He knew I had joined him because his shoulders relaxed. I loved that he could sense when I was near, the werewolf in him. I smiled at the thought.

I reached his side and didn't love the shadows I saw. "I heard you had a rough day."

"He claimed to love her. Loved her so much that her death sent him over the fucking edge, but he cheated on her."

"I thought your father wasn't really there anymore."

"He's not, but his ravings are memories of the past that he's twisted around. And the shit he was going on about today, he cheated on her. He was pissed that she got pregnant, so he punished her by fucking someone else."

That was surprising to hear since Brochan had said that from all accounts he was deeply devoted to Abigail.

He pulled a hand through his hair and moved away from me. "He didn't love her. A man doesn't love a woman then step out on her. Even angry that she deceived him, that wouldn't send him off to another woman. I don't know what he felt for her, but it wasn't love." He turned to me and his next words were so softly spoken. "If he felt what I do for you, he never would have walked out of the room let alone out of the house and into the arms of another woman."

"What are you saying?"

"I always thought his hatred of me turned him mad, but I think it was because he was mad that he treated me the way he did. I wasn't the cause of it, I was the outlet for it."

"That doesn't make what he put you through okay."

"No, but it explains it."

"And you needed that?"

"Logically I understood, but the little boy in me always thought it was me, something about me. It wasn't me."

Closing the distance, I touched his face because I knew how it felt to feel that way. "It looks like we both have dropped the weight of our pasts."

"Fucking finally," he said with a smile, but that faded when he touched my cheek. "There's a beast inside me. It's part of who I am…the savage part of my nature that allows me to do all the things I've done. Being with you has calmed those impulses, but it will come out from time to time. It's inevitable."

I knew who he was, loved who he was including the more savage part of him, so I teased him, "On the full moon most likely."

The smile was unexpected and really beautiful.

"So I've tamed the beast. I should put that on my resume."

He tossed me over his shoulder. I asked through my laughter, "Where are you taking me?"

"The lodge. The beast, he wants out."

"I swear, everywhere you look it is prettier than the last." I shared Cait's thoughts. We were at the pub having lunch.

"Brochan knows some places that are even more spectacular. If you can believe it."

"I can't, so I need to see these places."

"After lunch there are two last stops, one of which is Brianna's cottage."

"I was hoping her cottage was on the tour."

"And now that I officially own it, you can see the inside too."

My attention was pulled when the door opened. I was hoping Brochan would join us, but he was working on something. He wouldn't say what he was working on. It was a surprise. I both loved and hated surprises. It wasn't Brochan; it was Tomas. It had been a couple months; I wondered if he was over whatever it was that made him so creepy. He scanned the pub until he saw me. He looked smug.

Ethan started to stand. "Who is that asshole?"

I reached for Ethan's hand. "It's okay. Dude's a creep."

"I don't like the way he's looking at you."

"He's an asshole, but he's not worth it."

He settled back in his chair, but he didn't take his eyes off Tomas.

I braced because he'd be walking over here any second. I was sure he heard about Brochan and me, he was probably curious why I was back. But he never came over. He glared at the table, and then grinned before strolling out of the pub.

"That was weird."

"What?" Cait asked.

"He usually likes to gloat, odd that he didn't take the opportunity to rip into me about Brochan."

"Maybe he heard you're back together and it took away some of his fun."

I didn't think so. It was unnatural for him to pass on an opportunity to be a dick. I'd mention it to Brochan later. "Are you ready to see Brianna's place?"

Twenty minutes later, Ethan stood on Brianna's drive. Cait and I looked at each other a few times before looking back at him. "I've never seen that expression on his face," I said.

"Me either. Ethan, babe?" Cait inquired softly.

"This is perfection."

"Really?"

He turned to her. "You don't like this?"

"I love it. I didn't think you would. All the open space and grass and nature."

"I hate the city."

My jaw dropped along with Cait's. "Seriously? I thought you loved it."

"No."

"Why didn't you ever say anything?"

"Because you love it."

Cait laughed, "I hate the city."

Ethan looked adorable now because he was totally confused. "You do?"

Cait's attention shifted to me. "We are months away from getting married and we didn't know we hated the city."

"That is a pretty big thing to miss. Have you discussed children?" I teased.

"Yes," Ethan said on a chuckle. He looked back at Brianna's cottage. "I could live here."

"What about your job?"

"There are always jobs, but a place like this. I'm really glad she didn't take this from you, Lizzie." Envious eyes looked back at me. "You've got a little piece of heaven here."

After spending an hour at Brianna's we went to the ruins of the McIntyre estate. "What happened here?" Cait asked as we stood among the debris.

"This was where Brochan grew up."

They both knew enough about Brochan to know it wasn't a happy place. It still bothered me that Brochan kept it like this; I loved ruins, we'd toured through enough of them in Edinburgh, but this wasn't just ruins. It was a reminder. He was letting the past go, I hoped one day he could let this part of it go too.

Ethan moved around the remains as Cait joined me. She took my hand, but her focus was on the castle when she spoke. "Did you think when you met with Mr. Masters that him sending you here you would find the one person who understood your past because he shared a similar one?" She looked at me. "Do you think she knew? Aunt Brianna? Do you think she knew you two would end up together?"

A chill moved through me. In this place, this country, I could believe she did. "Her dying wish was for Brochan to show me kindness. She even wrote him a letter, one he didn't get until I returned to New York. She knew he would turn me away."

"I just got a chill. That's uncanny."

"Brochan calls her a witch."

"I got to tell ya, Lizzie, I think Brochan is right."

We were waiting on the drive when Brochan stepped from the house. He was dressed in his kilt, that whole beautifully sexy ensemble. That was definitely a sight I wanted to see more of. We were heading to a festival. I had dressed before Brochan so I could discuss paint colors for the nursery with Fenella and Cait.

"Holy shit," Cait whispered at my side.

"Magnificent, isn't it?"

"I want one."

I chuckled, "Ethan is right next to you."

She glanced over. "Not a Brochan, I want a kilt."

"For yourself?"

"No, for Ethan. Hey, Brochan, can you make this guy an honorary member of your clan so he can dress like that."

"I don't think it works that way."

"It should. Damn. I didn't think a kilt could be sexy but I stand corrected." She glanced over at me. "Does he wear anything under that?"

He did, but I thought it would be fun to fuck with her. "No."

Her jaw dropped as her eyes flew back to Brochan.

"You're wishing you had x-ray vision right about now, aren't you?"

"Hell, yeah."

The festival was in a town not far from ours. It wasn't so much a festival as it was an enchanted light show in the woods.

"I'd like to see the forest in the daylight. The trees are magnificent. I'd love to paint a few." Big and gnarly, a little scary with how the lights and shadows danced over them, but beautiful.

"It's an easy enough ride," Brochan said. His agreement brought a smile because a month ago he wouldn't have been so agreeable.

The men had been in front of us, but now they were trailing behind us. I took the opportunity to propose an idea to Cait. I wanted to discuss it with Brochan, but it might be moot based on Cait's reaction.

"With your wedding coming up I wanted to offer something to you and Ethan for your consideration."

"Oh, that sounds intriguing."

"I want to offer you Brianna's cottage."

Cait stopped walking. "What?"

"I know you have more clients than me, but with technology you can support them from anywhere. Ethan loved it and I love the idea that you are so close. I want my baby to have you in his life, Auntie Cait and Uncle Ethan, remember? I want to be a part of your children's lives. I'm sure there are legal things you'd have to do to live here, but we can work all that out. Think about it."

She hugged me so hard I had trouble breathing. "I don't have to. We would love that. Both of us."

"Really?"

"Yes! We were talking about it just last night. How amazing it would be to live here, hell, to get married here."

"But what about New York, Ethan's job and the arrangements you've already made for your wedding?"

"What about it? We have no family there. Ethan can always find a new job. We'll lose the deposit on the restaurant we settled on for the reception, but I don't care. My clients want to see me get married they can come here. I don't think I'd have to twist too many arms."

There had been one dark mark on the happiness I had found with Brochan, the idea that me moving on meant leaving Cait behind. I had thought it would be a long shot that she'd want to make a life here too. I wasn't sure I completely believed this was happening.

"Are you sure?"

"Absolutely. Ethan!"

"You don't have to holler I'm right here."

"Lizzie offered us the cottage."

His reaction wasn't feigned; they really did want this.

"Seriously?"

"Yes."

He had me off the ground and in a bear hug before I knew what was happening.

Brochan was a distance behind us. Cait took my arm as we continued on; I peered back to see Brochan was following but still keeping a distance. What was up with him?

"I hate to be greedy, but what are the chances we could have the reception at Brochan's?"

"I'll ask him, but I think he'll be fine with it."

I glanced at her and she was crying. "Hey, why the tears."

"I was so worried about losing you."

"I'm not going anywhere."

She smiled. "Now neither am I."

We continued on for a short distance when Cait tensed then looked behind us. She was probably wondering about Brochan's odd behavior too. "Is it just me, or do you have the sensation like we're being followed."

I thought she was teasing because Brochan, and now Ethan, were so far behind us.

"Seriously, the sixth sense I picked up living in New York is stirring something fierce."

I stopped moving. "You're serious."

"Yeah."

I looked back at Brochan. Was he sensing it too?

That was answered seconds later when two people jumped from the shadows. Ethan hauled ass toward us, I was guessing in case there were others, but I couldn't pull my eyes from Brochan. He moved with speed and precision. I'd never seen anything like it except in the movies. He throat punched one guy and he went down for the count. The other one, he toyed with, getting punches in here and there and then he did this round kick thing that sent the dude sailing into a tree. They were out, he walked to us, caught my hand.

"I think it's time we go," he said, but he was already dragging me from the woods.

"Muggers even here…unbelievable. You're more than a man of leisure, aren't you Brochan?" Cait sounded both awed and stunned.

I was stunned too, but for a different reason. I glanced up at him; his jaw was tight. "I recognized them, Brochan."

"Aye. So did I."

"Can you teach me how to do that kick thing?" Cait called. "That was fucking awesome."

I felt some of the tension drain from Brochan, but that was Cait.

"Aye, I'll teach you both."

"Sweet."

BROCHAN

Finnegan was driving Cait and Ethan to the airport. They were heading home. They had arrangements to make for their move. When we returned from the forest the other night, Lizzie shared what she and Cait had discussed. I was happy for her that her family would be in walking distance. I wasn't as happy about the prospect of people milling around my home for Cait's wedding, but Lizzie wanted it and I was discovering there was little I would say no to when it came to her.

Cait had peppered me with questions for the rest of the night about what I did prior to being a man of leisure. I didn't share. She didn't need to know.

Lizzie had recognized the fuckers that had attacked us. She was an artist, an observer, so she paid attention to the details. They were Tomas' friends. Why the fuck were they following us?

When I reached his house, he was outside smoking.

"Look what the cat dragged in."

I climbed from my car and moved right up into his face. "Why the fuck are you following us?"

He tried to act coy and as much as I wanted to beat it out of him, I tried a more civilized approach.

"I don't know what you're talking about."

I cracked my knuckles; fuck civilized. "I'm not asking again. Answer me, either the easy way or the hard way. I don't give a fuck which."

He saw what he needed to when the smirk fell off his face. "I don't have control over them, but if they took it upon themselves to knock the mighty Brochan from his pedestal, good for them."

Jealous. He was nothing but jealous. Of what?

"And that day in Edinburgh with Ashley?"

His expression gave it away. He didn't remember her.

"Why the fuck were you there?" I demanded.

He didn't answer, I moved closer. "I followed Lizzie."

My muscles hummed with fury. "Say again?"

"I followed her. I'm guessing you'd been to that pub before because Ashley was there, glaring at you like I was."

I hissed through my teeth, "Why the fuck follow Lizzie?"

"Because she picked you too. What the fuck is so great about you?"

Picked me too? What the fuck was he talking about?

"Even those who claim to care, they fucking lie. I'm done with it, all of it."

I was done with it too. I stepped even closer, he stepped back. "You don't have the balls to face me? Of course you don't. I handed you your ass with little effort when were just kids and we both know how I've spent my life. Kicking your ass would be unfair since you are at such a severe disadvantage."

Hate stared back at me.

"Stay away from me and mine. I'll ask only once." I turned and walked back to my car.

"She's tamed you. I don't fucking believe it. Brochan McIntyre using words instead of his fists."

I reached my car. "Come at me or mine and you'll see how fucking tame I am."

"Why are we doing this?"

Lizzie and I were in the front yard working on target practice."

"Because you need to know how to protect yourself."

"Why a gun? Why not karate or something?"

"Jiujitsu, that's a good idea. You still need to know how to fire a gun."

She seemed to sense it was important to me, so let it go.

"You're tense. You need to loosen up." I wrapped my arm around her waist and pressed into her thinking to distract her from her aversion to guns enough to get her to actually fire the thing.

"Keep touching me like that and I'm going to get really tense in an entirely different way."

I leaned in, brushed my lips over her ear then took a little bite. "I'll make you a deal. You give me an hour and I'll give you an hour." My hand moved down to her ass where I squeezed.

She was breathless when she replied, "Two hours and you've got a deal."

"Greedy little minx." I was already hard. It was a win-win for me, she'd learn to fire a gun and I'd get my hands on her body. "You've got a deal. Now let's try it again."

CHAPTER TWENTY

LIZZIE

Brochan and I were on the lane, walking the dogs. He was leaving for a few days. His project, the surprise, was well underway and still he wouldn't tell me what he was up to. And I had tried to get it from him, but the man could keep a secret. I tried again.

"Tell me about this project?"

"No."

"A hint?"

"No."

"And there is nothing I can do to persuade you to share?"

He looked wicked. "You can try, I'd enjoy your efforts." He pulled me up against him. "I'll be gone for three days. Fenella and Finnegan will be here, as will Champ and Boomer."

They had defected, following me wherever I went. Brochan preferred that, liked that I had our furbabies watching my back. Why he thought I needed that here, I didn't know.

"When you get back we'll start planning the nursery." Remembering Cait and Ethan's conversation and how they had missed some of the big stuff, I asked, "How many kids do you want?"

He didn't even hesitate. "Eight."

Eight? Was he…"No."

He laughed, "Five"

"Three."

"Okay, we'll start with three."

He checked his watch. "I've got to go."

It was only three days, but it was three days and two nights. We walked to the drive. Finnegan was closing up the trunk. Brochan shook his hand. "Thank you."

"Safe journey."

Fenella came running out. "I packed you some food, just in case." She thrust the food at him.

"I'm going to Edinburgh, not the Sahara."

"It doesn't hurt to be prepared."

He kissed her head. "Thank you."

Seeing Brochan showing kindness and affection to his parents, he really was healing. Finnegan took the food from him. Brochan caught my hand and pulled me away. He framed my face and kissed me, with tongue and teeth. I was a hot mess when he ended it. "That wasn't nice."

"To tide you over." He bit my lip. "If you plan on making yourself come, you better fucking call me. I want to hear that."

My legs went weak. "Now I'm thinking about it."

"Good. My plan worked. Call me."

"How soon is too early."

He laughed then kissed me again. "Nine. I'll be waiting."

I grabbed his arm and looked at his watch. "It's only three."

We walked back to his car; he kissed me again then climbed in. It was hard watching him pull away. I didn't know why I felt so funny about him leaving, but I had the weirdest sensation the shoe was getting ready to drop.

"Are you sure you don't want us to keep you company?" Fenella asked but she hadn't stopped yawning since dinner. It was almost eight, only an hour before I called Brochan. I hadn't thought of anything else. I'd never had phone sex. The idea of popping my cherry with Brochan had me in a constant state of arousal.

"I'm going to bed soon too."

"All right." She pressed a kiss on my head. "Sleep well."

"Good night."

"Night, lass," Finnegan said before he followed his wife out.

Boomer and Champ were sleeping by the fire. I should take them out before we went upstairs. That might be weird, phone sex with the dogs watching. They slept in the bed. We'd figure it out.

"Come on, boys. Let's go potty. We have a date with Daddy in an hour."

It was only October but it was cold. We weren't going far and still I pulled on my winter coat, hat and gloves. I grabbed a flashlight since the boys liked to dart into the woods and with their dark fur it was hard to find them. The moon was full. I would never again look at the full moon and not think of Brochan, my werewolf.

The boys were feeling playful, chasing each other into the trees. We had time, so I let them play as I walked along the path. Fenella had added mums to the gardens. It looked beautiful.

After ten minutes, the two hadn't returned. That wasn't like them. Thinking they trapped a rabbit, they'd done that before, I headed in after them since there would be no pulling them away from their kill. The flashlight caught them, they were definitely feasting on something. "What did you kill now?" I didn't like seeing the remains, it was nature and all, but it broke my heart. The rabbit had family too. The closer I drew my heart went into my throat because they were dangerously close to one of the drops.

"I think we're going to have to leash you at night. It's too dangerous out here in the dark. All right, you're done. Let's go back inside. It's cold."

We hadn't even taken a step and both of them started to growl deep in their throats. I jerked around for the cause, the beam from the flashlight landing on a shadow that moved. I gasped then turned to run. I felt hands on me, felt the hesitation before the shove. I heard the scream as the dog bit into my attacker, but I had lost my balance and the edge was right there. I fell over the side, a brutal slide as I was tossed and turned and scraped by rocks and branches. I landed at the bottom in a jarring hit. My hands immediately moved to my stomach. The baby. I ached everywhere. Tears fell as I cradled my stomach hoping to hold the baby there. I climbed to my feet, then lost my balance and fell back on my butt when Boomer and Champ came barreling down the side. My heroes. "We need to get back to the house," I told them as the three of us limped back in the direction of home. Five minutes later, I got turned around. It was so dark, even with the moon and the flashlight. Everything looked the same. I didn't bring my cell. I should have. My body ached and I felt cramps. The tears fell harder. While I fumbled my way home, I was losing my baby. We walked some more when a cramp so painful doubled me over. No, please no. I flashed the light around us and noticed the trees thinned ahead. We stepped into the healing circle. I couldn't go any farther. I curled up on the ground, bringing my knees up to my chest holding my baby inside me. Boomer and Champ curled around me. That was how Brochan found us in the morning.

BROCHAN

Nine came and went. I almost called her, I'd been half hard since I left her, but she had been sleeping a lot more lately. It was why I had suggested she call me. As much as I wanted to hear her voice, wanted to hear her moan and come for me, I'd let her sleep. I was only in Edinburgh because I didn't want her knowing what I was doing until it was done. I had finally decided what I wanted done with the old McIntyre land. I had a meeting with the contractors in the morning. There was another reason I came into Edinburgh, a stop I had made before I checked into the hotel. That was for Lizzie too. I wasn't getting any sleep until I took care of my problem. I rubbed my cock, memories of our last time in the lodge, naked, her on her knees in front of the fire, me behind her, driving into her, her tight pussy, the soft moans in the back of her throat, the way she held tight even after she came, milking my cock dry. My other hand worked my balls as I fisted my cock and really got down to business. The growl burned the back of my throat as I came on my chest. I still ached for her, but I climbed from bed and headed to the shower.

Jerking awake, my heart was hammering and I was soaked with sweat. A nightmare. Rubbing my hands over my face, I checked the clock. It was only three. I tried for sleep but something wasn't right. I took a shower but I couldn't shake the feeling that something was wrong. My cell rang. I snatched it up. "What's wrong?"

It was a hysterical Fenella. "It's Lizzie. She's not here and neither are the dogs."

My heart stopped. "When did you see her last?"

"Around eight last night."

It got cold last night, but she was damn lucky it hadn't gotten cold enough to be life threatening. I was going to tie the woman to me. "She probably got turned around again in the woods. I'm leaving now. Call the police, start the search. The dogs will bark if you call them." I hung up, packed up and was in my car ten minutes later. Why hadn't the dogs gotten her home? Mac and Ava came to mind and the possibility that Lizzie wasn't just lost caused a pain in my chest that was suffocating. I sped the whole fucking way home.

Pulling around the drive, it wasn't just cop cars but locals too, Blair, Bridget, Molly, Bruce and Fergus.

I jumped from my car. "Have you found her?"

Fergus was shaken, and knowing the man was a ballbuster, had the stabbing pain in my chest amplifying. "We're sweeping in a pattern, but so far…"

I didn't wait, running into the woods where they usually played. "Boomer! Champ! Boomer! Champ!" Why weren't they barking? Fear, an emotion I wasn't accustomed to, twisted in my gut.

I ran to the lodge and slammed open the door. "Lizzie!"

Empty.

I backtracked and headed to the loch. She wasn't there. Where the hell was she? Fuck. My hands shook as I pulled them through my hair. Think. Where the fuck would she be? The circle. She'd found her way there once; maybe she had again.

I broke into the circle then stopped and nearly went to my knees at the sight that greeted me. Three bodies curled around each other. Her boys were protecting her, but she was so pale and still. Boomer and Champ looked up when I dropped down at their side; they were shivering, but they were protecting her.

My voice broke when I whispered, "Lizzie."

I pulled off her glove; her hand was ice cold. Yanking off my jacket, I wrapped it around her. Her eyes fluttered open and tears filled my own because for a few seconds, I thought she was dead. Living a life without her, fuck that.

"The baby," she whispered. "I think I lost the baby." Curling into her, I pressed my lips to hers. Tasted her tears that blended with mine.

"Let's get you home."

"The baby."

"You're in the healing circle, mo leannan. You spent the night here."

Her sad eyes, wet with tears, looked hopeful. "Boomer and Champ?"

"Protecting their lady." I kissed her again then lifted her into my arms. "Let's get you home."

LIZZIE

Brochan stood by the bed, hands in his pockets as the doctor examined me. He looked exhausted. Dark circles had formed under his eyes, but those pale blues never left me. Boomer and Champ were sleeping next to me on the bed.

"You've got a lot of scrapes and bruises. Did you take a tumble?"

It was more than that, but I'd wait for the doctor to leave. "Yes."

"You need to be careful out there, lass. Maybe you shouldn't walk the woods at night. Especially not in October, the weather is very unpredictable. You're lucky it didn't snow. If your dogs hadn't been there, you would be in much worse shape."

Was he not mentioning the baby because it was bad news? I had to know, even not wanting to hear the confirmation. I had to know. "The baby?"

His old hand covered mine. "Your baby is fine. Nice strong heartbeat."

The tears slipped from the corners of my eyes.

"I'm ordering bed rest for the next few days." He stood and addressed Brochan. "She's going to be fine, they both are."

"Thank you, doctor."

Brochan walked the doctor out before returning and settling on the edge of the bed. "You got lost," he said as he brushed the hair from my face, rubbing his thumb over my cheek as he did. "Maybe I should tame back some of the woods."

"I didn't get lost. Boomer and Champ were playing, darting into the woods. They caught something, like they do. I went to bring them back…"

He touched my chin and held my gaze on him. "What happened?"

"Someone pushed me."

He morphed right before my eyes. Here was the beast and he was out.

"Pushed you?"

"Boomer and Champ bit him."

His voice was so soft, but it made the hair on my arms stand on end. "Someone lured you, waited for you and tried to…"

I hadn't thought of that. "You don't think the boys trapped something, you think something was waiting for them."

"Someone has been watching. Where were you?"

"The woods to the right of the drive, right near the drop."

He stood and moved with determined strides to the door.

"What are you going to do?" I asked, but I already knew.

Reaching the door, he looked back at me. The malice in his eyes caused a chill. "I'm about to get really fucking ugly."

BROCHAN

"How is she?" Fergus asked as soon as I hit the entrance hall.

"She's fine. So is the baby."

"Baby?"

I kept going, out the front door and into the woods.

"She's pregnant?"

I hadn't realized Fergus had followed me. "Yes."

He fell into step at my side. "Brianna always told me I was too harsh on you."

I didn't have time for this shit.

"Maybe…"

I interrupted him when I stopped walking because damn it I was pissed, he was here. Taking out some of this shit on him worked just fine with me. "What the fuck is your problem?"

"I don't like you."

"Yeah, I fucking get that part. Why?"

He moved into my face. "I remember the night she came home with the bruise."

"You think I did that?"

"She said no, but she wouldn't say how she got it. She was protecting someone and it was always you she protected."

That took some of the wind out of my sail. She hadn't mentioned my father, because that would have drawn suspicion, her being hurt by my father and the place burning down the same night. She was protecting me, again.

"It was my father."

"Blame it on a dead man."

"He's not dead. He's in a facility in Edinburgh…a mental facility."

His dumfounded look might have stirred a grin if I wasn't feeling homicidal.

"Where are you going?"

"Lizzie was pushed last night."

Now he was pissed. "Pushed? By who?"

"I don't know. But someone was waiting for her, knew her routine."

I saw what I was looking for; Fergus saw it too.

"Is that a steak?"

I was already standing at the edge, looking down at the drop. It wasn't far, maybe twenty feet, but it was steep and littered with rocks, branches and tree stumps. A wave of nausea moved through me. Lizzie was lucky she survived the fall with no more than some bruises and scratches.

Fergus joined me. "They could have killed her."

"That was the intention."

"Who? Who would do that?"

"I don't know, but whoever did left with a souvenir. My dogs bit the fucker."

"What are you going to do?"

I gave him a flat stare. "What I do best."

I watched from the shadows as Fergus approached Tomas. He didn't believe Tomas was capable of hurting anyone. I knew differently. I saw my confirmation when a bandage peeked out from under his sleeve. Fergus saw it too. That was all I needed to know.

I headed back to my car and called Gerard. After Edinburgh I had asked him to look into Tomas. I understood Ashley's motivation, but I didn't understand his. I got sidetracked with Mac and Ava, Lizzie, but now it was time to learn why Tomas O'Connell had such a hard on for me.

"I need to know what you've learned about Tomas O'Connell."

"Cliff notes version, he hates you and wants you dead."

"Then let's make it easy for him."

Lizzie packed a bag. Fenella and Finnegan were already packed. The staff was given a surprise vacation. I stood in our room, watching her…my eyes drifting to the little swell of her stomach. She'd been quiet since learning of my plan. We were cutting out the ugly and I was, just more graphically.

"How long?"

"No more than a week."

"Are you sure he'll come for you?"

"He'll come." I folded her into a hug. Her focus was on my chest. I lifted her chin. "I know we're cutting out the…"

I hadn't expected the hard look in her eyes. "An eye for an eye. If ever that applied. Just be careful."

I smiled then kissed her; there was a little beast in my beauty.

The full moon illuminated the navy sky as wisps of clouds moved over the pale sphere. The few times he cased the castle, the forest that wrapped around it had been a symphony of sounds—wolves, owls, crickets. Tonight it was as if the creatures that roamed the dark knew a more dangerous predator was on the hunt. He knew of a door that never was locked, he slipped inside. Without a sound, he walked up the stairs and down the hall. His palm was sweating from both nerves and excitement as he pushed open the door, raised the gun and squeezed the trigger, spraying the bed with bullets. Surprise furrowed his brow when he flicked the lights on to find the room empty but for a small piece of paper addressed to him on the nightstand. The first trickle of fear slithered down his spine. With shaking hands he unfolded it. Penned in dark red ink was written only one word.

Run

Panic coated his throat and the finesse he had entered with only moments earlier had fled. Bone-deep terror replaced it. He did as instructed and ran. Reaching the staircase, he felt the hair at his nape stand on end. He wasn't alone. The darkness took shape, staring back at him with ice-cold eyes.

BROCHAN

"You wanted me. Here I am."

Tomas' hand shook as he lifted the gun. I knocked it free; the gun skipped across the floor.

His terror filled eyes followed the gun before turning back to me.

It took everything in me not to snap his neck. "You could have killed her."

"I didn't mean to kill her. Just scare her."

One hard shove sent Tomas flying down the staircase. He landed in a heap, but he was still breathing. His head turned, fearfully tracking my approach, one step at a time. "How does it fucking feel?"

Grabbing him by the collar, I punched him in the face. He screamed. I punched him again and again and again. My hand ached; his screams had turned to whimpers and déjà vu slammed into me. My hand stopped mid-punch because I had been here before. Cycles. Fucking hell, this was another one. I shoved Tomas back to the floor and stepped away from him.

"You can rot in a cell." I reached for my phone and called the police.

CHAPTER TWENTY-ONE

LIZZIE

We pulled into the drive to find Brochan waiting for us. I had been a wreck for the last few days. I knew I didn't need to worry about him, but it didn't stop me. Tomas needed to be handled, whatever his deal was he'd crossed the line when he came at me. Why had he? I suppose it didn't really matter because he was now dealing with the consequences of his actions. However Brochan chose to handle Tomas I would have supported, but I was thrilled he'd opted to call the cops instead of taking the matter into his own hands. Though, from what I'd heard, his hands had definitely been involved.

Fergus parked, and I opened the door for the dogs. They ran to Brochan running around him, jumping on him. We piled out of the car, Fergus helping us with our things before he approached Brochan.

"I hear that Tomas O'Connell is in lock up on two counts of attempted murder."

"Aye."

"That's not really your style."

That comment from Fergus earned my full attention. He knew about Brochan?

He read my expression perfectly. "The whole town knows. He never hid it from us, actually taunted us with it. People keep quiet out of fear, but there was a healthy dose of guilt too. We knew what was happening and we did nothing, our silence helped to create the very monster we feared."

"He's not a monster."

Fergus offered his hand to Brochan. "No, he's not."

"He's a werewolf," I teased.

Fenella wasn't so formal; she walked right up to Brochan and hugged him hard and long. She cradled his face. "That's my beautiful boy."

She hurried inside to hide the tears. "You'll stay for dinner, Fergus."

She didn't wait for his answer.

Finnegan and Brochan shared a moment. There was love and pride in Finnegan's gaze before he broke the eye contact and reached for his and Fenella's bag. Watching them stirred an idea.

"I'll help you bring in the bags," Fergus said.

Brochan, the dogs and I remained. "How are you?" I asked.

"I wanted to kill him. I came so close, but I realized I was reacting again. We need to break the cycle, right?"

"I would have understood if…"

He held his hand out; I slipped mine into it. "I know."

It was hard finding a place to work. I didn't want the others to know what I was doing. I'd taken one of the bedrooms as a studio, not that Brochan wouldn't find me. I taped a note on the door to knock and not enter.

I was painting a portrait. I didn't usually sketch people, but I wanted a portrait of Brochan, Fenella and Finnegan. They were family and since I intended to continue the tradition of family portraits, we needed the first family.

A knock followed by, "Lizzie."

"One minute. I grabbed the cloth and covered the painting. "Come in."

Brochan looked at the covered easel as he closed the door. "You have your own secret."

"Yep."

He walked toward me as he yanked his shirt from his pants and pulled it over his head. His shoes were next then his jeans. Aches kicked off in all the right places.

"What are you doing?"

He stopped right in front of me and dropped his briefs. "Trying out my new profession as a nude model."

My clit clenched in a lovely spasm. "I just came."

His eyes went hot. "You better not have."

"You should climb on the bed."

He turned and I had to bite my lip to keep from biting his ass. In that slow, controlled way he had, he moved onto the bed like a big, lazy cat getting ready for a nap. He wasn't sleeping. Oh hell no.

"How do you want me?"

"That is such an open ended question, Brochan."

His smile was wicked. "I know."

I joined him, moving my hands over his body, his chest and shoulders, down to his abs, his thighs. I avoided his cock because once I got started there it was all over. His focus seared me as he watched me play. His voice was rough when he said, "You're a painter, not a sculptor."

"Hush, don't disturb a master at work." I straddled him and pressed down.

"What's the master doing now?"

"Determining how big a canvas I need."

"The biggest fucking one they make."

"Cocky. But feeling him swelling between my legs, he was right.

He grabbed my shirt and tossed it on the floor. "I don't usually paint in the nude."

My bra followed. "Learn." He flipped me onto my back and smiled as he worked my jeans and panties off.

Brochan's sated body was pressing me into the mattress, his cock still jerking inside me, my version of heaven. "What do you think about inviting the Stewarts to our home?" he asked.

His head lifted. My heart squeezed that he was ready to meet his mother's family. "I think it's a wonderful idea. Can I ask why now?"

There was the slightest hesitation before he said, "You were the link for Brianna to her sister. I'm that link to Abigail. I didn't get it before; I started to that day of the Highland games. Family isn't one dimensional and when Abigail died it wasn't just Finlay who lost her."

"Bent, not broken."

"We can't get careless. We have to be vigilante…"

He was thinking of Mac and Ava. "I know."

"We need to practice shooting some more. You're getting good, but I want you to keep it up. And it can't hurt to learn how to use a blade."

"A knife?"

"You're not always going to have a gun handy."

It was important to him and I needed to know how to defend the baby, and myself, so I didn't argue. "Okay. Is this party with the Stewarts your surprise?"

"No."

"There's another one?"

"Yes."

"And you still won't tell me?"

He rolled onto his back and my mouth watered seeing all that beautiful naked man knowing he was mine.

"No, but you're welcome to try."

CHAPTER TWENTY-TWO

LIZZIE

We sectioned off a part of our bedroom for the nursery. We painted the walls a silvery blue. Brochan and Finnegan were working on the crib and Fenella was hanging the drapes on the windows. I was painting a mural on the wall—an enchanted forest complete with fairies, elves, sprites, and the big bad wolf. I was working on the wolf's pale eyes when the memory had my hand going still. The book I had had as a child. I had wished for a big bad wolf to protect me. Maybe Brochan was right about Brianna. I was pulled from that when the men finished with the crib.

"That took far longer than it should have," Finnegan said as he and Brochan stood back and admired their work. The beige crib looked vintage but it was new. The heavy striped blue and beige silk of the drapes would also be used as a dust ruffle for the crib.

"I love it, but you are taking a chance using blue." Fenella had cautioned me when we were looking at color themes, but I knew it was a boy.

"It's a boy, Fenella. I don't know how I know, but I do."

"I believe you, really I do. Oh and that reminds me. I have something for you, Brochan. Lizzie found it. I had it polished."

Her eyes met mine as she pulled the medallion from her pocket. It looked brand new. Brochan's hand closed around it. "Where did you find this?"

"At the estate, in the rubble."

He was quiet for a few minutes, his expression thoughtful, then he turned to me and lifted the necklace over my head. The medallion settled between my breasts. Tenderness looked back from those pale eyes. "She'd want you to have that," he said softly. Brochan and I shared a moment then he announced, "Lizzie and I were thinking it might be time to connect with the Stewart clan."

I wasn't the only one to see Fenella's face pale when Brochan asked, "What's wrong?"

She tried to wave it off then stopped and confessed, "What if they're bitter that we didn't try to reach out sooner? I mean, we did raise you but it could look like we kept you from them."

"If they do feel that way, then we didn't miss anything all these years." I agreed with Brochan. Fenella still looked nervous.

"I think it's a good idea. There's a baby on the way and he has Stewart blood. Seems like a good time to mend the fence," Finnegan said then added, "And if they give us shit for doing the best we could, for giving Brochan a family and a home, we kick their arses from the house."

Silence before Brochan said, "What he said."

Fenella looked shocked for a second then laughed. "Okay." She checked her watch. "Oh, the roast. Finnegan, I need you to peel potatoes."

"My work is never done," he said then winked and followed her out.

I turned back to the mural. I loved it. I captured the tall pines that surrounded the castle; whimsical creatures darted in and out of them. There was a full moon above the forest. It felt enchanted and magical, it felt like home.

Brochan's arms came around my waist. "Is that wolf supposed to be me?"

"Yes."

"Where are you?"

"I'm not in the mural."

"You should be."

I twisted my head to him. "Why?"

He looked like a wolf when he grinned. "For the big bad wolf to eat."

BROCHAN

I stood in the library looking out at Lizzie playing with the dogs, they were playing tug of war, Lizzie was losing. Her stomach swelled now. My bairn. I knew now that my father hadn't been right in the head, not from the beginning, because I haven't even seen my child and the thought of bringing harm, of doing to my child what my father had done to me...he was a monster, a sick one.

I reached for my cell when it rang.

"Brochan, Rodney Danton. I lost eyes on Norah."

Annoying, but I'd expected that. Norah was shrewd; she'd have known she was being followed. I was surprised she'd allowed it for as long as she had, which meant she was getting ready to make her move. "When?"

"This morning. He thought she was home. He sat on the house like usual, but she didn't follow her schedule. He slipped inside; she was gone. He said it looked like she was going somewhere."

"Here." I'd been expecting that too.

"My thought as well. I don't think she intends to storm the castle, so to speak, but she's up to something," he replied.

"I agree. I'll have my guy look into her finances. Just how much she's in need of money will play into how she proceeds."

"Sounds smart."

"It might be a good idea if you come for a visit. More eyes."

"Wheels went up twenty minutes ago."

Canny motherfucker. "I'll have a car waiting at the airport."

"See you soon."

I disconnected then called Gerard.

"What's up?"

"I need you to look into Norah Calhoun's finances. How much, where she's got it invested, what her disposable income is."

"On it. I'll send it later tonight."

"Thanks."

"You just thanked me. What the hell is wrong with you?"

"Fuck off."

"That's better."

I disconnected. Norah had her own eyes on Lizzie, so to speak, but not anymore. Her coming here was inevitable, so was her next move. What remained a question was how she intended to make that move. Lizzie wasn't going to like hearing her mother was on the way. I detoured to the kitchen.

"Dinner will be done soon," Fenella offered.

"Lizzie's father will be arriving later tonight."

Fenella looked up from the bread she was kneading. "He is? I don't have a room ready."

I gave her a look. Every room was meticulous; she made sure of it.

"Okay fine, I want everything just right. It's Lizzie's father."

"Estranged father."

"That is why it is even more important that everything be just right."

I didn't want to add to the work she insisted on doing around here so I asked, "Do you need me to do something?"

Her expression softened. "Thank you for asking, but I'll handle it."

But she just said she...I didn't understand women at all. "Thank you." I said that almost like a question.

She looked like she might start to cry, so I hauled ass out of the kitchen by way of the back door. I heard Lizzie before I saw her.

"You're so handsome, both of you. Soon you'll have a little one to play with. He'll be able to keep up with you better than me. I'm tired all the time."

I rounded the house, then leaned my shoulder against the wall and watched her.

"I hope he looks like his daddy, that black hair and those pale eyes. My heart might not be able to handle two of them."

Her voice turned soft and I knew she was crying. She cried a lot these days. She had a hell of a row yesterday when she learned the shortbread was gone. She had been the one to eat it, but she wept so badly Fenella immediate baked another batch.

Lizzie rubbed her neck then turned. Her smile took my breath away.

"Speaking of the devil," she said as she strolled toward me.

"Talking to yourself again?"

"I was talking to the dogs."

It was the same thing in my mind, but I didn't argue.

She walked right into me and pressed her lips to mine. She was like a drug, just a taste and I wanted more, but we had to talk. Threading my fingers through her hair, I kissed her again, and then reached for her hand.

"I just spoke to your father."

Her head jerked to me. "You did?"

"Your father's guy doesn't have eyes on Norah."

Her hand tensed, I stroked the back of it with my thumb. "It was only a matter of time."

"Do you think she is on her way here?"

"Yes."

"What are we going to do?"

"Let her come, but I want you to practice your shooting."

"I had a feeling you would." She sounded so disgruntled I almost smiled. She wasn't going to like the next part. "I want you to carry."

"No."

"Lizzie, just until we know what's going on with Norah. We don't know what she's up to, we have to be prepared for anything."

"I don't want to carry a gun."

"I won't be with you every second, but your father will be when I'm not. I want you covered and I want you to be able to protect yourself and the bairn."

Her eyes narrowed. "Using the baby, that's low."

"I know. That's how strongly I feel about you having a gun."

"Fine, but just until this shit with Norah is over."

"Deal."

"I'm visiting Fergus tomorrow. Before we pack up Brianna's things, I want to make sure he has everything of hers he wants."

Cait and Ethan were taking the cottage. It would be a home again. Brianna would have wanted that. Lizzie thinking of Fergus was just her way. I brushed her cheek with my thumb. "Good idea."

"Fenella had some really great ideas for the wedding, including using the barn for the ceremony."

Wedding plans, that was a fucking buzz kill. I was giving up my peace for the day; that was my contribution. She chuckled, "That bad, huh? I won't bother you with the details."

I yanked her close. "Bother me with the details for our wedding."

She went completely still.

"Our wedding?"

She looked adorably confused. "Aye."

"But you never asked me to marry you."

I reached into my pocket and pulled out the ring, a simple emerald cut stone. It was the other reason I went into Edinburgh. Her eyes filled with tears. I lifted her left hand and held the ring at her third finger. She looked up in my eyes.

"Be the voice in the dark, Lizzie."

She touched my face. "And the one in the light."

My own eyes burned. "Aye."

Tears rolled down her face when she whispered, "Yes, I'll marry you."

I slipped on the ring and kissed it on her finger. She threw her arms around my neck. "I do love you."

Lifting her off her feet, I started for the house calling for the dogs. "We'll show Fenella and Finnegan, then I'll show you how much I love you."

"I like this plan."

LIZZIE

Resting my head on Brochan's shoulder, I stared at my hand. I still didn't quite believe it.

"When did you get this?"

"My trip to Edinburgh."

Glancing up, he was looking at my hand too. "When I got the call from Fenella that you were missing. I thought I'd tempted fate, like Mac, I reached too far."

Turning into him, I didn't like the shadows in his eyes. "You have to stop thinking that way."

"I know, but after how I have lived my life, finding a happy ending seems wrong."

"After the life you endured, I think you deserve a happy ending more than anyone." I sat up, took his hand and played with his fingers. "When I was little, I wished for you."

"What does that mean?"

"She was so cruel, but the day my father finally told her he was leaving her, they had a terrible fight. After he stormed out, she came to my room. Stood in the doorway and just stared at me so dispassionately. All the rage and anger my father had stirred in her, that was gone. She was ice, which made her words even more terrifying."

He cupped my chin and yet I felt his muscles humming. He was pissed. "What did she say?"

My eyes lifted to his. "She said she wished I was never born."

"Son of a..."

"I had been looking through *Little Red Riding Hood* and I wished that night for the big bad wolf to protect me from her. I had forgotten about that, well, maybe subconsciously I didn't."

Brochan had the oddest expression on his face.

"What?" I asked.

"I think we need to do some research on Brianna. Was she born or did she appear?"

"I think you might be right, but careful Brochan because you're starting to sound like me."

He pinned me under him.

"I think you deserve the happy ending. I think we both do," I whispered.

I took his kiss to mean he agreed.

Fergus' house was the same cottage I had spied my first day of sightseeing, the one near Brianna's with the stream that ran behind it. I understood why he didn't want to give it up. He was out front chopping firewood when I pulled up. He dropped the ax and walked to me as I climbed from the car.

"This is beautiful. I walked here when I first arrived and fell in love."

"First time I saw it, I had to have it," he declared.

"I understand why."

He pressed a kiss on my head then reached for my hand. "It looks like congratulations are in order." His eyes found mine. "Brochan proposed?"

It was a Brochan kind of proposal. I wouldn't have wanted it any other way. "Yes."

"Brianna would have loved that."

"I think she planned it," I muttered.

"I don't doubt it. Come, let's get some tea." He led us inside. We hit the living room and I stopped following. There were pictures everywhere. A lifetime captured in moments. "Can I look around?"

"Aye. I'll bring the tea out."

I didn't know where to start. There were pictures of Brianna and Fergus when they were young, like Brochan and I were now. Even then he was massive, towering over Brianna, but there was love. In every picture their love was the focal point. There were pictures of Brianna with another woman, her sister I was guessing because she had the same eyes. On another wall, it was a young Brianna and a baby, Norah. I stared at those pictures for a while. It was hard to believe that innocent babe could turn so ugly. Why? What happened? It was stupid, but I softened a bit toward Norah seeing that she hadn't been spawned. That at one time she'd just been a baby, sweet and innocent. Maybe like Brochan and me, something dark touched her, though I didn't know what because Brianna was nothing but light, a bright and beautiful light.

My heart tripped in my chest when I saw a picture of Brochan. He was young, a teenager, and there was a defiant look about him. He was angry, even then, but he was beautiful, so damn beautiful. An ache started knowing when this picture was taken, in the middle of his nightmare and no one helped except Brianna and the magnificent souls who became his parents.

"Are you enjoying my walls?"

"This is…" I had tears in my eyes; they were pretty constant companions these days. "Do you mind if I do the same? I'd love a wall like this in the nursery."

"Aye."

We settled on the sofa as Fergus served the tea.

"I wanted to share with you that I've offered my best friend, Cait and her fiancé, the cottage. Ethan fell in love with it when he was here. I hate for it to be sitting empty and I can't bear to part with it. Cait and Ethan are family, the only family I had before coming here. It feels right to give it to them."

"You don't have to convince me, lass. Family will be living there again. That's all that matters."

I was really glad he felt that way. "They want to keep the cottage pretty much as is, but I wanted you to go through it and take what you'd like."

He looked down but not before I saw the brightening of his eyes. "Thank you, lass, but Bri gave me all I needed."

"I'm taking her photographs." I looked at his walls. "A collage of snapshots for our baby so he'll know her."

He wiped at his eyes. "When are you packing up the cottage?"

"I'm starting tomorrow."

"I'll help you."

I hoped he would, hoped we could chat about her as we did. "I'd really like that."

I took a sip of tea. "Regarding Norah"

"She's like a bad penny."

"She dropped the suit."

He looked startled. "How did that happen?"

"My father persuaded her."

"Seems out of character for her to be so agreeable."

"He felt the same because he had someone watching her."

"And he no longer does." He understood when he added, "You think she's coming here."

"Yes. I wanted you to be aware. I don't know what she intends, if anything, but with her you can't assume."

"Aye. Thanks for the heads up."

"So, are you still planning a trip to Hawaii?"

"I think I'll hold off because there's quite a bit happening around here," he said then glanced down at my stomach. He reached for a folder on the table next to him. "But when I do go I have to decide where, but it's overwhelming. Maybe you'd like to help me?"

"Absolutely."

I returned home after spending a few hours with Fergus. He was right; it was overwhelming to decide where to travel in Hawaii. How did one pick among perfection? My father had been asleep when I left. He'd arrived quite late last night. When I entered the house, I heard voices coming from the hall and followed them. Brochan and my father were in the library. As soon as I entered, they both stood. My father smiled, then his eyes moved lower to my belly and he smiled even wider.

"Lizzie, you look well."

I walked to him and pressed a kiss on his cheek. "So do you."

"How was Fergus?" Brochan asked.

"He's going to help with packing up the cottage."

I joined them on the sofa. "His house has pictures everywhere. I'd like to do that for the nursery, a wall of nothing but photos of the family. I'm hoping Fenella has pictures of Abigail we can use. I won't be adding your father or Norah."

"I wouldn't want you to."

"So what's going on with Norah?" I asked because I knew it was what they'd been discussing when I entered.

"She caught a flight to Scotland last night."

I didn't like hearing that, but I had been expecting it. "Why now?"

My father leaned back on the sofa and crossed his legs. "Brochan's man, who I'd really like to meet because damn he's good, has learned in very little time that Norah is up to her eyes in debt."

A wave of cold moved through me. I recognized the sensation because I had felt it a lot as a kid. Fear.

"She has no money?"

"No."

"The woman can't live without money," I declared.

"No," my father confirmed.

"She's on her way here for money."

"Yes."

"What do you think she intends?"

"We won't know until she tells us," Brochan said.

"You're going to give her the chance?" I was incredulous. "Wait, have you heard from her?"

"Aye. She wants to talk." Brochan sounded so calm.

"With you?"

"A car is picking her up when she lands."

Those words brought me to my feet. "She's coming here? No."

Brochan stood, took my hands. "It'll be all right, mo leannan."

"You're bringing the devil to our door."

"The big bad wolf's door," Brochan whispered.

I couldn't smile at his tease because a woman I hadn't seen since I was ten was coming to my home. "I hope you know what you're doing."

He pressed a kiss on my head. "Keep your enemies close."

"Maybe I could see the nursery?" My father was trying to lighten the mood. It didn't work. I had a terrible feeling in my gut, but I tried for a smile.

"Sure."

CHAPTER TWENTY-THREE

LIZZIE

I hope he knows what he's doing," Fenella voiced my thoughts. We were in the kitchen, preparing dinner for Norah. She was on her way. She would be dining at our table, in our home, the place where I wanted only beauty and we were inviting the ugly in. "At least we have Fergus and your father here as well, more to hear her threats," Fenella added.

I looked up from the potatoes I was peeling. "You think she's going to threaten us too?"

"Why else come here?"

"Will we never be free of her?" I wasn't really asking that question. For twenty years she was out of my life, twenty years when I was struggling to find my way. And now I had found happy, more happy than I ever imagined, and she comes crawling back.

"Trust that Brochan knows what he's doing."

"Why are we making a meal? We should have gotten those microwavable dinners, or bread and water."

"Brochan was very specific."

I glanced at my watch. "I better get dressed."

I had just reached the door when Fenella called, "All will be well, you'll see."

I wasn't so sure of that but I tried for a reassuring smile.

Brochan stared out the window, his hands in his pockets. He turned to me and the shadows were back. I hated seeing them. I had stopped by the library before I went up to change. "I know we're cutting out the ugly, but this is ending only one way with your mother."

"Why do this at all?"

"Because you know better than anyone she won't ever stop." He had warned the more savage part of him would want out. It was that part of him that spoke now.

"I don't want that mark on you."

"I've so many already another won't make a difference."

It wasn't right. She was my monster, not his. I hated that love for me was going to have him walking right back into the dark.

Finnegan entered the library, my father on his heels. "There are a bunch of cars pulling into the drive."

No one ever came here. Brochan was as startled as me by the news when he strode from the library and down the hall. I caught up just as he opened the door to what looked like most of the town. I saw Bridget and Blair, Bruce, Molly, Mrs. Wilson, the butcher and the grocer.

Fergus stepped forward. "We did nothing when you were a child. We heard the rumors, but we turned a blind eye unable to believe one of our own could be such a monster. Only Brianna had the courage to step up and do what was right. Only she tried to break the silence." He looked behind him and saw the nods from the people standing in mass in our driveway. "Norah Calhoun is a monster."

Agreement called out from the crowd behind him.

"She only has power because of our silence. It's time to make some noise."

I never before and never again would see the expression on Brochan's face. It was as if the years had been stripped away and he was that young kid again, calling out in the dark for help and for the first time he heard voices calling back.

Fergus rallied. "Let's show Norah Calhoun that if you mess with one of us, you mess with all of us."

Brochan found me in the nursery sorting through pictures. The scene from earlier still caused my pulse to pound and my heart to sigh. Not that I thought it would help with our current problem. Even a town united wouldn't stop the snake from slithering in. I hated to my core that she was coming here, that her ugliness was going to tarnish the peace we had found.

He reached my side and studied the pictures, touching one of him as a boy holding a worm. He had been adorable as a toddler, happy, sweet and curious. "Where did you get that?"

"Fenella. She has so many wonderful pictures of you." I reached for one that I loved, a little baby Brochan getting his first bath.

"You're not putting that on the wall."

"Yes, I am. Your son's will go right next to it."

Any argument he had died. Tenderness looked back then he ruined the mood when he asked, "Are you ready?"

"No."

"She'll be here any minute."

"Let her stay outside. It's getting really cold tonight, maybe with luck she'll freeze to death."

He reached for my hand and pulled me from the room. "I don't like this plan. I want it so noted," I whined.

"It's noted."

"That had to have felt really good earlier."

"More than I can say."

We reached the great hall just as the doorbell rang. My stomach dropped. Finnegan went for the door as Brochan pulled me farther into the hall. It didn't escape my notice he stood in front of me. Fergus and my father joined us. Fenella appeared too, a united front.

The door opened and all the years between then and now vanished. I was that little girl again facing down my monster. Norah Calhoun strolled into our home without an invitation, as if she belonged there. Without even looking at Finnegan, she handed him her coat. "I'll have a martini, dry."

My hands balled into fists. She hadn't changed at all. That wasn't exactly true. She was older. There was evidence that she was trying to fight father time by the stretching of the skin at her eyes, her lips were fuller than they had been in her youth. Her hair was chemically treated and her figure, always rail thin, was a little wide in her stomach.

"The gang is all here," she sneered, her eyes landing on me. "Still struggling with weight I see."

Brochan squeezed my hand because he knew I wanted to punch her.

"You should fire your plastic surgeon. Are you purposely packing on the pounds so you can inject the fat into you lips?" my father said evenly from my side. I lowered my head and bit my lip to keep from laughing out loud.

"Dinner's ready," Fenella called from the doorway.

Fenella had outdone herself. I didn't understand why she would go to the trouble for a maggot. Brochan pulled out my chair, one right at his side, thankfully. It was only after I sat down that I realized we were missing a place setting, the one in front of Norah. Then I took in the offerings, juicy cheeseburgers, mashed potatoes with a pool of butter in the center and grilled cheese. My heart swelled. He'd remembered. I glanced at him; his focus was on Norah, but his expression was completely unreadable.

I whispered, "I love you."

He reached for my hand under the table and gently squeezed it, but he never took his eyes off Norah.

"Figures I did everything I could to get out of this place and I end up right back where I fucking started. And if that's not a big enough kick in the ass, my *daughter* has snagged herself a wealthy..." The way she eyed him made *me* feel dirty, "...man. I wondered how Elizabeth caught a man like you." She glanced around the table. "But it was pity I see."

She was being even more of a raging bitch than normal and I got that she was acting as she was as a defense, coming out of the corner swinging, but she was just such a cunt.

She dropped her elbows on the table. "Let's get right down to it, shall we? The cottage was my retirement plan. As Brianna's only heir I knew it would all come to me. My ex-husband deceived me with lies to get me to drop the suit and now I find myself in a position that I'm not comfortable with."

"Poverty," my father offered.

"I know the rumors about you, Brochan." Ice formed in my blood as she continued, "I'm willing to keep my silence for a small fee."

"Blackmail? How desperate," Brochan drawled.

"Whatever works."

"And what makes you think it'll work," he challenged.

"Life father, like son."

His next words were spoken so softly, which made them even more terrifying. "What do you mean by that?"

"It was so easy. He didn't want the baby, but then he shouldn't have fucked her. Heather didn't want to take advantage of the opportunity, but she was a stupid bitch. A hail Mary like that falls in your lap, you scoop it up."

"Who didn't want the baby?" Brochan's voice had dropped to a deadly whisper, but she was too high working her manipulation to realize how much danger she was in.

I went numb because I was beginning to understand the connection.

She sat back and savored the moment before she said, "Your father."

My heart broke as his body turned to rock. I squeezed his hand knowing how much her confession hurt him. She had blackmailed Brochan's father, had held his infidelity over his head. Stoked the fires of his obsession and madness. She had helped create the monster that had made Brochan's childhood hell.

"Your mother died and the money train stopped. Heather wanted to confess, had some stupid idea that he would love her, that she could step into his beloved, dead wife's shoes."

I had to speak up. Her logic was twisted, even then. "You are admitting you killed her?"

"I'm not admitting anything."

Then a thought left me cold as I touched my own belly. "What happened to Heather's child?"

She smiled but it wasn't pleasant. "Last I heard he is currently in jail on two counts of attempted murder."

Tomas. His jealousy made a horrible kind of sense; they shared a father but only Brochan lived in the castle. She lied to him, fostered his hate without sharing the horror Brochan lived in. She had manipulated him, turned him into one of her pawns. Another innocent, like Brochan and me.

"That's how you knew of the inheritance," Fergus said, turning my focus to him. "You kept your claws in him, turned him into your errand boy."

Brochan added, "You filled his head."

She didn't even try to deny it. "Another opportunity. He was easy to manipulate, just like his mother."

"Why?" I shouted. If I could get my hands on her...

"You never burn a bridge completely. Finlay McIntyre had been a cash cow, and now his son will be too."

I wanted to reach across the table and strangle her. She didn't care about anyone but herself. She really was a monster. But of all her crimes, knowing the part she played in Brochan's nightmare was the one I couldn't get past.

"How many times did you call Tomas, or write him, show him any kind of attention for him to so easily eat up your lies?" I asked.

She laughed. "Not a lot. The lonely can be quite needy. I did call his father before I left for the States, told him his other son was an orphan; would be left to the system. He didn't care. He wanted nothing to do with him."

Even through my fury, I felt fear because she had all but confessed. "How did you know he was an orphan?"

She didn't answer. She didn't have to.

"You killed his mom, didn't give a damn what happened to him, and then twisted him with lies. Wherever he ended up, he was in a far better place than Brochan."

She waved that off. "I cared more about what happened to him than I did about you."

"Why do you hate me so much?"

Something ugly moved across her face. "You were a mistake, a costly one. One I tried to correct."

My blood ran cold. I didn't immediately appreciate her cryptic comment. Brochan did. He moved so fast. He was around the table, pulling Norah from her seat by her hair. She wasn't cocky now. There was fear in her eyes. "You hired him?"

"Hired who?"

"The mugger." He released her like she was a disease.

It took me a second for his words to penetrate and even when they did, I still was having trouble understanding them. When it did finally sink in, I was sure my expression matched Brochan's murderous one.

"You hired someone to kill me?"

My father was on his feet. "You did what?"

Shaken but still on her mission, she actually had the nerve to laugh. "I should have hired your lover. He wouldn't have fucked up." She strolled to the door on unsteady legs. "I'm staying at the Inn since my home was taken from me. I'll wait there for your call. Five million dollars and I'm out of your life...." She looked back at us and smirked, "Until I run out of money."

We'd never be free of her. I thought of the life Brochan had lived, all the ugly, all the pain, but he didn't have to live in the ugly anymore. He had nothing but beauty awaiting him. I loved him so much that I was ready to sacrifice my own happy ending so that he would have his, with our son. I understood now the beast he spoke of, the savage part of man that stripped all of it away—right and wrong, black and white—who fed on only vengeance and a twisted kind of justice. I followed her and reached for the gun Brochan insisted I carry. A calm settled over me as my own inner beast woke.

"Mother."

She turned. Understanding came a second too late. I pulled the trigger. Her body jerked back before landing in a heap, blood coming from the single wound in the center of her forehead. Bile rushed up my throat, the hand holding the gun shook. Brochan grabbed the gun, but I just stared at her lifeless body as my own convulsed. Brochan held my hair as I twisted away and hurled.

Even fearing the repercussions of what I had done, I didn't have remorse for doing it. "I killed her," I whispered.

Brochan's big body trembled. "I would have handled it."

"We need to clean this up," Fenella and Finnegan were already on the move.

"We've got to get rid of the body," Fergus said.

"You've got to have someone?" My father demanded of Brochan.

"We have to call the cops," I insisted.

"No!" Brochan roared.

I touched his cheek, love for him pushing out everything else. "I don't want to start our lives together by covering this up, having Norah hanging over us even in death, pulling our family into it. I know you can make it all disappear, but it won't disappear for me. I did it. I'm not sorry I did it, but I have to face the consequences." And that broke me because we had come so close, but my mother had the last laugh. With one shot, the foundation we had been building on crumbled.

I waited in the library. Now that the adrenaline had faded, I was terrified. I didn't want to go to jail but I couldn't find it in me to be sorry I killed her. Better me than Brochan. I touched my belly, tears welled at the idea of losing time with them while I did twenty-five to life for murder. My only solace was Brochan would have our baby to love. He wouldn't be alone. He wouldn't be in the dark anymore. The first visitor arrived mere minutes after the shooting, but soon most of the town was in our great hall. There was a heaviness in the air, Norah's body was right there for all to see. I didn't understand why they were here until the police arrived.

I hadn't yet met the local police; it was so surreal I almost felt like laughing. I had never even gotten a speeding ticket and now my first time breaking the law, I commit murder.

He was older, in his sixties. He took in Norah before he moved into the hall. "All right tell me what happened here?"

Brochan stepped forward, "I shot her."

"No!"

I jumped to my feet but before I could say anything more Fergus shouted, "It was me, Seamus, I killed her."

I looked back at Fergus then Blair called, "No, I shot her."

Bridget was eating a grilled cheese, but declared with a full mouth, "I killed her."

"No it was me," Molly exclaimed.

Mrs. Wilson was sitting on the sofa. She looked terrified to be in the werewolf's lair, but her voice was very clear when she said, "It was me. I killed her."

Seamus stopped writing and looked around. "Did anyone else kill her?"

My father stepped forward, so did Fenella and Finnegan. I couldn't believe what everyone was doing. I had always wanted a place to belong, but I never imagined this. It felt so incredibly good, bittersweet because I finally found it and now I was going to lose it.

I inhaled then confessed, "I killed her."

"Yeah. And I bet Santa Claus took a shot too," Seamus muttered.

"No, it really was me."

"What was she doing here?" he asked.

"She was pissed Brianna left her estate to Lizzie," Fergus said.

"Yeah, I heard her say she was going to get what was hers, one way or the other," A woman I had never met chimed in.

"You remember poor Heather. Norah was the last person to see her. Suspicious how that poor darling died and how fast Norah left town," Mrs. Wilson said. "Bad egg that one."

It went on for an hour. Seamus threw up his hands and walked over to Brochan and me. "Let's talk."

We moved to the library. He stepped in, looked around before leveling sharp eyes on us.

"I don't know what happened here, but here's what I do know. Norah Calhoun was on my list for Heather Craig's death. I was never able to prove it even though I know she was responsible. Brianna Calhoun was a sweetheart and from all that I've heard, you are the spitting image of her." His eyes moved to Brochan. "I didn't believe Fenella when she came to me. I didn't believe your father could do the things they claimed. I was wrong and I've had to live every day since with the knowledge that I did nothing." He offered his hand. "I'm sorry."

Brochan took it.

Seamus touched his hat. "It's a clear case of self defense as far as I'm concerned. We'll get the body out of here as soon as possible."

I swayed not believing what I was hearing; Brochan dragged me against him and held me close.

Seamus started from the library but stopped and looked back, his eyes moving to my belly before settling on Brochan. "I'm guessing you're pursuing another line of work."

He knew too?

"Aye."

"See that you do." Then he walked out.

Hours later, the police had left, the coroner had taken Norah's body and Fergus and the rest of the town had gone home. The house was asleep, but I couldn't sleep. Standing in our room, I looked outside unable to believe what had happened. I'd watched all of it like I was standing outside of myself. I had killed her. I was supposed to feel some measure of remorse for that, but I didn't. How the town had rallied. I still didn't quite believe it. How Seamus had given me a free pass I believed even less.

Brochan came up behind me, his arms going around my stomach. "Are you okay?"

I turned into him. "I'm still having trouble believing it all happened, oddly not killing her. That felt real and right, but how the town stood up...for me. I don't understand."

He pressed a kiss on my neck. "Because they know what she was and what you are. It might feel wrong that you killed her, but right and wrong isn't that simple and the town is smart enough to know it."

I had thought similarly in the moment. Lucky for me they did too. They had given me my life, my happy ending. They may not have come through for Brochan as a child, but they had certainly come through for us. I changed the subject because it was going to take time for the events of the night to sink in and settle.

"Did you know the part she played with your father?"

His body responded first with how tense it grew. "No."

"There is no excuse for what your father did to you, but I understand why he went mad. Already worried about Abigail's pregnancy and then blackmailed on top of it, constantly reminded of his weakness."

Brochan brushed his thumb over my lips.

"Maybe we should request leniency for Tomas. He was a pawn too."

"You are a better person than me," he whispered.

"That's not true."

He sounded a little incredulous when he offered, "I wonder if Brianna knew of the connection between Norah and Finlay."

"You think it's possible?"

"I can't imagine she would have kept quiet about it, so if she did it wouldn't have been until later, maybe even when she attempted reconciliation, but it's an unbelievable coincidence that our parents had a shared history. That woman really was a witch."

"A good one."

"Aye, a good one."

I rested my head on his shoulder. "It could be something else all together." I looked up at him. "Maybe it was fate."

Those beautiful eyes warmed. "Fate...that I can believe."

Cait and I were in the white room. She and Ethan's wedding was in the morning. They had moved into the cottage, but Cait didn't want Ethan to see her until the ceremony. It had been a month since the Norah incident and though I had called Cait at the time, being here must have brought it all back for her.

"I can't believe that bitch. I can't believe she had the nerve to come here and blackmail you."

I still felt no remorse. I had made peace with it. She couldn't hurt me or mine anymore. I had told Brochan once sometimes it really should be an eye for an eye. After Norah, I appreciated better the truth of those words.

Cait reached for my hand. "Are you okay?"

"I am. I killed someone. Sometimes it sneaks up on me, but after everything she did, I'd do it again. She would have never stopped."

"I agree. That must have been hard for Brochan watching you..."

"He wasn't marking his soul for her. She was my monster to defeat, but let's not talk about her. Your big day is tomorrow. You seem very calm."

"After the last two months and all the work involved in selling our place, moving...the wedding is the icing on the cake, especially since you took care of most of it."

"Fenella did most of it. She had so much fun planning. Wait until you see the fairy tale wedding she's created." Brochan wasn't thrilled with all the nonsense, as he called it, but he was being a good sport about it.

"It's good practice for yours," Cait said, brushing her finger over my ring.

I didn't need the big wedding, didn't even really want one. A minister in the library sounded perfect. I just wanted Brochan.

I glanced at the clock. It was past two. "We need to get some sleep. Morning will be here before you know it." We climbed into bed and shut off the lights. We lay in silence for a few seconds before Cait whispered, "Thank you for my fairy tale wedding."

"You're the godmother to my son, seems fitting you should have a fairy tale wedding."

I knew her head turned to me even in the dark. Her voice broke. "I'd be honored."

"Brochan is asking Ethan to be the godfather."

"Oh Lizzie. Now I'm crying."

"I'm sorry."

"No you're not."

"You're right. I'm not."

Silence again before I said, "I'm so happy you walked into that diner."

She reached for my hand. "Me too."

Brianna's barn was lit with lights. Large arrangements of flowers flanked the front where the minister stood. White chairs were arranged in rows and divided by the aisle that was adorned with a white silk runner. Cait looked stunning in her gown as she stood up front with Ethan speaking their vows. My eyes were on Brochan, dressed in his kilt, his were on me. The minister announced husband and wife and after their first kiss, they walked hand in hand down the aisle. We'd all be heading to Brochan's for the reception. He pulled me up against his side and pressed a kiss on my temple before we followed the bride and groom down the aisle. Brianna had said there was magic here and all someone had to do was look to see it. I pressed closer to Brochan. He was my magic and I definitely saw him.

EPILOGUE

LIZZIE

The yard was teaming with people as the Highland games got started. I walked to the nursery to find Brochan standing over Brice's crib. He was wrapping his son in the McIntyre plaid. He knew I was there when he said, "I had once thought I had brought about the extinction of my clan." His eyes lifted to me. "Thanks to you, that isn't true."

He lifted his son, so tiny in his big hands. Brice looked liked his daddy, the same black hair and those beautiful pale blue eyes. I joined them. "I like seeing you wear my colors."

He'd had a sash made for me out of the clan's tartan. "I like wearing them."

"Are you ready for this?" he asked. The Stewart clan was in the great hall. Brochan had the great idea of having the reunion during the Highland games. It took the pressure off conversation but still allowed for the dialog. Fenella had grown more and more quiet the closer the day came. I understand her nervousness. She and Finnegan had it in their power to bridge the distance between Brochan and the Stewarts, but they had opted to respect the wishes of their son. She was right, but I could understand her being hesitant coming face to face with the family who had been denied Abigail's child.

"I am. Are you?"

"Yes. It is time to heal the wounds."

We'd been doing a lot of that since Norah's death. The town no longer treated Brochan like an outsider. He was still reserved and distant, that was his way, but like Cait's wedding, he tolerated his peace being disturbed for me, for our son, for our growing family.

He reached for my hand, holding our son against his chest, and we headed downstairs. As soon as we hit the landing all heads turned to us. It was a sea of plaids. The sight was awesome. Fenella and Finnegan moved through the bodies to join us. The patriarch of the family and Brochan's great uncle, Alastair Stewart, approached us. It wasn't hard to pick him out because like Fergus, the man was huge. As he approached his focus was on Fenella and Finnegan.

I felt myself brace, I couldn't image what Fenella was feeling. He then wrapped her into a hug. "Thank you." There were tears in the man's eyes. He was clearly not comfortable with showing affection because he awkwardly stepped back then offered his hand to Finnegan.

"Thank you for stepping in, for giving Abigail's child a family, a home."

It was like the whole room took a collective sigh. Alastair turned to Brochan. "'Tis so good to finally meet you." His green eyes turned to me. "And you." They settled on our son. "And who is the wee lad?"

"Brice Stewart McIntyre."

Alastair's head jerked up to Brochan, his eyes wet. "A strong name. May I have the pleasure of introducing you to the family?" Alastair asked.

Brochan replied with a soft, "Aye."

After the introductions, some went off to join the games and others gathered to get caught up on what they'd missed since they'd last seen each other. Brochan and I were with Alastair. He had been sharing about the Stewart estate, a trip I definitely wanted to make. The conversation turned when he grew thoughtful before saying, "Abigail chose Finlay. We tried to talk her out of it, but she loved him."

That was news. "Why did you try to talk her out of it?" I asked.

"He loved her, at least he believed he did, but it was too much, too consuming."

I had thought that once myself, obsession not love.

"When we learned she died, we reached out to Finlay. We tried to bridge the distance, tried to be part of your life. He wouldn't hear of it. At the time we thought he was bitter and angry that only after her death did we try for a reconciliation."

He didn't want to let go of Brochan because he needed an outlet for his madness. I took Brochan's hand; he linked our fingers.

"I'm sorry, son. I wish we had done right by you."

"That's in the past. I think it's time we think about the now."

"I agree. Thank you for this, for bringing us all together."

"I think my mother would have wanted it."

"Aye, she would have."

"Come." Brochan handed me Brice before Bethany Stewart, the oldest living member of the Stewart clan and Abigail's great grandmother, took his hand.

She led him to the sofa where someone handed her a photo album. Her delicate old hand lifted the heavy leather cover. I stood where I was, holding our son and watched; my heart so full it should have burst from my chest.

"This is Abigail. She loved pistachio ice cream. She would have eaten it for every meal. She liked the color blue." She looked into his eyes. "Pale blue, just like your eyes. She never learned to ride a bike, but she sang like an angel."

Brochan had given them the link to Abigail and for the rest of the afternoon they gave him his mother.

That night Fenella and I dropped onto the sofa. Finnegan fed the fire and Brochan got the whisky, and water for me since I was nursing. Fergus and my father were getting something to snack on. The house was filled with Stewarts, all of whom were sleeping.

"I'm exhausted, but what a good day," Fenella said as she took her glass from Brochan.

"It was. All those stories and the pictures...we have more to add to our walls, Brochan," I said.

He stood near the fire, swirling the whisky in his glass. He was lost in thought and after everything he had learned today, I wasn't surprised. "Aye." He took a sip of his drink then added, "She liked pistachio ice cream." His pale eyes turned on me. "So do I."

My heart swelled.

Fenella reached for one of the books Bethany had brought. I moved closer as we paged through it. "All the history."

Fergus and my father entered, carrying a tray of shortbread. "Good choice," I offered.

Fenella froze at my side; her hand even shook a little. I glanced over and her face was pale. "Fenella, what's wrong?"

"I think I'm more tired than I realize."

"Why?"

"Because that looks...no it couldn't be."

"What?" I asked.

Her wide eyes of wonder lifted to me. "That looks an awful lot like Brianna."

I glanced down at the very old photograph. "That's not possible."

Fergus was behind us in a heartbeat, his booming voice as incredulous as mine. "No, that's impossible, but..." His eyes grew bright. "Bri."

"Maybe she wasn't kidding about appearing on the moors," I whispered. My eyes met Fergus'. "I think you might see her again."

My focus shifted back to the woman standing in the back of the photo, not dressed in the Stewart colors, but someone close to the family like a nanny, a photo taken in 1886. A chill moved through me.

"She would have been over a hundred and fifty years old when she died," my dad said.

The only one not surprised was Brochan. He chuckled then kicked back his whisky. "I knew it." His eyes met mine and he smiled. "I fucking knew it."

FIVE YEARS LATER...

I stood with Fenella as we watched Brochan teaching Brice how to ride a bike. Every time the bike started to shake, Brochan was there to sweep our son up before he could fall. He wouldn't always be there to catch him, but that didn't stop him from trying.

My dad and Finnegan were with our two-year-old daughter, Bri, chasing butterflies. Her little legs were wobbly, but she was determined. "I can't tell you what joy it brings me to be standing here witnessing this beautiful scene." Fenella's focus turned to me. "You gave us back our son." She wiped at her eyes. "You saved him."

I pressed a kiss on her cheek. "We saved each other."

"Grammie, look!" Brice called.

"Oh, sweetie, look at you go," she called as she hurried after him.

I headed to Brochan who shifted his attention from our son to me, his eyes taking a leisurely study, settling on my stomach that was just beginning to show. When I was close enough, he had me pressed right up against him.

"He's a natural."

"He has a good teacher."

He curled his spine to look me in the eyes. "I love it here."

My heart filled hearing him say that because here was the surprise he had been working on, the one he refused to share with me. He had turned the McIntyre land into the Brianna Calhoun/Abigail Stewart-McIntyre memorial park. It was the town's center with birthday parties and weddings being held practically every week; even the festivals, including the Highland games Brochan hosted, were held there. A place that had been a painful and bitter reminder of how ugly humans could be was now a place of great joy and beauty.

"I love it too. So do the kids."

He looked wicked. "Speaking of the kids. They're busy with our parents, which means you and I have some free time."

Five years of marriage and an extremely healthy sex life and the man could still make me burn.

"First one to the car eats last," he said but then he lifted me into his arms and carried me to the car. "On second thought, no reason we can't eat at the same time."

My whole body felt those words. "You're a wicked man."

"A beast." He bit my lower lip. "And he wants to play."

We had found our own fairy tale; it was dark and twisted at times, but we had found our happily ever after or rather we had found happy at last.

ACKNOWLEDGMENTS

Finishing a book is always a bittersweet for me. I'm happy the story is done, but I always feel a little loss when I type *The End*. Luckily for me, I have people who are there to shine the light.

James, Caitlin and AJ, I love you.

My Beta Beauties. Friends that turned into family, those words are so true. Books brought us together, but we really are a family. I love you, ladies. Elsie, Markella, Devine, Dawn, Meredith, Tammy, Rosemarie, Yolanda, Sue, Ana Kristina, Andie, Raj, Michelle, Amber, Donna, Lauren and Audrey

Trish Bacher, *Editor in Heels*, thank you for the time and care you put into my books. One day, I hope we can raise a glass and celebrate in person.

Melissa Stevens, *The Illustrated Author*, who designed the cover, title page art, the interior art, formatted the paperback and ebook and created the e-files for Savage...working on the design of the book with you is my favorite part of the process.

Tracy Marks and Aaron Shedlock, thank you for the gift of your voices, bringing the characters to life for the audio book.

Ruth Martin, my personal assistant, you're wonderful. Thank you for all you do.

Kiki Chatfield, my publicist, I love you.

To all bloggers, thank you! Your continuous support, signing up for the reveals and promotions, sharing the teasers, just talking about the books, thank you, thank you.

A special thank you to The Next Step PR and Enticing Journey Promotions for hosting the tours for this book.

And lastly, to the readers. I wouldn't be here without you. Thank you for taking a chance on my books and thank you for coming back for more.

MORE BOOKS
BY
L.A. FIORE

THE BEAUTIFULLY SERIES...

Beautifully Damaged
Beautifully Forgotten
Beautifully Decadent
Beautifully Played: Coming 2018

THE HARRINGTON MAINE SERIES...

Waiting for the One
Just Me

LOST BOYS SERIES...

Devil You Know
Demon You Love: Coming 2018

SHIPWRECK SERIES...

Elusive
Title to be announced: Coming 2018

STANDALONES

Savage: The Awakening of Lizzie Danton
His Light in the Dark
A Glimpse of the Dream
Always and Forever
Collecting the Pieces

To learn more about what's coming, follow L.A. Fiore...

https://www.facebook.com/l.a.fiore.publishing
https://www.facebook.com/groups/lafemmefabulousreaders
https://twitter.com/lafioreauthor
https://www.instagram.com/lafiore.publishing

Contact me through email at:
lafiore.publishing@gmail.com

Or check out my website:
www.lafiorepublishing.com